THE WHITE LORD OF WELLESBOURNE

A Medieval Romance

By Kathryn Le Veque

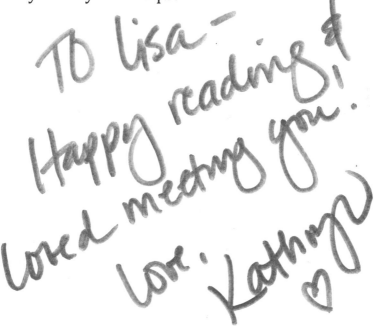

To Lisa –
Happy reading!
Loved meeting you!
love, Kathryn

Printed by Dragonblade Publishing in the United States of America

Text copyright 2006, 2014 by Kathryn Le Veque
Cover copyright 2006, 2014 by Kathryn Le Veque

Library of Congress Control Number 2014-008
ISBN 1494894874

Other Novels by Kathryn Le Veque

Medieval Romance:

The Wolfe * Serpent
*

The White Lord of Wellesbourne* The Dark One: Dark Knight
*

While Angels Slept* Rise of the Defender* Spectre of the Sword* Unending Love* Archangel* Lord of the Shadows
*

Great Protector* To the Lady Born
*

The Falls of Erith* Lord of War: Black Angel
*

The Darkland* Black Sword
*

Unrelated characters or family groups:
The Whispering Night * The Dark Lord* The Gorgon* The Warrior Poet* Guardian of Darkness (related to The Fallen One)* Tender is the Knight* The Legend* Lespada* Lord of Light

The Dragonblade Trilogy:
Dragonblade* Island of Glass* The Savage Curtain
  -also-
The Fallen One (related)* Fragments of Grace (related prequel)
*

Novella, Time Travel Romance:
Echoes of Ancient Dreams
*

Time Travel Romance:
The Crusader*Kingdom Come

Contemporary Romance:

Kathlyn Trent/Marcus Burton Series:
Valley of the Shadow* The Eden Factor* Canyon of the Sphinx

The American Heroes Series:
Resurrection* Fires of Autumn* Evenshade* Sea of Dreams* Purgatory

Other Contemporary Romance:
Lady of Heaven* Darkling, I Listen

<u>Note:</u> All Kathryn's novels are designed to be read as stand-alones, although many have cross-over characters or cross-over family groups. Novels that are grouped together have related characters or family groups. Series are clearly marked. All series contain the same characters or family groups except the American Heroes Series, which is an anthology with unrelated characters. There is NO particular chronological order for any of the novels because they can all be read as stand-alones, even the series.

Dedicated to my brother - a tall, blond hero in his own right, Bill Bouse III.

Contents

'One meets his destiny often in the road he takes to avoid it.'
                                        - Gaul Proverb

CHAPTER ONE

Early July, 1485 A.D.
England

The carriage had a bad axel and held a worse gait than that of a lame horse. For days she had put up with the rocking and lurching. Whenever the carriage came to a halt, she continued to rock and lurch long after it had stopped. Sometimes she thought her brains were about to come sloshing out of her ears.

Her patience had lasted nearly nine days. But it was eight days too many. Nearing a town nestled in the soft green landscape of Warwickshire, she could no longer stand the torture and she smacked the roof of the carriage several times until the driver pulled the horses to a stop.

The woman with the sloshing brains stuck her head out of the window. "What town is this?"

"Newbold, my lady."

"Thank God," she muttered. Then louder, "I will stop here. I must stretch my legs."

"But we are almost to Wellesbourne," the driver told her.

She ignored him. The door to the carriage was already open and the lady climbed out. Behind her, a contingent of four hundred soldiers had come to a halt, including three mounted officers. The shuffling of their feet kicked up clouds of dust from the dry road and the breeze, once so delightful, now brought the dust in the lady's direction. She fanned a hand in front of her face to be rid of the dirt.

"Look at me," she glanced down at her clothes, of the latest

9

fashion. "I shall be a dirty, dusty mess by the time we reach Wellesbourne. What will my new husband think of me?"

From the carriage door, a small covered head appeared. The lady's serving woman was an unusual shade of green as her feet gingerly found their way out of the carriage

"He shall think ye the most beautiful woman he's ever laid eyes on, m'lady." She nearly fell out of the door and would have done so had her mistress not prevented it. She straightened her girdle and looked at her surroundings. "My, 'tis warm in these parts."

The lady looked up from brushing the dust off her seamless surcoat, the ruby color peppered with brown specks. The land this far south was defined by rolling hills interspersed with flat plains now and again. Clusters of forests dotted the area. It wasn't nearly as lush or colorful as York, but there was charm to it.

"Whatever it is, I shall have to become used to it," she said, resignation in her voice.

Finished with the dust off, she refocused on the tavern she had seen as they had entered the outskirts of the settlement. It was a large establishment, surprising for such a small berg, and she thought it to be perfect place to refresh herself before proceeding to Wellesbourne. She did not want her future husband's first impression of her to be road-weary and famished. She would ease herself now to be presentable later. At least it seemed like a good idea.

"In there," she jabbed her finger towards the inn as she marched past the soldier who was her coachman. "Tell the men to rest while I am occupied. I shall not be long."

"In there?" he repeated, chagrined. "But that's a *tavern.*"

"Brilliant assessment, Strode."

He ignored her acerbic reply. "God only knows what kinds of creatures inhabit that place, my lady. 'Tis no place for you."

"If it does not have wheels on it and I can sit peacefully for a few moments, it is indeed a place for me."

He nearly sneered at her. "Do you have any money? They're

going to want coinage, you know. How do you expect to pay?"

She puckered her bow-shaped mouth, a snide retort coming to her lips but wisely refrained. Strode had been entrusted with the cash her uncle had given her and it would not do well to insult the man with the money.

"I will pay with the coin you so kindly give to me," she held out her hand. "A few pences, please? I promise that I shall be wise and thrifty."

"And if I do not give you the money?"

"I am sure there will be a man or two in that tavern who will gladly supply me with the money I need."

It was apparent she was going whether or not there were any objections. Strode leapt from the carriage and emitted a piercing whistle to several mounted soldiers to the rear of the carriage. Then he glared at the young woman he had known since birth.

"You shall go nowhere without escort, Lady Alixandrea," he said sternly. "Your uncle would have my hide if anything happened to you so close to your destination."

The Lady Alixandrea Terrington St. Ave lifted a well-shaped eyebrow at him. "God forbid."

It was a sarcastic remark, softly uttered. The mounted soldiers arrived and the coachman gave them instructions to stick close to the lady while she found rest at the inn. The men raised their eyebrows at the thought of the lady in a rough, untamed tavern, but they all knew that once Lady Alixandrea set her mind to something, there was no dissuading her. They had no choice but to follow or be left behind.

Gathering her skirt, Alixandrea set forth across the dusty road towards the timber and mortar tavern. Above her, the sky was unnaturally blue in the unseasonably dry weather and she thought perhaps that may have something to do with her unsettled stomach. Heat and travel could be an uncomfortable situation. Behind her, the maid shuffled like an old woman, kicking up more dust onto her new garment.

"Jezebel, pick up your feet," she admonished sternly. "And when we enter, I will do the talking, is that clear?"

The dark-eyed, dark-haired maid nodded. "Do ye want a bath, too?"

"A bath? In this place?" Alixandrea looked up at the hand-hewn sign that now hung above their heads. *Head O'Bucket.* "Would you look at the name of this establishment? I think I shall faint."

"Steady, m'lady."

"Steady it is."

The words were lightly spoken, lightly given. Alixandrea St. Ave was the last woman on the earth to give in to fits of fainting. She pushed the door open, giving it a good shove as it stuck on the hinges.

But her bravery was instantly tempered by the stench that immediately struck her; it was like walking into a garderobe. It was also quite dark, in stark contrast to the bright sunlight outside, and it took a moment for her eyes to adjust. Between the smell and the darkness, she was coming to reconsider her desire to visit this abysmal place. But one of the soldiers escorting her pushed the door open wider, thinking it was jammed, and she was forced to move forward.

There was one great room and little more. And it was surprisingly full. Alixandrea and her maid, followed by the soldiers, looked for the least obtrusive place to sit and quickly located a table near the door that was suitable. She noticed that all eyes in the place had somehow found her in the darkness. She wondered what they were thinking and how shortly her life would be in danger. In spite of what she had told her maid, she sent the woman in search of the barkeep in a hurry. She wanted to obtain her refreshment and get out.

As she sat and waited, with her soldiers close behind for protection, a great collective mass of appreciation was forming in that stuffy little tavern. When the door had opened and she stood there, illuminated by the bright sunlight, there were a few in the room that swore Heaven itself had opened up the door and an angel now stood in their midst.

Clad in a ruby-colored cloak with her glorious bronze-colored curls spilling over one shoulder, the angel in the doorway could only be described as magnificent. Her oval-shaped face was sweet and her eyes were the most amazing color of bronze, just like her hair; somewhere between brown and gold that flowed like sultry molten liquid. When she moved, she swished, as an angel's wings would have. And when she sat, it was with the aura of a queen.

There wasn't one man or woman in that room that wasn't instantly enchanted with her. She was obviously well-born, well-bred, and just this side of paradise. It wasn't long before someone approached the table.

"My lady," a soft, deep voice addressed her. "May I buy your meal for you?"

Alixandrea looked up into the face of a young man, perhaps a little older than her, with very short, golden-red hair. He had blue eyes and a square-jaw. It was a handsome appearance. And he was a big lad, which intimidated her a bit, but he seemed mannered.

"I am not eating, good sir," she said, avoiding eye contact with him. "I have merely come in to rest before continuing on my journey."

"Then allow me to provide you with your refreshment."

Before she could protest, he was whistling to the barkeep and motioning to the table. Alixandrea shook her head.

"No, good sir, I implore you," she said, more forcefully. "It is my wish to enjoy my rest without company, if you don't mind."

He looked at her as if he did not comprehend a word she was saying. Was it possible that there was a woman who did not want his company? His lips broke out in an easy smile.

"It is only because you do not know me," he said confidently. "I am Sir Luke Wellesbourne of Wellesbourne Castle. My father is lord over this fiefdom."

She looked at him intently. It was a struggle not to give away the surprise she felt. "Wellesbourne?"

He sat heavily next to her, taking the big earthenware cup from the barkeep as the man drew near the table.

"Aye," he jabbed his finger towards the smoking, sloppy hearth. "And that is my unsociable brother over there, brooding like a bear."

Her bronze eyes drifted in the direction he was pointing, noticing an enormous man sitting by himself, hunched over a cup. He was partially hidden in the shadows, enough so that she could not get a good look at him. Alixandrea's eyes lingered on the silent, hulking figure, a feeling in the pit of her stomach that she could not begin to describe. All she knew was that it disturbed her greatly.

"Who is your brother?"

Luke took a long drink from his mug. "The great and mighty Matthew Wellesbourne, favored of the king." He leaned near her, enough so that she instinctively tilted away from him. "Have you heard of The White Lord of Wellesbourne? Well, that would be him. But if you are thinking of inviting him to our table, do not bother. He is greatly troubled today. He would be horrible company."

The White Lord of Wellesbourne. She'd known that name for half of her life and the realization took her breath away. But how was it possible that he was here, *now*? He was supposed to be at Wellesbourne Castle; but then again, so was she.

Alixandrea stared at the dark figure, trying to get a better look. Although she thought she may have an inkling of the answer to her question, she asked anyway. "What is his trouble?"

"His wife is coming to Wellesbourne."

"And this is a bad event, I take it?"

"Aye," Luke took another drink. "Well, she is not exactly his wife. She is his betrothed. They were promised to each other years ago but he had been putting her off until her uncle laid his claim and told my father that if Matthew put off the marriage again, there would be serious consequences. So now, he is forced. He has come here to drown his sorrows in ale and wenches."

Alixandrea lifted an eyebrow, nodding her head slowly as if in complete sympathy. "My goodness," she said. "How utterly awful. Is his betrothed so terrible, then?"

Luke shrugged. "We do not know. But, then again, most noble women are some manner of terrible. But she comes with a large dowry and four hundred soldiers, so she must be worth something, eh?"

He laughed at his statement. Alixandrea smiled thinly. "Aye, she must be worth something," she agreed.

Luke licked the ale from his lips, his gaze steady upon her. "I am sure that if my brother had a wife like you, there would be nothing horrible about it. I would take you without four hundred fighting men and a sizable dowry."

He meant it as a compliment but it only served to further insult her. "How fortunate for me," she said, grossly tired of his company. The rolling carriage was starting to look inviting and she was suddenly desperate to leave. "If you will excuse me, Sir Luke, I will take my leave and continue my journey. Thank you for your company and fine conversation."

Luke put a hand on her arm, preventing her from rising. "You cannot leave so soon," he begged. "I do not even know your name."

Now it was her turn to smile, an ironic gesture. "I believe you already know it."

He blinked at her. "I do? Pray, lady, if thy name is Angel, then I do."

She stared at him, unwavering. "I have four hundred soldiers outside waiting for me as well as a sizable dowry. I am on my way to Wellesbourne Castle to marry my betrothed. Now, can you still say that you do not know my name?"

Luke's intoxicated blue eyes met her gaze for a long moment before gradually dissolving into an expression of horror.

"You...?" He pushed back in his chair and ended up toppling it onto its side. Luke was on his feet, babbling as he struggled to overcome his drunkenness. "My lady, I did not know. Forgive me, please. I had no idea."

She stood up, a small lady compared to the sizable knight. But her expression was the most powerful thing in that room at the moment.

"Either you are a complete fool or your brother truly has no sense of propriety that he would allow you to speak so," she snarled. "How many other people have you told that ridiculous story to? How many people will travel from this place spreading the tale of the heir of Wellesbourne's hideous betrothed?"

"No one, my lady, I swear it." He bellowed in the general direction of his brother. "Matt! A little help, please?"

By this time, Matthew heard the raised voices and glanced up to see Luke on his feet with the lady advancing on him. He'd seen her when she'd entered the inn, just like everyone else and, like everyone else, had been momentarily entranced by her ethereal beauty.

But he had no inclination to pursue her further and allowed Luke to behave as Luke was so capable of behaving. Now he was wondering what his brother had said to make the lady turn on him.

Matthew was far enough away that he had not heard their conversation although he had heard his brother's loud pleas for help. But he shook his head in response, turning back to his fourth cup of ale. Luke saw that his brother did not understand the severity of the situation and he made haste over to his table.

"Matt," he hissed. "Did you not hear me? We have… trouble!"

He was pointing at the lady. Matthew looked over at her again, a delicious goddess with porcelain skin. "What trouble could that be? Let me guess; she is a Tudor wench and you have seriously insulted both her loyalties and her parentage."

Alixandrea heard the "wench" portion and came to a halt. Luke shook his head, sickened at the course the conversation had taken.

"Nay," he whispered, hoping his brother would not take his head off for his stupidity. "She is your betrothed."

Matthew was lingering over his cup, his gaze distant. But the moment Luke spilled the words, his blue eyes took on the most peculiar look. It was as if he had suddenly become frozen, unable to think or move. One could literally see his fingers stiffening with tension and Luke was terrified that his brother was going to suddenly snap. Instead, he blinked his eyes in a slow, reptilian motion. It was a frightening gesture.

"Do you know this for a fact?" he asked steadily.

"I do."

"Did she tell you?"

"She said she has four hundred soldiers and a sizable dowry waiting for her outside, and that she is on her way to Wellesbourne Castle to marry her betrothed."

Matthew continued to sit immobile. Luke wasn't even sure if his brother was breathing. Finally, Matthew cast a long glance at his brother before looking to the lady.

She stood in the middle of the room, a vision of ruby and lustrous hair. She had the most beautiful face he had ever seen, delicate and sweet, yet with a hint of wisdom that was difficult to describe.

A cursory examination of the lady showed him absolutely no physical flaws as far as he could tell. But the expression she held was of indignant outrage, tempering his reaction to her presence.

"What did you say to her?" he asked his brother.

Luke was glad he was out of arm's range. He did not want a massive fist to come flying at him. "I... I told her that you were terrible company because you were awaiting the arrival of your betrothed whom you did not want to marry."

"Is that all?"

Luke winced, closing his eyes. "I said awful things."

"How awful?"

"She hates us, I know it."

Matthew did not want a fight on his hands from the onset. In fact, gazing at the lady, he wasn't sure he wanted a fight at all. He was rather taken aback by what he saw. The only appropriate thing to do was face her.

Matthew rose from his chair slowly, like the phoenix rising from the ashes, a massive man with equally massive shoulders on which to bear the weight of a kingdom. Everything about him reeked of power and command as his presence, once seated and inconspicuous, now filled the entire room.

It was a gesture not lost on Alixandrea. In fact, she had to suppress the urge to back away. She'd never seen such a sizeable man, even though he was in full armor which made him appear even larger. To her credit, she stood her ground as he approached. When he came within a few feet of her, he stopped.

"Lady Alixandrea?" he asked.

"I am the Lady Alixandrea," she not too subtly corrected the pronunciation of her name, *Alix-ahn-dray-a,* so that he would know for future reference. "And you are Sir Matthew?"

He lifted an eyebrow. "Aye," his deep voice was without force. "Forgive me, my lady. This is not how I had planned our first meeting."

Her lovely lips turned up at the corners cynically. "From what I understand, were it left up to you, there would be no first meeting at all. Just how did you plan it?"

Matthew could only imagine what his foolish brother had told her. *Awful things.* Unless Matthew wanted this marriage to be strained and conflicting from the beginning, he had to make amends. He had to undo the damage that Luke had done.

"Certainly not in a tavern with my brother drunk and me well on my way," he said. "I had hoped to meet you at Wellesbourne in the great hall where the appropriate introductions would take place."

She cocked her head slightly, studying him; he was a handsome man, not obviously beautiful, but in a rugged, masculine sort of way that was both powerful and intriguing. His pale blond hair was shorn tight against his scalp, curly and coarse. He had enormous blue eyes, a square jaw and gentle-looking features that were oddly out of place for a man of his fierce reputation. His ears even stuck out a little, giving him an inherently human quality.

But in that quality was something innately calm, although she knew that he was one of the most fearsome knights in the realm. He had been with King Richard on many campaigns against Henry Tudor's forces and had proven himself without question. She'd been hearing tales of The White Lord of Wellesbourne since she had been ten years old. It was a long time to hear of a legend.

So the man did not want to be married. There was no great crime in that. But she was disappointed. Somehow she had hoped that he would have longed to know her just as she had longed to know him. Her uncle had filled her with fairy tales of the man. Matthew had apparently been filled with horror stories of her.

"Then let us make the introductions now, however inappropriate," she said, trying not to sound too bitter. "My uncle Howard Terrington, Lord Ryesdale, sends his greetings. I am the Lady Alixandrea Terrington St. Ave and I have come with my maidservant, my manservant outside, and four hundred soldiers to be placed under your command. Such were the terms of the contract, my lord. We are fulfilling our pledge."

Matthew found himself watching her mouth as she spoke. Her lips were sweet and pillowy and lush. He suddenly felt very self-conscious, dirty and minimally drunk as he was, to be greeting this intriguing creature.

It was occurring to him that she was not at all what he had expected. The reluctance and bitterness that he had associated with this betrothal for so many years was quickly turning into something different. He did not know what yet, but it was different.

"And I am Sir Matthew Wellesbourne, Lord Ettington, heir to Wellesbourne Castle and sworn servant to our king, the illustrious Richard," he took another step towards her, keenly aware of their size difference; he was easily twice her width and more than a foot taller. "I welcome you to Wellesbourne and would ask the honor of escorting you to the castle, my lady."

She lifted an eyebrow. "Are you sure that doing so would not take you away from your ale and wenches, my lord?"

Now he knew what Luke had been telling her. He resisted the urge to grab his brother by the neck and squeeze.

"I think the ale and wenches can spare me." He extended a trencher-sized hand, clad in a heavy leather glove. "I would ask that you accept my apologies for a harsh beginning. Given the choice, it would have certainly not been my intent. May I guide you?"

She eyed him, her bronze eyes a maelstrom of fire, emotion and mystery. But she silently put her hand over his, a tiny mitt against his size. In doing so, it was perhaps a reluctant acceptance of his apology. Matthew tried not to stare at her as he led her from the tavern.

The sunlight outside was blinding. Matthew's eyes scanned the area, hawk-like, until they came to rest on a cluster of armed men a few hundred yards away from the inn. From a two-second perusal, he could see that they appeared to be seasoned, seemingly well fed and outfitted. That would translate into a strong contingent, he hoped. He led the lady in their general direction.

"I hope you had a pleasant journey from the north," he tried to make conversation, sensing that perhaps all was not forgiven yet.

"It was long, my lord," she said. "Long and bumpy at times."

He nodded. "Lack of rain has made the roads miserable."

"Indeed, my lord."

The small talk quickly died. Glancing behind, he saw that Luke had retrieved their chargers from the livery. The two soldiers and the skittish maid also followed in a suspicious group. Shortly, they reached the fighting men clustered in a grove of trees who now stood up from their various positions of rest as their lady appeared with a colossal knight on her arm. Strode, half-asleep inside the carriage where he was not supposed to be, shot out of the cab like a scalded cat.

"My lady," he rushed upon her, fully prepared to save her from the massive warrior even to his own death. "Are you well? Was there trouble?"

"No trouble," she told him. "In fact, the stop at this tavern seems to have been fortuitous. I would present you to Sir Matthew Wellesbourne, your new liege, and his brother, Sir Luke."

The foot soldiers, shocked from their momentary confusion, scurried to form a line for their new lord. Strode, his mouth gaping with surprise, bowed deeply.

"My lord," he said. "We were not told that you would meet us on the road. Forgive me if we did not rendezvous at the appropriate place or time. I had no..."

Matthew put up a hand. "Your orders were to take the lady to Wellesbourne, which is what you were doing. I just happened to be here and we met inside."

Strode stood up from his prostrate position, his eyes still full of confusion and, Alixandrea thought, fear. "I sent two men to look after her, my lord," he said. "She was not without protection. I have known the lady her entire life and would not dream of allowing her in such a place without proper escort."

He was babbling. Alixandrea cast him a long look, silently ordering him to shut his mouth. Matthew apparently did not notice. He was looking over the troops.

"Do you still have the full contingent of four hundred?" he asked. "None have run off or fallen ill during the trip?"

"We've lost none, my lord," Strode replied. "Would you inspect them?"

"Not now," Matthew said. "Wellesbourne is a little more than a mile to the south. I shall inspect them once we're in the fortress."

Alixandrea listened to the conversation, noting the interest in her betrothed's voice. It reminded her, yet again, of the truth of this marriage contract; he was marrying her for the money and manpower, nothing more. She was so foolish in that she had hoped he would have seen some value in her. She was no more than the soldiers and valuables she carried; she was a commodity. She would have to accept that.

She removed her hand from his. "If there will be nothing else, my lord, perhaps we should continue to the castle. The hour grows late."

He gazed down at her, watching the sunlight play off of her bronze hair. Gold, brown and copper glistened like a shower of light.

"A wise suggestion, my lady." He looked at Strode. "What is your name, man?"

21

"Strode, my lord."

"Very well," he nodded shortly. "Take the lady down this road, through the village, until you come to Wellesbourne. Stop for no one and make all due haste. These parts are not safe after dark, even to me."

Reaching over, he took Alixandrea's hand and tucked it into the crook of his elbow. She tried not to look surprised by the bold action; it was a claiming gesture. Silently, he led her over to the carriage, opened the door, and very kindly helped her inside.

All the while, Alixandrea kept feeling that same innate gentleness she first sensed in him. The man was fearsome by size alone, but deep down, she felt there was more. Perhaps it was something he did not like anyone to see.

Their eyes met briefly as she took her seat and the corners of his eyes crinkled, as close to a smile as she had so far seen. He'd remained stoic and emotionless to this point, and she thanked him with a dip of her head. As soon as Matthew removed himself from the doorway, Jezebel leapt into the carriage and the door slammed tightly. Outside, she heard a few barked orders and the carriage lurched, once again to reel and roll that last terrible mile to Wellesbourne.

As the carriage gained a sickening rhythm on the road, she was aware of her disappointment that he had not asked her to ride with him that last mile. Or she could have ridden her paltry in stride with his great warhorse, and all of the inhabitants of Wellesbourne would have seen that Matthew was indeed accepting this wife he had been expecting for ten years.

She could only imagine what all of Wellesbourne thought of her, the great chain of doom out to attach herself to Matthew and ruin his life. But he had not asked her, indicative of the level of enthusiasm he had for this marriage. She sank back into her seat, disenchanted and moody.

The horses were just gaining their stride when the carriage suddenly lurched to a halt. Unprepared, Alixandrea went skidding across the cab and hit her head on the boxy wooden headrest on the opposite seat. Stars burst in her vision and the blood began to flow.

"Oh, m'lady," Jezebel saw what had happened and rushed to her aid. "Here, take this kerchief. Press it on the wound or ye'll get blood all over yer dress."

The cut was on the right side of her forehead and stung. Alixandrea tried to put the cloth over the wound and steady herself at the same time. The world was still rocking even though the carriage had come to a halt. Trying to keep the blood out of her eye, she heard a voice from the cab door.

"What happened?" It was Matthew.

"The cab stopped too quickly, m'lord," Jezebel told him, trying to help her lady. "She hit her head."

The cab door opened and gentle hands were on her. Between Jezebel and Matthew, they managed to turn her around so that she was seated on the floor of the cab, her legs hanging from the open door. Though the kerchief covered most of her vision, Alixandrea could see Matthew's face looming close.

"Let me see."

His voice was low, full of serenity and reassurance. It disarmed Alixandrea so much that she actually obeyed him, allowing him to remove the kerchief so that he could see her head. He wiped her forehead a couple of times to keep blood from running into her eye as he inspected the injury.

His ripped off one of his leather gloves, tossing it aside. His big, warm fingers danced over her forehead and scalp, inspecting, but to Alixandrea, the sensation was something else altogether. Every time he touched her, some strange occurrence happened that sent bolts of heat racing through her body. She almost pulled away from him, but something inside her could not muster the will.

"It is not so bad, my lady," he finally assured her. "Just a little cut inside your hairline. Unfortunately, head wounds bleed heavily no matter how large or small. I am afraid you may have a bit of a bump."

Jezebel had produced a clean handkerchief, which she handed to Matthew and he pressed it back over the wound. Their eyes finally met and his expression relaxed into something pleasant and humane. She thought she might actually detect warmth.

"This is my fault, I fear," he said. "I ordered Strode to halt the carriage. It occurred to me to have you ride into Wellesbourne with me. Had I known my clever plan would see you come to harm, I would have never acted upon it."

He seemed genuinely contrite and she smiled. "'Twas not your fault, my lord," she said. "But I fear Strode is in for a beating."

She said the last part loud enough so her manservant could hear her. He was standing beside Matthew, blocked out of her view by Matthew's bulk.

"Forgive, my lady," he said. "'Twas an accident."

"Accident, my eye," she said snappishly. "You always stop this carriage as if the Devil has just planted himself right in your path. I have many bruises to attest to this."

Matthew glanced over at the beleaguered manservant. "Perhaps Strode requires some coaching in this area to perfect his skills."

While the manservant cowered, Alixandrea removed the kerchief from her head. It was spotted with blood, but the oozing had stopped for the most part. Matthew examined it again, realizing he was eager for another chance to run his fingers over her face. There was nothing about her skin and hair that wasn't soft and supple and utterly beautiful.

"Your hair should cover it adequately," he said, then looked her in the eye. "Do you feel well enough to ride with me?"

There was something in his tone that made her believe he might actually want her to. She handed the kerchief back to Jezebel.

"I am well enough, my lord."

He helped her from the carriage and led her over to his big dappled warhorse. The animal was muzzled to prevent it from biting everything that moved and Matthew made sure to keep his body between her and the horse. Luke stood at the animal's head, still reluctant to speak to the lady, fearful she'd not yet forgiven him for his behavior at the tavern. Their eyes met and he quickly lowered them, too fast to see the smile that played on her lips.

His hands went about her waist, completely encircling her. There was something to his touch that made her feel strangely giddy, but she attributed that to the bump on her head. She could feel the heat of his hands through her clothes, burning her. She did not dare turn to look at him, fearful that he would read her expression. He took a good grip of her and lifted her effortlessly towards the saddle.

That was when all hell broke loose.

CHAPTER TWO

The first hint that something was amiss was when the arrow hit Luke in the arm. At the horse's head, he grunted and pitched backwards.

Startled, Matthew lowered Alixandrea to the ground, knowing exactly what that arrow strike meant. He cursed himself for being stupid enough to find himself caught outside the gates of Wellesbourne in a vulnerable position. Their neighbor and Tudor ally, Lord Dorset, had been threatening them for weeks and he knew better than to allow himself to be caught in the open. But he just as quickly remembered that he had four hundred men at his disposal. Throwing his arms around the lady to shield her, he made haste for the carriage.

Even as he deposited her inside the cab, he was bellowing orders to the men at the rear. They responded to him quickly, confirming his initial observations that this was a seasoned crew. Strode clamored up onto the cab.

"Make haste for the castle," Matthew ordered in a tone that would have frightened God himself. "Stop for nothing."

Alixandrea did not have time to say a word to him before the carriage charged forward. Matthew was gone, preparing for battle. But she remembered Luke, lying on the ground with an arrow in him, and she stuck her head from the cab door.

"Strode!" she hollered. "Sir Luke is hit!"

She was gesturing to the knight, several feet away. Strode directed the carriage wildly in that direction, so hastily that a wheel caught in a hole near the road and ripped it right off the axel. The carriage collapsed onto one side, narrowly missing falling on Luke.

Strode was pitched off, rolling several feet away. But he was unharmed and called frantically to the women.

"My lady!" he cried. "Are you hurt?"

26

Her voice was muffled, annoyed. "No thanks to your driving."

If she was insulting him, then she must be well indeed. Strode crawled to the downed knight, listening to the howl of war around him as an unknown army emerged from the grove of trees to the northeast of the road. Metal hit upon metal as men met in battle. The peace of dusk quickly turned to chaos.

"My lord," Strode crawled up on Luke, helping him to sit. "Are you badly injured?"

Luke grimaced. "Not too," he said. "It is lodged in my arm. If you can get it out, I can still fight."

Neither one of them saw Alixandrea climb from the top of the wagon, exposing herself to flying arrows as she leapt to the ground. She fell to her belly, completely ruining her kirtle, and crawled to the men. She was horrified to see the arrow sticking out of the young knight.

"Dear God," she breathed, wanting to examine him but not wanting to hurt him. "Is it bad?"

"Not bad," Luke said as an arrow zinged overhead. "Remove this thing so that I may help my brother."

As if hearing his name, Matthew rounded the carriage astride his massive war beast. The creature's muzzle had been removed for the battle and Matthew's weapon was drawn. He was hardly recognizable through the menacing three-point helm that he wore.

"Get inside the carriage," he roared. "Luke, for God's sake, get her back inside where it is safe."

Luke nodded, acting as if he was still a fully functional knight and not an injured one. "Go," he said to Alixandrea. "Go before he becomes angry. Hurry."

The tone in his voice alone was enough to spur her back towards the carriage. They crawled through the grass and dirt, eventually reaching the carriage. Just as they did, a barrage of arrows peppered the underbelly and Alixandrea shrieked, instinctively putting her hands over her head to protect herself. Inside the cab, she could hear Jezebel scream in terror.

"We cannot chance trying to crawl in," she said. "They will

27

surely shoot us down the moment we try."

Luke had to agree. Many of the arrows seemed to be focused on the carriage. "Pull this arrow out of me," he half-grunted, half-demanded. "My brother needs my help."

Alixandrea and Strode looked at each other. There was reluctance in their faces, but they simply could not leave it there. While Strode held Luke by the shoulders, Alixandrea took a good grip on the arrow and yanked it straight back, straight out.

The ugly projectile fortunately came free in one pull, much to everyone's relief. Alixandrea wasn't sure if she could pull something like that from a man's flesh again. Though she'd been exposed to some manner of war her entire life, she had always been kept fairly removed from the horrors of it.

Taking the handkerchief that she had used to ease her own injury, she pressed it against the muscle of Luke's upper arm to stop the bleeding where the arrow had managed to wedge itself in through the mail and joint. He let her hold the cloth against him for about five seconds before rebelling.

"Enough," he pushed his way onto his feet. "My brother needs me."

With that, he was gone, racing around the side of the carriage, mounting his steed and galloping out of sight. Alixandrea and Strode sat in stunned silence, huddling against the cab for protection while the battle raged on. There was naught to do but sit and wait.

Wait they did, for a small eternity. The sounds of battle moved closer. It was difficult to tell the size of the enemy, but the men seemed to be fanning out because there was fighting in all directions.

The soldiers she had brought from Whitewell were some of her uncle's finest, extremely well trained. She knew they would fend off the enemy. However, as the fighting drew nearer, she began to grow concerned. She and her servants had no weapons should they be attacked. Her thoughts were lingering on perhaps finding a stick or rock or stone to protect herself with when a dirty, fighting body suddenly rounded the side of the carriage.

It was a foot soldier, but not one she recognized. It was a man with murder on his mind. As a scream left her lips, the soldier smacked Strode on the head and effectively neutralized him. He was on top of Alixandrea before she could take another breath.

His disgusting body, ripe with stench and dirty chain mail, writhed on top of her. Horrified and in a panic, she thrust her fist into his throat. Off guard, the man wretched horribly and released his grip long enough for her to break free. But she stumbled and he grabbed her surcoat before she could get away completely. He yanked her to the ground and began to overtake her once again.

Alixandrea was terrified. She struck the man, wrestled with him, even bit him on the wrist. She was rewarded with a sharp slap to her face. Suddenly, a body landed on top of her attacker and she realized that Jezebel had crawled from the carriage to help. But the soldier grabbed Jezebel by the hair and flipped her onto her back, knocking the wind from her. Alixandrea could hear her maid gasping for breath.

Renewed in her fight, she flipped over onto her stomach and struggled to get away from him. All he did was rip her kirtle and pull her hair. It was apparent what he wished to do. Alixandrea began to succumb to despair, knowing the man was far stronger than she and wishing she had a weapon. As he turned her over again, she noticed the arrow she had removed from Luke laying in the grass a few feet away. It was her only hope. She managed to throw herself in the direction of the projectile and grab it just as the lecherous soldier turned her over completely. She rammed the arrowhead straight into his eye.

Blood spurted everywhere. The man howled as he fell off of her, suffering through his death throes. There was blood all over Alixandrea's neck, chest, and in her luscious hair.

Blood was all that Matthew saw as he rounded the corner of the carriage. He, too, was covered in blood and he had a substantial wound on his thigh, but none of that seemed to matter. He practically fell off of the charger, ripping his helm off and tossing it to the ground as he went to her. He thought the blood was hers and horror filled him.

From the road heading south, they could hear what sounded like thunder. As Matthew fell to his knees beside her, Alixandrea did not realize that the roll of thunder signaled reinforcements arriving from Wellesbourne.

"My lady," Matthew demanded hoarsely. "Where are you hurt?"

She shook her head, sobs bubbling up until they spilled out all over. "He..," she gasped. "He did not hurt me. He tried, but I... I killed him. My God, I *killed* him."

Matthew let out a sigh so heavy that it was as if his entire body suddenly deflated. He put his hands on her shoulders to steady her; she was quivering violently.

"Let me see," he lifted her hair and checked her neck, shoulders and arms for damage. When he was convinced the blood wasn't hers, he met her still-terrified gaze. "Forgive me for leaving you unprotected. I did not realize Luke had left until I saw that his horse was gone."

She did not know what to say. All she knew was that she had killed a man and she could not shake the horror of it.

"He is dead," she whispered. "I killed him."

Matthew could see how shaken she was. Not knowing what else to do, he pulled her into his arms.

"You were brave, my lady," his lips were against her forehead. "Had you not killed him, he would have surely killed you. There is no shame in defending yourself."

She sobbed uncontrollably and he pulled her closer, perhaps just because he wanted to. "I did not want to do it," she wept. "He forced me to. I did not want to."

Matthew did not know what to say. He'd been in so many battles and had killed so many men that the act, the sight of it, did not bother him in the least. Such were the perils of war. But the lady was different; this was something new and horrifying and he felt tremendously remorseful for it. He should have been here to protect her, but he had left that duty to Luke, unaware his brother had run home for help. Then he had been caught up in his own mortal struggle. It took him some time to realize that the lady had been left unprotected. He was an idiot.

Behind him, he heard a growl and turned in time to see another opponent bearing down on him. On his knees with a woman in his arms was not the best position to meet an adversary.

Matthew unsheathed his sword with his right hand, turned to face his attacker and shoved Alixandrea behind him all in one clean motion. His foe was one of Dorset's finest and dispatching him was not as simple as a three-stroke kill. It took considerably more of Matthew's strength to slay the man that was trying very hard to kill him. The fight was brutal but eventually Matthew' skill and strength won out.

When the assailant lay dying on the ground, Matthew turned his attention once again to the lady. She stood back against the carriage, clutching Jezebel and struggling for composure. Strode had regained consciousness by this time and sat at her feet, nursing a sore head. As Matthew made his way back over to her, a knight suddenly roared up on a big red charger. The horse kicked up clods of earth, spraying it in all directions.

"Matt," the man demanded. "Are you well, man?"

Matthew paused, glancing down at his body, remembering the gash to his thigh. He nodded with some weariness.

"Well enough," he said. "How is Luke?"

"Fine," the knight said. "He rode back with us. Looks like Dorset's men again."

"I know." Matthew continued on towards Alixandrea. He reached out a hand to her, gently pulling her away from her frightened servants. "My lady, this is my brother, Sir Mark Wellesbourne. Mark, this is the Lady Alixandrea Terrington St. Ave. Take her back to the castle and make her safe."

Mark was in fighting mode but saw the seriousness in his brother's expression. He could only imagine what had gone on in the past several minutes; one look at the lovely lady showed that she had not been passed over in this battle.

He was, in fact, not surprised to see her. They should have

anticipated Dorset's men in the area, even though they had appeared to vacate a few days ago, and they should have doubly anticipated an ambush of the allied party. Although he wanted to stay and fight, he would obey his brother's wishes. He held out his arms.

"Give her to me," he said. "I shall return her home. Caroline will see to her."

Matthew swept Alixandrea into his arms, realizing the moment he touched her that he was very thankful she was in one piece. She was trembling; he could feel it through his armor. Their eyes met for a brief moment and he managed a weak smile before he handed her over.

"My brother will escort you to Wellesbourne," he said to her. "His wife will take excellent care of you."

Mark settled her in front of him, but she seemed reluctant to go. "But what about my servants?" she asked. "And my carriage? Who will...?"

"My men will get the carriage righted and send them on their way," he assured her. "Have no fear that all will be taken care of. Go with Mark now."

Having no further argument, she allowed Mark to settle her back on the saddle. He spurred his great red charger forward, galloping down the road to Wellesbourne.

Matthew stood a moment, watching them go, wondering why a thousand different thoughts and emotions were suddenly racing through his mind. He'd faced skirmishes like this before, countless times, and he'd only been focused on being victorious. But this battle had been different, and that the difference was currently riding to Wellesbourne with his brother.

***

Caroline Wellesbourne had made such a fuss over Alixandrea that one would have thought the Virgin Mary had walked right into their midst. Alixandrea was at a loss to understand why the woman was so thrilled to see her, but the few-minute trek from the steps of the keep, through the hall, up the spiral stairs and to the fourth floor told her why, exactly, the woman was so happy to have her.

Wellesbourne Castle was full of men, from top to bottom, and smelled like a pig sty. There were dogs everywhere, rubbish in the corners, and the great hall smelled of vomit and urine. The dogs freely used the corners of the room for the latrine. It was absolutely appalling. Caroline, overwhelmed and lonely, was clearly one of the only females in the entire castle and she was desperate for something fine and sweet and noble to remind her that such things did, indeed, still exist.

It had taken a long, hot bath and three servants to remove all of the blood and dirt from the battle. Caroline herself helped bathe her; she was sweet and overeager to help, and Alixandrea let her. Too soon the water grew tepid in the great copper tub and Caroline went in search of suitable garments since Alixandrea's were still in the carriage that had not yet arrived. Caroline reappeared with a soft blue robe, many layers of finely woven linen, and helped her new charge dry off and dress.

Truth be told, Alixandrea felt better than she had in weeks as she finally sat before the warming fire, running a bone comb through her long hair and allowing the heated air to dry it. It was good to be in something that wasn't rolling sickeningly over the road, and good to be in a place where she felt safe.

Caroline and the three servants continued to bustle in and out of the small chamber, sweeping out the dusty corners and making sure the linens and coverlet on the bed were moderately clean. Since they had not known in advance of her arrival, they made haste to make her comfortable. But she was already very comfortable and she finally put a stop to Caroline's frantic hovering when the woman decided that the mattress needed new straw.

"Truly, Lady Caroline, there is no need," she assured her. "The bed is fine. I will be most contented."

Caroline, a pale beauty with flaming red hair, did not look at all convinced. "But this straw is old," she insisted. "I do not even know when last it was changed. I would feel much better if we were to provide you with fresh stuffing."

Alixandrea shook her head, a smile on her lips. "My lady, you have been far too kind already. I would be grateful if you would simply sit and talk to me. It has been a long time since I have conversed with a lady."

Caroline's green eyes brightened and she did as she was asked. She was a tiny thing, quite a bit smaller than Alixandrea, and she took a seat upon a small three-legged stool that had been upended near the hearth. She faced Alixandrea with her hands folded neatly in her lap, waiting anxiously for her guest to begin the conversation. Alixandrea nearly laughed at her expectant expression.

"Tell me of yourself, Lady Caroline," Alixandrea said. "How long have you been married to Sir Mark?"

She blinked her big green eyes in thought. "We were married nearly two years ago, my lady," she said. "We met at the marketplace in Wandsworth, outside of London. My father is the Lord Mayor of Wandsworth."

Alixandrea tugged at the comb that had become stuck on a tangle. "Was it love at first sight?"

Caroline's pale cheeks pinkened. "Not quite," she said. "My father had to convince him that taking me as his wife was a good idea. Mark did not want to marry at all."

Alixandrea lifted an eyebrow. "That seems to be a Wellesbourne trait."

Caroline grinned. "Not with Luke. He wants to marry very badly," she said. "Now, tell me; did you meet with the enemy on the road and Matthew rode to save you? He is quite a knight. I know this because every time my husband starts telling stories about his valor in battle, he sends me from the room."

Alixandrea suppressed a smile. "He will not let you hear?"

"Nay. 'Tis too horrible for a lady's ears, he says."

And you believe that? Alixandrea did not say what she was thinking. "I met Sir Matthew and Sir Luke in a tavern at the edge of Newbold. We ran into each other, you could say."

"You were at the *Head O'Bucket?*"

"You know the place?"

"Only because the men go there when they want to get away from Wellesbourne. They have told me that it is a lively place with interesting people."

Alixandrea looked at her, aware that this woman may be slightly naïve, and slightly simple minded. Not that she was slow; simply that she seemed to have a rather gullible view of the world.

"It was certainly a busy place," she did not want to shatter the woman's illusion. "Have you never been?"

Caroline shook her head. "Mark will not allow it. He says that it is no place for a lady."

"He is correct. You are far too noble for a place like that."

It was a compliment that flushed her cheeks even more. Caroline wasn't sure how to respond; it did not occur to her to ask why Lady Alixandrea was at the place when it was allegedly too harsh for ladies. For lack of a better action, she stood up and took the comb from Alixandrea.

"Allow me, my lady," she offered.

Her small, white hands worked their way through Alixandrea's hair, expertly combing and fluttering the tresses so that the warm air dried them quickly. Alixandrea had an abundance of hair, wavy strands that ended just below her buttocks. Drying the mass would take a small eternity if not handled correctly.

"I used to do this to my sister all of the time," Caroline said after several moments of combing. "She had hair much like yours. I miss doing this for her."

"It has been a long time since you have seen her?"

"She died a few years ago in childbirth. She was sixteen years old."

"Oh," Alixandrea remarked softly. "I am sorry for you. I have never had a sister, but I can only imagine your grief."

Caroline forced a smile, but it was evident that the pain was still there. "I have the most beautiful five-year-old niece. Her name is Elinor."

"A lovely name," Alixandrea said. "It was my grandmother's name."

"Then we have something more in common."

Caroline had Alixandrea shift her chair so that the damp side of her head was facing the fire. She combed and fluttered furiously, drying out the heavy hair. Alixandrea was seated with her head slung back, staring up the ceiling, when the door to her chamber opened again. She thought it was the servants because they had been coming in and out with blankets and clothing and warmed mead. But then a voice spoke that sounded like the roll of thunder.

"I would speak with my lady, Caroline."

It was Matthew. Alixandrea sat up so fast that she nearly toppled from the chair, her bronze eyes focused on the huge man standing just inside the doorway.

He was still covered with blood, now dried black, and his face was lined with dirt where his helm had not protected his face from the elements. He met her gaze as if no one else in the room existed.

"Greetings, Matthew," Caroline said pleasantly. "'Tis good to see that you are not injured from the battle."

"Not overly," he said, forcing his attention away from Alixandrea to look at his sister-in-law. "If you would excuse us, please?"

It took Caroline a moment to realize that he wanted to speak with the lady alone. Her brow furrowed.

"I would not leave Lady Alixandrea unchaperoned, Matthew," she sounded as if she was scolding him. "'Tis not proper."

He had little patience for her propriety and struggled not to snap at her. Caroline was a delicate creature and he was unused to dealing with delicate creatures, especially since he was still in battle mode. He had been killing all afternoon and to snap a neck or bellow at a woman would have all been the same to him. He forced himself to calm.

"I promise that I will not harm or ravish the lady in any

fashion," he said. "Will that suffice?"

Caroline was obviously torn. "It simply isn't proper, Matthew."

"I know, love. But if you could just give us a moment, I would be grateful."

Caroline acted as if she were the last line of defense between her brother-in-law and the lady. She looked at Alixandrea, then back at Matthew again, before finally nodding her head.

"Very well," she said. "But I shall be right outside the door with my ear to the wood. And do not think for one moment that I will not come charging back in here if I hear anything questionable."

Matthew allowed the woman the illusion of power over this situation. So much of her life was beyond her control that he was content to let her believe she had the last word on something as simple as this. When the door to the chamber shut softly behind her, his attention refocused on Alixandrea.

Seated in the chair, her magnificent hair nearly dry and clad in a soft blue dressing gown, he was aware that his first impression of her had not been wrong. A door to heaven had opened somewhere and this woman had stepped onto the earth. He'd never seen anything so lovely and he paused a moment simply to stare at her. He could not help himself.

"I wanted to make sure that you did not suffer any ill effects from your adventure this afternoon," he said quietly. "It was, I would imagine, a harrowing experience to a refined lady such as you."

She smiled at him, vaguely aware that she was glad to see him. "Harrowing is an excellent term to describe it, my lord," she replied. "I see that you have made it out in one piece."

"Not for their lack of trying."

She laughed softly. "From what my uncle has told me, men have been trying to hack you to pieces for years."

"It feels like forever." *God, she is gorgeous when she smiles*, he thought giddily. "What else has your uncle told you about me?"

She shrugged lightly. "Only what everyone else knows; that you are a magnificent knight known throughout the realm as The White Lord of Wellesbourne. Even when I fostered at Pickering

Castle, I heard tales of your heroism. The young squires were raised on them."

"Surely you heard tale of others," he said modestly. "The empire is full of brave and cunning knights fulfilling their duty for the king."

She lifted an eyebrow. "That may be, but the more popular tales being fed to the men were of two particular knights. It was either The Dark Knight, who is said to rip men apart with his bare hands, or you, The White Lord, who is said to fight the enemy with all of the power of an avenging angel. You sweep through the land, smite all who oppose you, and vanish as swiftly as you came."

Matthew could not help it. The corners of his lips twitched with a smile at her dramatic reprisal of the stories that permeated the land. They got more dramatic with each mouth they passed through. Someday he might even come to believe them.

"Gaston de Russe, or The Dark Knight as you have called him, is truly a legend," he said. "I am simply mixed in with the rest of them."

She lifted an eyebrow. "Your humility is astonishing considering I have never known a knight to be anything other than completely full of himself."

He stared at her a moment, as if hardly believing she would dare insult the prodigious institution of knighthood, before finally breaking into snorts of humor. "I would say that is a fair statement," he said. Then his laughing abruptly stopped. "Just how many knights have you known?"

She grinned, something slightly mocking and even more evasive. "I meant the knights at Pickering and Whitewell. My uncle's fortress is full of knights who believe the sun would not dare rise or set without them."

He did not know why he suddenly felt a stab of jealousy at the thought of Alixandrea surrounded by dozens of brazen knights, all vying for her glorious attention. It further occurred to him that he had been an idiot for the past ten years, resisting Lord

Ryesdale's request for the marriage when he should have claimed her the very moment she came of age. Had he only known. Gazing into her rosy beauty, he could hardly believe she belonged to him.

"I see," he said after a moment. He took a few steps towards her. "My father has requested your presence in the hall this eve so that he may introduce you to the castle. As the Lady of Wellesbourne and my wife, you will be given all due respect."

She nodded. "I would be pleased to attend him, my lord, only... only my clothes do not seem to have arrived yet."

"They are here, in the courtyard. I told the servants to hold on bringing up your capcases until I called for them."

"My thanks," she said. He was standing there, looking at her with an odd expression on his face. She began to feel the slightest bit awkward. "Was there anything else, my lord? I should probably dress quickly if your father is expecting me."

His brow furrowed as if something puzzled him. Then he shook his head, turned around, and headed to the door. He was nearly to the panel when he came to a halt again and looked at her.

"May I ask you something, my lady?"

"Of course."

He began to retrace his steps towards her with deliberate thought. It was apparent he was grasping for words. "You and I have been betrothed for ten years."

"Aye, we have."

"And in all that time, did you have any reservations about this union?"

"What do you mean?"

"That, perhaps, you did not want to marry me?"

Her bronze eyes glittered in the firelight. "Do you mean did I have similar thoughts to your own?"

He came to a halt. "What do *you* mean?"

"You do not want to marry me, that much is clear. Luke was very plain. I suppose I should like to know what that reason's name is."

She was not only beautiful, she was intuitive. But it did not take a genius to sense his reluctance. He'd never tried to hide it.

"That reason was very long ago," he said quietly. "It no longer exists. And my reluctance to our union had nothing to do with her, at least not for the past several years."

"Then why the delay? Why the unwillingness? Why not just break the contract and allow me to marry another rather than wait for you?"

"*Is* there another?"

She was going to provide him with an evasive answer, but thought better of it. Ambiguity was no way to start a marriage she had waited long enough for. Besides, there was no point in lying.

"Nay," she replied softly. "There were a few who tried, but no one who caught my eye. I was, after all, promised to The White Lord. How could anyone compete with that?"

His blue eyes moved over her features, sensing her honesty. After a moment, his smile broke through. "They could not, of course," he said. "And thank God for it."

She met his smile but was a bit confused by his statement. "I do not understand."

He took a few steps until he was directly beside her, gazing down at her magnificent bronze-colored head. He could smell the scent of violets. It had been so long since he had smelled anything even remotely sweet or feminine that it almost made him light-headed.

"It means that we shall be married on the morrow and be done with any further delay. I command it."

She had to crane her neck up sharply to look at him. It was an uncomfortable position so she stood up, thinking it would be easier on her neck. But he was so tall that it made little difference.

"As you wish, my lord."

He was so close that she could feel the heat from his body. She could smell him, too. The combination made her head swim. And the way he was staring at her made her heart thump strangely.

She tore her gaze away, not knowing what else to do, wondering why she was feeling so strange. Her eyes inadvertently fell on his legs and she noted the big, dirty gash along his left thigh. It had bled a good deal and now the leg was covered with a layer of coagulated muck.

"You are injured," she bent over to gain a better look at the wound. "That should be tended immediately."

He looked down at his leg. He had very nearly forgotten about it. "I shall have it seen to." It was an automatic response. Then it occurred to him that she should want to tend it; as his betrothed, it was expected of her. "But if you should like to attend me, my lady, I would be honored."

She looked up at him and for the first time, he saw great uncertainty in her eyes. He'd seen nothing but complete confidence from this woman since the moment they met; therefore, the doubt was puzzling. "I fear... I fear that I would not do a very good job, my lord," she said.

"Nonsense," he stepped back and began unlatching his plate armor. "You will make a fine task of it."

She moved away from him as his armor fell off, half-frightened, half-entranced. She had only ever seen him with his armor on and even as he removed it, it made little difference in his overall size. He had massive arms, muscular and tremendously powerful. His chest was enormous, his waist slender, and his legs were the size of tree trunks. Stripped down to his stained undershirt and heavy linen breeches, there was nothing about the man that did not reek of absolute strength and power. He was magnificent.

It took her a minute to realize she had stopped breathing. When she resumed, it came out as an odd gasp. He looked over at her, standing several feet away.

"Where would you like me to sit?" he asked.

She responded like a dolt. "Sit?"

He lifted his eyebrows at her. "Aye, sit. Or do you want me to stand while you sew this gash?"

She suddenly grimaced, an expression between agony and

41

fear. "I... I have a confession, my lord. I pray that you do not think badly of me because of it."

"Think badly of you? I doubt it. But what is it?"

She shoved her finger between her teeth as if that would help bring forth the words. "Oooo...!" then she shook her hands with frustration. "I cannot sew your gash. I have never been able to do such things. My uncle said I was absolutely useless and he is correct. Such things make me ill. I know it is foolish, but I cannot help it. I am truly sorry, my lord. You deserve a wife that will be brave and tend your wounds. But I... I cannot do it."

He stood there a moment, staring at her. The room filled with a great shock of silence. Then, he erupted in snorts and giggles the likes of which Alixandrea had never heard from a man. He put his hands over his face briefly and when he pulled them away, his eyes were shining brightly at her.

"Thank God," he muttered. "I was feeling so completely inferior to you because I was convinced that you were utterly perfect. From the top of your glorious head to the bottom of your feet, you are an angel incarnate. But now I see that you have one flaw, just one, and it pleases me like no other."

She could not decide if she was flattered or insulted. She settled on flattery and smiled along with him. "I can do anything else for you, my lord, and surely will, but don't ever ask me to sew a wound. I would rather die a thousand painful deaths."

He was still snorting as he walked over to her and placed his trencher-sized hands on her head, cupping it. He gazed down into her lovely face, allowing himself to freely drink in the sight of her.

"Have no fear, my lady," he said in a voice that sent chills racing up her spine. "I do not think any less of you. In fact, I think more."

They were grinning at each other. Then, the grins slowly faded and something stronger took hold. Alixandrea's head began to swim again as his blue eyes bore into her. There was something in the way they flickered.

Somehow, he seemed to be drifting closer. She could feel his breath on her face. Her body began to tingle painfully, anticipation of something she could not yet feel or taste or see. But just as he loomed in close, he suddenly pulled back. His thumbs stroked her cheeks, once, and he dropped his hands.

"Caroline will sew the wound," he was walking away from her, leaving her weak and breathless. "In fact, she had probably heard all of this conversation."

He put his hand on the latch and yanked the door open. Caroline almost fell into the room. Her embarrassed gaze moved between Matthew and Alixandrea, having been caught eavesdropping.

"All is well, my lady?" she asked Alixandrea timidly.

Matthew lifted a blond eyebrow at her. "You know that it is." He gestured to his leg. "I require your assistance in tending this wound."

Caroline did not even look at it; she was too busy trying to recover her composure. "I shall go and get my things. Will you wait here?"

"Alone, with the lady? How improper."

Alixandrea hid a smile as Caroline blushed furiously.

"Enough of your torment, Matthew Wellesbourne," she snapped weakly. "Another spiteful word and you can sew your wound yourself."

His blue eyes twinkled. "How do you know that my lady will not tend it for me?"

Caroline opened her mouth, knowing the answer, but just as quickly knowing that she should not reveal it. To do so would be to admit she was listening to their conversation. In a huff, she quit the room. Matthew, smiling faintly, looked at Alixandrea and shrugged.

"I suppose I shall wait with here, if you do not object."

"I do not."

He watched her turn away from him and move closer to the fire. For the first time, he could get a good look at her figure without the layers of clothing and cloaks to hide it. He admitted that he had been curious to inspect her with all of the interest of one inspecting a new prize mare.

But with his first inspection, he got more than he bargained for; the firelight passed through the fine linen of the robe and silhouetted her body against the sheer fabric. Matthew knew he shouldn't look, as a gallant man would not have. But as a man who had just acquired something he had never imagined he would have, he could not stop himself; her legs were lovely and shapely, her torso slender. She put her arms up to comb her hair and in doing so turned slightly, and he could see the outline of her breasts and buttocks against the backdrop of flame.

He'd never seen anything so luscious or pleasing. To think that he would soon be claiming this woman bodily as his wife brought heat to his loins and he forced himself to turn away, fearful of his physical reaction to her. It was the most sweeping, instantaneous reaction he'd ever had in his entire life and the uncontrollability of it startled him.

"Are you going to have my servants bring up my possessions, my lord?" she interrupted his thoughts.

He was too embroiled in visions of her ripe body. "What's that?" he caught himself. "Aye, of course. Right away."

He left the chamber, perhaps too quickly, and descended the narrow stairs to the third floor. He did not go any further but shouted down the stairwell to the soldier on the floor below. When the soldier went to do his bidding, he remounted the steps, more slowly this time, and took a deep breath to steady himself.

He'd never known himself to be nervous, but he realized that was exactly what he was feeling. Something about the lady in the chamber upstairs unnerved him as no one else ever had. He had never wanted her, much less wanted to feel anything for her, but feel he did. It was something new and strange and unsettling, and he could not decide if he liked it or not.

Mounting the top step, he shook himself imperceptibly; *get hold of yourself, man*. She was a woman, like any other. Perhaps he was feeling this way because it had been so long since he'd found a woman attractive. It had easily been years and she was affecting him with her mere presence.

Matthew had faced battles since he had been seventeen years

of age as a full-fledged knight; nothing frightened him and certainly nothing unnerved him. But the introduction of this lovely lady had quickly circumvented the personal defenses he had practiced all his life. He had no defense against a beautiful woman. And he wasn't sure how to aptly deal with it.

He re-entered the room, mildly fortified, only to find her still standing in front of the fire with her delectable body delineated through the semi-transparent fabric.

He thought it best to wait at the top of the stairs.

CHAPTER THREE

Howard Terrington, Lord Ryesdale, had come from a long line of those who supported the White Rose of the House of York. His father and his fathers before him had battled beside Edward the Third, his son and grandson. In fact, Edward had granted William Terrington the charter at Whitewell to build a castle. Though it was more a fortified manor house, it was still formidable and anchored the main road across the Pennines from Lancaster, making it particularly strategic.

Whitewell had seen more than its share of action over the years, more skirmishes than actual battles. It wasn't preferential to move an army over the narrow, hazardous road that crossed the Pennines and straight into a battle, so most armies tended to travel far to the north or to the south to bypass them.

Whitewell's greatest threat came from the mighty Richmond Castle to the northwest, held by Edmund Tudor, Earl of Richmond. Since both castles were fairly isolated, they took no real part in the major battles in the war between the Roses, but Whitewell spent a good deal of time fending off raids and other forms of harassment. Here in the northern wilds, the Houses of Lancaster and York butted against each other, intertwined, and territories tended to blend like oil and water.

Howard was well aware of the rivalries, old, new, imagined and otherwise. But he considered himself far more shrewd than his ancestors in that he fully understood the power of his location. Since nearly the moment he took possession of the castle when his father died fifteen years ago, he only had his own betterment in mind. His ambition had started a few years ago when he had first been approached by an ally of the late Sir John Grey, a Lancastrian and relation to the Woodvilles. John Sutton, Lord Dudley, had been very clear in his mission; he was to secure Whitewell at any cost and when Henry Tudor sat up on the throne, he would make it well worth Howard's efforts. The Red Rose of Lancaster needed to secure the mountain pass, a short-cut from Lancaster to the Honour of Richmond, and they were willing to prostitute themselves in that effort.

All of this, of course, was unknown to the common man. Though Howard Terrington willingly climbed into bed with the Lancastrians at the promise of assuming some of Richmond's territories upon Henry's ascension to the throne, his Yorkist allies were none the wiser. No one questioned why armies of men were given passage over the Pennine road, mostly because the troops stationed at Whitewell were loyal to Terrington and simply did as they were told. If their lord ordered the road left unprotected, then they would oblige.

But there was more to Howard's greed. He not only wanted the wealth promised him, he wanted honor and glory, too. He was not a fighting man. He was a politician. When his only sister passed away and he became guardian of his niece, one look at the nine year old Alixandrea St. Ave and he knew that he had something to broker. He could see a beneficial marriage on the horizon, something to bring him the recognition he sought. So he brokered Alixandrea's hand like an auctioneer selling prize livestock.

Many prominent families had vied for the honor. John Sutton had made the final selection; Matthew Wellesbourne, son of Sir Adam Wellesbourne. The Wellesbournes had passed to Richard through his marriage to Anne Neville and were the prime forces in the king's arsenal. It was all the Lancastrian camp could have ever hoped for. They had planted a seed in the heart of Richard's strength. And that seed was Alixandrea Terrington St. Ave.

Not that she knew anything about it. She was a female and untrustworthy as most women were. Howard spent many years trying to set a marriage date so that he could move his niece and his contingent of four hundred highly trained Lancastrian-loyal men into the heart of the Plantagenet arena, but the House of Wellesbourne had continually put him off. It had taken ten years to place Alixandrea, and the sleeper army, where they belonged.

Now that the deed was done, it was time to set the plan in motion.

It was rainy this day, the first rain in quite some time, as he sat in his opulent solar at Whitewell. A fire smoked in the hearth and warmed wine ran aplenty. But he was not alone.

"She should be at Wellesbourne in a day or two," he said. "I anticipate her travel should take nearly two weeks, probably less."

He spoke to a man standing near the fire. He was a big man, attractive, a mercenary knight from Brittany who had served Henry Tudor for years. Sir Dennis la Londe was a feared assassin and a shrewd warrior, a volatile combination. Today, he was on an errand as a catalyst to greater things.

"I would agree," he said in his heavy French accent. "And your man; what was his name? Strode? He is aware of our intent, is he not?"

Howard nodded, studying the red liquid in his cup. "Very much aware. He has been instructed to unleash the troops the very moment the marriage takes place."

La Londe moved away from the fire, moving to the lancet windows. Rain dripped down on the sill, trickling down onto the floor. "Excellent," he said. "The time is upon us, Terrington. All that we have planned and hoped for is finally coming to fruition. Your niece's marriage could not have come at a better time."

La Londe often knew things that Howard did not. He was far more into Henry Tudor's inner circle than Terrington was.

"What do you mean?" Howard asked leadingly.

Dennis turned from the window. "I mean exactly what I said. There will be no long wait for our plans to come to pass. What will happen at Wellesbourne will happen with deliberate purpose to coincide with Henry's imminent arrival."

Although Howard had been hearing rumors about this for quite some time, it was the first confirmation he had received. It was what every Tudor ally had been waiting for. "Henry is finally coming? When?"

"Soon," la Londe said vaguely. Howard Terrington was not

someone he wanted to divulge everything to, at least not all at once. "Within the month we will unleash our army inside the walls of Wellesbourne and effectively cripple a great deal of the king's support. By the time Henry reaches England's shores, Richard's strength will be compromised. This is exact as Lord Sutton had intended, Howard. Bring down Wellesbourne and you cut off Richard's right hand."

"And weaken his resistance."

"Exactly. But there is more, *mon ami.*"

"What more is there?"

"Wiltshire and Pembroke are moving their armies to Shrewsbury. So are several other nobles. And do you know why?"

"Nay."

La Londe lifted an eyebrow. "Because it is the midsection of the country. Occupy it, fill it, create a noose around it and effectively cut off the north from the south. Separate Richard from his allies. And then the noose shall tighten as Henry arrives with his army of French and Teutonic mercenaries to assume his rightful place."

Howard could only think of what he would gain once Henry took the throne. "So it comes," he muttered, more to himself than to la Londe. "We've waited so long that I can hardly believe it. And to know that my niece will play a part in it..."

"As I said, her marriage to Wellesbourne could not have come at a better time," la Londe reiterated. "You should be congratulated. Your niece will accomplish what hordes of men could not. The fall of the White Lord of Wellesbourne will be a great feat."

It was why Howard had married her off in the first place. He could see that his place of respect with Henry Tudor would be assured. "Do not forget that, as the widow of Wellesbourne, she will be a very wealthy woman and much desirable as a reward to a worthy ally."

La Londe looked at him as if he was daft. "Why do you think I am here?" he said. "Never imagine that I have maintained my contact with you all of these years simply because I enjoy your company. I want something from you, Terrington."

Howard was astute enough to understand the implication. There could be no other choice. "You want my niece?"

La Londe nodded slowly, his pale-colored eyes narrowed and glittering. He was a terrifying man at times. "I have met the Lady Alixandrea. She is quite a prize. With Wellesbourne's wealth, she will be more than adequate compensation for my loyalties."

As much as Howard was fairly indifferent to his niece, he wasn't at all sure he wanted to see her wed to la Londe. But the man had indeed risked himself to support Henry Tudor's cause and had earned such compensation. In fact, it was only through such adequate recompense that la Londe sold his powerful loyalties.

"Fair enough," he said. He drained the last of his wine. "But we must veer back to the subject at hand; if Henry's arrival is as imminent as you say, then we must waste no time. The wheels must be put in motion."

"But the wheels are already in motion," la Londe barely let him finish before he was responding. "There are two purposes at heart, *mon ami*. Not only must we destroy the infrastructure of Wellesbourne, but in capturing the castle we must draw Richard's troops away from Henry's arrival. While some of the York allies are concentrated on regaining Wellesbourne, Henry will land in England and meet with potentially less resistance."

"My men will create a diversion."

"Precisely. And they must hold that diversion until Henry arrives."

"When will we know?"

"I would expect word to arrive within the next week. It is nearly June; Henry has been gathering strength for some time now. He plans to be on the throne by September."

Howard's cup was empty. He rose from his chair and collected the fine cut glass decanter that had been imported all the way from the Holy Land. The blood-red liquid swirled as he poured himself another measure and then a cup for la Londe. He offered the man the chalice.

"A toast," he said. "To plans well received and well executed."

La Londe lifted his cup. "To a prize worth having."

Howard drank deeply. He'd made a deal with the Devil and was very well aware of it.

***

The kirtle was a pale yellow and the sleeveless surcoat a deeper, richer gold. Unlike most women of fashion who wore a plackart from shoulder to chest as a sort of bib, Alixandrea's breasts were too full for such a thing so she had taken to wearing a whale bone corset instead. It wasn't unheard of in courtly fashion and supported her far more adequately. The problem was that Jezebel laced her into the thing as if she were tying up a pig to the spit. The more Alixandrea grunted, the harder Jezebel pulled until she was satisfied that the stays were correct and the lacings in the rear were property tied and left to trail. As a whole, Alixandrea already presented a lovely picture.

But there was more. Jezebel rolled fresh hose up each leg made of kersey, which was a lamb's wool blend, and fastened them with yellow ribbon. Then the slippers went on, made from damask and finely embroidered. Finally, it was time to tackle the hair, which the little maid did so quite ably.

She had become adept at the art of her mistresses hair and in little time, Alixandrea had a single thick braid draped over one shoulder into which a dozen yellow ribbons had been interwoven. Two golden hairpins in the shape of butterflies were placed strategically on her head, and the ends of the long kirtle sleeves were fixed with decorative weights to keep them properly draped. She wore no jewelry this night; she did not need any. By the time Jezebel was finished with her mistress, she was indeed a presentable sight.

Alixandrea stood there for a moment, gazing at herself in the polished bronze hand mirror that she had brought with her. Golden-brown eyes gazed back and thick lashes tickled her brow

51

every time she blinked. Jezebel bustled around her, picking up the robe from her earlier bath. She noticed her lady's distant expression.

"What is it, m'lady?" she asked. "Are ye not happy with yer presentation?"

Alixandrea shook her head and lay the mirror down. Beside her, on a small table that one of Lady Caroline's servants had brought in, sat a small alabaster pot of a mixture of beeswax and oil. Alixandrea was forever nibbling on her lips, a bad habit she had acquired; consequently, they were always cracked and bleeding. She smoothed the ointment on her lips to soothe them.

"I am," she sighed. "'Tis simply that this day... well, it has been exhausting. It certainly did not go the way I had planned. And now I must face the entire castle as Matthew's betrothed. I suppose I am just a bit apprehensive."

"But why?" Jezebel stood next to her, her arms full of clothes. "Ye're as lovely as an angel, m'lady. Can ye not see that Sir Matthew thinks so, too?"

Alixandrea looked at her. "He does?"

"Aye. He cannot take his eyes from ye."

"He can't?"

"Nay."

Alixandrea looked back at herself. She fussed with the little tendrils of hair that curled around her face, inspecting her features, wondering what he apparently found so fascinating. Jezebel went to put the laundry away and collected a small glass vial of perfume oil out of one of the capcases. She dabbed the scent of roses and violets on her lady's slender shoulders.

"There," she said with quiet approval. "Any man in this kingdom would be proud to have ye, m'lady. You go into that hall tonight and show those Wellesbourne men what they have been missin'."

Alixandrea felt much better with Jezebel's encouragement. The woman was her staunchest supporter and her harshest critic. "Will you be all right tonight while I am at sup?" she asked her.

"I shall find my way, m'lady. Have no worries."

Satisfied her maid would not starve, she stood up and began to pace around. The chamber was very small, hardly enough room for the bed, chair and small table, but it was comfortable and more than likely the cleanest room in the keep. Of that she was moderately sure. She started to chew her lip but tasted the ointment and stopped. Then she started to bite her nails, another bad habit, but Jezebel swatted her hands so she clenched them into fists and lowered them. By the fourth trip around the chamber, there was a soft knock at the door. Alixandrea froze as Jezebel opened the panel.

Four men stood in the very small landing just outside the door. She recognized Matthew right away, for he was the first one in the doorway. But what she saw amazed her; he had cleaned up from his harrowing day and stood in a pale linen tunic, leather breeches and massive boots. He wore no armor at all. His face was washed and she was sure from the smoothness of it that he had shaved. His blue eyes glittered at her as she came near, and the four men bowed deeply.

"My lady," Matthew said. "We have come to escort you to sup."

"And just who might 'we' be, my lord?"

"My brothers," Matthew indicated them in order. "Mark, Luke, and Johnny."

"Just the four of you?"

"That's all there is."

A faint smile played on her lips as she inspected the group; she recognized Mark only because she had met him earlier on their frantic ride to Wellesbourne. He was the shortest brother, stocky, with thinning black hair and a neatly trimmed black beard. Beside him stood Luke, who was as tall as Matthew but only half as wide. He smiled timidly when their eyes met. The last brother was one she had yet to see, a tall, slender young lad of perhaps twenty years with a head of wavy blond hair. John Wellesbourne had freckles all over his face and grinned shyly when she looked at him.

"A genuine pleasure, my lords," she dipped in a smooth curtsy.

"I am honored."

Matthew extended his hand. "If my lady is ready, sup awaits."

She allowed him to lead her from the chamber and assist her down the steps. In fact, Matthew and Mark made sure to stay in front of her, admonishing her to watch her step on the narrow stairs. John and Luke hovered just behind her, each vying for the spot directly behind her. The stairwell was too narrow for them to descend side by side, so someone had to go first and someone had to bring up the rear. Luke lost the battle when John finally shoved him out of the way and nearly made him lose his footing.

Another spiral stair led from the third floor to the second. This stairwell was wider, but it was nonetheless steep. Matthew walked backwards, making sure she kept a grip on him as she descended. It would not do for the lady to trip on her elegant gown and break her neck. He could see John and Luke fighting behind her, slapping each other around, but he ignored them. Like eager boys, they were immediately taken with the latest addition to Wellesbourne.

The second floor of the keep housed the enormous hall. There was a small entryway, into which the stairwell was built, and the main hall off of that. When the five of them got to the bottom of the stairs, Lady Caroline and an older man, stocky with thinning gray hair, were waiting for them.

Lady Caroline gracefully curtsied. "My lady," she greeted, reaching out to take her arm. "How elegant you look. I am so happy that you are here."

Alixandrea smiled at her; she was coming to like the lady. "I am happy as well. Thank you for your kindness."

"Allow me to present the patriarch of the Wellesbournes, Sir Adam," Caroline indicated the man next to her. "My lord, this is the Lady Alixandrea Terrington St. Ave, Matthew's wife to be."

Adam gazed at her a moment before reaching out and gently taking her hand. He covered it with his big warm palm. "I had no idea Matthew's betrothed would be so lovely," he said. "You must forgive us, my lady. Other than Lady Caroline, we are unused to such beauty in this place. Your arrival has both brightened and honored us."

"You are too kind, my lord," she said. "Everyone had been so kind to me. I am most happy to be here."

Adam smiled broadly, something he hadn't done in years, and tucked her hand into the crook of his elbow. Witnessing this, it occurred to Matthew that he would not be permitted to escort his betrothed into the great hall for everyone to see. His father would do it. But he made sure to walk directly behind her as the entered the pungent, brightly lit hall.

Wellesbourne Castle harbored something along the lines of five hundred men at any given time. With the troops that Alixandrea had brought with her, that number was nearly doubled. The feasting hall was reserved for senior soldiers, officers and knights, and there were about a hundred of them, all gazing at Alixandrea as she entered the room on their liege's arm. A group of traveling minstrels had sought shelter for the eve and stood in the corner, playing for their supper. But even the musicians silenced when the lady entered the room. It was the very same reaction that those in the tavern in Newbold had suffered; the moment she set foot in the room, no one could take their eyes from her.

Adam led her up onto the dais. A massive table was set upon it, full to bursting with food. The enormous hearth, at least eight feet tall, was directly behind them blasting heat in their direction. The brothers took their usual places at the table while Matthew took up a seat on Alixandrea's right side. Usually he sat at his father's right, but tonight that privilege was reserved for his future wife.

The introduction of Alixandrea was short and to the point. There wasn't much Adam could say that wasn't already obvious. Every man in the room was gazing hungrily at her. Matthew felt like a dog guarding his bone; he could see that this situation could potentially become deadly if he did not establish the rules from the beginning. "I would add one thing to my father's introduction of the Lady Alixandrea," his voice boomed when Adam was finished. "As you love and respect me, love and respect my wife. Know that she is mine and, as such, will be given all due reverence. Any transgression against her, no matter how small, will be forcefully dealt with. That is my word."

The men knew Matthew well enough to know exactly what he meant. He was quite fair and, on occasion, congenial with his men. He would interact with them where other knights of his stature would never dream of it. He had been known to roll the dice with them while on campaign and inquire on the health of even the lowliest soldier when warranted. For that, he was unique and for that, he was very much loved. He inspired a loyalty that most men could only dream of.

On that note, the meal was brought forth without further delay. Matthew offered to share his trencher with her before his father could make the suggestion and the old man glared at him. Matthew glared back. The dogs, having been relatively quiet in the corner of the hall, suddenly came to life as the food came out. Alixandrea watched the great platters being set forth across the table as Matthew reached out and grabbed the nearest knuckle of beef.

He laid it upon the trencher and handed her a knife. "My lady?"

She turned to look at him, seeing that he was offering her the first of the food. With a smile, she took the knife and cut at the well-browned meat.

"I hope this is to your liking," Matthew said.

"It looks wonderful," she pulled off a succulent piece and popped it into her mouth. "It is very good."

He smiled at her and ripped off his own hunk of beef. But there were more dishes being set down and Alixandrea studied each one with great interest until Matthew took the hint and began pulling all of the dishes across the table.

"This is peacock," he ripped a browned bird leg off of the body and put it on their plate. "And this," he tugged at a smaller bird leg, "is waterfowl. Swan."

She nibbled at the peacock. "Do you always eat this well?"

The corners of his blue eyes crinkled. "Only when we have very special guests."

Chewing, she watched him with a smile on her lips until he turned to look at her. "I am a guest, am I? I thought I was to be a resident. Was I wrong?"

He lifted his eyebrows as he reached for the wine. "Nay," he poured some sweet red liquid into her cup. "But your arrival is certainly an occasion."

"A happy one?" she teased.

"Aye."

She swallowed her food. Leaning in his direction, she put on her best serious expression. "Are you sure? We are not married yet, after all. I suppose you could still delay the marriage if you had a mind to."

Thoughts of her supple body silhouetted through the sheer robe by the firelight crossed his mind. "I have no inclination to."

"Surely?"

He sighed heavily and leaned into her just as she was leaning into him. Their faces were mere inches from each other. As she held a mock serious expression, he matched it.

"You are never going to forgive me for delaying our marriage, are you?"

"Eventually. But not today."

He could see humor playing in her eyes. "Are you always this vindictive?"

Her eyes narrowed, though it was in good fun. "This is nothing, my lord. You should see me when I am rightly angry."

"I do not ever wish to see you rightly angry," he assured her. "And in private conversation, you will call me Matthew. Or Matt. I will answer to whatever you choose."

A moment of jest had turned into a genuine moment of warmth. "As I will answer to Alixandrea," she said quietly. "Or wife. I will answer to whatever you feel is appropriate and worthy."

"Alixandrea is a very long name," his voice was low; he was enjoying her closeness. "Were you never called anything else? A nickname, perhaps?"

She thought a moment. "My mother used to call me Ali when I

was a child. But that was long ago."

He smiled. She smiled. He could not help himself from reaching up and stroking a finger across her soft cheek. "Ali is for a child," he murmured. "Alixandrea is for a woman, and a beautiful one at that."

He might as well have scorched her face, for that was the same effect his finger had upon her flesh. She could still feel the heat from it and it set her heart to racing. Their eyes held one another for an eternity of small moments until someone shouted encouragement to Matthew of a personal nature and he broke away, looking out over the room. To his right a table of his men were shouting at him to kiss his bride. He waved them off. He did not want their first kiss to be a spectacle.

Alixandrea returned to her fowl. A servant had set a marzipan subtlety in the shape of a little castle near her left hand and she commandeered a slice of it. Off to her right was an almond milk pudding with raspberries and sugared rose petals; she took some of that, too.

Matthew watched her as they ate, smiling when their eyes met. The wine was particularly good and she downed two cups of it in short order. With the music and festivities, she forgot about her harrowing day, only thinking of the wonderful life she was sure to have in this place. Matthew no longer seemed resistant to their union and she was doubly pleased. The White Lord she had dreamt of for ten years would soon be hers.

"Do you sing, my lady?"

The soft male voice came from her left. She turned to see that Adam was speaking to her.

"Somewhat, my lord," she replied.

"Excellent," he said happily. "Will you honor us with a song?"

She visibly blanched. "Now?"

"Please," Adam begged gently. "It has been too long since I have heard a fine lady sing. Caroline has many talents, but singing is not one of them."

Alixandrea glanced around the room of feasting, drinking men. They were loud and boisterous and she was intimidated. She caught Matthew out of the corner of her eye and she looked at him, trying to think of a way to gracefully decline the request. He could see her reluctance.

"Now is not a good time, Father," he said. "The lady has had a trying day. It is too much."

"Nonsense," Adam scoffed. "How difficult is it to sing a little song? I wish it."

Matthew did not look particularly pleased. "I do not think it would be wise."

"I *wish* it."

Alixandrea could see that there was no way out of the situation and she did not want to create a battle between them.

"Very well, my lord," she said. "What would you like to hear?"

"My Own True Love," Adam said without hesitation. "It was a favorite of Matthew's mother."

She stood up to leave the table. A glance at Matthew showed him to be still seated, his expression bordering on displeasure. She did not understand why he seemed so unhappy with his father's request. But he stood up, dutifully took her hand, and led her through the maze of drunk men to the minstrels on the other side of the room. Leaving her with the musicians, he took to the shadows but stayed nearby, mostly for protection against the drunken masses.

Alixandrea asked the minstrels to play the song that Adam had requested and the men heartily agreed. They were very young men, four of them, that had proven quite skilled with their talents. They played the vielle, citole, harp and flute. She turned to face the crowd as Mark and Luke whistled loudly for silence. The hall quieted somewhat as the men, and their drink, turned to the lovely vision in yellow standing against the north wall. Even the servants in the gallery above stopped in their duties to listen. The air quieted.

She had a captive audience. Alixandrea tried not to think of the hundreds of eyes staring at her. She had sung in an assembly before, many times, but this was different. She did not know these people and she did not want to make a fool of herself. She hoped they would like her.

The music began, the soft introduction of the many-stringed citole. After a few delicate bars, the words came.

O lovely one... my lovely one..
The years will come... the years will go...
But still you'll be... my own true love...
Until the day... we'll meet again....

Her voice was as pure as the ringing of silver bells, sweet and lilting and high. Her tone and pitch were perfect, in delicate combination with the haunting sound of the citole. There wasn't one person in the hall that hadn't come to a complete halt, in movement or in conversation, within the first few notes of her song. The second verse continued.

O lovely one... my lovely one...
My love for you... will never die...
My heart is yours... 'til the end of time...
When you will be...my own true love...

The song was over, though no one dared move. Alixandrea stood there, horrified that they did not like her song. But then the hall erupted in riotous cheering, so loud that she nearly had to cover her ears. She looked around and spied Matthew back against the wall behind her. He simply gazed at her, his face expressionless, before finally moving forward to claim her. She looked at him for some indication of what he thought of her talent. He gave her none.

He took her all the way back to the table where Adam sat with tears in his eyes. Alixandrea was flattered and concerned all at the same time.

"My lord?" she asked hesitantly. "Was the song not to your liking?"

Adam sniffled and wiped his eyes. He was drunk, that was true, but the song would have brought tears to his eyes even if he had not been. He put a big warm hand over her fingers.

"I have heard that song many times, my lady," he said. "I have never heard it sung quite so beautifully."

She smiled her thanks, turning to Matthew to see if she could yet gain a reaction from him. Wine in hand, he was gazing into his chalice.

"My lord?" she said softly. "Did you not like the song?"

He swirled the dregs and took a long drink. Then he looked at her. "I was wrong."

"About what?"

"You. You *are* perfect."

"I do not understand."

He sighed and set the cup down. "My mother used to sing that song to me," he said quietly. "I always thought it was the most beautiful thing in the world the way she sang it. But you... you sing it better than she ever could."

She sensed sorrow from him and wasn't sure why. "I am truly sorry if I have upset you," she did not know what to say. "Your father asked me to sing the song and I did not know that..."

He looked at her, the warmth back in his eyes. "You did nothing but sing that song more sweetly than anything on this earth. It simply reminded me of my mother and how much I miss her. You will sing many more times for me in the years to come."

"If you wish it."

"I do."

"Then I did not offend you?"

"Of course not."

Adam could not seem to stop weeping. He put his hand on her arm. "Will you sing the song again, just for me?"

Alixandrea looked to Matthew for guidance. His father was shedding tears and she did not want to aggravate it. Matthew sighed heavily; there was still displeasure in his voice in spite of his words to the contrary. "Sing it. It has been a long time since he has heard it."

She sang the song thirteen times that evening.

CHAPTER FOUR

"They are up to something; I can feel it," Matthew said ominously. "The Earl of Wiltshire has moved his men north to Nottingham. And there's word of more nobility moving their troops to the north, including the Earl of Pembroke, though that is no small surprise. Can you not see that all of this military movement signals a gathering, something great and powerful?"

It was dawn. The Wellesbourne brothers were gathered in the stale, smoky solar, huddled around a table covered with a massive, overly-used map. There were ink stains upon the vellum, which had also seen a dagger or two thrown into it for good measure. Pock marks littered the yellowed leather.

"Your instincts, as always, are without question," Mark said. "With Jasper Tudor moving his troops from Pembroke Castle, there could only be larger things on the horizon."

"Then you agree that something major is in the development."

"It would seem so. Dorset's activity against us for the past few weeks has indicated that something larger is on the horizon. Our spies have also indicated as much. But this sunrise has seen confirmation of that."

Matthew looked up from the table. "What do you mean?"

"Lord Sutton and the Earl of Somerset are on the move," Mark's voice was grim. "Two of our scouts returned this morning to tell us that Somerset has a contingent of a thousand Irish mercenaries sailing up the Mouth of the Severn. They'll make Gloucester in a few days."

Matthew listened carefully to his brother. He looked as if he hadn't slept all night, which he hadn't. But the lack of sleep had never dulled him.

"Do we know this for certain?" he asked.

"Certain enough," Mark said. "Thomas and Harl have returned with this news, and they are two of our most trusted."

Matthew recognized the names of the moles. They had been in Wellesbourne's service for years and were well versed in the world of intelligence gathering. Leaning against the massive map table, he ran his hand over his close-shorn hair. It was a pensive, if not weary, gesture.

"A thousand mercenaries," he muttered, more to himself. "Copious amounts of manpower are pouring into the heart of England. It is like watching a man bleed to death and not knowing how to stop the blood. It just keeps coming."

"So what do we do?" Luke asked.

"Obviously, the king must know," Matthew replied. "I shall question the scouts myself to make sure there is nothing else we should know before sending them on to Richard."

Mark nodded. "I thought you would want to. In fact, I tried to locate you last night when they arrived but was unable to find you."

"I was with Father."

A strange, if not disappointed, silence filled the air. It confirmed what they had all assumed, but it was Luke who finally spoke.

"You cannot blame her, you know," he said quietly.

"I do not blame her," Matthew said evenly. "But we should have known. I tried to stop him, but not firmly enough. I should have put a stop to it before it even started."

Mark and Luke passed long glances. "He was like this when Caroline first came to us," Mark said quietly. "The presence of a lady seems to unnerve him that way. But he got over it."

"Aye, he did, but at what cost?" Matthew began to show irritation, fed by his exhaustion. "It is not either one of you that sits with him all night, listing to him cry, holding him down when he tries to throw himself into the blazing hearth or hang himself with any piece of cloth he can find. I thought we were done with all of this madness, but that song undid what the past year of healing has accomplished. We do not need this chaos right now; we've too many other things that are far more important."

"I repeat," Luke said slowly, "that it is not her fault. She did not know how that song affects him."

"It releases suicidal depression and grief over a woman who died twelve years ago." Matthew looked at his brothers. "I am not going to go through this again, do you hear? I will lock him in the vault for the next twenty years for his own protection if he cannot come to terms with our mother's death. *I will not go through this again.*"

Mark and Luke remained silent, their eyes focused on anything other than their stressed brother. Matthew was right; he had taken the brunt of their father's insane grief over the past twelve years because Matthew was the only person who brought Adam a remote amount of comfort. It was an unpredictable madness, set off by the most innocuous things; a flower, a memory, a trinket... it was hard to tell what would throw Adam into a spin of despair. But they had all known that the song would be a major catalyst. It had been the favorite song of Adam and Audrey Wellesbourne. And Matthew had allowed it to happen; his anger at the moment was more at himself than anything.

"I am sorry you had to deal with his madness yet again." Mark wanted off the subject before Matthew became any more enraged. "Perhaps we should go see to the two scouts." He stood up, motioning to Luke to do the same. "Get some sleep, Matt. You will feel better after you have had some rest."

Matthew was still perched on the end of the map table. "Better," he snorted, savoring the irony of the word. "My father is locked in his chamber, tied down to the bed, I have an army of Irish mercenaries moving up the Severn, and tonight at Vespers I am to wed. When am I supposed to find the time to rest?"

Mark could see the haze of self-pity coming over his brother. Not that Matthew did not have every right, but at times it could almost be crippling. "I will see to Father," he said. "Luke will take care of Thomas and Harl so that all you will have to worry over his your wedding."

Matthew did not respond right away, sitting in moody silence as if mulling over the chaos of his life. Finally, he pushed himself wearily off the table. "Nay," he said slowly. "I will see to Father.

Above everything that is happening here at Wellesbourne, we need to return to London. We are needed there most of all, especially with Somerset moving mercenaries into the middle of England. Luke and Johnny can ready the men while the rest of us are occupied with other things."

"I haven't seen Johnny yet this morning," Mark said.

Matthew instinctively looked at Luke; he generally had a better grasp of the youngest brother's whereabouts than anyone. Luke nodded his head, slowly.

"I think I know where he might be."

"Find him. Prepare the men to leave."

The brothers disbursed, each going about his business. There was chaos at Wellesbourne and they had to do their best to control and channel it, for greater things lay ahead.

More than they would ever dream.

***

Alixandrea was awake at sunrise. Though the traumatic events from the previous day should have kept her in bed until the nooning meal, she was never one to lie around. Moreover, there was an entire castle that she was anxious to explore, a great new world she now found herself a part of. She tossed the covers off and leapt from bed.

She practically kicked Jezebel from her palette by the door, demanding the woman rise. While she brushed her teeth with a frayed, green hazel stick and a mixture of rose-flavored soda, Jezebel stirred the embers in the hearth into a soft glow and then began to throw open the capcases in search of suitable clothing.

Stick still in her mouth as she continued to brush, Alixandrea rummaged through the piles that her maid had extracted from the bags and settled on a pale blue lamb's wool sheath with a darker blue sleeveless surcoat. They weren't particularly impressive, but they were comfortable, durable and appropriate. Whilst investigating the filthy kitchens, halls, and other corners of the male-dominated keep, she did not want to have to worry about mussing her fine clothing. These were functional clothes.

After her teeth, she washed her face and hands in a basin of rosewater, hooting when the water was a bit too cold for her liking. Jezebel dried her off quickly and stood her in front of the warming fire to dress her. The first garment on was the soft blue sheath, fitting against her body like a glove and clinging softly to every delectable curve. The whale bone corset was next; Jezebel tied her into the contraption so tightly that she begged for release, just enough to breathe. The surcoat went over the top of that, secured at the back with a large sash that Jezebel fussed with until she had the perfect tie. The little maid then put her mistress' hair in two braids this day, neat and pretty and unfussy.

Dressing complete, she was more than ready to face the great mysteries of Wellesbourne. Jezebel tried to stop her from leaving the chamber unescorted, but Alixandrea would not listen. She did not want to be a bother when she could very well find own way around. Never once did she question her safety, which she probably should have, but her curiosity had the better of her. Everything was new and exciting.

Quitting the small chamber, she entered the dark, cold stairwell and descended to the third floor. She noticed there were two additional chambers on this level; one door was closed and the other was slightly cracked. Curious, she peeked into the barely-opened door and caught sight of a very messy, very odorous chamber. It smelled as if something had crawled into the room and died. The fireplace was cold and black. Nearly out of her line of sight was the corner of a bed and she could see that something was tied to the post. Peering closer, she noticed a foot.

Curious, not to mention slightly concerned, she pushed the door open a few more inches and was able to gain a clear view of the stripped bed. A man lay upon only the ropes that supported the mattress, his arms and legs bound to each post. It took her a moment to realize that it was Adam Wellesbourne.

She shoved the door open and entered the room. The old man lay with his eyes closed and she thought he was sleeping. Greatly troubled as to why he was captive, she leaned over to make sure he was at least uninjured. He did not seem to be, but he smelled like vomit. That was where the horrible stench in the room was coming from. She was about to untie one of the bindings when his eyes abruptly flew open.

"My lady," he blinked, surprised to see her. "What... what are you doing here?"

"I was passing by and...." She was more concerned for him than she was interested in explaining her presence. "Are *you* all right? Have you been injured?"

"I am not injured."

"Then why are you tied like this? Who has done this to you?"

The first binding fell away and his right arm came down. Most of the circulation had gone out of it and he feebly tried to move the limb around as she went for the bindings on his feet.

"Matthew," he said. "But it is not as it appears."

Alixandrea froze, her eyes widening. "Sir Matthew tied you up?"

"Aye, but he had to."

"He *had* to?" Her distress was turning to outrage. "What do you mean by that? He had to tie you to your bed, with no food and no fire? What kind of cruel, barbaric man is your son that he would do this to his own father?"

A foot came loose and he moved his leg around to regain the blood flow. "There are things that you do not understand," he said as his other leg became free. "In time, things will become clear. In time you will understand."

It was an evasive answer. It only served to infuriate her, perhaps because she thought now that her impressions of Matthew's gallantry and benevolence were only a myth. The man who had shown her such kindness was apparently the Devil in disguise. It was a sickening thought and a frightening one. She had been living on giddy dreams for the past several hours. It was horrendously disappointing to think that those dreams were about to turn into nightmares.

The sounds of big boots suddenly echoed in the doorway, sounding flat and hollow against the planked floor. Her fingers on the last binding, Alixandrea looked up to see Matthew standing in the doorway.

He had a shocked expression on his face. Startled, and more than afraid, Alixandrea moved away from the bed.

"You..." she hissed at him.

Matthew's brow furrowed. "What are you doing here, my lady?"

Alarmed, angered, she made a dash for the hearth and picked up the closest thing she could find, which happened to be the shovel. It wasn't much of a weapon but it was the best she could do. She rushed at him, wielding it in front of her.

"Get away," she growled, putting herself between Matthew and his father. "Get away from him or I swear that I shall fight you to the death."

Matthew wasn't sure what was going on and put up his hands, slowly. "I am unarmed, lady. Why do you threaten me?"

"Why do you tie up a defenseless old man?"

"Ask him."

"I did."

"What did he say?"

"That you tied him up. Why would you do such a thing?"

Matthew's momentary confusion faded and he began to understand what she must think of the situation. It still did not explain how she got here, but that would come later. He realized the need to diffuse the situation quickly.

"My lady, though your defense of my father is most noble, it is unnecessary," he lowered his hands. "What I did, I did for my father's own good. Ask him."

The Devil had a smooth tongue. He did not seem insincere or extreme, like the cruel fiend she had imagined would do such a thing. Now it was her turn to be confused. Keeping the shovel in front of her, she looked at Adam. "What does he mean, my lord?"

Adam finished releasing the bindings on his one remaining hand. He stood up, unsteadily, his gaze moving between the lady and his son. He almost did not answer her, but saw that he had little choice. She was about to take off Matthew's head if the situation was not quickly clarified.

"I have moments of madness, my lady," he said with quiet humiliation. "Matthew does this to prevent me from harming myself. My son does it to protect a foolish old man."

He began to weep, softly. It took Alixandrea a moment to realize that the situation was not as it had appeared, though there was no way she could have known differently given her initial impression. Slowly, she lowered the shovel. As she watched Adam sob, she suddenly felt very foolish.

"My God," she whispered, setting the shovel down. She looked at Matthew helplessly. "I did not know, my lord. I came in and found him tied up and assumed...."

She could not finish. It sounded stupid, even to her. Matthew came into the room when he was sure she was not going to whack him with the shovel and gently took her hand, kissing the palm sweetly. From shame to thrill all in a brief moment, Alixandrea's cheeks flushed warm at his touch. He simply smiled at her, dropped her hand, and went over to his father.

"Come, Father," he put his big arm across his father's shoulders. "Let us escort Lady Alixandrea down to the hall and break our fast. You will feel better when you have some food in your belly."

Alixandrea watched the interaction, sensing that there was a good amount of compassion from son to father. She suddenly felt doubly foolish that she had believed the worst out of the situation. As Matthew walked past her with his father, he reached out and took her arm.

"Come along, lady," he said. "Let us all become better acquainted."

Meekly, she followed them down to the hall. It was still strewn with bodies, men sleeping off the overindulgence of ale from the night before. The dogs snoring in the corner suddenly awoke with the introduction of new people and they rose stiffly, wandering over to the group as they entered the room. Not particularly fond of dogs, Alixandrea shoved one of the beasts away when it came too close. The others closed in on her, wagging their tails furiously.

They took a seat at the corner of the dais. A kitchen servant brought out a warm loaf of bread, dark brown on the outside and a soft, creamy color on the inside. Matthew took his knife and cut off a piece for Alixandrea and his father, and one for himself. More kitchen servants emerged a few moments later with drink, cheese, cold beef, and little cakes made from flour, raisins, eggs, and seasoning known as *blaunchpoudre*, a mixture of ginger, valuable sugar and other ingredients that gave it a bright yellow color. Alixandrea could taste the ginger in the cakes; it was her favorite.

"I must say, you eat very well at Wellesbourne," she said, anxious to change the subject from the events up in the chamber. "The meal last night was also exquisite."

"We spend a lot of time on campaign or out on the road one way or the other, eating only what we can carry with us or hunt," Matthew replied. "When we are home, we like excellent food. It has become a vice."

"I wish I'd learned the finer arts of cooking," Alixandrea said. "Our cook at Whitewell was nothing more than an expert on mutton. She could cook it twenty different ways, but it was always still the same – mutton."

"So you do not know the culinary arts," Matthew shrugged. "I am sure that you have other talents. Sewing, perhaps?"

"Nay, not sewing." She finished the last of her cake and bit into another. "I can draw a little. And I had the best garden in all of Yorkshire. It was a lovely place with an acre of beautiful flowers. I was very sad to leave it."

Matthew's warm expression faded and Alixandrea had no idea why. His blue eyes moved to his father; the man's face was buried in a knuckle of beef. Matthew watched, waited a few seconds more, and finally closed his eyes tightly when Adam's head came up. It was as if he'd been hoping the old man hadn't heard what she'd said. But he had.

"My wife had a garden," Adam said. "A very fine one. But it died when she did. It... died...."

His head went back into his food, but there were no tears. Simply the lethargic movements of a despondent man. Alixandrea looked at Matthew, her eyes wide with puzzlement. After a moment, Matthew stood up from the table.

"A moment, lady," he said quietly.

She allowed him to lead her to a semi-private alcove just off of the hall. Two enormous lancet windows soared above their heads, the cool air from the fresh new day blowing away the smell of dog feces. He stood very close to her so that his words would not be overheard.

"What did I do, my lord?" she asked before he could speak. "Whatever it was, I did not mean it."

He shook his head, putting a finger over her lips to silence her. They were very soft lips and he let his finger loiter, for just a moment. "I know you did not," his finger came away. "But you must understand something. My father still grieves for the wife he lost twelve years ago. My brothers and I have spent years dealing with his fits of madness, when he will drink himself into oblivion and spend the rest of the night trying to kill himself. That is what you saw this morning; I had to tie him up to prevent him from hurting himself. Believe me, if there was another choice, I would surely take it. But restraining him is the only thing that keeps him in check until the madness subsides."

She gazed up at him, her eyes wide with dismay. "But... he seemed fine yesterday. He seemed quite pleasant."

"He was until last night."

There was something in his tone; an alarm bell went off in her head. "Did I somehow contribute to his turn of madness last night?"

He smiled faintly. "The song you sang... it belonged to them. It brought back memories he was unable to cope with. And the garden issue is nearly as bad as the song. My mother loved her garden."

"I am so sorry," she whispered miserably. "Had I only known."

"Which is why I tell you now so that you will be aware. His behavior is not your fault, nor your responsibility, but we must

71

all be careful what we say or do around him."

She nodded resolutely. "I will, I swear it. And I will never sing that song again."

"Aye, you will." He was indecently close, feeling her body brush up against his torso. Thoughts turned from his father's condition to this woman he had so recently acquired. "You will sing it for me when I ask it of you. But for the future, be forewarned that any little item, no matter how small, can turn my father from a rational man into a grieving lunatic."

She could feel his heat; she hadn't noticed it initially, but now it was nearly overwhelming. It made her cheeks grow hot. The way he was gazing at her made her knees feel liquid and weak.

"Will you help me?" she asked, her voice a husky whisper. "With your father, I mean. You must help me learn what I can and cannot say in his presence."

"I will be more than happy to help you," his voice was a low rumble; he was much more interested in staring at her soft lips than talking about his father. "The problem is that it is sometimes hard to know."

"Then we shall all have to help one another."

He smiled, faintly, and put a finger under her chin, tipping her face up to him. He was so close that she could feel his breath on her face.

"Did you know that you are the most beautiful woman I have ever laid eyes on?" he whispered.

She shook her head, her heart palpitating wildly. It was apparent that their conversation about his father was over and another, perhaps more overwhelming, subject was at hand. It was something that had been waiting to be broached since yesterday and it was clear that he would no longer delay.

Matthew's lips were almost on her, but they just as quickly moved away. They lingered just out of reach in a maddening tease. He dipped his head towards her and she closed her eyes, waiting for the first taste of his mouth against hers. She'd waited ten years for this moment and she was going to savor every wild sensation, every devilish joy.

But his lips missed her mouth and gently touched the tip of her nose, one cheek, and finally the other. They moved across her forehead, brushing against her flesh, tenderly blazing a trail across her skin. His hands were on her face; she could feel his great warm palms on either side of her head, his fingers in her hair as his thumbs gently caressed her neck. She sighed raggedly, never having experienced anything so passionate in her entire life. She had, in fact, never been kissed. Her introduction to it was more than she could have dreamed.

"My God, you are sweet," he murmured, his lips against her chin.

Her reaction was to gasp, something between an actual word and a groan. She did not even know what that one word might be, only that it would be something encouraging. She'd never realized a man's touch could be so consuming.

Just as she opened her eyes to look at him, he descended on her, his mouth covering hers so firmly that he shoved her back against the wall with his force. Momentarily startled, she quickly regained her wits when she realized that she liked it very much. Her hands moved to his arms, to his shoulders, and finally his neck. Matthew licked her lips, inviting her to open her mouth for him, which she did so purely on instinct. Quickly, he invaded her with his tongue.

It was shameful, thrilling, lustful. Though Alixandrea had never known a man's touch, she fully acquainted herself with Matthew's. It was the most potent thing she could have ever imagined. His tongue moved deep, licked her, played with her, until she was left gasping. Then his mouth left hers and moved over her face again, exploring her with wild fervor. She completely lost her self-control, a limp mass in his arms to do with as he pleased. Matthew had her firmly in his massive arms, his mouth doing fiery things to her neck. She could have stayed like that forever.

But it was not meant to be. They gradually became aware of another male voice in the hall, a familiar one to Matthew. He pulled himself away from her and peered around the side of the alcove to see Mark speaking with their father. He looked back at Alixandrea.

He started to speak but could only manage a weak chuckle. Then he shrugged. "You will forgive me, my lady," he said huskily. "I rather lost myself."

She smiled, her lips chapped from his attention. "And I let you."

He lifted an eyebrow in concession. "After tonight, I will not have to apologize for taking liberties."

"What is tonight?"

"Our wedding at Vespers."

This was the first she'd heard. Her eyebrows lifted. "And you think to tell me now?" she said. "There is so much to do. I do not know if I shall have enough time to...."

He put his finger on her lips to quiet her, which only served to inflame him again and he stole a long, hot kiss before continuing.

"Have no fear," he whispered. "Lady Caroline is making all of the arrangements and a rider will be sent to Stratford to summon the priest. All you need do is attend."

She did not want to sound ungrateful. "I appreciate that you have already asked Lady Caroline to make the arrangements, but I would like to do it myself."

"Unnecessary. You will rest until tonight. I shall not have you so exhausted that you can hardly stand through the ceremony."

He meant well, she could see that. But the fact remained that she very much wanted to make her own preparations.

"Please, my lord, I am not trying to be difficult," she explained carefully. "But you must understand something; I have been waiting for this marriage for ten years. I have planned in my mind a thousand times over what it would look like, what I would wear, and the first meal I would serve you. It means a great deal to me to be able to do this for us. You know so little of me. I must take this opportunity to impress you as a wife should."

Matthew was coming to realize one thing very quickly; he could not refuse her anything. It was a frightening thought, but in truth, he did not much care. He'd spent so many years loathing the very idea of her that he felt guilty, especially when she had turned out to be such a lovely creature. Now there wasn't anything he would not do to make her happy. He *wanted* her to be happy.

"Very well," he said. "If it pleases you, then you have my permission."

She smiled brightly. "Thank you, my lord."

"Matthew."

"My lord Matthew."

He lifted an eyebrow at her and she giggled. "Come along," he took her by the elbow and led her from the alcove.

Mark and his father were in serious conversation by the time they reached them. The dogs flocked around Alixandrea once again but she shooed them away. Mark glanced up at his brother.

"There you are," he said. "I was just telling Father about our impending plans for London. He assures me that he'll be quite able to make the journey."

Alixandrea looked up at Matthew, silent questions in her eyes. *Plans for London?* Matthew's focus, however, remained on his father and brother.

"Did you find John?" he asked steadily.

Mark nodded. "Aye," he said. "He was right where we thought he'd be, in the stables with his new charger. Do you know that he's taken to sleeping next to it? I swear he'd marry that beast if he thought he could get away with it."

"Are he and Luke with the men?"

"Aye."

"Then we shall speak again tomorrow morning of our departure for London. Preparations should be well underway by then." Matthew focused on his father, sitting small and forlorn at the table. He made sure he caught his attention as he spoke. "The lady and I are to be wed tonight at Vespers. Father, I shall require your assistance."

Adam's red-rimmed eyes focused on him. "What is it?"

"I need you and Mark to ride to Stratford and summon the priest. It is important."

Adam nodded, a gesture somewhere between resignation and refusal. Mark slapped his father lightly on the shoulder.

"Come, Father," he said. "We've a long day ahead of us. We'd better summon the priest before Matthew changes his mind."

"I shall not change my mind."

Mark looked at his brother, a smile on his lips. "Oh? So you have accepted your fate, have you? Thank God. No more long nights of listening to you lament your dark future."

"My future has never looked so bright," Matthew took the lady's elbow, firmly, so that she would know it was the truth. "Come along, love. Let us get away from this imbecile."

Mark snorted as Alixandrea allowed him to lead her from the room. Not strangely, the dogs, which had been hovering near her the entire time she had been in the hall, followed. They were all wagging their tails furiously at her. It was hard not to notice; there were at least seven of them, four or five large ones and a couple of smaller. Matthew had to shove one of the bigger ones out of his way.

"Are these dogs always so solicitous?" Alixandrea asked.

Matthew shook his head. "Not at all," he looked around. "They must like you."

"Well, I do not like them," she looked at them rather fearfully. "Which brings about another point, my lo... I mean, Matthew."

He grinned as she caught herself. "What is that?"

She wasn't sure where to start and did not want to offend him. "This place," she lifted a hand in gesture. "How can I put this kindly? It... smells."

"So?"

She lifted her eyebrows. "It is extremely offensive. Every inch of this keep reeks of filth. May I ask a rude question?"

"By all means."

"I would assume that Caroline is chatelaine. Why does she allow this squalor?"

Matthew shook his head. "It is not her choice. She has tried to maintain Wellesbourne in a fitting condition. In the beginning, she worked herself ill over it. But it is difficult to keep up such standards when men do not follow them. I think she just gave up."

"I see. May I ask another question?"

"Is this one rude also?"

"That depends."

He grinned; he had an easy smile that came even more easily with her. "What is it?"

"I would ask that you allow me free reign to clean it up and maintain it. It is a disgrace, Matthew. For any visitors that might come here, I would be ashamed."

He'd never given much thought to the condition of the keep. It was what it was, and always had been. As he'd told Alixandrea, Caroline had tried to preserve it but the men and filth had overwhelmed her small spirit and she had eventually surrendered.

Then he thought back to the time when his mother was still alive; it had been a wonderful place then, fresh and fragrant, full of music and laughter. But when Audrey died, so did the warmth. Wellesbourne keep had gradually decayed into a stale, cold structure that housed men and dogs. They had all allowed this and saw nothing wrong with it, for the change had been so gradual he'd hardy noticed. In reflection, he could see Alixandrea's point. It was a miserable place.

"I would not want you to be ashamed," he said. "You are chatelaine now, as my wife. Do with this castle as you will. But I warn you; we are used to it as it is. We crushed Caroline's spirit and we could crush yours, too. If you wish to keep the place clean, then it may take some serious reconditioning and patience on your part."

She lifted an eyebrow. "Then we shall lead from the top. If I can have your cooperation, and your family's, then the men will see and obey."

"You have it."

She smiled. "I thank you." The moment had grown warm again. But there was also a bit of awkwardness with the silence until she broke it. "Where will you go now?"

He still had her by the elbow. His hand moved down her arm until it captured her fingers. He toyed with them, slowly, savoring the feel of her skin in his coarse palm.

"To the yard, where my men are," he said. "I will be with them this afternoon, but I will call for you right before Vespers. I assume you have enough to keep you busy between now and then."

"I do," she said, relishing the new sensation of his fingers fondling her own. "I must find Caroline to see what she has done so far."

"I'd check the kitchen. Last I saw her, she was speaking to the cook about tonight's menu."

Alixandrea nodded her thanks for the information. But there still lingered something on her mind and she hesitated before speaking. "When are you leaving for London, Matthew?"

Not an unexpected question given their conversation in the hall. But as he gazed at her, he realized that he could not, *would* not, leave her behind. An odd thought, considering it had never crossed his mind to bring her. Caroline had always stayed behind at Wellesbourne and he assumed that his wife would remain, also. But not now; not when he was just coming to know her. He wanted her with him.

"*We* are leaving before the week is out," he replied.

Her eyes widened with surprise. "I am going, too?"

"Did you think I would leave you here?"

Momentarily speechless, she fumbled over her words. "I...I do not know. The thought never crossed my mind. Why are we going to London?"

The easy smile flickered. "Do I need a reason to take my new wife to London to show her off? I shall be the envy of every man in the city."

Her pretty cheeks flushed. "I am sure there are far more lovely ladies in London, my lo.. I mean, Matthew. I am but a simple noble lady from the north. I have never even been out of Yorkshire."

"We are going to change that."

She did not know what to say to that. The past day of her life had been the most disappointing, angering, and thrilling that she had ever experienced. She could hardly imagine what the next fifty years held for her. Before she could think of a smooth reply, he took her chin between his index finger and his thumb and tilted her head up. She received a kiss to the cheek.

"You have a wedding to arrange, my lady," he said. "Can you find your way well enough in this place?"

"I shall manage."

"Good."

He winked at her as he quit the entry. She stood aside as Mark and Adam passed by her, having obviously been waiting for Matthew to separate himself from her. She hadn't even realized they had been standing there, waiting.

Alixandrea stood there for an eternal span of moments, her mind filled with nothing in particular. There was so much happening that it was difficult to grasp only one thought. But she knew her most predominant thought, at the moment, was happiness. It wasn't something she had oft felt, certainly nothing she had expected at this place. It was a peculiar, embracing sensation, one she could easily become accustomed to.

CHAPTER FIVE

The stables were dark, smelling of hay and urine. The horses shifted about restlessly as evening approached, sensing their meal was about to be delivered by the cowering stable boys who lived in fear of the massive war beasts.

They had to unmuzzle the animals in order to feed them, which could be something of an adventure. A couple of the boys had met with misfortune at the teeth of the chargers; one lad was even missing a finger. As the sounds and smells of evening descended, the stables were increasingly restless.

Strode was in the stable, tucked back in a far corner away from the entrance. He was tending to one of the matched set of carriage horses from Whitewell that had come up lame. The fetlock was swollen and tender and he was having a difficult time reducing the swelling. It was an expensive horse and he did not relish the thought of putting it down should it come to that. But a lame horse was of no service to anyone. It would be killed to provide food for the dogs if he could not heal it.

As dusk approached, he changed out the dressing for the eighth time since sunrise. The horse master had been kind enough to supply him with a soda mixture to include in the compresses, a blend designed to draw out the excess fluid. It was a useful concoction, but messy. It was all over his hands as he secured the compress. Just as he finished, a shadow behind him caught his attention.

Startled, he turned to see Jezebel standing just to the rear of the horse. Strode let out a long hiss.

"Woman," he growled. "Do not sneak up on me like that. I am bound to cut your throat before I know 'tis you."

Jezebel fiddled with her apron. "Sorry," she said. "I came to tell ye about m'lady's wedding."

"Well?"

"Tonight at Vespers."

His eyebrows lifted in a menacing manner. "That 'tis an hour away, at most. And you are just coming to tell me now?"

Jezebel had known Strode for a few years, having been his lover for the past two. He was a powerful man in the House of Terrington and she would do most anything for him, including betray the confidence of a lady who had been most kind to her. But she did not think of it that way; she could not see beyond her need to please Strode. Whatever he asked, she would do. Whatever he wanted, she would comply.

"I have been helping m'lady." She heard the threat in his tone and took a step back. "This is the first chance I have had to come tell ye."

Strode was on his feet. Grabbing her by the hair, he slapped her a couple of times. It was a brutal, sharp sound that echoed off the walls of the stable, startling the horses. Jezebel whimpered.

"Stupid cow," he rumbled. "You know what this means. You know what I have to do. I told you how important this was, but still, you fail me?"

She cowered from him, weeping. "I know," she sobbed. "But this is the first chance I have had. M'lady needed me and I could not get away."

He still had her by the hair, pulling the faded brown strands. He had a wild look to his eye. "I must get to the men," he muttered. "Key soldiers, those in command of the rest. They must be prepared to strike at the very moment the church bells peal. It will be their signal to erupt from within. And then, we shall have such chaos..."

He let go of her hair as he trailed off. Jezebel rubbed her face where he had struck her. "What are you going to do?"

Strode's initial sense of panic at the thought of his orders coming to fruition so quickly died into a slow burn. He calmed himself; he was a good soldier and used to quick decision making. That is why Lord Terrington put him in command. He would not fail at this most important task no matter the wench's incompetence. It would not cost him his glorious showing.

"Go back to the lady," he told her. "I will do what needs to be done."

Jezebel was still rubbing her face. "Are ye going to be in the church?"

"My direct orders are to kill The White Lord; therefore, I must be in the church. As the lady's attendant, it is my right and no one will be the wiser to my purpose unless you open your trap and levy suspicion against me."

"I shall not say a word."

"You'd better not." He glared at her. "What about Lady Alixandrea? Have you spilled anything to her? The two of you do an awful lot of chattering."

"I have never said a word. She knows nothing."

He continued to glare at her as if trying to intimidate her into changing her story. But the woman stood firm. "Well and good for you, then. Traitors are dealt with in such ways and I'd have no hesitation in slitting your skinny throat."

Jezebel knew he spoke the truth. She thought she was being clever in hiding her fear, but she wasn't. He could read it in her eyes. "Ye won't hurt m'lady, will ye?" she asked timidly. "She doesn't deserve to be hurt. She hasn't done anything."

He snorted. "Foolish woman. I would sooner kill myself than harm a hair on her head. But she must stay out of my way when I move on Wellesbourne. I will not have time to pick and choose my targets."

Jezebel's weeping had faded. She wasn't particularly comforted by his declaration not to hurt the lady, but then again, she was a single-focused creature. All she knew was that she had completed her task as Strode had asked of her when he had pulled her deep into the circle of intrigue that seemed to flow throughout Whitewell like a disease. *You will tell me when this wedding is to happen so that we may confiscate Wellesbourne Castle in the name of Henry.* Everything about Whitewell stank of hatred against Richard, of the fall of the Red Rose. Aye, she had completed her task. Her reward was marriage to Strode, an elevation of her station. All would look more favorably upon her now. She had done what he had asked.

Hand still to her red-welted face, she slipped past him. Strode watched her disappear into the approaching dusk, a waif of a thing that did not matter much to him. She could die tomorrow and he would not be heartbroken. But for the moment, she served a purpose. And that purpose was to feed him information. He left the stables in her wake, heading for the Whitewell troops housed in temporary quarters just inside the main gate.

The stable was left still and silent but for the snorting of a horse now and again. They were becoming increasingly impatient for their evening meal. In the growing darkness, a head suddenly popped up in one of the stalls that housed a big blond charger. It was difficult to make out who it was until the shape came from behind the horse and stepped out into the fading light. Straw stuck out from the figure's pale blond head, the blue eyes reflecting shock in the twilight.

John Wellesbourne had heard everything.

***

Her wedding dress had been her mother's. It was a white confection of silk and linen, woven with strands of real silver thread. Across her midsection was an elaborately embroidered belt of crystals and silver beads, absolutely gorgeous and glistening. The neckline was off the shoulder, the sleeves long, emphasizing her slender neck and shapely torso. Jezebel had pinned her hair up with silver pins and had braided strips of white ribbon into the bronze curls. If ever Alixandrea had looked like an angel, today was the day. As the sun set, the hour of Vespers quickly approached and she sat in taut anticipation of the evening's events. The arrangements were made, the hall readied, and there was naught else to do but wait.

Under her earlier supervision, and with Caroline standing silently by, the great hall had been transformed from a smelly room of dogs and dirt into a warm place with fresh rushes and a blazing fire.

Although it still smelled of dogs and probably would until the floors had been washed a few times, she was moderately satisfied with its current state. It had taken a small army of house servants to achieve it, some of whom now had a permanent job in keeping the floors of the great hall clean. Alixandrea wasn't a heavy-handed chatelaine; she preferred to accomplish her needs through positive encouragement and kind directives. At least for the moment, it seemed to be working.

The dogs who populated the hall were another problem altogether. Seven in all and a litter of pups, and they seemed to like Alixandrea a good deal. The moment she walked into the room, they were on her and continued to follow her around as if she held all the answers to their doggie dreams. She had resorted to tricking them to go outside into the kitchen yard; when they followed her from the hall and out into the yard, she dashed back inside the keep and slammed the heavy oak door. She heard them whimpering outside but that was of no matter; dogs belonged outside, in her opinion, and outside they were going to stay.

It had been an interesting afternoon to say the least. She felt that she was becoming moderately acquainted with the four story keep and she also felt that she was settling comfortably into her position at Wellesbourne. Caroline had been company all afternoon, following her around more than actually helping. Alixandrea could see what Matthew had suggested of the woman; she wasn't particularly strong willed, and she definitely was not a leader. She was rather meek, a little flighty, and a sweet simpleton as Alixandrea had observed earlier. There was no way this woman could stand up against five grown men and a castle full of soldiers.

They had parted ways a couple of hours before Vespers so that each could dress for the ceremony. Jezebel had been nowhere to be found when Alixandrea arrived in her chamber, but the maid made her appearance shortly thereafter with a big copper tub and servants bearing hot water. After her mistress was bathed, she brought her mistress honeyed wine in an effort to calm any nerves she might be feeling for the evening's events.

The wine was very sweet. Cup in hand, Alixandrea stood in front of a large bronze mirror that she had brought with her from Whitewell. The reflection gazing back at her was confident, relaxed. She was rather pleased with the way she looked and hoped Matthew was pleased also.

"I wish my mother could see me," she murmured, smoothing at the skirt. "She would have been blissfully happy. This was her gown, you know. She married my father in it."

"I know," Jezebel watched her as she twirled and posed. "Ye look lovely, m'lady."

"Do you think so?" Alixandrea put the goblet down to fix a ribbon in her hair. "What do you think of the hall? I had them clean it up. Does it look much better?"

"It does, m'lady."

"I hope Sir Matthew thinks so. I hope he..."

She was interrupted by pounding on the chamber door. It was loud, almost angry. Jezebel flew to the door and opened it. Mathew stepped into the room, with Mark standing in the doorway behind him. Alixandrea noticed right away that both men were still dressed in the clothes they had worn earlier, certainly not clean or ceremonial garments that one would expect for a wedding. By the expression on Matthew's face, she could sense his ominous mood from where she stood. She was about to ask him if anything was amiss when he spoke.

"Something has come up, Lady Alixandrea," he said, his voice deep and cold. "I am afraid that our nuptials planned for this evening will be indefinitely postponed."

Alixandrea felt as if she had been hit in the stomach. *Indefinitely postponed*? She could feel the blood draining from her face and it was a struggle to maintain her composure.

"Is there a problem, my lord?"

"Nothing that concerns you."

She did not believe him. "My lord, if I have done something offensive...."

"I did not say that you did."

"Even so, your attitude clearly demonstrates that I must have done something. Why else would you cancel our ceremony?"

He cut her off. "I will repeat my statement that it is not your concern. And you will ask no more questions on this matter until such time as I decide it is a subject worthy of further discussion."

Alixandrea did not say another word. She stared at him, her sultry bronze eyes asking a thousand questions that her lips could not. He was absolutely final in his manner, a brutality and harshness emanating from him that she could never have imagined he was capable of. She simply lowered her head in submission. Before she could lift it again, the door slammed and he was gone.

She stood a moment, shocked and sickened. She could not imagine what she might have done to offend him so. Everything had been so pleasant between them, up until just a few hours ago. Then she remembered the hall, now devoid of dogs and feces, now cleaned as she had insisted. Perhaps he did not want it cleaned even though he told her that she could do as she pleased. Perhaps he was really hoping she would leave it alone, but like a meddling female, she had not. She had insisted the hall have her signature upon it as the new chatelaine. Aye, that must be her mistake. There could be no other.

Slowly, she turned from the door, the dress swishing as she moved to the nearest chair. Jezebel still stood near the entry, her brown eyes wide with astonishment at what she had just witnessed. It took her a moment to find her tongue.

"M'lady," she began hesitantly. "I would not be too upset. Perhaps there are more important things happening right now and he cannot think on a wedding."

Alixandrea waved her off weakly. "'Tis all right, Jez," she said quietly. "He did not want to marry at all. Perhaps... perhaps he has come to fully realize that. Perhaps I have done something so horrible that he can never forgive me."

"He has to marry ye," Jezebel insisted. "He has a contract with yer uncle. To break that contract would be to bring about your uncle's wrath."

"I understand that. But he does not want to marry right now."

"Demand yer rights, m'lady. Don't let him put you off like this."

"I will not force him."

Jezebel watched her lady slump in her chair, like a silken dove whose wings had just been clipped. It was only a matter of moments before the tears came. The mood of the room was heavy with sorrow and disappointment, so thick that it was palpable. It was suffocating. The little maid turned to the door.

"I shall go get ye a good draught of ale," she said firmly. "Ye need something stronger than wine."

Alixandrea did not even have the strength to respond. She continued to sit in the chair, wiping the tears that streamed down her cheeks, wondering if she would ever be able to right what she had apparently wronged.

***

Matthew and Mark were in their father's chamber, just off the third floor landing. Adam sat in the corner, silently, watching his two sons as they peered from the cracked door. It was like watching two cats lie in wait for a mouse.

After several long minutes of watching and waiting, Matthew apparently saw something. He sank back against the wall nearest the door, his massive frame hidden by the shadows of the dark room. Mark was peering through the crack between the doorframe and the joints that held the door. They all heard shuffling on the third floor landing, a wisp of a shadow that passed through the light and was just as quickly gone. After what seemed like an eternity, Matthew finally moved out of the shadows.

"There she goes," he whispered to Mark. "Luke and John will catch her downstairs and follow her to see where she goes."

"She's going right for that manservant to tell him that the wedding is off," Mark said quietly. "You can bet on it."

"Let's hope so."

"What do we do in the interim?"

"We wait. Our commanders know what is going on. They'll keep an eye on the Whitewell troops. The next few hours should be very confusing for them when the church bells don't peal." Matthew pushed the door open wider, eyeing the stairwell to make sure the maid was gone. "I want you out on the wall to keep an eye on what is going on in the ward. I will join you shortly. But right now, I do believe I have some explaining to do."

They both knew what he meant. Mark wriggled his eyebrows. "Best of luck."

"I may need it."

Matthew mounted the stairs to the fourth floor two at a time until he reached the top floor. Softly, he rapped on Alixandrea's door. He waited a nominal amount of time for her to answer and when she did not, he carefully pushed the door open.

The small room was warm and cozy. His blue eyes found Alixandrea seated in front of the hearth, her head in her hand. Gazing at her, he felt extremely guilty for what he had done. But it had been necessary. There was a spy in their midst, something he did not quite understand yet but soon would, and he had to deal with it on a moment-by-moment basis. Until he had a better grasp, there was no other choice. He only hoped that the lady could forgive him.

"My lady," he said softly.

Alixandrea nearly jumped from her seat. The sight of her red-rimmed eyes nearly drove a knife through his heart. She was on edge, her bronze eyes eager, anxious, and sad.

"My lord," she said quickly. "I thought it was the maid. I apologize for not answering the door."

He put up his hands. "No apologizes, please," he said. "For 'tis I who must apologize to you. What I said earlier... I am very sorry if I upset you. But if you will allow me to explain, you will see that it was necessary."

He could read the emotions rolling across her face. Shock, surprise, relief... and finally curiosity. She shook her head, puzzled.

"I... I do not understand, my lord."

"Matthew."

Her expression folded into one of extreme confusion and a

little frustration. "Matthew?"

His easy smile sparked. "Aye," he said softly. "Would you sit down? I should like to speak with you."

Woodenly, she obeyed. He pulled up the small three legged stool that lay propped against the hearth, settling his massive body atop it. As he looked at her, they were eye level and he could read the distress in her face. With regret for having caused it, he reached out and took her soft, warm hand in his great palm. Alixandrea watched him warily.

"I must ask you something," he said quietly. "I would appreciate an honest answer."

"Of course."

"How much do you know about the politics of Richard and Henry?"

Her confusion did not ease. It only grew. "I know that they are bitter enemies and that both lay claim to the throne, and that this war between York and Lancaster has been going on since the days of my grandfather."

His smile broadened. "Very simply, and very well, put. Whom does your uncle support?"

"Richard, as you do."

There was no hesitation in her answer. Gazing into her eyes, he sensed total truth, or at least, what she believed to be the truth. John said that the maid had mentioned that Alixandrea had no knowledge of the subversion going on. It was the one thing that truly vindicated her. He'd seen some smooth liars in his time. Had the maid not unknowingly supported Alixandrea's lack of knowledge of the situation, he could have had a devastating circumstance on his hands. He was very glad he did not.

He began to caress the fingers in his warm palm. "I want you to listen very carefully to me. But know this before I begin; I do not lie, and I would certainly never lie to you. What I am about to tell you is total truth and you will accept it as such."

"Without question."

He took a deep breath, wondering where to begin. "I did not mean anything I said tonight. We are indeed going to be married, as planned. But I had to do what I did for a very good reason."

She visibly relaxed. But there was bewilderment coupled with the relief. "I do not understand. Why would you...?"

He put up a hand so silence her. "It would seem that somewhere in the past few years, your uncle has become loyal to Henry Tudor. I do not know how, when or why, but my brother was witness to a very interesting exchange between your manservant and your maid this afternoon. Many things were said. Many treacherous things."

Her eyes widened. "Jezebel? And Strode? What *kinds* of things?"

"Evidently, your maid is spying on you," he told her. "She reports back to your manservant about what is going on between you and me. She reported to your manservant this afternoon that you and I were to be married at Vespers, whereupon your manservant told her that he must give the information to the Whitewell army so that they would know to attack when the church bells rang."

Alixandrea was beyond surprised. "Attack whom?"

"Wellesbourne, I would assume."

She stared at him. Then, she slowly shook her head. "Your brother must be mistaken," she said softly. "I have known Strode and Jezebel for many years. They are faithful and loyal servants."

"Aye, but to whom? To you? Or to your uncle? Alixandrea, if your uncle has influenced them, it is no reflection upon you. But it is clear that he is using you for some seditious purpose. What was originally proposed as an alliance now appears to be meant for infiltration. If what my brother heard is correct, and I have no reason to mistrust him, then your uncle means to destroy Wellesbourne."

Her mouth was hanging open in shock. She was staring at him so intensely that he wasn't even sure if she understood him. But after a small eternity, she closed her mouth and her eyes. It was almost as if she could not bear to look at him any longer.

"You are certain of this?" she whispered.

"As certain as I can be without discussing it with your servants first-hand."

"What are you going to do?"

He sighed. Most fighting men were able to remove their emotion from decisions. Matthew had never been able to do that. Although he had perfect judgment and always went with his instincts, still, there were times when his emotions could cause doubt. He'd lived all of his life with the fact that he was an emotional man.

"I will do nothing."

She looked at him. "Nothing?"

He shook his head slowly. "For the moment. I will get to the heart of this subversion in my own time and in my own way. A perfect example was tonight; I told you the things I did so that your maid would go running back to your manservant and report to him. And that's exactly what she did."

"How do you know?"

"She left your room very shortly after I did, did she not?"

"She said she was going to get me ale."

"I can say with a great degree of certainty that she is not in the kitchens right now."

Alixandrea suddenly understood. She was sickened "She is with Strode?"

He nodded slowly. "Undoubtedly telling him that the wedding has been cancelled."

The revelations were nearly too much take. Alixandrea suddenly smacked the arm of the chair with an open palm.

"She is spying on me," she hissed. "How could she do this? I thought she loved me."

"Who is to say why people do what they do? But now that you know, you must be very guarded with her. What she knows, your manservant knows. And what he knows gets to the army and, more than likely, your uncle and whomever he is allied with. And because you are to be my wife, you will be privy to valuable information. I have the confidence of the king. Your uncle and his allies are more than likely counting on this to serve their cause."

She was ill with the realization. He made it sound very logical and she could not deny that Jezebel's behavior, at times, could make her believe this. Suddenly, many things made sense.

"When I was young, when my uncle and your father were in discussions for the marriage contract, I remember there was a man who came to Whitewell often." She thought back to that time, hazed by the years gone by. "He was short, with silver hair and pocked skin, and my uncle seemed to cower to him. It was very strange. Although my uncle called him John Law, I heard them talking privately once and my uncle called him Sutton. I did not think anything of it at the time, but now it seems to make sense. They used to discuss politics and marriage endlessly. After the marriage contract was brokered, I never saw the man again."

Matthew listened to her closely. His expression never changed. "If your recollection is true, then your uncle has been involved with Tudor much longer than I suspected."

"Why? Do you recognize the man I described?"

"Possibly. Sir John Sutton is a very close ally of Jasper Tudor. He is married to a daughter of Lord Clifford, also another Lancastrian supporter. Did he also walk with a limp?"

"He did."

"Then it was indeed John Sutton."

Alixandrea gazed at him, a sense of overwhelming guilt sweeping her. "Then it seems that I have brought something dark and rebellious into the House of Wellesbourne. No wonder my uncle was so eager to marry me into this household."

His smiled returned and he patted her soft hand. "Had I known what prize I would be acquiring, I would have been equally as eager."

She looked surprised. "Why would you say that? I have brought doom to your family. You should send me home right away."

"Are you mad? It would give your uncle the right and opportunity to wage war against me. Besides, I have no intention of sending you anywhere. You belong to me and I intend to keep you."

"Are *you* mad?" she softly snapped back. "Do you not

understand that something horrible has followed me here? I will not be the cause of your downfall, Matthew. I would rather die."

He was genuinely touched. He did not know why he should believe her, but he did. Reaching out, he gently touched her cheek.

"Trust me when I tell you that I will not fall," he said softly. He did not tell her of Strode's specific instructions to kill The White Lord; he thought that might be too much information for one night. "You and I will be married and I will deal with this insurrection from within my ranks. Wellesbourne soldiers are loyal to the core. Four hundred Whitewell men cannot contend with a thousand Wellesbourne men."

"But what about Jezebel and Strode?"

"I am not nearly as concerned with Strode as I am with your maid. She hears all, sees all. Say only what I tell you to say in front of her and nothing else. You must detach yourself from her. Perhaps if I were to position Caroline in such a way that she would act as your lady in waiting, we can displace your maid so that she will be ineffective. As for your manservant, I will deal with him appropriately."

"How?"

"When the time is right."

He seemed decisive and calm about the situation. His manner eased her tremendously. Above all of the bewilderment of the disclosures, Alixandrea realized one thing; she was very glad they were still to be married.

"Thank you for... well, thank you for clarifying things," she smiled weakly. "When you came in earlier to announce that we would not be wed, I will admit that I was disappointed. I am so glad that it was not the truth."

His features softened. "I am truly sorry to have caused you any sorrow. But it was necessary."

"I see that now."

"I am simply sorry that you seem to be a pawn in something that should not involve you."

"I have faith that you will guide me through it."

He kissed her, then. He could not help it. He knew it was not proper and that he needed to get out of the chamber before the maid returned, but he was very glad that things were well again between them. Before the kiss became too heated and he lost control, he pulled himself away.

"Come along, now. My father and brother are waiting."

"Waiting for what?"

He held a hand out to her, pulling her to her feet. "Us, of course. There can be no marriage without a bride and groom."

Her eyebrows rose. "We are still to be married tonight?"

He led her to the door. "My father and brother brought the priest back from Stratford this afternoon. I'd hate for the man to have come all this way for nothing."

"But what about my servants?"

"Can you keep a secret?"

The light of excitement began to gleam in her eye. "Of course."

His smile returned and he took a moment to study her closely. His gaze moved over her face, memorizing every curve, every line. He would do it every night until he could close his eyes and envision her perfectly, this woman he would be married to. He still found it unbelievable.

"I am afraid that I do not have the luxury of infinite time this night," he said quietly. "Because of the situation, I will more than likely be up all night watching Whitewell's army for signs of insurrection. But have no doubt that this wedding will indeed take place and our time to come to know each other, as husband and wife, will indeed come."

Alixandrea's response was to return his smile. She frankly had no quick answer; anything she could think of sounded too naïve or too embarrassing. It was a surprise conclusion to an evening that had been full of surprises. With Mark, Caroline and Adam Wellesbourne as witness in Adam's smelly, cluttered bower, The White Lord of Wellesbourne became husband to the Lady Alixandrea Terrington St. Ave Wellesbourne.

His wife sat up all night, watching him on the ramparts from her small chamber window.

***

It wasn't a garden as much as it was an overgrown yard filled with dead, dried things, bugs, and other sundry creatures. Upon close inspection, however, one could see that it had once been very well planned and lovingly maintained. There was even a small pond in the middle of it for all manner of water plants. A bench and massive bronze sundial sat near the north wall. Aye, at one time, this garden had been a marvelous place.

Alixandrea had found Audrey Wellesbourne's patch quite by chance. She had been trying to escape the dogs that someone had let back into the hall. When the beasts had followed her out into the yard and she had attempted her escape back inside again, the door jammed. Stuck, with several happy dogs closing in, she made a dash for a small gate built into a dividing wall just to the west of her position.

The gate had been old and rusted, but the latch had lifted and she had been able to escape the onslaught of canines. Now, sad doggie faces looked in between the slats of the iron grate as she stood in the middle of the dead garden.

It was close to the noon meal as Alixandrea gazed back at the dogs, wondering how to get out of the enclosure without being mauled. Smells from the kitchen wafted on the breeze and she was hungry. She'd fallen asleep just before dawn, having spent the entire night watching Matthew's blond head from her bower window. She was somehow fearful that the Whitewell soldiers might somehow create a ruckus and she was worried about her new husband. She could not help but feel that this was all her fault, and in that guilt lay protectiveness. It wasn't as if The White Lord could not fend for himself, but if her uncle's soldiers were going to create havoc, she would make it her business to try and stop them, foolish as those thoughts were. She could not let such a thing happen without a fight on her part.

But it had been an exhausting night of watching and waiting. She had only been awake an hour or so, lured down to the hall by the smells of bread. Jezebel had been nowhere to be found, not an unusual occurrence but now one that made her deeply suspicious. Then the dogs had chased her from the hall, those happy, licking beasts that seemed so attached to her.

Fortunately, the temperature outside was mild enough that she could remain without need of a cloak or heavier clothing. Dressed in a pale linen sheath with long sleeves and a soft wool surcoat of the same off-white color, she took a seat on the old bench and sat in the weak sunlight. She assumed the dogs would tire of waiting for her and go away, so she decided to wait them out.

The warmth of the sun was faint, but it was wonderful. It seemed to heighten her exhaustion and she closed her eyes, soaking it in. She hadn't seen Matthew yet this morning and wondered where he was. Though she was married to him only last night, he had disappeared soon after the ceremony and she'd not spoken to him since. But she's had the benefit of catching glimpses of him up on the wall walk all night. It had been comforting. Leaning back against the bench, she closed her eyes and dozed in the sun.

The sounds of the creaking gate startled her. Alixandrea sat up quickly, her eyes opening to see young John Wellesbourne approaching. He smiled shyly at her.

"Good morning," he said. "Sorry to disturb you, my lady."

She returned his smile. "Good morning, Sir John. And you did not disturb me in the least."

"I was passing through the yard and saw you in here. Matt is looking for you."

She stood up from the bench, pointing to the gate. "I came in here to get away from the dogs. They seem to like me."

John glanced back at the mutts lined up against the iron entry. "I have never cared much for them."

"Nor I. Why do you suppose they are intent to follow me?"

He shrugged. "It cannot be because you smell like food. Perhaps they are simply seeking a friendly face and you have one."

"Perhaps."

She studied the youngest brother for a moment; she'd only met him one other time, yesterday upon her arrival to Wellesbourne. He was a tall lad, as were most of the Wellesbournes, but he seemed very quiet, a softer, meeker, more introspective version of his eldest brother. And he was very young.

"Well," she said after a moment. "I suppose I should go and find your brother now."

"I shall escort you."

"Will you fight off the dogs, too?"

He grinned. "Have no fear, my lady. I shall save you."

She returned his grin and he flushed violently. Humored, she allowed him to open the gate for her and kick away some of the dogs.

"That was your mother's garden once, was it not?"

The moment she opened her mouth, she was suddenly regretful. If Adam Wellesbourne was still devastated by his wife's death, she had no idea how the rest of the family felt. She should have been more sensitive. But John merely nodded his head without a hint of distress.

"Many years ago. After she passed away, Father would not touch it, nor would he let anyone else. It eventually died away."

"A pity," she said. "It looks as if it was a lovely place, once."

"It was."

"How did your mother die?"

"In childbirth."

Her eyebrows rose. "Truly? Wasn't she rather old to be having children? She already had four grown boys by that time."

John's head bobbed up and down. "I was nine years of age when she passed away. Matthew was twenty-two, Mark was twenty, and Luke was thirteen. I remember the day that it happened clearly; Mother's time came early. She lay in bed for three days trying to deliver the child but she died with it still inside her. Father buried her in her garden. She was not quite forty years of age."

Alixandrea looked at him, dismayed with understanding. "That is why your father will not touch the garden."

"Exactly. She lies at rest there."

They reached the door that led into the kitchen and Alixandrea paused, facing her new brother-in-law. "John," she said slowly. "Do you think your father would be horribly offended if I revitalized your mother's garden? As a tribute to her memory, of course. It just does not seem right that something she loved and tended so carefully should be allowed to lie dead. It seems to me that it should be kept living and beautiful as a reminder of her."

John's expression changed from curious to doubtful to hopeful and back again. "I... I do not know, my lady. My Father is... well, he can be..."

She put a hand on his arm. "Say no more. Your brother has already explained such things to me. I will speak to him about it to see what he thinks."

John visibly sighed. "That is wise, my lady. But... well, if you would like my opinion, I think it is a good idea. I used to spend a lot of time with Mother in the garden when I was very young. I'd almost forgotten, it seems so long ago. But... but I should like to see Mother's garden live again."

She smiled at him as he led her into the kitchen, fighting off the amorous dogs as they went. By the time they entered the hall, all of the Wellesbourne brothers and Lady Caroline were gathered at the long table, huddled in a cluster. Alixandrea met Matthew's eyes over the top of the group and, for a moment, she would swear until the day she died that sparks literally flew. She could not have looked away from him if she'd tried.

His rugged, handsome face relaxed, as if all of his troubles just suddenly vanished at the sight of her. He looked exhausted, but not too tired to walk over and meet her.

"I see Johnny found you." He was careful not to reach out and touch her, no matter how badly he wanted to. "Where were you?"

"The dogs chased me outside and I was locked out." She wondered why he'd not yet made a move to take her hand or otherwise greet his new wife. "Your brother said that you were looking for me."

"I was." He cast a long glance at John, who wisely took the hint and left them alone. "Where is your maid?" he asked quietly.

"I am not sure, she was not in my chamber when I awoke," she answered back, also quietly. "Why? Is something wrong?"

He shook his head, glancing casually around the hall to make sure there were no obvious signs of them being watched. "The last she saw of the two of us together was when I postponed our marriage. We must be careful how we behave in public. For all your maid knows, I am still gravely displeased with you and with the prospect of our marriage. I do not want her to think otherwise."

"Is that why you did not take my hand just now?"

He lifted an eyebrow at her. "You'll never know how difficult that was for me. As I stand here and look at you, I want to take you in my arms so badly that they ache."

It was a sweet thing to say. "Can I at least smile at you?"

"Not in public."

She was genuinely disappointed but understood. "Very well. So what do we do?"

He did reach out then and took her by the elbow, gently leading her back over to the table where his family was congregating.

"You will spend time with Caroline," he said softly, evenly. "I would have the two of you be constant companions right now."

She tried not to appear too disillusioned. "Will I not be seeing you at all, husband?"

He froze and looked at her. After a moment, he fought the smile that threatened. "I never thought I would like to hear that word where it pertained to me."

She hadn't thought much about saying it; it was simply the truth. "And now?"

"It is like music to my ears." She started to smile and he feigned a glare. "None of that. Stop it this instant."

She had to put her hand over her mouth. "I cannot help it."

"You must," he commanded softly. "Go with Caroline now. I will find you later."

She nodded obediently; Caroline was seated just to the right of her husband at the edge of the table and smiled when she saw Alixandrea. She stood up, took her new sister's hand, and led her from the table. But Alixandrea cast Matthew a final glance before leaving the room entirely. It was a longing gesture, a new one filled with hope and anticipation. His eyes lingered on the empty doorway a moment.

"Matt?"

Someone was calling his name. He turned around to see Mark looking at him. A short perusal of the faces around him showed that they were all grinning to some extent. He knew why and cleared his throat.

"I am sorry, I did not hear what was said."

"I know," Mark replied, his gaze moving over Alixandrea. "They have way of doing that to you, do they not?"

"Who?"

"Women."

Matthew's easy grin flickered. He wasn't going to play stupid when they could all figure out that he wasn't entirely displeased with this marriage. He really should have been embarrassed considering he had spent ten years denouncing it, but he found that he wasn't in the least.

"Not all women," he said. "Just one in particular."

Luke snorted, John grinned, and Mark just shook his head.

"Let's get back to the subject at hand, if I can tear you away from thoughts of a hazel-eyed goddess," Mark eyed his eldest brother deliberately. "We were discussing our movement for London."

Matthew shrugged. "Nothing has changed. We leave in two days."

The brothers glanced at each other. "What about Father?" Mark asked the question they were all thinking.

"He will be ready to ride."

Adam was up in his chamber, seated next to the cold hearth in something of a stupor. He hadn't moved since Matthew's wedding last night. The brothers were taking turns keeping an eye on him, but remarkably, he'd not yet gone to drink yet. He was simply sitting, lost in a haze of grief and thought. But he was not alone; a Wellesbourne guard was posted right outside his door should he be needed.

"But what if he's not?" Mark persisted quietly. "Matt, we don't know what kind of effect this wedding will have on him."

Matthew sighed with irritation. "He's known this day would come for ten years. He cannot be shocked or surprised by it. As long as we keep the liquor away from him, it is my hope he can rationally deal with whatever feelings he may be sensing." He reached over and took half a loaf of bread that was sitting on the table; besides being exhausted, he was also famished and he took a healthy bite. "Mark, did you send Thomas and Harl on to London as we discussed?"

"Aye," Mark replied. "They left yesterday and should arrive in a couple of days, God willing."

"Good," Matthew swallowed the bite in his mouth. "Luke, what of the army?"

"They are prepared," he said. "They're ready to mobilize and move out within an hour. Just give the word."

"Excellent." Matthew took another bite. "And Johnny; the condition of the wagons and auxiliary detachments we are taking with us?"

"All ready," John, though meek and introspective most of the time, was nonetheless a logistical master. He considered details even the most seasoned of men might overlook. "We've rations, a smithy and a surgeon ready at your command."

Matthew nodded, satisfied. "Add a carriage to the entourage."

His brothers looked at him. "For what?" John asked.

Matthew met their curious gazes. "For my wife. She is going to London with us."

For a moment, no one said a word. A woman on a battle march was unheard of and it had certainly never happened in the world of the House of Wellesbourne. But no one was brave enough to voice what they were thinking, at least not yet.

But Mark finally spoke. Someone had to. "It is not safe for a woman on the road, Matt. You know this. Moreover, we're a fully armed battle contingent and a prime target for an oppositional army. What happens if we're engaged before we get to the safety of London? Do you want another happening like we had a couple of days ago with Dorset's men?"

"There will be twelve hundred men," Matthew replied steadily. "There will be plenty of men to protect Lady Alixandrea should it come to that."

"But what about the men from Whitewell?" Luke wanted to know. "You cannot possibly think to leave them here, which means they must go to London, too. Do we really march to London with four hundred rebels in our midst?"

Matthew wasn't used to being questioned, especially by his brothers. He found himself fighting down irritation. "Have you lost faith in me, brother?"

Luke shook his head. "Nay. But I am asking a valid question."

Matthew's initial reaction was to become angry at his brother's doubt in his judgment. But that would accomplish nothing. Still, he was offended and forced himself to calm.

"Last night after we discovered Ryesdale's plans for insurrection, I sent a rider to Oxford," he said. "Gaston de Russe's army is camped just outside of the city. I have asked de Russe to ride for Wellesbourne, meet our army, and ride into London with us. With The White Lord of Wellesbourne uniting with the army of The Dark Knight, all of England will tremble in fear of us. So you see, brother, even if the men from Whitewell decide to revolt, twelve hundred additional men under the command of de Russe will ensure that our army stays stable and powerful."

The uniting of two legends. It was like the army of Cuculainn uniting with the army of King Arthur; there would not be a man in England that would not look upon the alliance as invincible. Luke looked at Mark, who merely shrugged. They had no more questions of their brother. John wasn't concerned with the implications of the strategies as much as he was the logistical issues of bringing a woman on their march.

"We will have over two thousand men," he said to his eldest brother. "She will need her own contingent of guards unless you plan on being with her every moment. And she will need her own tent, and bathtub, and..."

Matthew put up a hand. "She is my wife, John. She will be in my tent. As for the rest of it, I leave it up to you; however, I will hand-select the guard that will be assigned to her protection."

"Won't they become suspicious if you do not select Whitewell men to guard her?" John asked. "They came with her, after all. It would only seem logical to select them to guard her."

"It will be a chance I shall have to take," Matthew replied. "No one from Whitewell, including her manservant, is to be allowed anywhere near her. I don't care how you do it, John, but you keep that man away from her. Assign him something so remote that there will be no chance of him coming into contact with her."

"Perhaps we should just leave him behind with the maid," Mark suggested. "We can cut the troops off from the manservant, as he apparently gives the commands, thereby lessening the chance of revolt."

Matthew thought seriously on the suggestion. It was a good one. "That is certainly something to be considered."

Finished with his bread, he moved to pour himself some watered ale. The brothers settled down to the benches now that they were comfortable with the conversation and a plan of action was being formed. There was much that lay ahead, and much more to do. Matthew sat next to Mark, across from Luke and John.

"Now," he said. "To discuss the situation once we reach London."

CHAPTER SIX

Though she was supposed to be with Caroline, Alixandrea ended up in her chamber. Caroline wanted to sit before her massive loom and continue her needlework, a giant cohesion of color and birds and other creatures, but Alixandrea had no talent in such things. She found it boring.

She did, however, have some talent with drawing, mostly the flowers that she had grown in her garden at York. So she went up to her chamber, a floor above Caroline and Mark's, and went in search of her drawing case. All she could find were clothes and other assorted items and realized that not all of her cases had been brought up. It was a small chamber and it appeared as if only the necessary cases had been brought up and placed in the small alcove off of the chamber. She would have liked to have asked Jezebel where her drawing supplies were, but the woman was missing. Still. Frustrated, bordering on angry, she went in search of her maid.

There was another small chamber across from hers with a bed and other clutter in it; it was empty of human life. Down the flight of stairs was Caroline's chamber and Adam's right across from her. Still no maid. Descending to the second floor, the great hall was to her left and she could see Matthew seated with his brothers at the great table. She stood there a moment, watching his strong profile from a distance, hardly believing she was married to him. She did not feel married. Tearing her eyes away from him, she peered into the small room off to the right, a solar with a massive table in the center of it and a well-worn map spread out across it. The room was empty. Puzzled, wondering where to start looking next, she suddenly caught movement out of the corner of her eye.

She had barely seen the twitch, but it had been unmistakable. Nearly out of her line of sight was the large gallery that lined the upper portion of great hall. Tall, tapering lancet windows were embedded in the wall all around the room, hanging just above the gallery to allow ventilation and light into the chamber.

Alixandrea took a couple of steps towards the entry of the great hall, watching the gallery above. The balcony-like protrusion was built of wood with wide guardrails lining it. However, there was just enough room to be able to see between them. And she could see someone on the walk.

The narrow staircase to the gallery was just inside the hall. Silently, quickly, she darted to the entrance and slipped up the first two steps. Matthew hadn't seen her, but John and Luke did, as they were facing the stairs. She put a finger to her lips to silence them. Then she pointed the same finger at them and twirled it in a couple of circles, indicating for them to turn away from her and put their focus back on their brother before he turned around, too. Like obedient children, they did as the lady told them, but she could tell they were uncertain about it.

When she was sure they would not look back at her and give her away, she shimmied up the steps until she reached the top. Down on her hands and knees, she peered around the side of the guardrail and had a clear vision of whatever might be on the gallery.

It was Jezebel, down on her knees, watching the men through the slats in the railing. Alixandrea's heart sank; if she ever had any doubt of what Matthew had told her, it was quickly dashed. Her maid, the woman she trusted, was spying. She had probably been there for some time. Though Alixandrea would allow the woman to explain, she could see no other explanation. She thanked God that Matthew hadn't shown her any affection when she walked in the room, for it would most likely be filling Strode's ear right now. Matthew had known exactly what could have happened and had made sure they were careful. Their lives had depended on it.

Anger filled her, so much so that she stood up. She was not going to hide from this affront. The only way off the gallery was the stairs she had just mounted, so there was nowhere for

Jezebel to go. She began to walk towards her maid.

"Jez," she said in a normal speaking tone. "What are you doing up here?"

The little maid turned to her, startled. From her angle, she'd never seen her mistress mount the stairs. Her wide brown eyes were huge with shock and she leapt to her feet.

"M'lady," she stammered. "I... I was looking for ye. I haven't seen ye this morn and I thought...."

Alixandrea walked right up on her. It was an effort not to reach out and strangle her. "So you look for me, hiding up here in the gallery?"

"I did not want to bother the lords, m'lady. I thought you might come in to join them."

"Then if that's true, you already saw me in here a few minutes ago. Why did not you announce yourself?"

Jezebel's face turned red. By this time, the men below had heard the voices and had turned to see where they were coming from. Matthew was actually on his feet. Alixandrea caught his movement out of the corner of her eye and when she turned to look at him, Jezebel suddenly pushed past her.

In her panic, the maid misjudged her own strength; an intended brush against the lady pitched Alixandrea right over the thigh-high railing. Only the quick reflex of grabbing the banister as she went over the side saved her from falling twenty feet to the cold, hard floor below.

Alixandrea shrieked with terror as she dangled high above the floor. Matthew bolted faster than he had ever moved in his life, running for the gallery stairs like a madman. Luke followed him while Mark and John rushed over and positioned themselves underneath the lady, hoping to break her fall if she lost her grip. They held out their arms, waiting, hoping to God that no one would be killed.

Jezebel ran right into Matthew as she tried to escape down the stairs, screaming as he grabbed her and practically tossed her onto Luke. Luke roughly took the maid as Matthew raced onto the gallery. It wasn't a long gallery, but Matthew swore it was the longest run of his life. It seemed to take forever, knowing he was running as fast as he could yet hardly appearing to make any ground.

He could see Alixandrea's fingers around the top of the railing and he aimed for them, reaching out, finally coming upon her and grabbing her wrists.

"I have got you." He almost pitched forward himself in his haste but managed to hold his balance. "It is all right, I have got you."

He effortlessly pulled her up, straight into his arms. Alixandrea grabbed hold of him, panic in every breath, every movement. When she finally realized that she was safe, the tears came. Matthew held her tightly.

"Is she all right?" Mark called up.

Matthew took her face between his two hands, looking into her wet eyes. "Are you well?" his voice was shaking.

She nodded. He pulled her back into his powerful arms. "She is well enough," Matthew said to his brothers. "Simply scared."

By this time, Luke had Jezebel down on the floor. The maid was weeping uncontrollably. Over the top of Alixandrea's head, Matthew caught sight of the woman.

"Take her in the solar," he growled. "Do not let her out of your sight. I shall join you shortly."

Luke nodded, yanking the woman out of the hall and listening to her cries echoing against the walls. Luke wasn't hurting her in the least; she simply knew she was in a great deal of trouble. Matthew listened to her cries fade as he rocked Alixandrea in his arms gently. The woman was shaking terribly.

"Are you truly all right?" he asked into her hair. "You did not hurt anything?"

She sniffled, struggling for calm. "Nay," she said, her nose stuffy with crying. "I am well enough."

He pulled back just long enough to look her in the face, just to make sure she wasn't lying. When their eyes met, he smiled bravely at her. "Then why don't we get down from here?"

She wholeheartedly agreed, clinging to him even as they

descended the stairs. She was unsteady and Matthew directed her to the nearest bench. Mark and John crowded around them.

"Did she shove you, my lady?" John asked anxiously. "Did she do it a-purpose?"

Alixandrea shook her head as Mark shoved a chalice of ale at her. She took a long drink even though she did not much like ale.

"She was trying to escape me," she gasped. "I don't believe she purposely tried to shove me over the side."

Matthew was sitting next to her, straddled across the bench. His blue eyes were soft with concern. He watched her hands shake as she took another drink of ale.

"As long as you are all right, that is my utmost concern."

Alixandrea's bronze eyes fixed on him. "But she knows that we suspect her now. Why else would she try to run?"

Matthew shrugged casually, his big hand reaching out to clasp her arm comfortingly. His voice was deep, rich, reassuring. "All she knows is that you caught her spying. I doubt she knows the extent of our knowledge and how it relates to Strode and the army."

"Then what are you going to do with her?"

"Throw her in the vault as punishment for nearly killing you. After that, I do not know. But we can at least keep her isolated from your manservant in the vault and he will have no further source of information. Your little maid has just given us an excuse to cut out the eyes and ears of those inside Wellesbourne who have been sent to do us harm."

She sensed that he thought this event, such as it was, had a positive side. Slowly, her shaking lessened and she began to feel better, though still exhausted. The past few days had been most taxing. With Matthew's strong hand still on her arm, she finished the ale and set the empty cup aside.

"If you will excuse me, I think I should like to rest a while," she said. "It has been a busy morning."

Matthew stood up with her. "Come along, then. We shall get you settled and then I will return to see what I can glean from your maid."

Hand on his, she paused. "You are not going to hurt her, are you?"

He gazed down into her magnificent bronze eyes. "Would you think me capable of such a thing?"

"Nay," she shook her head, suddenly ashamed. "I did not mean it the way it sounded. It is just... Jezebel has been with me a long time. I know she must be punished, but I...."

She trailed off and he clutched her hand, leading her out of the hall. "Trust me that I will do what is best."

"I do."

She was still shaking in spite of the fact that she had calmed somewhat. In her mind, she could still see herself falling from the balcony and the thought rattled her; consequently, the trip up the spiral stairs was slow going.

When they reached her chamber, Matthew led her inside and closed the door softly behind her. The bed drew Alixandrea's attention and with a fatigued sigh, she fell atop the mattress without so much as removing her shoes. Matthew stood by the door.

"Your exhaustion is understandable," he said with some compassion. "It seems that all you have known is chaos since setting foot on Wellesbourne land."

She shifted on the bed so that she was looking at him. "Aye, 'tis been a bit chaotic. First there was the battle the day I arrived...."

"... and the feast the first night, followed by the wedding that almost never happened..."

"... and now I almost plummet to my death from the gallery banister. Is there anything else that could possibly happen to me?"

He grinned. "Let us hope not."

She sighed heavily, her nerves finally at rest. Truth be known, Matthew seemed to have a great hand in helping her ease. His presence was comforting and calming.

"Hopefully, whatever bad fortunes that seemed to have befallen me will have run their course by now," she said. "I am not sure how much more I can take."

"Nor I," he said, chuckling softly when she rolled her eyes in agreement. "Shall I leave you now to rest, wife?"

Alixandrea pondered the question. It suddenly occurred to her that they were truly alone, without any threat of interruption or spying. Not even Caroline could protest their being alone, as she had been witness to their marriage.

Her heart suddenly began to race, wondering if he meant what she thought he meant. She did not know if she was ready for such a thing, especially after the events of the past few minutes. But the more she thought on what he perhaps might be suggesting, the more the thoughts of her chaotic first days faded. She wasn't so exhausted, after all. She could feel her cheeks grow hot with a little fear, and a lot of anticipation.

"Do you want to leave, husband?"

"Nay."

He did not hesitate as he walked into the room. She sat up on the mattress, gazing up at him as he came to a halt beside the bed.

"Do you know that I sat up all night, watching you on the wall?" she said. "I was afraid something horrible was going to happen to you."

He lifted a blond eyebrow. "So you would watch it happen?"

"Nay," she shook her head. "I wanted to stop it. If it was going to come from the men of Whitewell, then I felt it my duty to stop them."

"And just how did you intend to do that?"

She shrugged. "Short of throwing projectiles out of my window or howling at the moon, I really don't know. I had hoped that if it came to that, some marvelous idea would come to me."

"Then I thank God that my life did not depend upon your brilliant defense plan."

She laughed softly, knowing he was right, knowing it had been foolish of her. But she had no idea how much her gesture, however small, had touched him. He reached down, gently touching her chin, her cheek.

"I know you were awake," he said in his soft, rich voice. "I watched you all night, too, through that very window. Not much of a way to spend a wedding night."

She shrugged, lowering her gaze coyly. "I would not know, my lord. I have never had a wedding night."

"I shall see what I can do about that."

He sat down on the bed next to her. He was such a large man that the small wood and rope bed frame creaked dangerously. Alixandrea barely had time to look at him before he was descending on her, his lips clamping down over hers and his powerful arms winding around her body.

As it had the first time he kissed her, the heat and fervor of the passion between them overwhelmed her senses and she could do naught but submit to his tender ambush. He kissed her softly, joyfully, succulently. She was barely aware when he laid her back on the bed, his mouth still against hers, his arms embracing her tightly.

His hands, as large and calloused as they were, nonetheless possessed the gentlest touch she had ever experienced. They caressed her back, her arms, moving to her face and neck and stroking her skin tenderly. His lips moved to her cheeks, her ears, suckling her neck as if it was the most delectable morsel. The sensations were overpowering and Alixandrea surrendered completely, losing herself in the maelstrom of heat he created.

"I am sorry," he suddenly pushed himself up onto one elbow, his face looming over her. "Perhaps this is too much for you. We barely know each other, after all. I am simply a stranger who is now your husband. If you would prefer to leave this intimacy until we come to know one another better, I understand. I do not want to hurt or frighten you, but I swear that I cannot keep my hands off you. Something about you... it causes me to lose control and I am a man unused to such lack of discipline."

Alixandrea gazed at him; the man was nearly too good to be true, apologizing for his weakness. Any other man in his right mind would have taken her on the spot, without question or regrets. She was not so naïve that she did not know that. She was older than most brides and had therefore been privy to much talk in that arena. The servants at Whitewell and Pickering had been quite free with dispensing their knowledge.

"You have not hurt nor frightened me so far," she said softly. "I am your wife, Matthew. It is your right to claim me."

"I know what my rights are. I was attempting to consider your feelings."

"It feels good so far."

He eyed her, seeing a double meaning in her words. He took it as encouragement. A grin spread across his face and he lowered his head, his lips hovering a hair's breadth above her own.

"Are you sure?"

"I am sure."

"Then let us see if we cannot make it feel even better."

His tongue invaded her mouth. More attuned to it this time, she invited him in, her own tongue playing timidly with his. He laughed low in his throat and his hand left her shoulder, moving down the swell of her breast. Focused on what his hand was doing, she closed her eyes as his lips suckled her chin and moved along her jaw line.

His fingers were moving between her breasts, drawing a sensual outline around the left one. She could feel him moving across the rise of her breast, into intimate territory, and she flinched when he found her sensitive nipple. He smiled against her flesh and his big palm closed in over her ample bosom. It was more than a handful for him.

He caressed her a few times, acquainting himself with the softness of her delicious body. Alixandrea had never experienced something so electrifying and a groan escaped her lips. Ignited by her response to his touch, Matthew suddenly pulled her to a seated position and unfastened her surcoat as quickly as his big fingers would allow. He pulled it up over her head, leaving her in her soft sheath. Almost simultaneously, he removed his tunic, bearing his massive chest.

Dazed, Alixandrea stared at his broad chest, the muscles bulging and his skin a lovely golden-pale color. She hardly noticed when he unfastened the stays of her corset and the thing popped free. He could not pull it off of her so he yanked it over her head. In his haste, her hair caught in the metal stays and they ended up laughing as he unwound her hair from its tangle.

"Sorry, love," he said as he deftly unwound the mess. "This wasn't part of my master plan."

She giggled as the hair came free and he tossed the corset aside. He paused a moment, gazing down at her. He could not help the smile on his face. Though it was normally close to the surface, it seemed perpetual when she was around.

"I have never in my life seen such a sweet face," he murmured. "Every time I look at you, I can hardly believe that you are real."

She did not know what to say. His words made her feel warm and wanted, more than she could have imagined and better than she had ever hoped for. The White Lord was hers, and she was his, and both seemed very pleased at the prospect.

Still dressed in her sheath, Matthew lay his wife back down on the mattress, the thin layer of linen the only barrier between their bare skin. He could feel her taut nipples brushing through the material, rubbing against his chest, and it nearly drove him mad. He laid his body atop her so that he wasn't crushing her and also so one hand could have free rein; when his lips latched onto her soft earlobe, his right hand went to work.

His fingers snaked underneath her sheath, lifting it up as he went. Her skin was like velvet to his rough-hewn fingers, and he literally had to stop himself from trembling as his hand trailed up her thighs to her buttocks, moving further to her hip. When the sheath came up as high as her groin, he felt her hesitate and modestly try to keep it from coming up any further. His lips left her earlobe and went to her mouth, kissing her until she could hardly take a breath. It distracted her enough so that he was able to lift the sheath to her waist. His mouth still on hers, he put both hands underneath the sheath and lifted it over her head in one clean motion.

In the same action, he lifted up the side of the coverlet, covering her enough for modesty so that she would not feel exposed. It was a considerate thing to do, but Matthew, unlike most men, had always been intuitively considerate. Perhaps it was his mother's influence, the gentle Audrey; whatever the reason, he was thoughtful in a way that Alixandrea would benefit from. She never felt exposed or uncomfortable as Matthew covered her and removed his boots and breeches. Somehow, it all came off in the heat of passion and soon they were both nude beneath the turned up corner of the coverlet.

Matthew never said a word as his mouth returned to her, only now it explored beneath her neckline. Her shoulders, the swell of her breasts, and her arms were all targets for his tender lips. Alixandrea lay there, smothered by his enormous body and tented with the coverlet, feeling the predominant emotions of comfort and satisfaction and something she could not yet define. Having never been intimate with a man, the painful tingling in her arms and legs was something she'd never known, and every time he suckled her skin, it made her want to gasp. A few times, she did. But when Matthew's mouth latched onto a nipple, she achieved an entirely new level of sensation she'd not yet conceived of.

His hot, moist mouth nearly brought her off the bed. He put his hands on her arms, holding her to the mattress as he suckled. First one breast and then the other; Alixandrea's head was spinning with exhilaration. Matthew's attentions were becoming more and more insistent as he held her down while his mouth ravaged her. Soon he released her and his hands joined in the plunder. Alixandrea lay beneath him, too upswept with the new experience to be of much use. But when his hand moved to the fluff of soft curls between her legs, she instinctively flinched.

"'Tis all right, sweet girl," he murmured. "I promise that I will be gentle."

His voice, so soft and soothing in her ear, gave her courage. It also sent chills up her spine. Everything was so new and consuming. She would have to trust him; he'd not failed her yet. In fact, he had gone out of his way to make sure she was secure.

"I trust you," she whispered.

He shifted his body so that he wedged himself in between her luscious legs. His hands were on her, everywhere; he could not seem to touch her fast enough, tenderly enough. She was so delectable that he was like a starving man at a feast; everything was appealing. He wanted to gorge himself. But he had to remember that she was oh-so-new to this, and that constant reminder tempered his rampage.

But not entirely. He wanted to feel himself inside of her. He kissed her hard as he eased into her, feeling her slickness against his member. He played with her, easing in, withdrawing, making way further and further inside of her each time. Finally, he could stand it no longer and he pulled back and drove hard, seating himself deep inside of her. The most she did was draw in a sharp breath; there was nothing more. No crying, no hysterics. Relieved, encouraged, his kisses softened against her mouth as he slowly began to move.

It had been a long time since Matthew had been with a woman. So long, in fact, that he could not remember when last he touched female flesh. But gazing down at Alixandrea's face, it was as if no other woman had existed before her. It was a struggle not to erupt immediately into her sweet body; he wanted to savor it, to feel it, and he wanted her to do the same.

In the soft afternoon light that drifted in through the lancet window, Matthew gazed down at her body, shielded by the coverlet that covered them both; her breasts were round and firm and peaked, her stomach flat, her slender legs parted to receive him.

It was too much to take. He shouldn't have looked at her. One hand supporting himself and the other hand on her buttock, his thrusts grew more insistent. He knew his pleasure was coming quickly and he did not want to stop it. The hand on her buttock moved between them and he stroked the damp curls, feeling the place where their bodies melded.

Gently, his fingers played with her and he could feel her body stiffen beneath him. Another few strokes with both his maleness and his fingers and Alixandrea gasped loudly, her body arching against him. He lost himself, spilling within her, driving home with all of the power and passion he was feeling.

Too soon, it was over. Too soon, their bodies cooled and their passion banked until they lay in a heap, intertwined, dozing away the minutes as the world went on around them. The calm after the storm had arrived, and it settled heavily.

Yet Alixandrea was not asleep. She lay beneath Matthew's enormous body, thinking that of all the things she had imagined this moment would be, it did not compare with the reality of it. She had heard the female servants telling stories of pain and devastation at the hands of inept men. But Matthew was not inept; he had been kind and considerate and gentle and, above all, he had made her feel things that she had never imagined to exist.

"Are you well?" his mouth was against her forehead. "I did not hurt you, did I?"

She tilted her head back, looking up at him. The more she saw of this man, the more handsome he became. It wasn't so much in his physical appearance, for she had seen men that were more beautiful. But he had a certain quality she could not quite put her finger on that made him absolutely irresistible, far more attractive than any man she had ever known.

"Nay," she said softly. "You were quite gentle."

"I'd hoped to be. I did not want this to be a bad experience for you, as it is with some."

"It wasn't." She snuggled against him, daring to be bold and pressing herself against him. He was big and warm and safe. "Would it be possible to stay all day here?"

He laughed, low in his throat. "It would be my most ardent desire, but alas, I cannot. I am mobilizing an army and..."

This time, she put her fingers on his lips to silence him. "Say no more, husband. I know that you are a busy man with much demand for your time and attention."

He kissed her fingers. "But none more important than you."

She gazed at him a long moment before laughing softly. "How can you say that," she asked, "when you have only known me for two days?"

He put a massive arm behind his head, resting on it. "Because you are my wife. It matters not if I have known you two days, two months, or twenty years. By virtue of your station, you will always be important to me."

She sat up, clutching the coverlet to her chest. With her mussed bronze hair, sweet face and creamy skin, he was indeed in danger of staying there all day. He reached out, pushing a stray lock of hair from her face.

"This is a contract marriage, Matthew," she said softly. "You do not have to say things that you do not mean. You are not obligated to pay me lip service."

His eyebrows lifted. "Is that what you think I am doing?"

Her head wagged back and forth, slowly. "I did not say that you were. But as we have both acknowledged, we've known each other only two days. We know so little about one another. How can you make declarations of my importance without even knowing me?"

"I told you. As my wife, you will always be important, even if we grow to hate one another."

Her bronze eyes were fixed intently on him. "I pray that it never comes to that. I promise you that I will do all in my power to ensure that this marriage is pleasant for the both of us."

He toyed with the ends of her hair. "I hope it is much more than that."

"What do you mean?"

He shrugged, those big shoulders lifting. "Though we have known each other a very short time, I have seen much that I like during that time and very little that I don't. I may be many things, but a bad judge of character is not one of them. My life has depended on it. I would be willing to wager that you are a woman of good character."

She was beginning to feel that wonderful warmth again, something he seemed so capable of creating between them. "Even though I do not like to tend wounds?"

He laughed softly. "Aye, even though you do not like to tend wounds."

"And even though I do not like to sew?"

"Aye, even that."

Her gaze continued to linger on him, drifting over the enormous bicep near his head, the muscular build of his bare chest. Being a proper lady, she should have been embarrassed faced with the bare flesh of a man, but found that she was not. She rather liked looking at him.

"What do you like to do, Matt?"

His easy smile turned gentle; he liked hearing his name come out of her mouth. "What do you mean?"

She shrugged and lay back down beside him; he gathered her into his arms and held her close. "I mean just that," she said softly. "I like to tend flowers and sometimes I like to draw. What do you like to do in your leisure time?"

He thought a moment. "I have been a sworn knight since I was seventeen years of age," he said pensively. "All I have known is war since that time. Seventeen years of battles. I suppose there hasn't been much time for leisure."

"But if there was time, what would you do?"

He tickled her nose. "Probably spend it with you."

She giggled and swatted at his hand. "Aye, but doing what?"

He snorted, burying his face in her neck, his hot hands once again moving down the hollow of her slender back. "Doing what we just did."

She laughed softly, pushing at him. "Be serious. I am attempting to get to know you, husband. You could cooperate."

He pulled back and looked at her, though the blue eyes were still full of humor. Errant strands of bronze hair were in her face and he pushed them aside to get a better view.

"Sorry," he said, though he really wasn't. "I suppose if I had to think of one thing I like to do, 'tis to go fishing."

"Fishing?"

"Aye. I used to do it with my father when I was a lad. In fact, I could fish before I could walk. There is much peace and serenity to fishing, far removed from the cries and violence of the battlefield. Fishing, to me, has always signified peace because I learned it at such a young age before I even learned to wield a sword."

"I have never been fishing."

"Then we shall have to remedy that."

She grinned at him, a joyful smile which he easily returned. He wanted nothing more than to make love to her again, but he refrained. Better to bask in the wonder and joy of their first time together. She was his wife now and he looked forward to a lifetime of opportunity to further acquaint himself with her lovely mind and body.

She fell back asleep in his arms. Though Matthew did not sleep, he stayed with her and did not move a muscle.

CHAPTER SEVEN

It was dawn. The battlements of Wellesbourne were bathed in pink light as the sun began to rise, basking the green countryside of Warwickshire in warm, soothing shades. From his post on the wall, Matthew could see a three-point buck in the distance, finding his morning meal.

Birds flew overhead, singing sweetly to greet the new day. He glanced up at the lavender sky; perhaps the birds always sang so sweetly and he just hadn't noticed. But this morning, he found pleasantness in nearly everything. He had left his wife still sleeping in her small bed, warm and cozy, and for the moment, life was good. It was surprising to realize that there was an agreeable side to his existence, far removed from the war and death he was so accustomed to.

But that was until Mark and Luke arrived. The middle Wellesbourne brothers looked dismal and tired. It was usual, when the army was housed at Wellesbourne Castle, for Mark and Luke to take the night watch. Matthew and John usually patrolled during the day, and with Matthew, sometimes all night as well. But last night, Matthew had found great comfort sleeping next to his wife in her small bed. By his brothers' expressions, he guessed that it had not been a quiet patrol.

"Greetings, brother," Mark said as he approached.

Matthew pushed himself up off the wall where he had been leaning. "Good morn," he acknowledged. He looked between Mark and Luke. "Why the grim faces?"

Mark and Luke came to a halt, Luke rubbing his eyes wearily. "We received a rider from Warwick last night," Mark said. "The Earl of Oxford has made it to France, apparently quite welcomed by Henry Tudor. He brings with him the de Vere fortune to support the French mercenaries that Henry must pay for in his quest to claim the throne. This is bad news, Matt. It gives Henry more powerful barons than we would like."

The pleasant morning quickly dissolved. Matthew sighed, his gaze drifting over the landscape of his beloved Warwickshire. "Did you tell the messenger to return and tell Warwick that Somerset and Sutton are moving Irish mercenaries up to Gloucester?"

"Aye."

Matthew pondered a thousand courses of action that the latest news could take. "Last we heard of de Vere, he had laid siege to St. Michael's Mount and was attempting to rouse all of Cornwall into a Lancastrian uprising," he said. "When did this end?"

"A few weeks ago," Mark replied. "De Vere has been fleeing Richard's forces since that time. Somehow he's escape to France."

"And his fortunes with him."

The brothers fell silent, each lost to their own particular thoughts. Matthew's jaw ticked faintly, indicative of his level of concern.

"We must return to London immediately," he said finally. "Too much is happening for us to remain here any longer. Richard will require our strength and counsel."

"They are all up to something," Luke muttered. "You were right when you said it two days ago, Matt. Something big is happening."

Matthew was already heading for the gatehouse and the narrow spiral stairs that led to the ward below. "Notify John and the men. We move out within the hour."

Luke nodded shortly and fled down the stairs in front of his brothers. Mark followed Matthew to the ward.

"What about Father?" Mark asked.

Matthew shrugged. "What about him? He was sleeping soundly in his room this morning when I left the keep. We kept the drink away from him yesterday, so I would presume that he would be able to ride."

Mark was silent. Matthew knew his brother well enough to know when something was bothering him. "What is it?"

"What do you mean?"

"I know you, brother. Your silence is full of something, doubt or disapproval, I cannot be sure."

Mark glanced up at his brother, his eyes so dark that they were almost obsidian. He was the only brother that favored Adam in that regard; the rest of the Wellesbourne siblings possessed their mother's blue eyes.

"I thought you were with Father last night," he said. "Had I known that you were not, I would have stayed with him myself."

Matthew snorted. "I have a new wife and you think I spent my evening with our father? Think again."

"But he's still brittle, Matt. I am not comfortable with him being left alone."

It was an old argument between them. Mark could impart guilt on Matthew like none other; Matthew, on the other hand, would accept it. They loved each other dearly, would defend one another to the death, but they could still trade barbs and insults like brothers could.

"Then you stay with him," Matthew snapped softly. "I told you that I am not going to go through this again and I meant it. He's a grown man; I have played nursemaid for twelve long years, Mark. I am tired. It is time for you to shoulder some of the burden."

"You are unfair," Mark was trying to keep his temper. "I have shared this burden with you many a time. But we all know that Father responds better to you than to any of us."

"And that makes it my sole responsibility?" Matthew came to a stop, glaring at his shorter, stockier brother. "I have far too much on my mind to deal with this insanity right now. Wiltshire and Pembroke have moved their armies north to Nottingham, Somerset and Lord Sutton are due in Gloucester any day at which time they, too, will move north, presumably to Nottingham, and Oxford and William Brandon have both fled to France to join Henry's forces there. Something massive is brewing, Mark, larger than anything we can comprehend. When my mind should be focused on that, you are angry because I did not spend the evening sitting with my father who has less control than a weak woman and the constitution of a skittish cat."

Part of Mark knew that he was correct, but the other part was genuinely concerned for the state of their father. He knew Matthew was concerned too, deep down, but the man had enormous responsibilities staring him in the face that the others did not.

"Fine," he said shortly. "The rest of us will try to handle Father. But if something happens to him, something awful, know that the ultimate responsibility should have been with you."

"I am not the only son of Wellesbourne," Matthew boomed.

"But you are the only one he'll listen to!"

They faced off against each other, fury in their expressions, emotions running rampant. Mark jabbed a finger at him.

"I know what this is about," he hissed. "Your new wife has you else occupied, so much so that you would forget your duty as Adam Wellesbourne's eldest son."

A fist came flying at Mark. He wasn't fast enough to duck and Matthew's crushing blow nearly took off his head. He went spinning off balance but somehow managed to keep his feet. Blood dripped from his nostrils as he looked up to see his brother bearing down on him.

"Do not ever accuse me of dodging my duty as a Wellesbourne," he stopped short of striking his brother again; he simply stood over him and growled. "I have given more to this family, king and country than you can possibly imagine."

Mark wiped the blood from his nose. "Your obligation is to protect your father, especially from himself."

Matthew's blue eyes were like ice. "You will not tell me what my obligation is."

Mark just shook his head and turned away. Matthew called out to him before he got too far.

"Did I hurt you?"

Mark paused. "No. But it was a good hit."

Lips pursed with regret, and a lot of disgust, Matthew went over to him and tilted his head up, peering up both bloody nostrils.

"You usually duck faster than that," he grumbled.

"I did not see the fist until it was too late."

"You are slowing down in your old age."

Mark smiled in spite of himself. "And you are growing edgy in yours."

"I am sorry."

"So am I."

They parted ways as they had done a thousand times before. Sometimes Matthew came away bloodied, but most of the time it was Mark. It had been thus since they had been small boys. All of the things they said and did to each other, they had made a vow never to part angry, and they never had. While Mark went to see to the army, Matthew made way for the keep.

The first stop he made was at his father's chamber.

***

Alixandrea was fully dressed when Matthew came for her. He had expected to wake her, for it was shortly after dawn, but she was sitting by a brightly blazing hearth sipping warmed milk with nutmeg. When she saw him enter the chamber, she smiled brightly. Matthew nearly melted.

"This morning sees you well, I hope," he said.

She nodded. "It does. And does it see you well, also?"

"It does."

He went to pull up the small stool that sat against the hearth. He sat next to her, gazing at her beauty as if nothing else in the world existed. Had he been thinking with his rational mind and not his besotted one, he would have realized he was completely smitten. He'd known the lady four days and already, he could not imagine life before she came to Wellesbourne. It was as great as the difference between heaven and hell.

"I am glad you are awake," he said. "It would seem that we must leave for London sooner than I originally planned. How long will it take you to be ready?"

She lifted her eyebrows. "I have hardly unpacked since my arrival. 'Twill simply be a matter of loading my cases onto the wagon again."

"We do not need to take everything. Only those items which are necessary."

"How long are we staying?"

"That is hard to say."

"Then everything is necessary."

He lifted an eyebrow. "We will be traveling swiftly and lightly. I cannot spare the time or manpower to lug around all of your worldly possessions." When she opened her mouth to protest, he put up a hand to silence her. "Whatever you may leave behind, we can purchase for you in London if necessary."

She gazed at him steadily before a grin spread across her lips. "Then I shall leave everything behind."

"Everything?"

"Aye. When will I have another opportunity to purchase fine new things, in London no less?"

He could see she was teasing but he cocked a stern eyebrow at her. "So that's your plan, is it? Marry me and spend my fortune?"

She laughed softly. "Fortunate for me that you did not suspect my true motives before we were wed. Now it is too late."

"We'll see about that."

She continued to giggle. He reached out, grabbed her behind the head, and kissed her soundly. She tasted so good that he kissed her again, this time long and hard. The warmed milk in her hand almost ended up on the floor; Matthew caught it before it could spill, though some drops ended up on him.

"Sorry," he set the cup aside, wiping the liquid off his hand. "I got carried away."

She licked her lips, tasting his passion on her. "You have my permission to get carried away any time you wish."

He wriggled his eyebrows at her. It was an open invitation and he knew that he was a fool not to take it.

"Would that I could take the time to spend with you right now as we did yesterday," he touched her cheek gently. "But the duties of the day are already dictated. I would not rush through our time together and make so little of it. Time spent with you, coming to know you, is time that deserves all of the respect I can give it. And I cannot do that right now."

She nodded in understanding. "Then it is best that you go about your duties and leave me to mine, for I would keep you here all morning." She stood up, her cheeks turning a delightful shade of pink as she fumbled for the correct words. "I cannot explain this, Matthew. I cannot explain why I have no fear or reservation about you and why what happened between us yesterday, which should have rightfully distressed me, did nothing of the sort. I feel as if I have known you my whole life, as if you are something that has always been with me and I feel you as a part of me. I want to spend all of my time with you, whiling away the hours as if nothing else in our world exists. We respond to each other so easily, so readily. Can you not sense that?"

He reached out and took her hand, a warm, soft thing. "Of course I can," he said huskily. "Do you think this has been easy for me the past few days, knowing I should be focused on my duties but finding myself unable to think of anything other than you? My brothers think I have gone mad. Maybe I have. But if this is madness, then I happily accept it."

Alixandrea was coming to realize that Matthew always knew the right thing to say. He wasn't like her uncle, hard and selfish, or like most men she had come in brief contact with. There was something beyond the surface, something deep.

"As do I," she said. "Let us be mad together."

They stood there a moment, grinning at each other. It was silly and completely wonderful. Matthew knew he had to get back to his duties and did not relish the thought of leaving her, even if only for a few moments. He was dangerously close to forgetting his duties completely, just as Mark had accused him.

Maybe his brother had been right. Frankly, he did not care if Mark was right or not, but he did know what was expected of him. It was a struggle to focus.

"As much as I would like to stay here and gaze at your beauty for the rest of my life, I am afraid I have more pressing tasks elsewhere," he said. "I will send Caroline and a few servants to help you organize your cases."

"Caroline was already here," she said. "She helped me dress this morning. Which reminds me...."

"What?"

"Jezebel," her smile faded. "Have you... what have you done with her?"

His smile faded also, his professional persona taking over. "She is still in the vault under orders that no one but Wellesbourne guards be assigned to her. Strode is not allowed near her."

"Have you seen him since yesterday?"

"In the stables. One of your carriage horses is lame and he has been tending the animal."

"I have not seen him since I arrived here, but that's not unusual. He is not a house servant."

"He will be going with us to London."

Her eyes widened. "He will? But... but won't that be risky? If he discovers that we've been married..."

"I would rather have my enemy close than leave him here at Wellesbourne to usurp my soldiers and open the gates for an invasion force." He could see how worried she was and he took her in his arms, gently. "Have no fear; your manservant will not last long against me. He will trip himself eventually and I will be there to pounce."

She gazed up at him, her body warm and fluid as she delighted in his embrace. "But what of Jezebel?"

"She stays in the vault, accused of making an attempt on your life. There she is, and there she will remain until I decide otherwise."

"And then what?"

His eyebrows lifted. "And then I send her back to Whitewell. She'll not stay here."

Alixandrea was about to ask another question when shouting from the ward caught Matthew's attention. Her window faced the main gate of the castle and the sounds easily traveled, even four stories up. He released her and went to the window, peering into the void below.

"What is it?" she asked.

His blue eyes were focused, like ice. In fact, his entire body seemed frozen as he viewed the scene below. Then, he suddenly shifted on his big legs and made haste for the chamber door.

"Visitors," he held out a hand to her. "Come along, love."

She jumped to do his bidding. "Who is it?"

The corner of his lips flickered. "An old friend."

He did not say any more and she did not ask.

***

Gaston de Russe was known as The Dark Knight. Along with Matthew as his "white" counterpart, he was the most legendary knight in the realm during these ominous times of royal turmoil.

Whereas Matthew had been given his name in reference to his widely known benevolent character, The Dark Knight was aptly named for a demeanor that sparked nothing short of blind terror. The man wasn't cruel; he had never crossed that line into such darkness that men feared him for his brutality and vile conduct. But he had been known to rip a man apart with his bare hands on the battlefield and other horrific tales that were fit only for the heartiest of soldiers. The name Gaston de Russe struck fear into the hearts of all men, Lancastrian or York.

Alixandrea knew of him only by reputation. As she'd heard tales of The White Lord all her life, so had she heard tales of his dark counterpart. Matthew had mentioned Gaston's name as they had quit the keep and entered the bailey, but she truly had no idea what to expect. When the mighty gates of Wellesbourne swung wide to receive her guests, the first thing that caught Alixandrea's attention was a knight astride a coal black charger.

But it wasn't just any knight; as large as Matthew was, and he was enormously large, the knight astride the black beast was even larger. He wore well-made, horrendously heavy plate armor and a helm that sported massive spikes jutting from the sides of it to not only intimidate the enemy, but to prevent them from grasping him about the head. He had hands that were easily twice the size as a normal man's, wrestling the fire-breathing charger with one hand while directing his men into the keep with the other.

She watched him with something of morbid fascination, this extraordinarily massive man who spoke no words yet ordered his troops about more efficiently than most. All he did was point and his men leapt to do his bidding.

There were two more knights accompanying him, one man astride a large gray charger and the other aboard a roan. They were knights of the highest caliber, their weapons expensive and their armor well used. The knight on the roan headed straight for Matthew, flipping his visor up as he approached. Alixandrea could see that the very handsome young man was smiling at her husband.

"Wellesbourne," the knight boomed. "Tis good to see your ugly face again."

Matthew grinned. "Your cousin should have drowned you at birth," he growled. "Who let you out of your cage?"

The young knight snorted. "We received your urgent missive. Gaston thought it was important enough to ride at full speed from Kidlington."

"That is a forty mile trek since last night. Your men must be exhausted."

Sir Patrick de Russe, the young and dashing cousin of Gaston, passed a glance over the troop of men that was pouring into the bailey. "You forget that these are de Russe men," he said. "They have been driven harder than most. Forty miles over several hours is not unusual for them."

The knight on the gray charger rode up, dismounting. He was tall and slender, with an indefinable elegance in the way he moved. He unsheathed a gauntlet, used the free hand to unlatch his visor, and then pulled the helm off. His blond hair was flowing to his shoulders, his hawk-like face bordering on unhandsome, though not unkind. He looked right at Alixandrea; she swore the man's eyes were so blue that they were white. But his gaze just as swiftly moved to Matthew.

"My lord Wellesbourne," he greeted; his accent was heavy and Nordic. "We came as fast as we could."

Matthew put out a hand and clapped him on the shoulder. "'Tis good to see you, Arik." He indicated Alixandrea, standing next to him. "Meet my betrothed, the Lady Alixandrea Terrington St. Ave. My lady, this is Sir Arik Magnesson, de Russe's right hand."

Arik's gaze was an appraising one. The man missed nothing. He bowed elegantly. "My lady. Sir Matthew is indeed fortunate."

She smiled, somewhat timidly. "A pleasure, my lord."

Patrick was still nearby on his roan. Hearing the introductions, he dismounted swiftly and approached Alixandrea.

"I am Patrick de Russe," he took her hand boldly and oh-so-gallantly kissed it. "If I can be of any service, lovely lady, do not hesitate to call upon me."

Matthew lifted an eyebrow at him. "Hands off, whelp. The lady is spoken for."

Patrick dropped her hand and grinned. He was excruciatingly handsome when he smiled. "Of course, my lord Wellesbourne. I meant no disrespect."

Matthew simply grunted at him, a manner or mood that Alixandrea had only seen from him once before. He'd displayed the same behavior when she had been introduced to his men on the first day of her arrival. He had made clear his territory, and he was doing it again now with Patrick. The thought made her take a step closer to Matthew, just to put some distance between herself and the brash young knight. Perhaps Matthew knew something sinister of him that she did not.

The man on the coal black charger was suddenly before them. Like a shadow, he had just appeared and now he hovered before them on the dancing destrier. He dismounted his beast and passed him to a waiting groom, removing one of the heavy mail gloves he wore and, like Arik had done, unlatching his three-point visor.

Alixandrea watched him approach, somewhat taken aback at

the sheer size of the man. She'd never seen a human so massive in her entire life. The sword sheathed against his mammoth saddle was almost as long as she was tall and probably weighed nearly as much.

"Where is the danger, Matt?" he asked as his visor swung open. "I rode at full speed because I expected to see this place swarming with Henry's allies."

Matthew wasn't intimidated by de Russe in the least; that much was abundantly clear. His easy smile creased his lips.

"You do not read your missives very carefully, do you?" He met the huge mitt that was extended to him in greeting. "I think all you do is hear the name 'Henry' and all else fades into hateful madness."

Gaston's expression did not change and when he spoke, it was in a voice that bubbled up from the bowels of Hell. "No truer words were spoken," he agreed. "Nonetheless, I was under the impression that you needed assistance."

"I think you were looking for an excuse to leave Kidlington. I furthermore think that you have not seen battle in a few months and were hoping for some action here for I know, quite clearly, that I did not ask for aid."

Gaston gazed steadily at Matthew, who was shorter than him by nearly half a head. As tall as Matthew was, it was truly a statement of de Russe's size. After what seemed like an eternally tense pause, during which Alixandrea was understandably terrified, the corner of the knight's mouth twitched.

"How well you know me," he growled. "If there's no fight here, then I say we make one."

Matthew laughed. Alixandrea stood next to her husband, fighting the natural instinct to back away from the enormous knight that growled and grunted before her. De Russe fought off a grin as Matthew snorted, giving Alixandrea an opportunity to study him.

Though she could only see his face, he was clearly an attractive man, something of a surprise given his giant size. He had eyes that were the color of smoke, hidden beneath heavy dark brows, a straight nose and a firmly square jaw. She could see a scar running from the corner of his left nostril, all the way back along his cheek and disappearing underneath the mail hauberk. When he finally did break out in a smile, however brief, his teeth were straight and white. Her initial observation of The Dark Knight gave him something of a human quality, not the horrifying phantom she had heard tale of.

Matthew had her by the elbow, startling her from her train of thought. "My lord, allow me to introduce you to my betrothed." There was pride in his voice as he spoke. "This is the Lady Alixandrea Terrington St. Ave. My lady, be pleased to meet the mighty Gaston de Russe, my dearest friend and ally."

Alixandrea dropped into a graceful curtsy, aware that her knees were shaking and hoping it wasn't obvious. "My lord, 'tis a pleasure to meet you."

When she straightened, Gaston was gazing at her in the same appraising manner that his man Arik had possessed. His smile was gone.

"My lady," he said shortly before looking back at Matthew. "I am famished. Show me Wellesbourne hospitality before I faint from starvation."

Matthew led the way inside Wellesbourne, his hand gently gripping Alixandrea's elbow. He apparently saw nothing wrong with the way de Russe had greeted her, but she felt very insignificant. The man obviously did not like his first impression of her.

When they reached the entrance, Matthew took them all inside the small solar off the entry. He held on to Alixandrea so that she could not leave. In fact, he seated her next to the well-used map table. The Wellesbourne brothers had been in the great hall and had seen the party come in from the yard; Mark greeted de Russe and his men warmly. Luke was given a slap on the head by Arik and John was given such a greeting that he blushed furiously. The redder his cheeks became, the more Patrick teased him. It was obvious that there was great camaraderie between all of them.

At Mark's bellow, servants appeared with wine, bread, and a half a wheel of white, tart cheese. Alixandrea watched de Russe pour himself a full goblet, downing the contents in two swallows, and the pour himself another. Somewhere in the drinking he removed his helm, revealing dark hair that had been shorn up the back of his skull and left long to fall over his eyes in the front. He raked his hair back along his scalp as he drank the second cup. She thought it was a rather exhausted gesture.

As the others tossed around light conversation, Alixandrea continued to watch Gaston. For some reason, she found him fascinating. He remained fairly aloof from the others, content with his wine, observing rather than participating. His smoky gray eyes were piercing, all-consuming, all-seeing. She was unnerved by them and clearly curious why Matthew had brought her into this room full of knights. He was still standing next to her, speaking to Arik on the new Belgian charger he had purchased last year. Gently, she tugged on his arm until he finished his conversation and looked at her.

"Perhaps I should go," she whispered. "You will surely want to speak to these men of things that would not interest me."

He shook his head. "You will stay." He raised his voice. "My friends, I would thank you for coming in spite of the fact that you have not fallen into an immediate pit of war and blood. Given time, however, you may get your wish."

"Speak plainly, Matt," Gaston said over the rim of his cup. "What goes on here that you would send for me?"

Matthew lifted a pale eyebrow at him. "I asked you to rendezvous with my army upon the road to London. 'Twas you who so brashly rode to Wellesbourne to save me from myself, apparently." As the others snickered, Matthew grinned at de Russe and continued. "In truth, we have something of a volatile situation on our hands and your presence is not unwelcome. I would have you understand the situation."

He launched into the tale of Strode, Jezebel, Howard Terrington and the possible marriage broker of John Sutton. Though Matthew delivered the story with neutrality, still, it was a treacherous and shocking account. Alixandrea could not help but feel responsible, as she had brought this all down upon them, unknowingly as it was. Matthew even told them of their secret marriage and the reasons for it. By the end of the story, the de Russe men were sober, serious. Gaston set his cup down.

"So you have a sleeper army within your men," he said. "At a specific command, they are to erupt from within and wreak havoc."

"Exactly."

De Russe's smoky eyes were cloudy with thought. "Who would have thought Howard Terrington capable of this?" he muttered, with some disbelief. "The man is a rabid supporter of Richard. He has given more money and men to the cause than most and Whitewell has held the road to Richmond for more years than I have been alive. Are you sure of this, Matt? Not that I doubt you, but it is an amazing turn in loyalties, I must say."

Matthew shrugged. "I have refrained from questioning the manservant Strode for fear of causing suspicion among the Whitewell men. I do not want them to think that anything is amiss, at least not yet."

De Russe looked pointedly at him. "Now that my men are here to reinforce your lines, I would invite the rebellion. I frankly do not want to march the entire way to London waiting for an uprising with each step. If we get it over now, then we'll all sleep better."

"True enough. But rather than risk the lives of our soldiers, we can simply separate the Whitewell men from the rest and give them the opportunity to swear fealty to me or meet their fate."

"You are too kind, Matt. You shall be tucking them into bed with feather quilts next."

Matthew grinned. "Hardly. I am simply trying to protect Wellesbourne and de Russe men from any unnecessary fighting, within the walls of Wellesbourne no less. As well planned as we might attempt such a thing, it could still veer out of control. I do not want to risk my men or my castle if we can reach a peaceable end instead."

De Russe grunted, possibly in agreement. "If it comes to a battle, I shall personally take delight in dispatching the leader; what was his name?"

"Strode. But we should not be too hasty about killing him. I personally would like to find out what else he knows."

"As always, the Peacemaker."

"If there is a peaceful solution to the end, I will take it."

"As you wish."

Alixandrea had been sitting quietly, listening to all that was said. She was trying to be as detached as possible, knowing that Strode and Jezebel had been in some sort of plot against her and Matthew, but the fact remained that she had known these people for many years. She had trusted them without question and her affections were still attached.

She must have sighed and not realized it, for Matthew suddenly spoke to her. "Did you have something to say, my lady?" he asked.

She looked up from where she had been fidgeting with her hands in her lap, only to see that everyone was looking at her. She shook her head. Then, she nodded. "I know what Sir John heard and I know what you explained to me, and I further was witness to Jezebel's actions in the gallery, but I must say that I am having a difficult time understanding that my servants would plot against me."

"It is not against you," Matthew said quietly. "It is against me and against Wellesbourne."

"Even so, I cannot truly believe they would do this," she said, more insistently. "I want so badly to talk to Strode to have him explain what John heard. Perhaps it wasn't what he thought at all. Perhaps there is a perfectly reasonable explanation for all of this."

"Then send for him."

De Russe's voice was a growl. They all looked at him. When he noticed their attention, he recollected his wine cup and poured himself another drink. "Send for the man. Let us question him here, in front of everyone, and make sense out of this."

Matthew's gaze lingered on Gaston a moment before casting a nod in John's direction. "Go tell Strode that my lady wishes to speak to him. He's probably out in the stables with the lame horse."

John quit the solar. Alixandrea sat there, looking at the faces in the room, wondering if some of them did not distrust her, too. The situation looked so suspicious that she could not blame them.

"What do *you* know about this, my lady?"

Gaston must have been reading her mind. She gazed steadily at him, strangely no longer afraid of him.

"Only what Matthew has told me, my lord," she said. "My servants have been loyal and dedicated to me, never indicative of something dark and sinister behind them. Perhaps that is why I am having such a difficult time grasping this."

"So you knew nothing about your uncle's shift in loyalties?"

"Politics has never been of interest to me. But to answer your question, I knew nothing. Perhaps because I am not the suspicious type, but upon reflection, there are things that I now question."

"Like what?"

"His unexplained trips," she searched her memory carefully. "Visitors in and out of Whitewell at strange hours, people I did not know. He would simply tell me they were travelers, but when they stayed at Whitewell, I never saw them and they always seemed to leave in the dead of night. I suppose if I was the mistrustful kind, those things would lead me to believe that my uncle was up to something."

Gaston gazed at her a moment longer as if his mere attention would force her into confessing. Out of respect for Matthew, however, he would not push the subject. It was obvious that Wellesbourne was smitten with her. Perhaps he would believe whatever she told him, but not de Russe. He was different. He had never trusted women and had never gotten along with them, so feminine wiles did not work with him.

Alixandrea met his gaze until he looked away to refill his cup.

He did not believe her; that much was clear. She would have been deeply insulted had she not had the prudence to realize that these men's lives depended upon whom they could trust and whom they could not. These men in the room were closer to the king than most, the core of Richard's defenses against Henry Tudor. And she had brought the rebellion right into their midst.

Before she could wallow in guilt, John reappeared with Strode. The young manservant from Whitewell appeared unruffled as he entered the solar, even after he saw all of the knights in the room. He focused curiously on Alixandrea.

"My lady," he said. "You have sent for me?"

Before she could answer, Matthew put a hand on her shoulder to silence her and to indicate that he would do the talking. He took a step forward, placing himself between the lady and the servant. It was a protective gesture, one not missed by de Russe.

"Tell me of your orders from Terrington," Matthew said with a hint of hazard in his tone. "I understand that he instructed you to do something once the lady and I were married."

Strode's blue eyes flickered. His gaze moved between Alixandrea and Matthew. "My orders were to deliver the lady to Wellesbourne, my lord."

"And then what?"

"I do not understand, my lord."

From the corner, silent John suddenly found his mouth. "I heard you say that you were to kill my brother when he wed the lady. I heard you say that you would give the order and the men from Whitewell would attack!"

Strode's expression morphed queerly. He had been initially startled by the outburst, just as quickly put on guard by the contents.

"Who told you such thing?" he said. "I would not...."

"Your accomplice, the maid, is in the vault and has admitted all," Matthew told him. "We know what your orders are. She told us of your directive to kill me and to unleash your army within my ranks. My brother also heard you tell the maid of your plans. You may as well confess and I may be merciful."

The veins on Strode's temples bulged as he struggled for composure. "I do not know what that simple minded woman has told you, but I am not a traitor. I would never,...."

He never got the chance to finish. Matthew's massive hand shot out, grabbing him around the throat. Strode struggled against him, but it was of no use. Matthew was twice his size, twice as strong, and many times more deadly.

Alixandrea could not bear to watch; she lowered her head, closing her eyes from the vision of Strode's purple face.

"Lies will not be tolerated," Matthew growled. "Confess the truth and we will show mercy. Continue along this path of fabrication and your death with be a slow and painful one."

"I did not...!"

Matthew's grip tightened. More struggling went on as Strode's life began to slip away. His face went from purple to blue. He was coming to lose consciousness. Not one man in the room seemed uncomfortable, but Alixandrea was nearly sick. She could hear him gasping. As the sounds of strained breathing filled the room, Matthew suddenly let go of Strode long enough to clobber him on the side of the head with a massive fist. Strode staggered against the wall.

"You have been ordered to unleash a sleeper army within these walls," Matthew rumbled. "Confess and I may show mercy."

Strode put up his hands to fight back, but it was like watching a lamb against a lion. He had no chance at all. Matthew reached down, grabbed him by the shoulders, and literally tossed him to the middle of the floor. He bore down on Strode before the man could crawl away, grabbing him around an ankle and hurling him against a wall.

"Tell me what I wish to know and I will cease your agony," he told him as he grabbed him by the arms. "What were your orders from Terrington?"

He paused long enough to give the man the chance to reply but when it was obvious that he refused to speak, Matthew threw him into a chair. The furniture collapsed under the force. Mark and Luke, who happened to be standing nearby, simply took a casual step away as if there was nothing to be concerned over. Matthew reached down, this time grabbing Strode by the hair. Pulling his bloodied head up, he looked him in the eye.

"Next time, I shall toss you through the window."

There was no doubt that he meant what he said, and they were two stories up. Strode struggled weakly against Matthew as the man heaved him toward the long lancet window. When he realized he was about to end up twenty feet on the ground below, he let out a cry.

"As you... *say!*" he croaked.

Matthew immediately dropped his hand. Strode fell to the floor, a horrible rasping coming from his throat. He rubbed his neck, looking up at Matthew, at Alixandrea. Her eyes were still tightly closed, her face turned away. Instead of fear, his expression was full of surrender.

"It does not matter now if you know or not," he said, his voice hoarse. "My life is at an end in any case."

"Tell me of your orders."

He took a couple of deep breaths before answering. "To... to kill you after you wed the lady. Then, as the church bells rang in celebration of the wedding, my men were to attack Wellesbourne from within in hopes of gaining control of the castle."

"Is that all?"

"That is everything. I was to hold the castle until reinforcements arrived."

"Who were the reinforcements?"

"That was not made clear to me, my lord. I was only told to hold the fortress."

It was just as John had said, plain and without misunderstanding. Meanwhile, Alixandrea had opened her eyes when she realized that he was no longer being thrashed to death.

"Why have you done this?" she asked, almost painfully. "What have I done that you would try to harm me in such a way?"

He shook his head, hand still on his swollen neck. "This has nothing to do with you. Your uncle gave me orders. It is my duty to carry them out."

"It is your duty to kill my husband?"

Strode wiped the blood trickling out of his mouth. "It is my duty to serve your uncle."

"And who does he serve?" Matthew asked.

Strode knew better than to lie. "Henry Tudor."

If there had been any doubt lingering in her mind about the truth of Strode's involvement, it was dashed in that moment. "I trusted you," she whispered, her anguish evident. "You were like family to me. How could you do this?"

Strode did not have an answer. It was apparent that he wasn't particularly spiteful or hostile towards her; he was simply doing as he was told. Mark picked him up roughly, shoving him at Luke with the order to take him to the vault. Patrick de Russe followed Luke and the prisoner from the solar, leaving a somber group behind.

De Russe was nursing his wine while the others stood around, not knowing what to say. It was clear what had happened, and even more clear what needed to happen. Matthew leaned down next to his wife, taking her hand gently.

"Perhaps you would like to go and rest now," he said softly.

She was shaken but not senseless. She felt more anger than anything. But she appreciated his kindness, marveling that the hands that so tenderly held her could have been so brutal against Strode.

"I... I still need to collect my cases for London," she tried to focus on something else, anything but what she had just witnessed. "Perhaps you can send a few servants to carry them down. Strode usually...."

She trailed off, rolling her eyes as she realized that Strode would no longer help her with anything. She put her hand on his arm.

"What are you going to do with him? And with Jezebel?"

He patted her hand, leading her towards the door. "I am going to send them back to your uncle with a message."

"What message?"

"That is for me to determine." He pushed the door open for

her, the stairs to the third floor a few feet away. "Go and rest now, love. I shall be up shortly."

She did not argue. Her mind was rather full of things at the moment and she needed time to reflect. The moment she set foot in the foyer, the dogs in the hall came rushing towards her, encircling her with their happy, hairy wagging.

Matthew watched with a grin on his face; he'd not given much notice as to how much the dogs liked her, but he was starting to. And she was becoming more accustomed to them; at least she wasn't kicking them away as she'd done in the past. She even reached down to gingerly pet the giant wolfhound on the top of the head. Tongues began licking at her and she pulled back. As she ascended the stairs, the wriggling pack followed.

When Matthew went to her chamber an hour later to see how she was faring, he found seven dogs sleeping contentedly outside of her door.

CHAPTER EIGHT

Rather than invite an uprising as de Russe had suggested, Matthew took his own advice and separated the Whitewell men from his army, corralled them in an area of the bailey that was heavily watched by Wellesbourne men, and announced that he was aware of the orders from Lord Ryesdale.

He further informed them that their leader was in the vault and there was no other option for them but to swear fealty to The White Lord or die. With Gaston de Russe and his army of cutthroats hovering nearby, there wasn't one man from Whitewell that did not believe him.

Fealty during this time to the foot soldier was nothing more than swearing loyalty to the man who provided ample food and shelter. It wasn't a conviction as much as it was with the nobility; therefore, the decision was fairly simple. The seasoned soldiers of Whitewell knew when they were defeated; they could see it all around them, in the faces of de Russe's men, and in the faces of the brothers from Wellesbourne.

When Matthew promised them new weapons should they join his army, it was a decision made all the more uncomplicated. Most swore their allegiance without further prodding. Those that refused were put in the vault with Strode and with that, Matthew considered the situation peacefully resolved. It was a much better state of affairs than it could have been.

Settling the situation and putting closure on it allowed him to focus on the task at hand. He'd been trying to get to London for quite some time and would be put off no longer. Unlike some, Matthew had no problem traveling after dark. No one in their right mind would dare attack the army of The White Lord, made even more powerful now that The Dark Knight rode with him. It was therefore an unconcerned task to have the army and ancillary units readied by early afternoon for departure.

Loading up his wife, however, had been something of a process. She was convinced that she needed at least six trunks out of the nine she had brought with her to Wellesbourne. Nothing Matthew could say could dissuade her. Moreover, she insisted that Caroline go to London as well when it was Mark's practice to leave his wife behind.

It created something of a stir; Mark did not want Caroline along, probably because he could not openly pursue the ladies as he liked to do. But Matthew did not tell Alixandrea that; it wasn't his way of doing things and furthermore he did not think she needed to hear it. What his brother did was his own business, so long as it did not affect his performance as a knight.

Early afternoon was passing into midafternoon as Alixandrea finished packing her last two cases. These were the ones that held her undergarments, belts and jewels and were most important. Matthew stood by the door with Luke and Patrick, waiting with increasing impatience for his wife to finish. Mark, Caroline, John, Adam and Gaston were already down in the ward, waiting. Everyone was ready to go but Alixandrea. Matthew finally sent Patrick down to tell Gaston to move out; by the time the wagons moved at the end of the column, they would be in the ward with the cases loaded on board.

"My lady," Matthew said with more patience than he felt. "We are out of time. Close the cases so we can load them."

Dressed in a cardinal red surcoat with a gold kirtle and dual-color sash around her slender waist, her lovely hair was pulled back at the nape of her neck to keep it out of her way. She fussed with a twisted belt, finally giving up and tucking it back in the case. Around her, the dogs had somehow made it into the chamber and they lay in various positions around her feet and on the bed. Alixandrea moved around them as if she did not even notice them.

"You can take this one." She slammed the lid of the case and Luke immediately moved forward to pick it up. She watched him heave it onto his broad shoulders. "Be careful with that one, Luke. The stays on the lid sometimes come undone. I do not want my pretty things all over the dirt."

"Aye, my lady."

He shuffled out of the door and Alixandrea turned to her husband, smiling brightly. Matthew returned her smile, feeling like an idiot. It was hard to become annoyed with her when she was so sweet and lovely.

"We really must go," he said. "Is that the last case?"

She looked at the smaller one next to her. "Aye," she said. "I just want to make sure I have everything."

He stepped over a sleeping dog and closed the lid of the case. "You *have* everything," he told her. When she opened her mouth to object, he spoke quickly to drown out her words. "I told you that we can buy anything that you may have forgotten or may need."

"But...."

"No 'buts'. We are leaving *now*."

She stuck her lips out in a pout, more for show than real distress. He kissed her swiftly once, twice, before taking the case on his shoulder and her in his other hand. As they quit the chamber, the dogs stretched, stood up, and followed.

In the ward, he tossed the case onto the wagon that also contained a myriad of other necessities, food and materials to repair the weapons included. The massive gates of Wellesbourne were open and the army was already moving through them, kicking up clouds of dust. In the carriage that was now being driven by a Wellesbourne soldier and not Strode, Caroline sat waiting for her. Matthew escorted her over to the waiting cab.

"You shall have a contingent of men with the carriage," he said. "In my stead, you will do what they tell you. Understood?"

She nodded. "Where will you be?"

"At the head of the column."

The thought of not seeing him did not sit particularly well, but she did not say anything. He was a busy man and his attention was required on more important things. She had Caroline to keep her company whilst they traveled.

"Then be safe, husband," she said softly. "Caroline and I will ride quite happily together."

He gazed into her lovely face and completely forgot himself. He took her in his arms and kissed her, only to be rewarded with hoots of approval and whistles from the men around them. He looked at their smiling faces, realizing they still had no knowledge that he had actually married the lady. For all they knew, he was taking liberties that he should not have been. And, shockingly, she was letting him.

"Can a man not kiss his wife?" he boomed.

The men whistled and shouted congratulations, then dutifully quieted. Their liege was a fair man who showed them a good amount of camaraderie, but they were as always respectful of him. If he wanted to kiss the lady he called his wife, so be it.

Matthew loaded her up into the cab and secured the door himself. He chased the dogs off that seemed intent to follow Alixandrea's every move. His last vision of her was a radiant smile that seared deep into his heart, and of the dogs that sat in the ward looking dejected as she rolled away.

As he collected his charger from a nervous groom, he began to think that never in his life had he known such happiness. Aye, he'd been content his entire life, with the satisfaction of a spotless reputation, power and talent. He'd always taken pride in the fact that he served with his father and brothers, a family unit that enjoyed status among the nobility.

But never had he known true happiness, like the giddy sensations he had known over the past few days. He never knew such things had existed, but exist they did. And it all centered around the beautiful young woman he had been so reluctant to marry.

***

The trip from Wellesbourne to the outskirts of London hadn't been nearly so long as the trip from York to Wellesbourne. Even so, by the second day, Alixandrea remembered why she hated the infamous carriage so much. She might as well have taken a ship that traveled upon the open sea. Even though she was used to the rolling somewhat, it still made her nauseous, and Caroline was even sicker than she was.

Still, they'd never once complained to their husbands. Matthew made sure they found shelter each night and saw to it that his wife had a bed to sleep in, and she never let on just how awful she felt. In all, the trip to London had been a miserable affair and the ladies had been very glad to reach their destination.

Caroline perked up on the fifth day when they reached the perimeter of the city. Her father was lord mayor of a town just to the east of the road they traveled upon, but Mark would not allow the time for a visit. He promised her that he would consider it once the army reached London, but for now, they were eager to reach their destination. Caroline was disappointed but understood.

As Alixandrea watched Mark and Caroline interact, she was coming to think that Mark did not harbor a great deal of affection or respect for his wife, which was truly a pity considering how Caroline felt about him. She had noticed it before but it was more evident even now.

London seemed to start long before they reached the heart of the great city. They passed through miles of villages, most of them a very short distance from each other, and the children would run out to watch the army pass. Alixandrea found herself watching the children just as they were watching her, each curious about the other. Most of them were dirty little urchins, but surprisingly well fed. She saw no evidence of blatant poverty and starvation. At one point, she smiled and waved at one of the little boys standing on the side of the road. He was a cute child. He responded by throwing a rock at her.

The action made her laugh. She sat back in her seat and chuckled. She was about to venture another look from the window when a massive dappled charger suddenly pulled alongside the cab. She recognized her husband's steed and stuck her head out of the window.

"Well?" she asked him. "What is it? I am busy charming the locals peasants, so be quick about it."

Inside the cab, Caroline burst into laughter but Matthew had no idea what she meant. He flipped up his visor and looked at her.

"What mischief is this?" he demanded.

She just grinned at him, a playful gesture. "Nothing, my lord. Just a joke."

He lifted an eyebrow. "A joke?"

"Aye," she explained. "I smiled at a little boy back there and he threw a rock at me."

Matthew's head snapped sharply to the rear, his blue eyes narrowing. "Which child?"

She shook her head. "I am not going to tell you because he was probably three years old and terrified. You have better things to do than punish a three year old."

He looked at her, not entirely pleased with her answer but allowing it to go unchallenged. He held out his hand, an invitation for her to place her fingers in his palm, which she did so gladly. The mailed glove was cold as he clasped her warm flesh.

"We are an hour outside of Windsor," he told her. "We will be staying at Rosehill, my aunt's residence near the castle. My father has already gone ahead to announce our arrival."

"Which side of your family is your aunt from?" she asked.

"She is my father's sister. The Lady Livia Wellesbourne St. James married a man of some wealth and has chosen to live near the city all of these years. She will be very happy to meet you and, I warn you, will try to stuff you with all manner of treats. If you get too fat to shove through the door while we stay here, I swear I shall divorce you and leave you in London."

She giggled. "I promise, I shall not eat too many."

He winked at her. "I really would not divorce you."

"I know."

They smiled at each other a moment, the easy warmth settling between them. Matthew finally brought her hand to his lips, kissing it softly.

"I only came back to tell you this," he said. "I must return."

"So soon? You only just arrived."

"Believe me that I would stay if I could, but duty calls. And Aunt Livia will expect to see me at the very first or she might try to box my ears."

He left her with a smile on her face, watching him ride all the way back to the front of the column. He sat so strong and tall in the saddle, like the legend she had heard tale of. Only now the legend was reality, more than she would have ever dreamed it could have been. When he was out of sight, she settled back in her seat, not realizing that Caroline was watching her closely.

"I have known Matthew for two years," Caroline said quietly. "I have never seen him like this."

Alixandrea looked at her. "Like what?"

Caroline shrugged lightly. "Smitten," she said. "Anyone can see that he is absolutely enamored with you."

Alixandrea's smile broadened. Though it was only Caroline's opinion, she dared herself to hope. "As I am with him."

Caroline gazed steadily at her. A weak smile finally creased her face. "It was always my hope that Mark would feel towards me the way Matthew feels towards you. You are most fortunate."

So the woman wasn't oblivious to the way Mark responded to her. Somehow it hurt Alixandrea's feelings to know that. She put her hand out, taking Caroline's tiny cold fingers in her palm.

"Perhaps he will," she said encouragingly. "'Tis not too late."

Caroline laughed bitterly. "He does not hold any affection for me, my lady. He never has. We've not had any children because...."

She trailed off, her cheeks suddenly flame-colored. Alixandrea could not let it go; it was apparent the woman needed someone to talk to. Two years in a house full of men with no one to confide in must have left her horribly lonely and in need of companionship. She had sensed it the first day she arrived.

"Because why?" she asked gently. "You may tell me, Caroline. I would never tell anyone."

Caroline met her gaze. There was pain in her eyes. "He... he has stopped performing his husbandly duties," she whispered. "He stopped nearly a year ago. Oh, I know he goes to the *Head O'Bucket* and I know why. I am not as stupid as everyone would think and I further know why he does not want me to come to London. Did you think I did not know that? I do, you know."

Alixandrea did not know what to say. "Oh... Caroline," she murmured. "How can you be sure of this? He is your husband, after all. Surely he would not shame you."

Her expression was unnaturally hard. "There was a baby born to one of the servants a few months ago," she said. "Mark and his brothers happened to be back from London at the time. If there is a birth at Wellesbourne, I am the one to tend it. It is my duty. But Matthew would not let me tend this one. I did not even know about it until the child had been delivered and then Matthew tried his best to keep me from seeing the child. But I did. A delightful little girl with nearly black eyes and hair. She is the spitting image of my husband."

Alixandrea felt sick inside. She could only sit there, holding Caroline's hand. With the warmth of the comforting touch, Caroline's confession came tumbling out.

"Matthew was only trying to protect me, I know that," she continued. "He has always shown me such regard. But there are some things that even he cannot protect me from."

Alixandrea listened to her, thought on it a moment, and finally shook her head. "I do not know what to say that would bring you comfort. Anything that comes to mind sounds trite or naïve. Have... have you ever spoken to your husband about this?"

"Nay. But I know that he would tell me that it is none of my affair."

"And the others know? All of the brothers, I mean, and Adam as well?"

"Of course. But they do not involve themselves in what does not concern them."

The cab lurched and rolled over the particularly bumpy road. Alixandrea continued to hold Caroline's hand in silence, glancing out the window now and again, lost in thought. She tried not to hate Mark Wellesbourne for his behavior, but it was difficult. She also knew that it was not considered outlandish behavior for a man to take a mistress, or several, even though he was married. It was shameful. She could only pray that Matthew would never do such a thing to her. The mere thought of it made her feel sicker than she already did.

"Well," she tried to sound positive without sounding unsympathetic. "Perhaps we can change things. Perhaps we can get you some new clothes in London, things so beautiful that Mark will not want to look anywhere other than at you. And perhaps we can do your hair differently, and add a little jewelry. We can certainly try, can't we?"

Caroline was torn between resignation and the inclination to agree. She'd never confessed such things to anyone and it was a new experience to have a woman's advice on the subject. "Perhaps."

Alixandrea smiled at her, forcing away the melancholy of the past few minutes of conversation. "We shall find the best dress makers and the finest stylists in all the city. We'll make you a ravishing creature."

Caroline did not say anything. She simply returned Alixandrea's smile, unconvincing though it might be. They sat in silence until the blue ribbon of the Thames came into view and the brownstone and thatched roof houses of the London commons appeared as thick as trees in the forest. In spite of their conversation and gloomy thoughts, the excitement of having finally reaching Windsor overshadowed everything.

They had arrived.

***

The walls of Whitewell's keep were wrought with tension. Not only did Lord Ryesdale have his evening meal interrupted, but it was interrupted by the last person he expected to see. His gut hurt at the sight and his food, the fine venison he had hunted that day, was pushed away. He could not believe what he was seeing and demanded an explanation in front of the entire hall. Though it was only a few servants and soldiers, still, it felt as if he was confessing to the entire world. Now everyone knew of the failure of Strode Levingsworth.

But none more so that Howard. He heard his manservant's tale, his eyebrows lifting with each passing word. By the time the man was finished, Howard was ready to explode.

"He sent you back to tell me this?" he demanded. "He dares to threaten *me*?"

Strode stood before his liege, head down, waiting for the blows that were about to befall him. The ride north to York had been a particularly dismal one and he thought, many times, of abandoning his course. But he had been at Whitewell since infancy and it was the only home he had ever known. He had nowhere else to go. He could only hope that Lord Ryesdale could forgive him his failure.

"He said to tell you that he has taken your niece and your men and that you should count yourself fortunate that he doesn't burn Whitewell down around your ears."

Howard's eyes bulged. "More threats?" he gasped. Then he charged Strode, as the man had expected, striking him across the face. As the servant fell to the floor, Howard hovered over him. "What went wrong? How did you foul up my orders, you stupid fool?"

Strode cowered beneath him. "The maid," he said; it was the only thing that came to mind. "She must have told him everything, for surely, it did not come from me. I was faithful, my lord."

"Where is she?"

"She ran off, my lord. I have not seen her since we were released."

Howard was nearly beside himself with fury. His first instinct was to take it out on Strode, the man who had failed him, but for some reason he refrained. His anger took the form of twitching and shaking, directed inward until his heart pulsed wildly and his head swam.

"Ten years," he growled, shaking his fists. "We have waited ten years for these plans to come to fruition and at the critical moment, you fail me. Ten years of planning wasted."

"It was not my fault, my lord," Strode slowly got up from the floor. "I swear that I did everything you told me, up until the last. Somehow, Wellesbourne discovered our plans, but I swear to you that I did not tell him. I never gave us away."

Howard clenched his fists so hard that his jagged nails cut into his palms. "Ten years," he muttered again. "My God, we waited so long and now..."

He went off into a corner, muttering to himself. Sweat beaded on his forehead despite the chill of the room. It was a large room, well appointed, fitting for Howard Terrington's arrogance. Strode backed himself up near the door as if preparing to run out should Howard strike at him again. He watched his liege mumble and hiss, frightening sounds that dribbled of madness.

"What would you have me do, my lord?" he asked. "Please. All you need do is ask and it will be done."

Howard acted as if he did not hear him. He muttered a moment longer before coming to an abrupt halt. Then, his head came up and he looked at Strode as if something fantastic had suddenly occurred to him.

"La Londe," he hissed. "I'd nearly forgotten."

Strode wasn't following him. "My lord?"

Howard threw up his hands. "Dennis la Londe!" he roared. Hastily, he staggered from the hall to the alcove just off the main chamber. He moved to the enormous desk that nearly filled the room, toppling a chair as he did so. He grabbed at the inkwell and quill, scrambling for a sheet of vellum. Strode watched him curiously.

"What are you doing, my lord?"

Howard began fiendishly scratching on a small piece of vellum. "I am fixing your mistake," he hissed. "Dennis la Londe left for London four days ago. He should be arriving within the next day or so."

Strode still did not understand. "My lord?"

Howard slopped spots of ink all over the table as he wrote. "God's Bones, Strode, you know la Londe. We must send word to him that your attempt on Wellesbourne's life was unsuccessful. With The White Lord in London, and la Londe in London, the possibilities are staggering."

Strode was beginning to come clear now. "You will have Sir Dennis assassinate him?"

"That is an ugly word," Howard scribbled. "Let us say that where you failed, la Londe will not. I do not know what we shall do about the rest of our plan, for there is no diversion now to distract Richard while Henry lands upon England's shores. But I will let la Londe worry about that. He must know that Matthew Wellesbourne is in London and that Wellesbourne Castle remains intact. Get this message to him."

"I shall take it myself, my lord," Strode said, eager to be of service and reclaim his liege's good graces. "I shall not fail."

Strode did not fail in delivering the message. He caught up to Dennis la Londe on the northern outskirts of London and faithfully delivered the missive. What he did not know, however, was that the vellum from Terrington also contained his death warrant. Once he completed his task, la Londe was to kill him in punishment for his failure.

Strode suspected, as he lay bleeding to death on the open road, that his liege and the world had indeed turned against him.

***

Rosehill
Near Windsor, England

Livia Wellesbourne St. James had never had any children of her own, which is why she nearly went into seizures at the sight of her four nephews. Though Adam was her only brother, the two had never gotten along particularly, but she loved his sons. As she squealed in delight, men in armor invaded her well-tended house and tracked dirt over her hall.

Matthew had already met his aunt, as he had told Alixandrea he would. He always had to be the first to greet her, otherwise she would throw fits. With Matthew properly kissed and embraced, he could leave his brothers to the domineering attention of their only aunt and go about his business.

While John and Luke were on the receiving end of liquor-smelling kisses, Matthew went back for Alixandrea. As Caroline wait for Mark, Matthew helped his wife from the cab so that she could get a good look at the manor house. Alixandrea could not help but be awed at the sight of it; the place was enormous, far larger than the castles she had been accustomed to. She stood for a moment just outside the door, her gaze falling upon the well-manicured grounds, lush garden, and masonry walls.

The manor house was fortified, sitting on the opposite side of the Thames and about a mile to the east of Windsor Castle. It had vast lawns behind the high walls and the house itself had a main house plus two massive wings. She studied the structure, oblivious to the dark clouds littering the sky above. As rain drops began to pelt the dirt, Matthew tried to coax her inside. But she stood for a moment as the wind whipped up, smelling the fresh air and observing the awesome surroundings.

"This place is enormous, Matthew," she commented. "What on earth did your uncle do to acquire all of this?"

"He was a nobleman by birth and had a gift for trade," he replied, looking up at the threatening sky. "He had a fleet of ships that sailed the known world, trading goods from all ports. It would be fair to say that he was successful at it and it would be furthermore fair to say that he was probably one of the richest men in England."

"I take it that he has passed away?"

"Six years ago. But he left all of this," he swept his arms out over the expanse of yard, "to my aunt, who in turn has willed it to me upon her death."

Alixandrea realized that it meant it would be hers, too. But it was too overwhelming a thought and she had not the mind at the moment to ponder it. She was exhausted from her trip. As she turned for the entry, she noticed that the vast majority of the army was still beyond the gates.

"Are they going to camp out there?" she asked.

Matthew had her by the elbow, glad she had decided to move out of the increasingly foul weather. "London is still several miles away and de Russe is taking the army on to the city limits."

"He is not staying here with us?"

"Nay."

"A pity. He seems like a lonely man. I was hoping to get to know him better."

Matthew almost smiled at the irony of the statement. "I would be surprised if he let you. He is not one to make friends easily, especially with women."

"I sensed that. But it has not deterred me."

Matthew did smile, then. They entered into the dark, cool entry hall, a massive two-story chamber with an enormous iron chandelier hanging above their heads. At first glance, she could see that it was a far different place from anything she had ever known. Where rushes and dogs littered the floor of the fortresses, fine carpets that had been brought all the way from Persia covered the polished wood floor of the entry. She could see muddy boot prints on it, knowing it had to come from the messy Wellesbourne men. Crystal candle sets spread throughout the entry hall gave off an enormous amount of refractive light. Alixandrea was understandably overwhelmed.

"God's Bones," she gasped. "I have never seen anything like this."

Matthew had seen it before, too many times to count, and was immune to the wonderment. But he agreed with her.

"I doubt you ever will," he said. "My aunt maintains a level of living that God himself is envious of."

She lifted an eyebrow at him. "After the filth of Wellesbourne Castle, how is it you manage to stay here and not ruin the place?"

He laughed softly. "My aunt would beat me." He pointed at the dirty rug. "Even that will not escape her wrath once the joy of our arrival wears thin."

A squeal suddenly filled the air. Alixandrea looked over to see a round, rosy woman rushing towards her, arms outstretched. Livia Wellesbourne St. James was an enormous woman with wobbling chins and painted cheeks. She wore a garment of layers upon layers of the finest silks, with studs and embroidery to a gaudy degree. She threw her fat arms around Alixandrea and nearly strangled her.

"So this is your lovely bride, Matthew?" Aunt Livia held Alixandrea at arm's length, inspecting her closely. "She is exquisite, darling. Absolutely exquisite!"

Matthew felt a pride he'd never before experienced. It was strangely fulfilling. "Aye, that she is," he agreed. "The Lady Alixandrea Wellesbourne, this is the Lady Livia St. James."

"Psh," Livia hushed him. "We need no introductions. I can see that she belongs to the House of Wellesbourne. Welcome to Rosehill, dearest girl. What is your name again?"

Alixandrea fought off a smile; the woman was giddy, dramatic, and scatterbrained. "Alixandrea, my lady."

"Darling," she hugged her again, releasing her from her stifling embrace but not quite letting go. She put an arm around her shoulders. "You have married the crème de la crème of Wellesbournes, my dear. Matthew is our shining star. We will expect many strong babies from you."

Alixandrea smiled weakly, looking to Matthew and silently pleading for his help. She could hardly believe the old woman had jumped into such a delicate subject. Matthew just grinned a moment before taking pity on her.

"Auntie, we've only been married a few days," he said. "You must give us time."

Livia glared at him. "I would have news of an impending child before you leave London, Matthew. I am an old woman and haven't time for your foolish delays. You have made me wait quite long enough for this marriage."

Matthew clapped his hand to his forehead in a gesture of disbelief before removing his wife from his aunt's overbearing embrace. "Good God, Auntie, to the Devil with propriety and subtlety, is it? You are going to terrify her."

Livia was reluctant to let Alixandrea go but had no choice as Matthew pulled her free. She was preparing a sharp retort when Mark came through the entryway with Caroline on his arm. Then, her attention was focused on another hapless couple.

"And you!" she screeched at Mark. "You have been married to your lovely girl for two years. Where are the children, Mark? I vow that if you do not produce a child within the next year, I shall leave you out of my will completely. Do you hear me?"

Mark had less humor about his aunt's gripes that Matthew did. Caroline flushed furiously as Livia gregariously embraced her. Alixandrea leaned in to Matthew.

"She is going to crush Caroline," she whispered urgently. "Save her!"

Matthew leaned down. "I am afraid that no one can save her now. We shall just have to hope for the best."

Alixandrea wiggled her eyebrows, struggling not to laugh. Livia, as well meaning as she might have been, was both appalling and hilarious. Mark did not fight to take Caroline back as Matthew had, so Livia kept her arms around Caroline as she led her into the lavish hall where all manner of food await. The furniture in the room was the finest that money could buy; the seats of the sumptuous chairs were stuffed with feathers and the tables were costly and matching. As soon as Alixandrea entered the hall, she came to a sharp halt.

"What is wrong?" Matthew asked her.

She had a queer expression on her face. Her hands splayed as if feeling for something in the air. "No dogs," she hissed. "There are no dogs pawing at me. What shall I do?"

Matthew grinned broadly. "Disoriented?"

"Horribly."

He was enjoying a laugh with his wife, removing her cloak and laying it upon the nearest chair. Their revelry was interrupted, however, when he heard his brother's voice beside him.

"Matt," Mark said quietly. "Look at father."

Matthew's gaze moved to the massive carved buffet sideboard

that lined the south side of the hall. Adam, so quiet for the past two days, stood with a wine bottle in one hand and a goblet in the other. While they watched, he poured and drank the entire contents, twice. Mark looked at Matthew, who looked disgusted and resigned. He took a step in his father's direction, but Alixandrea stopped him.

"No," she said quietly. "Allow me."

Matthew shook his head. "Nay, love. I shall deal with him."

She put her hand on his arm. "Please do not take offense to what I am about to say, but you have dealt with this for many years with little result. Perhaps you can let me try. Perhaps a woman will have a better touch with his grief."

Her words were reasonable, softly spoken. Matthew glanced at Mark, who simply shrugged his shoulders. Matthew did not think it was such a good idea, either. However, against his better judgment, he agreed.

"Very well," he said quietly. "Try if you must."

She gave him a brief smile and was gone, moving across the fine carpets and wood flooring with grace and elegance. Matthew watched her cross the room, simply because she was so entrancing. She moved like an angel in her blue surcoat and luscious bronze hair. Every minute of every day that passed and he came to know her better, the more captivated he was by her.

While he and Mark watched, Alixandrea approached Adam and said a few words to him. Adam seemed to look at her with a blank expression, but she said a few more words, smiled, and gently pried the bottle out of his hand. Then she took the cup, setting both down on the table.

A few more words were exchanged between the two, though the brothers could not hear what was being said. Finally, Alixandrea put her hand in the crook of Adam's elbow and, with a large smile, led him away from the table. The last Matthew and Mark saw of Adam, he was actually smiling as he allowed Alixandrea to lead him into the next room. They were talking; or, at least, Alixandrea was talking and Adam spoke up now and again. And then they were gone.

"Where are they going?" Mark asked.

Matthew shrugged; frankly, he was still surprised that his father gave up the alcohol without a fight. "I do not know."

"Should we follow?"

"Nay." Matthew shook his head, but from expression it was apparent that he was unconvinced. "They will not go far."

Unconvinced, Mark nonetheless lost himself in the food that Livia had presented. The Wellesbourne brothers could eat more than the population of a small village, and Mark had been known to put away ghastly amounts. Only Matthew wasn't eating at the moment, standing by with his ale in his hand, his gaze lingering on the door that his father and wife had just left through. But that only lasted a few minutes before his curiosity got the better of him and he was compelled to follow.

The room they had disappeared into was another receiving room, as lavishly furnished as the one he had just left. There was a door off to his right, half-open, and he assumed it was the path to follow. Matthew found himself wandering the halls of Rosehill until he came across a door leading to the gardens outside. He almost walked past it until he heard voices coming from the other side. Opening the door, he walked straight into Alixandrea and Adam, seated on a wide covered porch, watching the heavy rain fall.

Alixandrea smiled up at him. "Greetings, husband," she said. "Come and join us."

Matthew's gaze moved between his wife and his father. Adam looked amazingly composed while Alixandrea just looked cold. Their breath hung heavy in the air as the inclement weather drizzled around them.

"What are you two doing out here?" he asked. "Father, 'tis cold out here for her. She needs her cloak."

"Then go and get it," Adam told him. "Be a good husband as I entertain your wife."

It sounded suspiciously like a command. Matthew lifted a disapproving eyebrow but said nothing. He went back to retrieve Alixandrea's cloak and when he returned, it was to the sounds of her sweet voice filling the misting air. When Matthew heard the song, he froze.

I dreamt that you loved me still
And loved me forever and a day.
From beyond the mellow sea
I felt your spirit calling to me
And I dreamt that you loved me still.

It was a beautiful song, made more beautiful by her sweet, lilting voice. Matthew looked to his father for his reaction, noting that he seemed rather distant. He had frankly expected an explosion given the fact that the song Alixandrea had just sung contained yet more personal memories. A glance at his wife showed her with a smile on her face, looking straight at Adam. She reached out and put her hand on the old man's arm.

"Is that how she sang it?" she asked. "'Tis such a lovely song. Did she sing it often?"

Adam nodded. "I could hear her singing it about the keep. She used to sing it to the boys when they were babies."

"Ah," she said knowingly. "A perfect song for babies, as it is soft and soothing. But it is a beautiful song for lovers. The words have such meaning."

Adam seemed to have difficulty knowing what to feel, or how to react. He started to get up. "I would like something to drink," he muttered.

But Alixandrea kept her hand on him, keeping him in his chair. "You do not need drink, my lord," she said gently but firmly. "Stay with me. We shall remember your wife fondly so that whenever you think of her, you will do it with joy. She *was* a joy, my lord, as I said earlier. She was not something to be associated with endless pain."

Adam looked at her, unsure how to respond. It had become such a habit for him to correlate his wife with agony that he could hardly remember any other way. Alixandrea's concept of remembering the joy and not the pain was almost incomprehensible. It almost made him angry.

"When she was alive, she was my joy," he said. "But her death did not bring me joy. You may not deny me my grief. 'Tis my right."

Matthew listened carefully to the exchange. He had indulged in the very same discussion, too many times to count. His answer was to become angry and try to verbally beat some sense into his father. But that had never worked. Perhaps he was too frustrated to be effective any more.

But Alixandrea was new to all of this; she was of a new mind, new blood, something that Adam might respond to. Matthew had told her that he thought she was of good character. The next few moments might determine just how good of character she was.

Alixandrea could see Matthew from the corner of her eye, suspecting that she knew his thoughts. It wasn't that she wanted to prove anything to him, for she did not; but she did want to help Adam. He seemed very much in need of it.

"May I ask you a question, my lord?" she asked.

Adam nodded, half-heartedly, apparently not too interested in any question she might have. But she delved on. "What was your wife like?"

"Can you not see that it pains me to speak of her?"

"Please. Tell me."

Adam scratched at the sides of his chair; not having a cup in his hand gave him nothing to do, nothing to hold on to. "She was full of all of the goodness in Heaven," he said, bordering on agitation. "She was sweet and kind."

"Did she have spirit?"

"Of course."

"Did she give you her opinion or tell you when you were wrong?"

"That she did."

"Then she was a woman who knew her mind."

"Aye, very much."

Alixandrea leaned towards him. "Did you respect her for her thoughts?"

He looked at her, mildly outraged. "Of course I did. Audrey was a brilliant woman with a great mind. Her guidance was unparalleled."

On his arm, Alixandrea's hand tightened. "Then tell me this, and you must be completely honest. What would she say to you if she saw that you were grieving like this for her twelve years after her death? Would it please her? Would she wish it of you?"

He looked at her as if she had lost her mind. "What do you mean?"

"You know exactly what I mean. What do you think Lady Audrey would say if she knew you had made attempts on your own life out of grief?" When Adam refused to answer, she did it for him. "If she is the kind of woman you say she is, then she would be furious with you. Absolutely furious. Don't you think?"

Still, Adam refused to answer. He was looking at his lap, the ground, anything but Alixandrea's piercing bronze eyes. She shook him gently. "Look at the situation from another point of view. What if it had been you who had perished? Would you want Audrey to spend the next twelve years destroying her life because of her grief? Would you want her to commit suicide because of it? Of course you would not. Why would you think that she would be pleased by the inordinate grief you have shown over her passing? I have a feeling she would go to fisticuffs over it."

Adam did not know what to say. He was speechless, confused. He stood up sharply, yanking his arm out from under her hand. He stood on the edge of the porch roof, watching the rain fall. Alixandrea stood up and went to him.

"Please do not think me harsh," she said quietly. "'Tis only that I know that if I were to die, I should not want my husband to waste his life grieving. That would only hurt my memory, clouding it with agony and pushing aside all of the happiness we had together. I would want him to live and love again. To think that perhaps I could have taught him that during my life would have made it all worthwhile."

Adam did look at her, then. "Taught him what?"

She smiled, a beautifully soft and knowing gesture. "That life is a gift to share with others, for too quickly it is gone."

Adam continued to stare at her, his dark eyes glittering with unchecked emotion. After a moment, he turned and disappeared into the house. Alixandrea watched him go, her gaze falling on Matthew when Adam left her sight. Matthew was still holding her cloak; he held it out to her when their eyes met. She smiled weakly.

"I do not know if I did any good at all, but I tried," she turned so that he could put her cloak around her shoulders. "Sometimes it takes a stranger to help where family cannot."

He leaned down, putting his lips against her ear. "You *are* family."

His hot breath made chills race down her spine. "Only in the marital sense. He does not truly know me yet."

"He will."

His arms went around her, creating a safe, warm envelope against the rain and chill weather. So easily, they were coming to respond to one another, his arms around her and her contentment in his touch. They stood a moment, watching the water fall across the great green expanse of the garden. It looked like a sea of glittering emeralds. Alixandrea snuggled back against him, feeling his hard armor against her but comforted just the same.

"So your aunt expects babies right away, does she?"

Matthew laughed softly in her ear. "I was hoping you had forgotten about that."

She joined in his laughter. "How could I? The woman basically told me that I am a brood mare. I am not sure how to respond."

Matthew cradled her, the falling rain reflecting in his blue eyes. "You are most certainly not a brood mare. But an heir would not be unappreciated. Besides, the fun is in the practice."

Her cheeks grew warm. Though bodily she was no longer a maiden, in her mind, she was still relatively innocent.

"We shall see." She pulled herself gently out his embrace. "Shall we go back inside? I am famished."

He took her by the elbow, guiding her towards the door. "My aunt wants babies before we leave this house. That doesn't give us much time. I think we should go practice instead of eating."

"Matthew!" she scolded softly, blushing furiously as he laughed. "Be quiet. Someone will hear you."

He grabbed her just inside the doorway. It was dark and chilly, the only light from the gray skies outside the door. His blue eyes bore into her.

"I doubt there is anyone in this house that believes I have not yet consummated this marriage," he growled. "But if there is anyone foolish enough to think that I have not yet taken what belongs to me, then God have mercy. One only has to look at us to know that this marriage, however short it has been, agrees with us both."

His warmth and closeness made her giddy, her heart thumping loudly against her ribs. She was sure he could hear it. "It does, doesn't it?" she whispered, watching him nod. "But... well, I was wondering one thing."

"What is that?"

She made a face as she thought about how she would phrase her concern. "It is my understanding that women; that is, some women, wear a wedding ring to signify that they are, in fact, married. Would it be too much to ask for a small one?"

Gazing into her lovely face, Matthew began to feel the familiar guilt creeping into his veins. But instead of keeping his thoughts to himself about it, he found himself telling her. "You must forgive me for being so poorly planned for this marriage," he said. "I never even thought to buy you a ring."

"If you feel strongly about it, you do not have to."

"I feel strongly that I have been a fool about this entire situation, but you already know that. I must see the king on the morrow but when I am finished, I will take you to the Street of the Jewelers in London and buy you any ring you wish."

She smiled. "Truly?"

He kissed her on the tip of her nose. "Truly."

"But what about you?"

"What *about* me?"

"Men have been known to wear wedding rings as well. Will you not wear one?"

Three days ago, she would have never asked him such a question. But today saw an entirely different situation and she felt comfortable asking him. He paused a moment, thoughtfully, before slowly nodding his head.

"If you wish it."

"Only if you do."

His easy smile spread quickly across his face. "How could I not? Every man in London will know I have married the most beautiful woman in the land."

Her smile, oddly, faded as she continued to look up at him. "And that is another question that has been on my mind. What if I wasn't beautiful? What if I was the horrible hag you had expected? Would you still wear one? Or do you only wear it because I am beautiful and you want to show everyone how well you married?"

It was an astute query; he should have expected it. She was not only lovely, she was intelligent, and seeing his quick change of heart about their marriage over the past few days, she should have rightly wondered to the cause. It made him feel shallow. Perhaps he was, but there was more to it than that.

"Mayhap that would have been the truth the day I met you," he admitted quietly. "But over the past few days I have come to see that your beauty is not only on the outside, it runs very deep within. Physical beauty isn't much without the beauty of soul to go with it and you, my lady, have both. When I say you are beautiful, I mean that you are beautiful everywhere. I told you that I believed you to be a lady of good character. I wasn't wrong."

Once again, he managed to say the correct thing. She felt foolish for even questioning him. "May I say, then, that I am very proud to be Lady Wellesbourne."

"And I am very proud to be your husband."

It was a sweet moment. She chuckled softly. "You would not

have said that a week ago."

"A week ago I was an idiot."

Timidly, she reached up to touch his stubbled face. Even without his conventional male beauty, there was something extraordinarily attractive about the man that grew on her by the moment. The French term for it was *un certain quelque chose*; a certain something. Matthew, from nearly the moment she had met him, had that certain something that made him irresistible.

When she touched his face, he closed his eyes at the first flutter of her fingertips. It was an oddly invigorating gesture. Both hands came up and she gently clasped both sides of his face, studying this man whom she was married to. Matthew did not even open his eyes; he simply leaned forward and kissed her.

His lips were soft and warm, his tongue demanding entry into her mouth. She responded to him more quickly this time, becoming more comfortable with his attention. She had fast learned to like it. He picked her up, holding her against him, her feet dangling off the floor as their kisses became more heated. The small entry they were standing in was dark, cold, and empty. There was a tiny cloakroom off to the left; he pulled her into it and closed the door.

He tossed her cloak off, letting it fall to the floor. He wore full armor, putting him in a logistically difficult position for what he wanted to accomplish. But he backed her against the wall, continuing to kiss her as he went to work on his armor.

Alixandrea, swept up by the fervor that was swirling between them, instinctively began to help him with his pieces of protection. It was strange that neither one of them said a word, each one knowing what the other was thinking, each one a willing participant.

When his plate armor came off, he bent over at the waist and Alixandrea pulled his mail coat off over his head. The hauberk went on the floor beside it, as did the linen shirt he wore beneath. Stripped to the waist, it wasn't good enough for him; he grabbed Alixandrea with tender brutality and deftly stripped her of her surcoat.

The corset and girdle followed, leaving her in her sheath. The entire time, it seemed to her as if his mouth never left her, but she knew at some point it must have. All she could feel or think or taste was the lust that had built up to frenzied proportions. She'd never known such a thing. When Matthew snaked his hands underneath her shift and lifted it over her head, she wasn't even concerned that she was naked, standing in Aunt Livia's West Hall cloak room. All she cared about was Matthew and his heated touch.

Matthew was so consumed with her that he was blinded it by it, but not so much that he did not notice that she was stark naked but for the stockings she wore. Tied to each thigh with a pretty blue ribbon, he very nearly lost his mind with the erotic vision.

Taking her in his arms, he continued to kiss her as he lifted her up against him. She wrapped her legs around his waist as a child would have done. With one hand, he managed to lower his breeches. Putting her back against the wall, he eased her down onto his waiting erection.

Alixandrea moaned softly as he invaded her body. She was sore from the previous day, but the pain of his insistent entry only served to enhance her glorious sensations. Matthew tried to be gentle, but it was incredibly difficult. He eased into her until he was seated. Then, with her back against the wall and both hands on her buttocks, he began to move.

The thrusts were gentle at first, erotic and slow. She was as slick as the rain that covered the ground outside. But his passion was demanding and his movements became faster, hotter, wetter. A hand moved to her full breasts, gently fondling the creamy skin. Her legs tightened around him as he gained momentum, thrusting in rhythm until he could only hear her soft gasps in his ear. The hand on her breasts moved back to her buttocks, clutching them tightly as if to never let her go.

Harder and faster he went, feeling her legs tighten around him, until her body suddenly stiffened and her soft crying lingered in his ear. Feeling her tight walls draw at him, he spilt his seed deep inside her delicious body.

But it wasn't over. There was still heat. He was still moving and she was still gasping. He could not seem to stop moving, milking their passion for every last ounce it was worth. He felt her release at least twice more around him, her body shuddering with delight and her cries soft in his ear. But when the movements finally slowed and their wits returned, he fell forward against the wall, making sure she was protectively clasped in his massive arms. It wasn't that he was exhausted; it was that he was unbelievably content. He was still having difficulty believing it was all real.

"Are you all right?" he asked softly.

Her face was in the crook of his neck. "Aye," she said, muffled against his flesh.

His hands caressed her. Then he snorted. "I am happy to report that we are well on our way to granting my aunt's wish."

She suddenly lifted her head. "Will they be looking for us?" she asked, concerned. "We should probably...."

He kissed her, quieting her words. "They will not come looking for us if they know what is good for them." Nonetheless, he stood up and slowly let her slide to the ground. "But, in good taste, we should probably get dressed and join them."

She smiled, going for her shift. Her knees were wobbly and he laughed when she bobbed and weaved. He even held out a hand to steady her as she picked up her clothing, to which she was grateful.

They dressed in warm silence; Matthew would reach out to touch her every now and again, almost as if to convince himself she was still here, still real. He needed help with his mail coat and hauberk, which she somewhat awkwardly provided. She'd never dressed a knight before. When they were finally dressed, they just stood a moment, gazing into one another's eyes.

"God, you are beautiful," he murmured.

She smiled modestly. "As you are also quite handsome, my lord."

He snorted and opened the door, ushering her back out into

the cold, dim hall. A swift perusal of the area showed that there was no one about. They were still quite alone. He took her hand and tucked it into the crook of his elbow as they headed back to the main hall.

"Of all my brothers, I am not the most handsome," he said. "Luke has that distinction. Women cannot seem to get enough of him."

"Perhaps he has what people would consider physical perfection, but it 'tis you who has the true essence of male attractiveness," she said. "However, I would not put too much stock in Luke's appearance. You are also quite attractive, physically. You have beautiful eyes."

He grinned. "I have never heard that before. Dare I believe you?"

"You'd better."

They smiled at each other as they reached the door that would lead them into the brightly lit hall where food and wine await.

"Would you like to know something?" he asked softly.

"I would."

"I think I could grow to be very fond of you."

She feigned shock. "Of me?"

His smile seemed to fade and a strong warmth took hold deep in his eyes. Whatever was brewing behind those soft blue orbs reached out to grab her.

"Absolutely," he whispered.

Alixandrea did not know what to say. By the tone of his voice, there was nothing she could say that could give either one of them any greater hope that their marriage was indeed destined to be a pleasurable thing for them both. When he brought her hand up to his lips and softly kissed her fingers, her cheeks turned delightfully pink. If she'd been reluctant to allow herself to feel true happiness before this moment, she realized that she was no longer afraid. She would permit herself to feel it.

The door in front of them suddenly flew open and the light from the hall nearly blinded them. Matthew opened his mouth to berate whoever had enabled the action, but Mark's serious face caught him by surprise.

"Matt," he was breathing heavily, as if he had been running a great distance. "We've been looking everywhere for you."

"Here I am," Matthew said calmly. "What is it?"

One word sent them all into the deepest levels of apprehension.

"Father."

CHAPTER NINE

The nearest physic was six miles to the east. John and Luke had already gone to fetch him, leaving Rosehill in a panic.

Adam was lying in an upstairs bedroom with Mark and Matthew to staunch the bleeding from his mouth, ears, and tend what they presumed to be several broken ribs. The broken bone sticking out of his lower right leg had already been semi cleaned and splinted by Caroline and Aunt Livia's majordomo.

With all of the chaos going on around them, no one could explain how Adam had ended up under the wheels of a coach. The more Matthew worked to stabilize his father, the more he realized that he knew the answer to that question. Adam had finally done it. Though Matthew did not want to believe it, there seemed no other explanation. Guilt such as he had never known seeped into every pore of his body. He could not believe he'd finally made good on his threats.

Alixandrea stood outside of the chamber door, watching her husband gently feel his father's torso for damage and fighting off the sick feeling that she had caused all of this. She'd tried to help Adam when Matthew had warned her he was fragile. For all of her good intentions, it seemed that she must have triggered a stronger desire for death within the man. He'd run out and thrown himself under the wheels of the Whitewell carriage that she and Caroline had been brought to Rosehill in. The coachman had been taking it around the side of the manor to the livery when it had happened and, eager to be done with his duties, had been going at full speed at the time. He'd never had time to stop.

The coachman was down in the hall, weeping quietly in a corner. Alixandrea remained outside of Adam's chamber while family members worked feverishly to aid him. Distraught from watching Matthew work on his father, she wandered down the corridor until she came across an open window. It was still raining outside. There was a wide enough sill to sit on, and she sank heavily.

Rain whipped in, dampening her neck and arm. Gazing out over the gray and green landscape, she had never felt so awful in all her life. She wondered what Matthew as going to think of her now, the woman who had goaded his father into attempting suicide. The past few days had been better than she had ever hoped for. Now, because of her arrogance, her stupidity, it would all come to a crashing halt. Matthew had been right to not to want to marry her. Perhaps he had always known best. Now she'd done this.

Tears filled her eyes as she listened to the sounds of commotion a few doors down the hall. Something was happening inside that room and Matthew was in a state; something about Adam not being able to breathe. Mark was in the corridor, bellowing for a knife and she resisted the urge to go see if she could help. Mark's eyes found her, bitter black things, and she averted her gaze in shame. She wasn't any good with blood or pain. It would be better if she stayed out of the way.

Alixandrea stood up and began to walk, unaware that Mark was following her from a distance. She passed through the corridors of Rosehill and somehow ended up outside. It was still raining, beastly weather that wrought havoc over the land. The rain pummeled her as she walked without her cloak, sloshing across the wet drive and into the green lawns beyond. Mark, having stopped short of following her out into the foul weather, watched her from an upstairs window until she disappeared into a grove of trees. Then he went back to his father.

Alixandrea wandered desolately. Seconds turned into minutes. Minutes turned into hours. The rain finally stopped and the sun peeped out from behind the dark clouds, weak though it might be. Alixandrea's mind lingered on the room she'd left behind, where a man lay dying because of her.

Why did she have to interfere? Why could not she have listened to Matthew when he told her that his father was fragile? She had always been headstrong but it had never gotten her into trouble. Until now. Matthew would probably never speak to her again, of that she was certain. She was coming to feel the grief that Adam had felt on the passing of his wife, maybe not so severely, but certainly it was there. Matthew would undoubtedly banish her. Now she would have to live without him.

At some point, the sun started to set. Alixandrea was freezing in her wet garments, her lips blue and teeth chattering, but she did not notice. The pain in her heart was too heavy to notice anything else. The Thames was off to her right; she could see glimpses of the blue-gray waters in the distance. Had she possessed any courage, she would have gone and drowned herself in penance for her sin. But she could not muster the strength or courage to walk in that direction.

She continued on her present course, stumbling through the unkempt fields, far away from any roads that she could see. Like a drunkard, her head was swimming and it was increasingly difficult to move her feet. But she did not care what happened to her; she would be grateful if God would allow her to drop dead at this moment.

It was too much to take. She could no longer keep her wits or her strength. Stumbling to her knees, she pitched forward into the wet green grass. Her last coherent thought before darkness claimed her was wishing that God would be merciful and this was the end of it.

***

"He is in a bad way, but I think he shall live."

The surgeon was a large man with a bad smell about him, but Aunt Livia affirmed that he was the best physic in the area. Matthew did not much care for the man, but he seemed to have done a well enough job with Adam. The old man's leg was neatly cleaned and re-splinted, his ribs bound, and he was breathing easier thanks to the incision Matthew had made near his ribcage. A broken rib had punctured a lung and Matthew had known enough how to ease the condition.

At the moment, he seemed to be resting comfortably. The sun was setting outside and a bright fire burned in the hearth, creating something of a hopeful mood in the chamber.

"What about his leg?" Matthew asked. "It was a bad break."

"It was. Providing the poison stays away, he should keep it and walk again."

Matthew was satisfied. Giving the physic a few gold coins for his troubles, he turned back to his father as Luke escorted the surgeon from the room. Matthew checked his father's pulse, lifted an eyelid and, content with what he saw, allowed himself to breathe a sigh of relief. Whatever foolish attempt his father had made was not going to claim him, at least not at the moment.

Mark and John were in the room, seated in various corners. Caroline had come in and out, bringing water and bandages and drink to those involved in Adam's care. Aunt Livia, unable to stomach the sight of her brother, had taken to her bed, leaving the house somewhat quiet. It was always quite when she was still, always bordering on happy chaos when she was about.

For the first time in hours, Matthew's mind was able to expand beyond the immediate needs of his father. His thoughts moved to the evening, perhaps some food, and a warm bed with Alixandrea beside him. He hadn't seen her since the onset of events, but knowing how she felt about blood and wounds, wasn't surprised nor offended. He assumed she had found a warm, quiet corner in which to wait. He suddenly found himself looking very much forward to seeing her.

"I should find my wife and tell her he will be all right," he muttered. "Mark, keep a vigilant eye while I am gone. I shan't be long."

In the corner, Mark stirred. "By all means, go find her," he rumbled. He had neglected to tell his brother that he had seen his wife wander away earlier in the day. In fact, he had been deliberate in his withholding. "Tell her that her attempts to keep you occupied while our father tried to destroy himself thankfully did not come to fruition."

Matthew froze, his narrowed gaze turning to his brother. "I

can only hope that I did not hear you correctly."

Mark's nearly-black eyes glittered with the twist of the flames. "You heard me."

Matthew did not say anything for a moment, but the expression on his face morphed into one only seen in battle. The hardness, the fury, was indescribable.

"You will come out into the hall with me."

John leapt up from his stool in the corner. "He did not mean it, Matt. He is upset. We are all upset."

"I meant every word," Mark snapped. "Had Matt not been so preoccupied with his new chit, none of this...."

Matthew was already flying across the room. John was a big lad, but not big enough to stop his brothers from battling. Nonetheless, he bravely threw himself between Matthew and Mark before Matthew could get a good hold of him.

"No, Matt," John pleaded, struggling to hold his eldest brother at bay. "He doesn't know what he's saying. He is frightened and tired."

Matthew sandwiched John between himself and Mark. He had hold of Mark's shoulder, the other hand grabbing his neck.

"Never again will you slander my wife or accuse her of something that is not of her doing," he hissed. "If I ever hear another negative word out of your mouth about her, I shall kill you."

They knew he meant every word. Mark managed to move his head enough to get Matthew's hand off his throat, winding both of his hands around John to get at Matthew's face.

"I am not saying anything other than the truth," he snarled. "You allowed her to speak with father when you knew what might happen. You allowed her to provoke him into this... this madness. And see what has happened?"

"I was there when she spoke to him. She said nothing that you and I have not said over the past twelve years. He was, in fact, responding to her far better than he ever responded to us. I will not allow you to blame her for this."

The punches began to fly then. John wisely stopped trying to prevent such a thing and yanked himself out of harm's way.

"Stop it!" he shouted. "You'll hurt each other! You'll hurt father!"

Matthew slowed his actions but he still had a good grip on Mark. Mark, for his part, had given Matthew a lovely bloodied lip. Rather than throwing any more punches near their father's convalescent bed, Matthew started pulling Mark from the room; he was so much stronger than his brother that the battle was a little one-sided. But Mark was a scrapper and would not surrender easily.

John saw what was happening and once again tried to intervene. He rushed forward, attempting to remove Matthew's hands from Mark's body.

"Stop it," he pleaded. "Now is not the time for this. Father is injured and we do not need either one of you injured, too. Stop it, I say!"

By now, the commotion had roused part of the house. A few Rosehill servants stood in the hall, fearfully watching the tussle going on inside. Caroline, having been tending Aunt Livia, had been summoned by a frightened maid. When she came to the doorway, she shrieked in dismay.

"Matthew!" she gasped. "Mark! Stop it this instant!"

Matthew and Mark stood just inside the doorway, wrestling with each other more than actually fighting. Neither one of them was listening to reason; they seemed more intent to see who could wrangle the other to the floor and Matthew had a substantial advantage. Mark finally stumbled and bumped his father's bed; Adam's body jolted. More grunting and struggling between the brothers ensued until a familiar voice drifted upon the air.

"Matthew," Adam rasped. "Mark, cease this folly. Have you both gone mad?"

In mid-battle, the brothers froze and stared at their father. Struggles instantly forgotten, they went to his bedside.

"Father," Matthew said quietly, wiping the blood from his lip. "You had us very concerned. How do you feel?"

Adam's eyes were barely open, his lips pale as he spoke. "I can see how concerned you were, fighting at my bedside. What idiots I have raised."

The brothers did not even bother looking at each other, knowing he was right but neither one willing to admit it. Mark put his hand on his father's arm.

"Thank God you have survived," he said, sounding more like a frightened child than a man. "What on earth possessed you to throw yourself in front of a carriage? How could you do that?"

Though barely lucid, Adam managed to give a good attempt at a scowl. "Dolt, I did not throw myself in front of the carriage. I just did not see it."

Matthew did look at his brother, then. For all of the awful things Mark had said, Matthew almost shouted his relief that Alixandrea had nothing to do with it. But Mark did not look at his brother; his attention remained focused on his father.

"Then... it was just an...?" He could not seem to say the words. It did not make sense to him. "How could you not see a racing carriage?"

Adam's eyes closed. "Easy enough when the mind is elsewhere," he murmured. "I must have wandered into its path, for I remember little but a strong blow. How badly am I hurt?"

"A few broken ribs, a broken leg," Matthew said. "What had you so distracted that you would wander into the path of a moving carriage?"

Adam did not open his eyes. "Many things, Matthew. You heard your wife; she had much to say to me. Am I going to recover?"

It was apparent he did not want to elaborate on what had him so distracted that he would put himself in danger. Matthew let it go, for now. Frankly, he was relieved on so many levels that it was difficult to focus. "The physic says you will heal."

"I shall heal if you two will stop fighting in my chamber," Adam muttered. "Get out of here, both of you. When I am well enough, I shall beat you both severely."

He drifted off to sleep without another word. With a lingering, hostile glare at his brother, Matthew quit the room. He found Caroline standing in the hall.

"Where is my wife?" he asked her.

The redhead shook her head. "I do not know, Matt. I have been with Aunt Livia for some time."

Unworried in the least, Matthew set off to find his wife. In the doorway, Mark watched him go, now more than ever determined not to tell him what he knew. The woman had been the cause of too much misery in their lives. They were better off without her. Moreover, there was some sick sense in Mark that did not want to see Matthew happy. Why should Matthew be happy with his wife when Mark was, in fact, not? There was too much jealousy and bitterness in Mark to be kind to Matthew at the moment. He wanted to see his brother suffer.

An hour later, Matthew still had not found Alixandrea. Mark got his wish; Matthew was indeed suffering.

***

When she awoke with her face pressed against the wet grass, it was night. In the sky overhead, a night bird sang somewhere and all was still across the land. Unsteadily, she pushed herself up, disoriented. The moon cast some light on the landscape but she did not recognize any of it. She remembered Adam's accident and she remembered walking in the rain, but little else.

Her legs were weak and wobbly as she stood up, wondering where to go. Off to her right were a few outbuildings in the distance and what looked like a church. She could see the rise of the bell tower. Deciding that would be the best place to go, she staggered in the general direction.

The field stopped and she ended up on a road. The church was further than she had thought and it took her some time to reach it. Her delicate slippers were not made for the water, dirt and walking that she had forced upon them and they were nearly falling off her feet by the time she reached the church. She banged on the door, as much as her strength would allow.

The door was a long time in opening. The great iron hinges that held the oak door to the masonry structure creaked and groaned as the panel opened slightly. A suspicious head appeared, the crown shaved, indicating a monk. He was small, pale, and dirty. Alixandrea opened her mouth to speak but ended up coughing instead.

"Brother," she rasped. "I am in need of shelter for the night. Will you help me?"

The monk peered at her. "We are not an inn, my lady."

"I am not looking for an inn. I am in trouble and in need of your help."

"What manner of trouble?"

"Please. I am lost."

He took another look at her, noticing she was wet, disheveled, and looked as if she had met with some misfortune. After a reluctant moment, he stepped back and opened the door wider.

"Come in," he said.

She stumbled in the door. The sanctuary was cavernous and dark, smelling of mold. The monk held the only taper in the entire place. After he bolted the door, he looked at her rather curiously. She was shivering and pale.

"Now what, lady?" he asked.

He was either very stupid or very annoyed. She guessed the latter. "A fire might be nice. And something to dry myself with, if it is not too much trouble."

If he heard the sarcasm in her voice, he did not let on and motioned for her to follow. There was an alcove on the west end of the church that was apparently used for a common room of sorts. It was very small, with a table in the middle, a weak fire in the hearth, and clutter all around. The monk indicated for her to sit, which she did so gratefully, pulling the stool near the fire so that she could warm herself.

The monk just stood there, staring at her. Then he disappeared. Alixandrea coughed and shivered, relishing the blissful warmth from the blaze. She almost did not care where the monk went so long as she was out of the cold. He was a bit of a snip, but it was of no matter. Her harsh thoughts were quelled when he returned shortly with a massive pile of material, very course linen in a bunch. He held it out to her.

"You need to get out of those wet clothes, my lady, or you'll catch your death," he said. "You may wear this while your clothes dry."

She wasn't sure she wanted to take her clothes off, but upon reflection, decided he was correct. She was already coughing. She accepted the garment from him.

"Thank you for your kindness, Brother."

She swore he blushed as he left the room, closing the heavy door behind him. The door groaned in protest, poorly hung, and jammed against the floor as he finally yanked it shut. When he was gone and she looked around to make sure there were no holes by which to watch her, she gingerly unrolled the garment he had handed her.

It was a robe like the monks wore with a hole for the head, long sleeves, and yards of course fabric. Very quickly, she stripped off her wet garments and practically jumped into the robe, more from modesty than from the chill of the room. The rough material scratched her skin, but it was warm and dry, and to the Devil with comfort. She hung her heavy surcoat and under-things around the hearth so that the warmth would soon dry them. Reclaiming her seat on the small stool, she huddled near the fire, continuing the process of drying herself out.

With the heat, her exhaustion magnified. Her eyelids began to droop, her head to bob. She did not want to fall asleep in this strange place, even if it was a church. She did not trust her surroundings. She wanted to dry off, reclaim her clothes, and press on. Where she was going, she hadn't a clue yet. All she knew was that Matthew surely did not want her now and her life with him was ruined. Perhaps her only choice was a place like this, gloomy and depressing and dirty, as a servant of God. She could imagine no other option.

With the shock of the situation wearing off, depression began to set in. If only she had kept her mouth shut, if only she had done as Matthew had wished. She should not have interfered. But she was only trying to help. She and Matthew had been building such an amazing relationship, more than she had ever dared hope for. The White Lord of Wellesbourne had been hers, if only for a brief moment until she dashed everything to bits. She could not believe she had ruined it all because of her arrogance.

Her exhaustion and distress finally claimed her, for the next thing she realized, the door was opening and she was startled awake. The monk was standing just inside the doorway with a cloth in his hand, filled with something she could not quite see. Instead of handing it to her, he timidly placed it on the table near her as one would place food in the cage of a wild animal. He remained standing by the door just in case he needed to bolt.

"I thought you might need something to eat," he said. "There is cheese and some bread. It isn't much, but at least it is something."

She gazed over at the yellow cheese and crumbling brown bread. "My thanks," she said. "You have been very kind."

He nodded his head, once, as if he did not wish to discuss his kindness. Something about it made him uncomfortable. He stood and fidgeted.

"What manner of trouble do you have?" he suddenly blurted.

His uncouth manner almost made her smile. He had changed from his earlier suspicious approach to something of curiosity. Alixandrea picked up the cheese and took a grateful bite.

"Family trouble," she said, her mouth full.

The monk looked puzzled, uncertain. "What did you do?"

She lifted an eyebrow at him, insulted by his question, but that was until she realized that she really did *do* something. She shook her head, averting her gaze as she spoke. "Things I should be ashamed of. I... I need sanctuary. I have no place to go."

The monk looked stricken. "You cannot stay here, my lady," he said. "We cannot... that is to say, we do not have a place for you."

"Then where should I go?"

He took a step inside the room, apparently not so concerned now that the lady was going to jump up and bite him. "There is an abbey in Twyford," he said. "Perhaps the Sisters of St. Jerome would be able to help you."

It sounded reasonable. "Where is Twyford?" she asked.

"A few miles to the west. If you take the road that cuts through this town, you will come upon it within a day."

Alixandrea's heart sank as she realized where her destiny lay. Clearly, she had no other choice and, quite clearly, she must spend the rest of her days doing penance for Adam Wellesbourne's death. It was her fault as surely as she had murdered him with her own hands.

"Then to Twyford I will go," she said, the slight cough that had been plaguing her for the better part of the morning again bubbling up. "When my clothes are dry, I shall depart."

He nodded, still standing a few feet away from her. She resumed eating her cheese and bread, not looking at him, wondering what he was doing. She could feel his curious eyes on her, moving across her back, down to her feet, and sliding across her head. It was an eerie feeling, like unseen bugs about her. She almost scratched herself out of sheer discomfort.

"You can stay and rest if you wish," he finally said. All of the suspicion was gone from his tone. "The day proves ugly. You should wait until the weather clears."

"My thanks," she said softly.

"Are you running away?"

She looked at him sharply; it was as if he was thinking aloud, blurting out questions that were better left unasked. After a moment of staring him down with her piercing bronze eyes, she turned back to the fire.

"That is none of your affair."

It wasn't; he knew that. Awkwardly, he turned back for the door. He was almost through the opening when her soft voice stopped him.

"If any knights come to the door inquiring for me, you will tell them that you have not seen me. Is that clear?"

"Knights?" he exclaimed fearfully. "Are they after you?"

She shook her head at him as if he was an imbecile. "They will not kill you or burn the place down around your ears," she said.

"You will simply tell them that you have not seen me."

The monk did not look entirely clear or convinced in his actions, but he nodded anyway. Shutting the door softly behind him, he left the lady to her bread and cheese.

The cough was gaining. By the time she finished her food, a slight fever had started, though she did not notice. Laying her head down on the rough, worn table cluttered with old bowls, an iron fork, and other implements, Alixandrea drifted off into a fitful, dismal sleep.

CHAPTER TEN

"I cannot imagine that she willingly left," Gaston said. "Henry's agents are well aware of our arrival and they are also well aware of your custom of staying with your aunt when you visit London. It is quite possible they staked out Rosehill and abducted your wife."

"How would they have even known I was married?"

"You said yourself that Terrington's loyalties have shifted. It is quite possible that all of Henry's allies know of your marriage to her by now, long enough for plots to be in the works, at any rate."

A night and day of searching for Alixandrea had left them no further along than they had been the moment they had realized she was missing.

Matthew was positively distraught; it had been Luke who had sent word to Gaston to return to Rosehill at once, and upon his return, he found a man he'd known for twenty years to be in a state he'd never before seen. Matthew might have been the more congenial of the two, the more benevolent, and, Gaston was sure, the more deadly, and based upon that experience, he'd never known the man to be anything other than perfectly controlled. This disheveled man before him now was a stranger. Matthew's countenance had the usually-composed Gaston unsteady, more in sympathy for his friend than for his display of weakness. It distressed him to realize that emotions could do such a thing to a man, even one as strong as Matthew.

"But that would not make any sense," Matthew argued weakly. "Her manservant was supposed to kill me. For all Henry's people know, I am dead. Why would they stake out Rosehill and abduct my wife to use against me if they are presuming I am dead?"

Gaston's smoky eyes were hard. "You sent her manservant home with a message. Did you not think that message has been conveyed?"

Matthew shook his head sharply. "That was a week or so ago. There hasn't been enough time for Lord Ryesdale to spread that word that the assassination attempt was thwarted."

"So you think."

Gaston did not agree with him; that was clear, on many levels. Matthew did not have the stomach to argue with the man at the moment. His agitation grew.

"Have it your way; they staked it out and abducted her," he growled. "We have searched the countryside for her but the rain has conveniently washed away any trail we might have followed. I would hazard to say that they have not killed her outright and in that I take comfort. Knowing how they think, I am sure that they would rather use her against me. A dead wife will gain them nothing."

It was the same thought every man in the room had. Gaston's gaze moved between Matthew and Luke, sensing their genuine distress. John was the same, only more naked in his display of sorrow. Strangely, Mark was the only Wellesbourne brother that did not seem concerned as the rest of them did. Sitting next to Matthew, he seemed, in fact, rather detached from the whole thing. It was odd behavior from the usually-loyal Mark.

And with that realization, Gaston began to suspect Mark knew more than he was telling. Though he could hardly believe it, Mark's body language said otherwise.

But he would not question him in front of Matthew. The man hadn't eaten since yesterday; he was edgy and irritable, his face pale and unshaven. Any disruption might send him over the edge, especially one involving Mark. He would defend Mark to the death against all accusations and then turn around and kill him all in the same breath. Now was not the time. But the time would come.

"If she has been abducted, then she is well away from this place," Gaston finally said. "Any further searching would be in vain. It would be my suggestion that we contact the Bishop of Ely."

Luke looked at him as if he had completely lost his mind. "John

Morton?" he repeated, incredulous. "Why would you contact a man who virtually licks the soles of Henry's feet?"

"Because he would know," Matthew answered before Gaston could reply. He looked pointedly at his brother, his blue eyes somehow dimmer, void of the joy that he had so openly displayed over the past few days. "John Morton is a man of the Church. Though he has chosen his loyalties, he still must act within the guidelines of the Church and, hopefully, provide us with honest answers. I would trust him over any other of Henry's dogs."

"Exactly," Gaston finished. "I will ride for Ely immediately. It should take me a few days to reach him, but I will find out what I can."

Matthew shook his head. "You shall not go, my friend. We have enough brewing here to keep you more importantly occupied. She is my wife. I shall go."

Gaston would not stop him. Matthew would be useless to him in his current state; it was better that he take care of his personal matters and steady himself. Without another word, Matthew quit the room, presumably to prepare himself for the long journey to Ely. Gaston shot Arik, his second in command, a long look, suggesting that Arik accompany Matthew. The big North man silently slipped from the room in pursuit of The White Lord. Mark was the next one to quit the room in silence. Gaston walked after him.

Mark went outside, heading for the stables, when Gaston caught up to him.

"Mark," he called quietly.

Mark stopped suddenly, turning to face Gaston. By his expression, he was clearly surprised. "Gaston, you startled me. What is it?"

Gaston stood head and shoulders taller than Mark; the short, stocky Wellesbourne brother had to crane his neck back to look him in the face.

"Matthew's wife," Gaston's voice was low. "What do you know about her disappearance?"

Mark's dark eyes cooled. "Nothing."

"You are lying."

Mark lifted an eyebrow. "Choose to believe what you will. But I would be lying if I said that I was distressed."

Now it was Gaston's turn to lift an eyebrow. "Why would you say that?"

"Because I am not sorry, Gaston. She is the reason why my father is lying on the edge of death."

Gaston had heard the story of Adam's mishap from Matthew upon his arrival. It was one more horrific event in a day that had been full of them. But he was at a loss to understand Mark's point of view.

"Why would you say that?"

Mark's ruddy face tightened. "You know how father is, how he has never gotten over the death of my mother. Matthew allowed that... that *woman* to intervene and the result was my father throwing himself in front of a racing carriage."

"Matthew said that your father told him it was an accident."

"Pah," Mark waved his hands at him and began to stomp off with Gaston trailing after him. "He can say that all he wants, but I know the truth. She drove him to it. She tried to kill him."

"Matthew said no such thing."

"Of course he would not!" Mark came to an abrupt halt, as did Gaston. He glared at The Dark Knight. "He's hypnotized by her, de Russe. You have known Matthew for twenty years. Have you ever seen him like this? He's been completely seduced by that woman and doesn't have the clearness of thought to realize it."

Gaston's expression remained cool. "You did not do anything with her, did you?"

Mark shook his head. "No matter what I think or feel, I would not lay a hand on her. But I am not going to pretend I am concerned when I am not. She can keep running for all I care. We'll be well rid of her and back to normal, as we were before she came."

A twinkle came to Gaston's eye. "*Keep* running? Why would you say that?"

Mark's expression twitched. He seemed to lose his confidence as he averted his gaze. "A figure of speech."

"You are a very bad liar."

"Have it your way, then."

There was something about Mark's change in manner that made Gaston believe very strongly that Mark was somehow involved in the lady's disappearance. "You know far more than what you are telling me."

Mark snorted. "You are mad."

"I do not think so."

The veins on Mark's temple throbbed as he struggled to reclaim some of his poise. "I am only concerned with my father, and he is Matthew's responsibility. Matthew's head hasn't been in the right place since the day that woman arrived."

"Your father is the concern of all of his sons, including you. Do not place such a heavy burden on Matt's shoulders. It is unfair. And it shows how unwilling you are to accept any responsibility, yet you are more than willing to blame others for their failings."

Mark's response was to turn on his heel and continue to the stables. Gaston allowed him to go, watching the man until he disappeared from view. He had known Mark Wellesbourne for many years and had never known him to be a liar. Still, he was convinced the man knew something he wasn't telling. His attitude toward Matthew's wife bore watching. He wondered if Matthew was aware of it.

He thought one more perusal of the area was in order before returning to Windsor. Even though he had told Matthew it was futile, still, he would do it for his own peace of mind.

***

The lady was very ill.

The monk watched her sleeping fitfully, her head on the old table, and wondered what he should do. His superior was on a trip to Bracknell and would not return for several days. Meanwhile, it was the monk and a couple of orphans to take care of the small church. Now he was faced with the added burden of an ill woman.

The sun was starting to set, signaling the onset of Vespers. He would soon open the sanctuary for the faithful that would come for their evening prayers. The lady was in the small alcove directly off the main sanctuary and he did not wish for her to be seen.

Uncertain and fidgety bordering on panic, he closed the door to the alcove and was horrified when he could still hear her coughing through the closed door. He wondered if any of the faithful would hear her and report to his superior that he had allowed a woman in the place during his absence. He would be whipped for sure.

The two orphans, boys around ten and twelve years of age, had begun to light the tapers around the small, barren sanctuary. The weak light from the setting sun permeated the thin lancet windows carved all around the top of the sanctuary. Even with the glow of the candles, it was a gloomy place. A crude wooden altar served as the divine brokerage for God's holy blessings.

The monk donned his crude service robe and went to stand in the sanctuary as the faithful began to trickle in. It was mostly elderly, crossing themselves at the door before wandering further into the chapel for their prayers. They were the poor, the servants of the nobles that comprised the congregation of his poverty-ridden church.

The monk had dreams long ago of being a great bishop in a great cathedral, but his dreams had only brought him here. Sometimes he was angry at God for placing him in this destitute place, but in truth, he had become fond of his parishioners. He stood next to the door, watching them filter in, hearing the faint coughing of the lady in the room behind him. It got to the point when she would cough, he would cough, hoping to cover up her sounds.

More people began to enter as the sun finally dipped below the horizon. When he was sure most of the faithful had arrived, he moved to close the door. But blocking his path was an armored man so massive, so terrifying, that he filled up the entire entry.

The monk screamed like a woman. Then he slapped a hand over his mouth to silence himself as the helmed head turned in his direction.

"You." A massive gloved finger was beckoning to him. "Come here."

The monk forced his quaking legs to move. "Yes, my lord?"

The knight's armor creaked and groaned as he moved towards him. He sounded, and looked, like the Devil himself.

"I am looking for a woman," he said. "She may have passed through this church, or possibly this town. Have you seen any strange women about, well dressed and fine?"

The monk thought of the lady's orders to him earlier: *tell no one you have seen me.* But even as he mulled over her command, thoughts of the massive knight snapping his skinny neck came on far more strongly. He had no intention of dying for a woman he did not know. With a squeak in his voice, he threw his arm in the general direction of the alcove.

"In there," he croaked.

The enormous knight blew past him, practically kicking open the door. The small, cramped room displayed the lady in the middle of it as if a light shined directly down on her, pointing her out. The knight threw back his visor as he went down on one knee beside her.

Alixandrea's face was flushed, beads of sweat on her forehead. Gaston could see that she was gravely ill. He ripped off a gauntlet and put a hand to her face.

"Christ," he hissed.

"Yes?" The monk replied, hovering back in the doorway.

Gaston shot him an irritated glare. "Not you," he hissed. "I meant her; she's burning up. How long has she been like this?"

The monk was wringing his hands. The faithful, having seen the knight enter, now began to crowd up behind the monk. It was a nervous little group.

"I... I do not know, my lord," he said truthfully. "She came to me early this morning and told me that she was in trouble. I allowed her to come in and dry herself."

Gaston had heard enough. Looking around, he spied some manner of blanket thrown in a heap in the corner. It was filthy but it would have to do. He grabbed the material and tossed it around the lady's shoulders. Gently pulling her up into a seated position, he tried to wrap her in it but she awoke, groggy and disoriented.

"Hands off me," she did not recognize Gaston and slapped him straight across the face. "Unhand me this moment!"

Her strike stung, but he did not flinch. He knew she wasn't thinking clearly.

"'Tis all right, Lady Wellesbourne," he said quietly. "I am taking you home to your husband."

Her eyes were wide, unfocused, as he swept her up into his arms. "Husband?" she repeated as if she did not recognize the word. By the time Gaston had her out into the sanctuary, she began to struggle. "I cannot go home. No! Put me down!"

"You must go home," Gaston said calmly. "Matthew is worried sick."

"No," she gasped. "Please do not take me home. I cannot go!"

The monk found his voice, and for some reason, his courage. He tagged after them. "Where are you taking her?"

"Home," Gaston ducked a hand that came at his face. "To Rosehill."

"You... you will not punish her, will you?"

Gaston merely cocked an eyebrow at the monk, as if the man were insane. It was enough to stop the monk in his tracks, watching as the massive knight took the struggling lady from the church. He was going to follow but thought better of it. His guilt began to grow; as a man of God, he should have stopped this. But as a mortal man, he valued his life more and had no wish to tangle with the enormous warrior. He let them go.

A few men, including Patrick de Russe, were waiting outside when Gaston burst through the door with the lady in his arms. Patrick's eyes bugged out at the sight of Lady Wellesbourne.

"Jesus!" he exclaimed, leaping off his steed to assist his cousin.

"You found her!"

"Aye, I found her," Gaston grunted as she pushed against his neck. "She's ill and requires a physic. Ride for Rosehill and make sure one is waiting for us. And for God's Sake, send someone to bring Matthew back. Tell him we have his wife."

Patrick snapped orders to the nearest soldier, who went on the run. He carefully took the squirming lady from Gaston so that Gaston could mount his charger. Lady Wellesbourne smacked him a few times, too, for good measure. She had nearly gouged his eyes out by the time he handed her back up to Gaston.

"She's on fire, Gaston," he said quietly. "I could feel her heat against me, even through this mail."

Gaston's expression was grim. "I know."

He gathered his reins and tore off without another word. Patrick leapt onto his destrier and the entire party followed The Dark Knight at a raging pace.

***

She never did tell him why she could not go home. All Gaston could get out of her was crying and coughing, and finally silence. She slept against him heavily, like a boneless body, which made it tricky when he dismounted his charger with her in his arms once he reached Rosehill. She was dead weight and he was very careful not to drop her.

Having been notified by an advance soldier from Gaston's party, Caroline and Lady Livia met them at the door, screeching over Alixandrea's condition. The entire house and hold was in an uproar as Livia directed Gaston to take her upstairs to the first bedroom on the right. Even as he mounted the stairs, servants raced around him, carrying all manner of healing medicaments and other implements. By the time he reached the bedroom with the massive carved bed, it was full of people. It looked like a convention.

Gaston exploded. "Everyone *out*," he bellowed. "Only the physic and Lady Caroline will remain. The rest of you; be gone!"

Orders from The Dark Knight were not meant to be disobeyed. Aunt Livia tittered like a hysterical bird as her ladies escorted her from the room. Caroline stood on the opposite side of the bed with the same physic that had tended Adam after his accident. She was surprisingly composed. Gaston approached the bed and gently lay Alixandrea upon the goose-stuffed mattress. She was incoherent as Caroline began to gently remove the dirty blanket that covered her.

"Where did you find her, my lord?" she asked as she peeled back the cloth.

Gaston stood back as the physic went to work on her. "At a church in Oakley."

Caroline slipped the blanket off as the physic held the patient up off the bed. "What in God's name was she doing there?" she asked, baffled. "What happened?"

Gaston went to stand at the end of the bed. "I do not know, my lady. She has been confused since I found her." He watched them toss aside the blanket and fumble with the course monk's robe she wore. "I will be waiting outside, Lady Caroline. I would speak with you when you have Lady Wellesbourne settled."

He left the room, closing the door softly behind him. A quick perusal showed a corridor crowded with people. Aunt Livia was seated upon a small silken chair with one of her ladies fanning her face.

"Gaston," she gasped. "Where did you find her? Do you know that Matthew has been in a panic?"

"I do indeed, Lady St. James," he said. "I found her in a church in Oakley, a few miles from here. I do not know how she came to the place. The lady is quite incoherent, as you saw. I could not get an explanation out of her."

"She's going to die," Livia suddenly began bawling into her fine silk kerchief. "She's going to die and Matthew will have no heirs! Oh, the pity!"

Gaston had known Lady Livia for many years. She had always been the supreme example of over dramatics, but they tolerated her because she had a kind and generous heart. Matthew thought a good deal of her; therefore, so did Gaston. But her hysterics were trying his patience.

"She is not going to die," he said steadily. "She should be well in a day or two."

The door from the chamber suddenly flew open and Caroline stood in the opening. She began snapping orders at the servants hovering about.

"Bring me cold water and rags, and plenty of both," she said. "We must bring her fever down. And bring me fresh clothing for the lady."

Gaston had never heard Caroline speak in such a manner. She was usually a quiet, meek lady because that was what her husband liked. The lady before him was taking charge and he liked the change.

"A word, Caroline," he said quietly.

As the servants rushed off, Caroline followed Gaston several feet down the corridor so they could speak privately. His manner seemed odd and she sensed that.

"What is amiss, my lord?" she asked him.

He paused, gazing down at her. "I am not sure," he said. "Something Lady Alixandrea said to me. Do you have any idea why she feels she cannot return to Matthew?"

Caroline's brow furrowed. "Cannot return to him?" she repeated. "I have no idea. Is that what she said?"

"She did," he replied. "She said that she could not go home. And what in the hell was she doing in that church?"

Again, Caroline shook her head, baffled. "I truly would have no idea, my lord," she said. "Perhaps Matthew can answer that better than I. Perhaps... perhaps they had a quarrel."

Gaston wriggled his brows, no closer to discovering the lady's reluctance to return home than he was a moment ago. "Perhaps," he said. "Has someone gone after Matthew?"

She nodded. "John and Mark rode after him several minutes ago. Matthew and Luke left for Ely a few hours ago."

Gaston's thoughts turned to Matthew's state of mind, his travel plans. "And, no doubt, they were riding hard. It will take some time for Mark and John to catch them. I do not expect we shall see Matthew until late tomorrow at the earliest." He looked at Caroline. "How is Lady Wellesbourne?"

Caroline knew what he meant; he was asking if she thought the lady would survive long enough for her husband to return. "She is ill, my lord," she said. "Beyond that, I cannot say."

The servants were returning with cool water and rags. Caroline left Gaston standing in the corridor as she returned to her charge.

Only time would tell.

***

"Gaston," someone was shaking him awake. "Gaston, we need your help."

Gaston had been asleep in a chair in the corridor outside of Lady Wellesbourne's room, his head leaning back against the wall. It was pitch black, the night silent and still. He had no idea what time it was. When he opened his eyes, he found himself gazing into Caroline's pale face, her features illuminated by the small taper in her hand. He was instantly concerned.

"What is it?" he asked.

"Come," Caroline began to walk back into Lady Wellesbourne's room, motioning for de Russe to follow. "Please, come and help."

He was up, following her into the room with such speed that he nearly ran her over. The first thing he saw was Lady Wellesbourne laying on the big bed, her skin the same sickly shade as the sheets. She was ghostly pale.

The physic was leaning over her, his fingers against her neck, feeling her pulse. The lady was twitching and rolling and would have pitched herself off the bed had the physic not stopped her. Then she rolled to the other side, mumbling incoherently, and the physic reached out yet again to prevent her from throwing herself onto the floor. It was exhausting just to watch her.

"Has she been this active all night?" Gaston asked, incredulous.

"She is delirious," Caroline whispered, leading him over to the bed. "We must cool her down, but we cannot get her to stop moving. I am not strong enough and the physic cannot hold her and tend her at the same time."

"What do you want me to do?" Gaston asked.

"Get on the bed and hold her," the physic answered. "She must be held still with considerable strength so that we may get medicine in her and cool cloths on her. She is rolling herself to death."

Gaston did not ask any further questions; he went to the head of the bed and pulled the lady up into a sitting position. It was like trying to grab hold of a waterfall; she was sliding and tumbling in every direction. While the physic and Caroline held her forward, Gaston managed to get in behind her and then the three of them lowered her back against Gaston's broad chest.

Seated in between his legs, Gaston took her right hand in his right hand, her left hand in his left hand, and wound her own arms around her body. His legs acted like a fence, holding both her lower body and legs confined. He shifted around slightly, settling them both comfortably. He had a feeling the lady's state would get worse before it would get better and he wanted to have a good hold of her.

"Good," the physic could see she was adequately restrained. "Now, we must get some bark brew down her. 'Twill ease this fever."

Alixandrea's head was against Gaston's shoulder, her bronze hair spread out over them both. Gaston used one arm to wrap her in a bear hug while one hand went across her forehead, holding her back against him and effectively trapping her head. The physic poured some potion down her throat as she coughed and sputtered.

"There now, lady," the physic put the phial down. He looked over at Caroline. "The cold cloths, lady. Cover her in them."

As Alixandrea struggled weakly against Gaston's embrace, Caroline and the physic proceeded to completely cover her in cold, wet rags. From her neck to her toes, she was enveloped in them.

At first, she became semi-lucid and protested viciously; it was too cold and she was going to kill them all given the chance. But her objections faded as exhaustion and illness claimed her, and soon she lay quietly shivering against Gaston's powerful body.

For his part, Gaston had remained stoic and silent throughout the ordeal, fighting improper thoughts when they occasionally entered his head. The lady was sweet and supple and he could understand Matthew's infatuation with her. Gaston's own wife had never felt this marvelous against him, cold bitch that she was. He had wondered from time to time what it would have been like to have been married to a woman he hungered for. During the course of the night as Lady Wellesbourne lay against him, he was coming to understand what it might have been like. He envied Matthew.

As the cold light of dawn filtered through the covered windows, the lady finally quieted but for an intermittent twitch now and again. All was still, calm and quiet. Gaston was awake, his chin resting against the top of Alixandrea's head as he watched the room lighten with the sunrise. Caroline, too, was awake, diligently changed the rags that soaked Alixandrea's body, rinsing in cool water and placing them back against her searing skin. As the birds began to chirp on the windowsill, the physic rose stiffly from his stool and put his hand against the lady's forehead.

"She is still burning," Gaston muttered to him.

The physic did not reply. He went back to the clutter of paraphernalia he had brought with him and pulled out a small wooden bowl with part of the rim cut away. Gaston watched as the man put Alixandrea's hand in the bowl and nicked her wrist with a small flint. Blood began to seep into the bowl.

Bloodletting was never a good sign. It was what some would call a last resort. Gaston had never liked it because he thought it weakened an already weak body. Perhaps the physic was reading his mind, for when he spoke, it was in tones only Gaston could hear.

"It might do well to send for a priest," he murmured. "The lady cannot take much more of this and it is best to be prepared."

In spite of his hushed voice, Caroline heard him. Her eyes widened, her hands frozen in place above a wet rag she was replacing.

"No," she hissed. "You will not give up. She will live."

"I am not giving up," the physic said. "But we must face truths. The lady is burning with fever and soon her body will surrender. It is the way of things."

"No," Caroline said, more loudly. "Not Alixandrea. Matthew will be here soon. He will tend her when he returns and she will live."

Gaston could see that she was growing agitated. "No one is giving her over to God just yet," he reached out and put a massive mitt on her arm, comfortingly. "But prayers could not hurt. That is what the physic is suggesting."

Caroline was torn between resentment and sorrow. She put the cool rag on Alixandrea's leg and muttered angrily all the way to the door. "She is not going to die," she told them. "I forbid you to say such things."

"Of course, angel," Gaston said calmly. "But send for a priest and his prayers just the same."

When she quit the room, she left behind a mood of sorrow. No one wanted to think the worst. After a moment of reflection, the physic motioned to Gaston.

"She's no longer struggling, my lord," he said. "You may get up and leave her to the bed."

He was sorry to have to let her go, but he did as he was told. Laying the lady gently down to the feathered mattress, he took a moment to gaze at her lovely face, praying that Matthew would make it back soon. He did not want to be the one to tell Matthew that he had found his wife, only to have her die before he returned. No, he did not relish that thought in the least.

The sun continued to rise in what was a beautiful morning. No hint of the rain and clouds of the past few days remained. Caroline came back into the room and resumed her duties, as did a few servants, collecting soiled linens and generally cleaning up.

Gaston stood by the window, watching the landscape, listening to the bustle of the chamber as people came and went. Someone stoked the fire. A glance at the lady every now and then showed her to be gray, sweating, and still. Even gravely ill, she was still a lusciously beautiful woman. Gaston found himself wishing fervently that Matthew would hurry.

By late morning, his prayers were answered.

CHAPTER ELEVEN

Exhausted from hours in the saddle and days without sleep, Matthew's first look at Alixandrea had him falling to his knees beside the bed.

He could hardly believe what he was witnessing. Lying upon the damp sheets, her delicious bronze hair stuck to her moist forehead, he knew just by looking at her that she was on death's door. No one had to tell him anything specific; he just knew.

But in spite of everything, he was so glad to see her, so overcome with emotion, that he gathered her into his arms and buried his face deep in her neck. He'd only meant to hug her. But something unexpected happened. The next sounds that filled the musty chamber were those of his profoundly pitiful sobs and he was unable to stop them.

Gaston hadn't seen the break down coming, but he wasn't surprised. He chased everyone out of the chamber except for Caroline and the physic. Caroline stood next to Matthew, weeping with him. Because he was crying, she was crying. His display had weakened her already-taxed emotions.

Gaston stood by the door, never more deeply sorry for someone in his entire life. He and Matthew had seen so much life and death together, but never when it was this close. If Richard and Henry and the allied forces throughout England could only realize that The Dark Knight and The White Lord were men of flesh and blood and feeling, all might be lost. To the world, these were men with steel where their hearts should have been. If it were known that they did, indeed, feel pity or pain, then the land would be set upon its ear. Only within the confines of this small chamber were they allowed to show any emotion.

Hesitantly, Gaston went to his friend. The man was sobbing deeply into his wife's pale neck. He put a hand on Matthew's shoulder.

"Matt," he whispered. "Put her down, man. Let the physic have her."

Matthew was having a difficult time controlling himself. The dam had burst and his feelings were flooding out all over the place, his shock and exhaustion and anguish finding an outlet.

"What happened to her?" he wept. "Where did you find her?"

"At the church in Oakley," Gaston gently pulled him back as the physic pried the lady loose and laid her back upon the bed. "She was ill when I found her. I do not know how long she had been that way."

Matthew wiped furiously at his eyes, his nose. "But I do not understand any of this," he said. "What was she doing there? How did she get there?"

"The priest said she had come to the door, telling him that she was in trouble," Gaston replied steadily. "Other than that, I cannot tell you any more. The only person who can supply all of the answers is your wife. But she did say something strange to me."

Matthew looked at Gaston with his red-rimmed eyes. "She spoke to you?"

"Aye. Long enough to tell me that she could not come home."

Matthew's pale brows drew together. "She could not come *home?* What nonsense is that?"

Gaston shrugged. "Perhaps only the ramblings of a sick woman," he said. Then he peered more closely at Matthew. "The two of you did not have a row, did you?"

"Never."

Gaston had no reason to doubt him. He looked back at the lady on the bed. "Then it must have been her sick mind talking."

Matthew was still in his armor. He began removing pieces, tossing them against the wall with a clatter and bangs. He was fatigued and drawn, but the sight of Alixandrea brought renewed vigor to him.

There was an odd sense of urgency to his movements and Caroline had to jump aside at one point or risk being struck by a flying piece of armor. It smacked against the wall, leaving a gouge in Aunt Livia's wall covering that she had ordered from Paris. French artisans had carefully plastered the painted linen to the walls. It was the first of its kind in the area, now with a black mark on it.

But Matthew hardly cared. He ripped off his mail and let his weapons fall where they may. He ended up in his soiled linen tunic and leather breeches. He could not get his greaves off without removing his boots, and he had no mind to do that yet. He simply wanted to be near his wife without all of the fortified protection. He kicked aside a piece of shoulder armor that was in his way, an unusual action from a man who normally took great care of his expensive protection.

"Perhaps you should sit and eat something," Caroline had been watching his sharp movements and it concerned her. "You look as if you could use a bit of sustenance."

Matthew shook his head. "I am not hungry."

"Please, Matt."

He picked up his mail hauberk from where it had fallen and tossed it back against the wall with the rest of his armor. "Perhaps later."

Caroline looked at Gaston, who merely shook his head. They both watched as Matthew went back over to the bed and sat his bulk upon a small stool that the physic had been using. Taking one of Alixandrea's hands into his great palm, he brought it to his lips and sat, staring at her, as if afraid she were going to disappear. Caroline went back to her task of placing cooling rags on Alixandrea. Gaston stood there a moment, knowing there was nothing further he could do.

"Matt," he said quietly. "I shall be outside if you need me."

Matthew turned to look at him. He had an expression on his face that Gaston had never seen before.

"I haven't the words to thank you," he said quietly. "Without you... she would not be here."

Gaston's lips twitched into an exhausted smile. "You would have done the same for me."

"Without question. But I still cannot adequately express my

gratitude."

"No need. But I will say one thing."

"What is that?"

"She is worth every effort."

He quit the room, leaving Matthew flattered and oddly jealous at the same time.

***

It was snowing. At least, that was what Alixandrea thought. In her dream, it was freezing. There was snow on the roof of the keep at Whitewell and snow inside as well. It was in her bed. She dreamt that she could not find anything to wrap up in. It was so cold that she was shaking. And when the stark reality of consciousness claimed her, she was shaking so badly that her teeth were smacking together.

But the chill wasn't the reason she had awoken. Someone was talking to her, speaking in tones that could only be described as agonized. Her eyes slowly opened, moving unsteadily to the source of the sounds.

He was hobbling because one leg was broken and he was leaning heavily on crutches that his youngest son had fashioned for him. He shouldn't have been out of bed much less attempting to walk. But Adam Wellesbourne was nonetheless standing beside Alixandrea's bed, one hand clutching her clammy fingers as he offered soft prayers to a God he had forsaken long ago.

"...and I swear that if you allow this woman to live, I promise I will never again attempt to take my life as I have so often sworn to do," he murmured. "She has brought life back to the House of Wellesbourne. 'Twould be a cruel thing to do to Matthew if you were to take her from him. From all of us. Please, God, hear my prayers. Let this woman live. Alixandrea, *you must live!*"

It took her a moment to realize that she was not looking at a ghost. Shocked, she opened her mouth to speak when something buzzed loudly in her right ear.

Groggily, she turned her head slightly to see Matthew's head down on the bed beside her, snoring softly. His big arm was thrown over her body protectively. She could not see him very well, but he appeared to be seated, his head and upper body resting on the corner of her mattress. And he was sleeping like the dead. She looked back at Adam, the apparition she still could hardly believe.

"Sir... Adam," she rasped. "You are alive?"

It was most definitely a question. Adam's eyes flew open, the dark orbs looking at her first with surprise and then with such joy that words could not adequately describe it.

"My lady," he gasped. "You are alive!"

She blinked, slowly reorienting herself. She had a suspicion that she was at Aunt Livia's home, but had no idea how she came to this bed. In fact, she remembered very little after Adam's accident. Everything was a blur, seemingly weird and distant.

"Of course I am alive," she whispered. "But, more importantly, *you* are alive. The last I saw, you had been badly injured."

The conversation had snapped Matthew from a deep sleep. His head came up, sharply, his focus instantaneous. Such were the traits of a seasoned knight. But the moment he saw that Alixandrea was lucid, the battle-ready expression on his face washed with such astonishment that he very nearly fell off his stool. He grabbed her by both shoulders as if fearful she would slip away.

"You are awake," he breathed, his gaze moving over every delicious feature of her face. "My God... you are actually awake."

"Aye," she wasn't quite sure why he was so shocked.

"How do you feel?"

She blinked, becoming more oriented. But she felt strangely weak when she tried to move. "I... I am not sure," she said softly. "Has something happened?"

Matthew put his hand on her forehead; she was no longer hot. He sighed heavily with relief, with gratitude. It was enough to bring tears to his eyes again, but he fought them. "You have been ill, love," he said quietly. "Don't you remember?"

She shook her head, but glanced down at the cold cloths still covering her body. She was reminded of how cold she was and she gingerly picked one up to inspect it.

"You were with fever," he told her. "We had to do that to bring down your temperature."

"I am freezing," she whispered. "Please take them off."

He began yanking them off of her, throwing them to the floor. The entire area around the bed was littered with wet rags in little time. Adam still stood beside the bed, dodging the wet cloths as Matthew tossed them about.

"We were worried for you, my lady," the old man said. "We feared the worst."

Alixandrea refocused on him, still surprised to see him. "And what of you?" she murmured. "The last I saw, you were lying in bed, gravely injured."

Adam smiled. "I was. But it is not my time yet. So here I am, recovering, and a prickly burden to my sons."

Alixandrea's bronze eyes fixed on him, heavy with emotion. "Sir Adam," she said softly. "I must say something. I am sorry if I said anything that would cause you to... well, harm yourself. It was never my intent. I only thought to...."

Adam cut her off, his brow furrowed. "Is that what you thought?" he was mildly indignant. He looked at Matthew, standing on the other side of the bed and listening carefully to the conversation. His indignant stance left him. "That is what they all thought, my sons. They thought that I had thrown myself in front of a racing carriage. But I did not. I simply did not see the thing until it was too late."

Alixandrea closed her eyes, tightly. A single tear popped from her left one, trailing down her temple. Matthew saw it.

"What's wrong, love?" he asked softly, wiping the tear away with his thumb. "Why do you weep?"

She burst into tears, as much as her weakened state would allow. "I thought I'd killed him."

Matthew was back on his knees, his hands warm and gentle on her arms, her shoulders. "Why on earth would you think that?"

She could not stop the tears. "Because he was so upset when I spoke to him about your mother. You had warned me, Matthew. You had told me he was easily upset, but I did not listen. I thought I could help him. I was afraid I'd driven him to desperation with my clumsy attempt."

Matthew was genuinely baffled. She was so distressed that he took her carefully in his arms, holding her against his chest. She seemed so light, so weak. He pulled her closer.

"You did indeed help him," he murmured into her damp hair. "What happened was an accident and nothing more." He held her back so he could look into her pale face. "Is that why you ended up at the church? Did you run away because you thought you had caused his death?"

She sniffled, tears easing as she found strength in Matthew's powerful arms. When he held her, all was right in the world again. She tried to think on what he was saying, but the more she thought, the more it did not make much sense to her.

"I do not know about a church," she said. "I... I remember your father's accident. I remember walking outside. I kept walking... I remember that I was upset in thinking I'd finally driven your father to kill himself. But I do not remember much more than that. What happened to me?"

He could tell by her expression that she was being completely truthful. He gathered her up against him again, so incredibly grateful that she was alive. God only knew what could have happened to her had the fortunes not been kinder.

"It doesn't matter," he whispered. "All that matters is that you are here, and you are going to get well. I shall not leave your side, I swear it."

"Then you are not angry with me for upsetting your father?"

"He was not upset. You helped him more than you know. And what happened to him was an accident."

"My own stupid fault," Adam put in.

Alixandrea pulled her face from Matthew's shoulder, looking over at her father-in-law. He seemed well enough. Every horrible thought she had over the past day, or few days that she could remember, seemed like a nightmare. She leaned back against her husband, relieved and spent.

"Then I must tell you how glad I am to see you," she said to Adam. "For I never thought to again."

Matthew kissed her forehead, lingering over it, allowing himself one last stab of fear and pain at the events of the past few days. It was over, thank God.

"Nor did we, you."

***

London wasn't anything she had imagined it to be. Living far to the north as she had all of her life, she had built up a vision of the city that was something akin to Heaven. She had imagined finely dressed people everywhere and streets paved of gold. As she rode in the carriage just behind her husband's war horse and the outskirts of the berg loomed into view, nothing could have been further from the truth.

The dirt streets were full of mud, the gutters fragrant with human feces, urine, and in many cases, animal carcasses. After the heavy rains of the past few days, the sun was had come out, heating up the earth and creating a stench that had to be experienced to be believed. The men could smell it, but it did not offend them as it did the women. It wasn't long before Alixandrea and Caroline gave up their sight-seeing, pulled their heads back into the carriage, and plugged their noses.

Adam was still on the mend and did not make the trip. Matthew, Mark, Luke and John were in full battle mode, however, and rode in various positions around the carriage, surrounded by the fifty men-at-arms that Gaston had left behind at Rosehill.

Gaston had returned to Windsor several days prior when it was clear that Alixandrea was going to reclaim her health. From Windsor, he had moved their troops to London. Whatever activity was taking place at this particular time was taking place at the Tower of London, and the great stone bastion beat with a pulse as the heart of England.

It had been nine days since Alixandrea's brush with the

horrendous fever. She had regained her strength quickly, eating whatever Aunt Livia would put in front of her. She also quickly discovered that the old lady did not spend much time with the females of the Wellesbourne family; her time was spent with her beloved nephews. Matthew said it was because she craved male attention and it was clear that Aunt Livia did not like to share their attention. Whatever the case, she had been present during Alixandrea's recovery only to force food down her throat. Alixandrea's impression of her was, as of yet, undetermined. She could not decide between thinking her to be a sweet old woman or a self-absorbed shrew.

On this fine and sunny day, Alixandrea felt better than she had in a long while. If the stench hadn't been so bad, the day would have been perfect. She could look out of the carriage window and see her husband's legs as he rode astride his charger. True to his word, he hadn't left her side since she had emerged from her fever except on rare occasion.

Even now, he kept dipping his head down to catch a glimpse of her in the carriage as if to make sure she was still there. His actions made her smile.

"You keep watching me as if I am going to disappear," she said to him the next time he dipped his helmed head. "I promise that I am not going anywhere."

She could not see his expression because his visor was down. He slowed the charger so that he could move closer to the window.

"I know this carriage makes you ill," he said. "I am simply making sure you are well."

She leaned out of the window, gazing up at him. The sun was bright and she squinted. "I am well," she assured him. "When will we arrive at the Tower?"

"Shortly," he said. "But I thought you wanted to visit the Street of the Jewelers."

Her expression bloomed. "I do," she exclaimed. "When will we be there?"

Luke was a few paces behind Matthew, listening to the

conversation. "Soon enough, my lady," he answered before Matthew could. "But I can assure you that there will be nothing within those stalls that can compare with your beauty. You put the finest adornments to shame."

Alixandrea grinned as Matthew turned his helmed head in the direction of his brother. "Luke, I swear that if I hear you flatter my wife one more time, you and I shall come to blows. I am the only one who may flatter her. Do you comprehend?"

Luke put up a hand in surrender, but Alixandrea was sure he was smiling.

"Were I not married, I am sure your honeyed words would have worked their magic," she told him. "As it is, I fear you have only roused my husband's anger."

"That is not hard to do, my lady, where you are concerned."

She continued grinning at Luke as the knight waved to her and slowed his charger, enough so that the carriage passed him almost completely. It was clear that he did not want to provoke his older, bigger brother, in good humor though it might be. They all knew that Matthew had been particularly sensitive lately where his wife was concerned. Alixandrea looked up at her husband.

"You did not have to be so cruel to him," she said.

"I was not cruel."

"Will you not lift your visor when you are speaking to me? I feel as if I am speaking to a statue."

His response was to flip his visor up, his blue eyes twinkling at her and a smile playing on his lips. "Better?"

She nodded. "Verily. Now, tell me; after the Street of the Jewelers, where are we going?"

"To the Tower."

"And then what?"

He sighed, lifting an eyebrow. "Do you always ask so many questions?"

"I do. Please do me the courtesy of answering."

He scratched his cheek with a great mailed glove, glancing about as if he was thinking of a reply. "Well," he began, "I suppose you could say that I have a surprise for you."

Her eyes lit up. "A surprise? What is it?"

"De Russe has informed me that the king has arranged a tourney in celebration of the summer season. It seems that it is becoming an annual event, for he has done the same thing for the past two years. In any case, the tourney will be the day after tomorrow; a vast, vulgar spectacle of knights and pageantry. You have never seen anything like it."

She clapped her hands in delight. "And we are going!"

"I am competing."

Her eyes widened and her hands froze in mid-clap. "You are competing?"

He nodded. "This is an enormous tourney and any knight worth his weight in salt pledges to compete."

Her excitement, so strong at first, suddenly banked into something dark and brooding. She simply nodded her head, trying not to show her true feelings.

"I am sure you will do fine," she said quietly. "I.. I am looking forward to the spectacle."

He was far more astute than she gave him credit for. "Nay, you are not," he growled. "What is the matter?"

She shook her head and sat back in the cab. "Nothing, truly."

The next thing she realized, the cab door was flying open and Matthew's bulk was in the door. Reaching out, he grasped her by the arm and pulled her out. Somehow, he managed to remount his charger with her in front of him. It could not have been very easy if she hadn't been somewhat cooperative, and she suspected that she had. In fact, she had gone quite willingly.

Seated in front of him with his massive arm around her, she settled back contentedly. She had grown so accustomed to him by her side day and night, almost since they had met, that she was coming to crave it.

"Now," he rumbled in her ear. "Why did you look as you did when I told you that I was competing in the tourney?"

She thought about being evasive but was coming to realize that did not work with him. "It is foolish, really."

"Let me be the judge of that. Why do you not want me to compete?"

She sighed heavily, realizing she would have to tell him. "'Tis silly."

"Tell me."

She settled back against him, pressing herself more closely into his armor. Even though it was cold and hard, still, Matthew was on the other side of the protective metal lining. She swore she could feel him.

"When I fostered at Pickering, the earl held a tournament," she began quietly. "I was perhaps twelve years old at the time. We had a knight in service at the time, a man sworn to the earl and, by all accounts, a very fine man. In any case, he competed in the tournament and made it to the final round. We were all so proud of him. But as we sat and watched, this fine, strong knight was brought down by a lance that split and ran great shards into his face and neck. He lingered for four days before finally passing on. It was a horrible death."

He understood, somewhat. "So you do not want me to compete."

She turned to look at him, his sweaty face underneath the raised visor. "Matthew, I cannot bear the thought of a mistake or an accident and losing you to an injury that simply did not have to happen. I would just... die."

His blue eyes glittered at her. "I have competed in many tournaments and have yet to be badly injured in one. In fact, I have won more times than I have lost. But I have never had anyone in the lists cheering for me as you will. The thought of it makes me very proud."

She did not have the courage to ask him not to compete. To do so would be to display doubt in his abilities as a knight. She turned around and faced forward.

"As you will make me proud, I am sure."

His lips were suddenly on her ear, kissing her softly. In spite of the fact that his metal helm was knocking her softly in the head, Alixandrea closed his eyes blissfully as his lips moved across her lobe.

"I will not compete if it will upset you," he whispered. "I only want to make you happy. I could not bear it if you were miserable."

She put her arm up, encircling his neck as his lips moved to her jaw. His warm mouth was sensual, warm, inviting.

"I will not be miserable, Matt," she murmured. "But I would be lying if I said that I am not concerned for your safety."

"Matt!" Mark was hailing him from the opposite side of the carriage. He reined his big red charger around so that he could gain a look at his brother. "The Street of Jewelers is coming up on the left. I shall take the men on to the Tower."

Matthew moved his mouth from his wife's neck, being careful not to shout in her ear as he replied. "Leave me a contingent of ten and take the rest."

"Can I come, too?"

They had almost forgotten about Caroline, sitting quiet and lonely in the carriage. Both Matthew and Alixandrea looked over and smiled at her.

"Of course, darling," Alixandrea said. "In fact, perhaps Mark will join us."

Caroline shook her head even as Matthew called out the invitation to his brother. Mark did not reply directly, but he muttered orders to John, who, along with Luke, continued on to the Tower as Mark, Matthew, Alixandrea, Caroline and ten men at arms lingered behind.

The Street of the Jewelers wasn't a particularly large place. It was, in fact, rather small. Situated in the heart of an avenue surrounded by plaster and thatched-roof row houses, it was full of people and stalls. Some merchants seemed to work out of their shops, but still others had lean-to's up against the walls. And, oddly enough, it did not smell. The dirt avenue was swept and relatively clean.

Matthew lowered Alixandrea gently to the ground. As she stood there and gaped at the bustling site, he dismounted behind her and handed the reins over to the nearest man-at-arms. Over to their left, Mark dismounted his steed, rather testily, and opened the carriage door for his wife. That was as far as he went to help her. She had to climb out of the cab herself.

If Matthew noticed his brother's behavior, he did not let on. He took his wife's elbow and began to guide her towards the stalls.

"Now," he said. "What will it be? A gold ring? A silver ring?"

Alixandrea was so excited that she could barely contain it. "I am not sure. I will have to see some examples and make a selection."

The first shop they came to was a dim, crowded place that smelled of odd incense. An old man with a strange cap on his head was there to show them his selection of fine jewelry. There were red stones, white stones, green stones, and stones that had many colors in them. Matthew and Alixandrea inspected the rows of fine rings in his carrying case.

"Here is a gold band," Matthew had to remove his gauntlet so that he could pick up the jewelry. "It is rather nice."

She glanced at it. "Too plain."

He lifted his eyebrows and put it back. As he was sifting through some of the others, she held up a silver ring set with several diamonds. It was a slender, pretty band and she slid it easily on her slender, pretty finger.

"This one," she announced, holding it up for all to see.

Matthew looked at it; it was a lovely, glittery ring. "Are you sure? There are many other shops. Perhaps we should look some more before making a decision."

She shook her head. "Nay," she said. "I like this one."

He wasn't going to argue with her. If she liked it, she liked it. "Do you want to look at anything else? Necklaces, perhaps?"

She took her eyes off the wedding ring long enough to glance at the other items the old man had. She veered off course and ended up back at the rings. Matthew watched her pluck a thick silver band from the collection. She looked up at him.

"Do you like it?" she asked timidly.

He lifted an eyebrow. "It is too big for you."

"I meant for you."

After a brief moment of realization, he snorted and removed his other gauntlet. He held up his left hand to her.

"Put it on."

Grinning shyly, she shoved the ring onto his enormous finger. He held his hand up, looking at it, acquainting himself with the feel of it. "It is as if it was made for me," he announced. "A perfect fit."

"Truly?"

"Truly." He kissed her, taking another look at her ring. "And this one is as flawless and delicate and beautiful as you are."

She smiled modestly; his compliments were coming to mean a great deal to her whereas once, she was suspicious of them. Matthew put his arm around her.

"Now you must pick out something else, otherwise I will feel very foolish," he said.

"Why?"

"Because we have only been here a matter of minutes and you have already made your selection. Caroline and Mark will think I have forced you into a quick decision simply to be done with it."

"We cannot let them think that," she leaned against him, gazing up into his strong face. "By all means, let us visit other stalls."

Matthew paid for the rings and they emerged back onto the avenue with their new-found adornments. As Alixandrea excitedly showed Caroline, Mark went over to his brother and peered at his ringed finger. He lifted an eyebrow and shook his head.

"Why did you let her talk you into that?" he snorted.

Matthew was not oblivious to how his brother felt about Alixandrea. It had been increasingly apparent since their father's accident, even though she had clearly been exonerated of any wrongful actions. Though Mark had mostly kept his opinions to himself, there were times when the truth broke through. Yet his behavior did not seem isolated simply to Alixandrea; he had been increasingly hostile to his wife as well. The more the wives were around, the more unhappy Mark seemed to be. Matthew knew his brother well enough to know why.

"I am proud to wear this," he told his brother. "If you had any sense, you would wear one, too."

Mark looked at him as if he'd lost his mind. "Why?"

Matthew lowered his voice. "Because you are married and I would ask, for the duration of this trip, that you at least act as if you are. I do not want to hear tale of your indiscretions with your wife in residence with you."

Mark's dark eyes cooled. "My activities are of no concern to you and you have always respected that. I would ask that you continue to do so."

"Not with Caroline present. What you do when she is at Wellesbourne and you are out and about is your business. But while she is here with you, I would expect you to honor your vows to her. If nothing else, to preserve the woman's dignity. She has tolerated far too much of your roving ways and has never said a word. The least you could do is show her a measure of respect while we are in London."

Mark did not back down. "You may give the orders on the battlefield or within the family, but when it comes to my marriage, I draw the line. You will not order me about in my own marriage."

"I will say no more," Matthew growled. "But I will tell you this; if Caroline comes to me in tears because of your lack of discretion, you will hear from me and it will not be pleasant."

Mark shook his head. "You have been married two weeks and you think to lecture me? You are the last person that I would take marital advice from."

"My marriage seems to be starting far better than yours did."

"Give it time. You have had a woman or two in your bed during your visits to London."

"Not while I was married."

Mark suddenly jabbed an angry finger in Alixandrea's direction. "By the law, if not by the law of God, you have been married to that woman for ten years and I know for a fact that you have bedded many a wench during that time. In fact, you cavorted quite seriously with Mena for a solid year without regard to your betrothal. So think not, brother, to lecture me on the sanctity of marriage when you smashed yours into the dirt for many long years and did so happily. Your self-righteousness makes me sick."

Alixandrea and Caroline, by now, were listening. With Mark's raised voice and Matthew's body language, it had not been difficult to hear or see what was going on. Alixandrea took the full brunt of Mark's last sentence, vicious and stormy as it was. He may as well have physically struck her; it would have done far less damage.

Alixandrea's gaze traveled between her husband and Mark before silently, with dignity, making her way back over to the carriage that sat parked along the edge of the avenue. Without a hind glance, she climbed inside and closed the door. With tears in her eyes, Caroline followed.

Matthew stood there a moment before closing his eyes, sickened by what his wife had heard, knowing the heated words had devastated her. He could not muster the strength to become angry with his brother; Mark had said nothing that was untrue.

Wiping a weary, remorseful hand over his face, he followed his wife's path back to the carriage. Looking in the cab window, he could see Alixandrea seated with her head hanging down. He could not see her face, but he could only imagine her expression.

"Alixandrea," he said quietly. "Mark was angry with me. He spoke... out of turn. If I could take back his words, I would surely do so simply to ease your heart."

Her slender shoulders shrugged. "It is of little matter."

It wasn't of little matter and they both knew it. "I am truly sorry if your feelings were hurt," he said. "Had I known he was going to explode at me, I would have stopped him before his words could reach your ears."

Her head came up and he was struck by the pain in her bronze eyes. He tore his gaze away from her long enough to look at Caroline.

"Will you leave us a moment?"

Caroline obediently climbed out of the cab. Matthew helped her to the street. He then climbed into the carriage, causing the thing to lurch dangerously under his weight. He was far too big to be in it. But he wasn't about to leave Alixandrea like this.

"Nothing he said was a surprise to you," he sat across from her, gazing into her pale, sorrowful face. "I cannot change the past, much as I would like to. But it was wrong of Mark to throw it in your face like that. He's angry with me, and because of it, he is trying to get back at me by hurting you."

She inhaled a long, deep breath. Her eyes moved to her new ring and she toyed with it, absently. "So her name was Mena."

"Aye."

"So now the reason has a name."

He sighed. "I told you that the reason no longer exists. I meant it."

"Were you in love with her?"

"I thought so at the time."

At least he was being honest. She could not fault him that. "Did you want to marry her?" she asked.

He lifted an eyebrow thoughtfully. "Strangely enough, not particularly. I thought that I was too young to marry. I did not want to marry anyone."

"Especially me."

"Especially you."

A tense hush fell over them, each lost to their own thoughts. Matthew was praying she would forgive the distress and Alixandrea was struggling to do so.

"We've known such joy over the past few days, Matt," she said softly. "I suppose I would like to think that we have both waited all of our lives for this time. I know I did. But I am also well aware that you did not. Hearing her name spoken... it was a bit of a shock. It somehow made her more human, not just a faceless, nameless ghost from the past."

He leaned forward, elbows resting on his knees. "I have said it before and I will say it again. I was a fool. Mark was right; I treated our betrothal horribly. I disrespected all that it should have stood for. I did not want to marry you and it was my own personal rebellion to live loosely before the bonds of matrimony could tie me down." He reached out, gently taking her hands and holding them tightly. "But do you know what? I was wrong. I was so wrong that I cannot even begin to comprehend what a complete idiot I was. Though the past cannot be erased, I will make you this promise for the future; I swear on my oath as a knight that I will never stray, that I will never disrespect you, that I will always be kind to you, and that I will love you for the rest of my life as deeply as any man has ever loved a woman."

Tears suddenly spilled over in her eyes as if a bucket had been dumped. They literally coursed down her cheeks. Matthew moved to sit beside her, taking her into his arms and ignoring the extreme rocking of the carriage. He held her close, his lips against her forehead as she wept softly against him.

"No tears, love," he murmured. "We have much happiness ahead of us. I swear that I will do my best to always give you joy."

She looked up at him, her cheeks wet, and he pulled his thumbs across her face to dry the tears. "You do give me joy," she whispered. "And I will love you too, until I die."

He smiled faintly at her, warmed by her words, warmed by the moment between them. Whatever feelings had been developing between them had now come full circle, anchoring deeply into their hearts, never to be cut loose. He did not care what his brother thought; he adored the woman and would be plain about it. His grin broadened.

"I do love you," he murmured.

"I love you, too."

He laughed softly before kissing her, so deeply that she had to pull away from him so that she could take a breath. He continued to kiss her, every part of her face and flesh that his lips could come into contact with.

"I will tell you this every day, so you had better become used to it," he murmured.

Her hands were on his face, his neck, as he forcefully kissed her. "It will never become tiresome, I assure you. Tell me with every breath you take and I shall be glad to hear it."

"Then do not let Mark, or anyone else, remind you of my horrid past. It is of no matter. All that matters is that I am your husband now and I worship you."

She nodded, overwhelmed by his attention, and he finally pulled away. He sat a moment, gazing at her.

"Do you know that I have never seen such a sweet face?' he asked with a twinkle in his eye.

She simply grinned at him, her lips red from his furious kisses. Matthew finally climbed out of the carriage and mounted his charger. He did not replace his left gauntlet; the hand and the ring remained exposed to the world the entire way back to the Tower.

CHAPTER TWELVE

The Tower of London was an enormous complex with catacombs of chambers, passages, halls and towers. A concentric fortress, it had gone through several building renovations since its original construction on the banks of the Thames beginning in the year 1066.

Alixandrea was overwhelmed with the sheer size of the place as Matthew brought their party through the gaping front gate, passing through the double-portcullis entry and then passing through another gate that led to the vast inner ward. Once through the second gate, he made an immediate left and headed for one of the massive inner towers. She would later learn that it was called the Wakefield Tower.

In the center of the courtyard sat an enormous pale-stoned structure four stories to the sky. Narrow, cylindrical towers marked the four corners, topped with turrets that were littered with black birds. Sun glinted off the roof, creating flashes of light. Matthew helped Alixandrea from the carriage and she nearly fell, not paying attention to where her feet were placed as she absorbed the enormity of the keep. It was mesmerizing. Matthew grinned as he helped Caroline from the cab.

"The White Tower," he told her before she could ask.

Alixandrea poked a finger at it. "That is the White Tower?"

"Aye."

It was a struggle to keep her mouth from hanging open. "It is colossal. I do not know what I had expected, but surely there is nothing larger in the world."

The men were moving around them, gathering capcases and other materials from the carriage. Alixandrea had to step out of the way or risk being run down by over-eager soldiers.

"I shall take you to it after we've had a chance to settle," Matthew said. "I would assume you would like to rest a while before this eve."

She turned to look at him. "What is happening this eve that I will need my rest?"

"A feast, of course. And I am sure that Richard will request an audience."

Her eyes widened. "The king?"

The corners of his mouth twitched as he pulled a small valise out of the cab and handed it to a waiting servant. It was as much of an answer as he would provide. Alixandrea had to remind herself yet again that The White Lord of Wellesbourne was at the right hand of the king. Until this moment, none of that had seemed real. It was tales she had simply heard of the man; now, however, she was about to become acquainted with the reality of his station. It was a heady awareness.

Mark suddenly rounded the corner of the cab, ripping off a gauntlet in a sharp move. His visor was raised, his dark eyes glaring like shards of obsidian. It was clear that he was still boiling over his confrontation with Matthew earlier.

"Caroline," he barked. "Come with me."

Matthew's smile faded as he watched Caroline meekly pursue her husband. Alixandrea watched also, almost daring Mark to make eye contact with her. He seemed to have an inordinate amount of hostility and she did not understand why.

"He is not angry with her, is he?" she looked at Matthew. "What has she done?"

Matthew's gaze lingered on his brother until the man disappeared from view around the side of the cab.

"She's done nothing," he said simply. "Come along, love. Let us get you settled into our rooms."

He took her hand and tucked it into the crook of his elbow. Alixandrea followed him to the enormous tower and into the stone-arched entry. It was cool and musty inside. They ascended the steps to the second floor, took a turn, and opened up onto an enormous corridor. It seemed to go on forever. They walked a nominal amount of time before coming to a great carved door, which was already open. There were servants milling around inside as Matthew ushered her into the room.

The chamber was done in the blue and white colors of the Wellesbourne crest, with expensive chairs arranged neatly in the center. A wide-mouth hearth blazed over to her left and a large tapestry of a knight astride a white horse covered one wall. There were all manner of plush furnishings that were unknown in the more austere, battle-oriented castles that Alixandrea had known. This place was made for comfort. Properly awed, she gawked as she studied the room.

"It is beautiful," she gasped. "Do you truly warrant such richness?"

Matthew grinned. "I am content in the knight's quarters, but somehow, I was issued these rooms at Richard's insistence. I rarely use them."

She shook her head, once again reviewing the opulence. "A pity," she sighed. "I have never seen such luxury. I fear I may become accustomed to it and grow irreversibly spoiled."

Coming up to stand behind her, he wrapped his arms around her, his face in the side of her head as he inhaled the delicate scent of her hair. "You would be the one person to truly justify such lavish attention," he said. "I would like to spoil you."

His hot breath against her head sent chills bolting down her spine. "Careful what you say. You may regret it."

"Never."

They shared a moment, briefly, before separating. There were too many people about and the nature of their relationship was still too new for blatant public displays of affection. Besides, Matthew did not want to create a spectacle for gossip-mongering servants.

As he moved to retrieve a small case that had been set on the floor, Luke and John were suddenly in the door, making their presence known by kicking aside one of the chairs that was too close to the entry. It crashed to the floor, taking a small table with it. Alixandrea frowned at the brothers, moving to right the table as John steadied the chair.

"You two are a pair of wild bulls," she said. "You must be more careful."

John grinned contritely while Luke, oblivious, went straight for Matthew.

"Much is going on, Matt," he said, his tone laced with quiet urgency. "The king would see you now. Gaston is already with him."

Matthew handed the case over to his wife. "You have been here a matter of minutes and already you know this?"

"Richard saw you come in through the gate," Luke replied.

At that moment, Mark's head popped into the doorway. "Matt," he said. "We've been summoned."

Matthew glanced over at his dark-haired brother; they were back in professional mode, the disturbances of earlier in the day forgotten.

"So I have been told," he said. He looked at Alixandrea, standing a few feet away with the case in her hand. She had been listening to the conversation. "I am afraid that I will have to leave you alone for a little while. Will you be all right?"

She nodded. "Of course. I have much unpacking to do."

"Good." His easy smile returned, briefly, and he gave her a wink. "Make sure that you do not leave this chamber until I return for you."

"Why not?"

"Because I ask this. Please."

There was something in his tone that precluded further argument. Alixandrea nodded her head, watching as her husband and Luke quit the chamber. John followed them out, giving her a small wave as he did so. She waved back and the door closed, leaving the chamber oddly still. There had been so much commotion just a few moments before that the sudden stillness was unsettling.

It took her a moment to get herself moving, realizing there was a lot of work to be done and no Jezebel to assist her. She had no idea where Caroline was. But standing just to the left of the chamber door were two female servants, workers at the Tower. They stood there, uncertainly, obviously waiting for direction.

She put her hands on her hips.

"Who are you?"

The first maid, a tiny woman with gray hair and very few teeth, bowed sharply. "Ann, m'lady."

The second woman, not quite so old and a little plumper, did the same. "Mary Joan, m'lady."

"Are you responsible for these chambers?"

"These and the three other Wellesbourne chambers when the lords are in residence, m'lady."

"Very well," Alixandrea said crisply. "As Lady Wellesbourne, you now take directives from me. Help me to get unpacked, and quickly, for I have a busy night ahead."

The women flew into action, an organized assault on the cases still left in the main chamber. They picked up what they could and disappeared into the door adjacent to the hearth. Alixandrea followed them into the smaller chamber beyond; there was a massive bed frame with only a mattress, a large wardrobe against the wall, and little else. Compared to the sitting chamber, the room was fairly plain but comfortable enough.

"We've not yet had the chance to make your bed, m'lady," Mary Joan said. "We only learned of your arrival a short time ago."

Alixandrea waved her hand at her, unconcerned. "I have no need for the bed at the moment. It can wait. But I do need to unpack and find my gold brocade surcoat."

The women nodded, throwing open the trunks and cases and beginning to lay forth garments to be put away. Alixandrea moved to help, but realized they were efficient in what they were doing. They did not need her help. In fact, they looked rather confused when she made the attempt. Not the least bit offended, Alixandrea wandered back out into the sitting chamber.

After a few minutes of drifting around, inspecting every piece of new-found furniture, she poured herself a measure of sweet red wine from the decanter in the corner and planted herself in one of those magnificent chairs. Feeling somewhat like the Lady of the Manor, deposited into affluence she had never before imagined, she settled down with her wine and her chair to enjoy the rest. It was just coming to dawn on her what being the wife of The White Lord of Wellesbourne would truly mean. And the thought was overpowering.

The next she realized, the sun was set, the room dark, and Mary Joan was waking her from a deep sleep.

***

"Henry has not yet left the shores of France, though all intelligence tells us that it is imminent. I fear what this summer will bring."

The voice was soft and somber. It also happened to come from the King of England. Richard III sat in his small solar, just off his bedchamber, a place that was both comforting and convenient and safe for him. He did not travel the halls of the Tower too often, for it had become a dangerous place with rival factions vying for control. Sometimes it was more dangerous than even the most violent parts of the city. These days, he tended to stay to his well-guarded chambers, but when he did go out in public, it was surrounded by a host of knights. He would take no chances.

The king had called his most powerful knights to his side as soon as they arrived at the Tower. Like an eager child, he was determined to see them and after the usual social pleasantries, he delved straight into business.

Much was at stake and there was no time to waste. Matthew leaned against the wall near the hearth while Gaston stood on the opposite side of the room, arms crossed and massive legs braced. Luke, John and Mark stood somewhat in the shadows, as did Patrick and Arik. Also present was Francis Lovell, Lord Chamberlain of the Royal household and one of Richard's closest advisors. He was young, intelligent, and loyal to the bone. But he was more a politician than a warrior, with sage advice for those who would actually see the field of battle. And as a ward of the Earl of Warwick, he had connections that were unsurpassed, making him an invaluable ally.

"When Henry does sail, we shall be ready for him, Your Grace," Matthew said quietly. "He has a sufficient build up in Gloucester, as we discussed earlier. And you have received our earlier intelligence, so you know as much as we do at this time."

"Something is building," Richard said quietly.

"Agreed," Matthew said. "But we are unsure what, exactly, it might be."

"Surely you have an opinion, Sir Matthew," Lovell spoke, moving to stand next to the king. It was an almost protective gesture. "Your military expertise is beyond question. Surely you have formed a judgment."

Matthew was silent a moment, his attention moving to Gaston. De Russe met his gaze steadily, and Matthew was fairly certain that, based upon all intelligence given at this time, they had come to the same conclusion. He felt confident speaking for them both.

"Henry will not land upon the shores of England," his voice was low and steady. "To do so would be foolish since the country is so blatantly divided. He cannot be guaranteed the support he requires. But Wales is not divided in the least; it is Beaufort's country and it is my estimation that he will make landfall in Wales, move east to his mother's property to gather her armies, and then sweep into England through the Marches and on to Gloucester to collect the mercenaries there. By that time, he will have acquired a substantial force and in perfect position to strike the heart of England."

Richard looked at Matthew with something of fear and resignation. "Where do our forces stand against him?"

Matthew lifted his eyebrows as he shifted on his big legs. "Warwick moves south to Gloucester, Norfolk moves west from his holdings, and de Russe and I move northwest. There are other armies poised to join us, but those are the main body of your forces at this time. We will converge on him and destroy him."

"Just like that?"

"In theory, Your Grace."

Richard folded his hands, his long, thin fingers wringing against each other. Then he stood up; he was short, rather pale and thin, making him appear older than his years. He liked to think that he was a great military tactician, when in fact, he depended on others to feed him ideas that he could claim as his own. He'd never seen a true battle, but insisted he controlled military engagements by virtue of his wishes. His military career was, at best, lackluster, which is why he depended heavily on men like Matthew Wellesbourne and Gaston de Russe. They were the heart of his forces.

"London is crawling with Tudor loyalists," the king muttered. "My glorious tournament is full of them. 'Twould seem they wish to make a statement against me and my allies by competing on the tournament field."

"Victory shall be yours, Your Grace," Gaston said, his voice low and reassuring. "I am competing, as is Matthew. There is not a man in London who believes any of Tudor's fools can outshine us. If a statement is what they want, a statement is what they shall have. We shall crush them."

Richard knew he had the strongest knights in the realm at his side. But he also knew that Henry Tudor had many powerful men in his favor also.

"Robert Montgomery is in London, champion of Somerset," he said. "So is one of Neville's men, Artur de Soulis. And Dennis La Londe has entered."

Matthew and Gaston exchanged surprised glances. They had not yet heard this.

"He serves Tudor directly," Matthew said. "That is a fairly audacious statement to have him compete."

"I saw him earlier today, here at the Tower," the king moved across the carpeted floor, his fine slippers making soft noises across the threads. He stopped at the window, glancing down to the courtyard below and watching the ravens feed. "He is big and he is dangerous. I am extremely uncomfortable with him residing within these walls."

"Do you wish for us to remove him, Your Grace?" Gaston asked.

Richard nodded without hesitation. "He stays here as a guest of Lord Grey of Northumberland. I want him removed."

"As you wish, Your Grace," Gaston replied. "I will see to it personally."

Richard felt better immediately. He turned away from the window, facing the room full of powerful men. Seeing their confident faces gave him courage. "Then it is settled," he said. "I will see you all at the feast tonight. I have a new cook all the way from the Holy Land and am anxious to show off his talents. Matthew, I understand that your have brought your new wife to London."

Matthew nodded. "I have, Your Grace. She is eager to meet you."

"As I am eager to meet her," Richard's gaze lingered on him. "I saw her from my window earlier when you arrived."

"I am sure you will approve of her, Your Grace."

Richard simply nodded. "Gaston's wife is also here," he said casually. "I am looking forward to more fair companionship than your own this eve."

Matthew looked strangely at Gaston, who refused to meet his eye. Only when they were out in the corridor with no one else around them did he speak.

"I thought Mari-Elle was in France," Matthew said.

Gaston watched his boots as they moved along the ground. "She was. She returned a few weeks ago. I have only made contact with her so that I could see my son."

"And how is Trenton?"

Gaston actually smiled. "Growing large. He is seven years old now."

"And Mari-Elle?"

Gaston's smile left him. "Still the same cold bitch she has always been."

Matthew did not want to get on to the subject of Gaston's wife. They had been pledged as children, married at a very young age, and completely resented each other.

Mari-Elle was high bred, cultivated, vain and cold. When Gaston married her, he had inherited her fortune, but it had been a price too high. It had taken almost ten years to produce their son, a boy in the image of his father. Considering the lovers Mari-Elle kept, Gaston had wondered if the boy was even his until he grew older and there was little doubt. He clearly adored the child. But Mari-Elle kept a separate life from her husband and kept the boy with her. The moments Gaston actually spent with him were precious and few. Gaston's marriage had been one of the main factors in Matthew's reluctance to marry Alixandrea; he had seen what a contract marriage could do. He never wanted to find himself in the same position.

"Well," Matthew continued after a moment's pause. "I look forward to seeing the lad. Will he be at the feast tonight?"

"Probably not," Gaston replied. "Mari-Elle keeps him locked away from me whenever she can."

"Then perhaps Alixandrea and I can visit him another time," Matthew tried to stay positive. "As it is, I suppose we shall be seeing Mari-Elle tonight."

"Unfortunately."

Matthew had nothing more to say on the matter. He felt deeply sorry for his friend; he always had, but such was the way of things. They came to a fork in the corridor; Gaston was to the right and Matthew to the left. They paused a moment to face each other.

"Until tonight, then," Matthew said. "I am looking forward to scoping out the room."

Gaston grinned. "No doubt. Speaking of such, I do believe I shall go find la Londe and throw him out into the streets."

"Need help?"

"I think I can take on la Londe by myself."

Matthew spread out his arms tauntingly. "But it would be so much more entertaining if we both did it."

Gaston laughed. "That may be, but I think I can do this without you. Go back to your wife and I will see you tonight." His smile suddenly faded, as if something had just occurred to him. "Matt, I hope that I am not speaking out of turn, but I would say something that has been concerning me for some time."

"What is it?"

"Mark does not seem too fond of your new wife."

Matthew's good humor fled. "I know," he said evenly. "I suspect he is upset with me because I have actually found happiness in my marriage where he has not."

Gaston shrugged in a gesture suggesting it was indeed possible. "Back at Rosehill he seemed very upset because you were not tending Adam every minute of every day. He further seemed to think that Adam's accident was your wife's fault. I would watch him if I were you."

"Mark?" he repeated doubtfully. "That is madness. He would never harm her."

"Maybe so. But I can promise you that he knows more about her disappearance from Rosehill than he told you."

Matthew's face clouded with confusion. "Why would you say that?"

"Because when I questioned him about her disappearance, a slip of his tongue gave him away. He told me that, although he knew nothing of her disappearance, she could keep running as far as he was concerned. It wasn't so much what he said, but how he said it. He saw something, Matt. I am not sure what it was, but he saw her leave Rosehill and I believe that he made a conscious choice not to tell you."

Matthew could only stand there and shake his head, slowly, as if reluctant to believe the worst. "You must be mistaken."

"Ask him. Oh, and Matt?"

"What?"

"Nice ring."

With that, The Dark Knight turned on his heel and moved down the dim corridor, heading for his chamber. Matthew stood there a moment, watching the massive figure disappear from sight. Only then did he turn on his own path, his mind full of their conversation.

He knew that Mark had no particular liking for Alixandrea and he furthermore knew why. But Mark was his brother, and they had seen much life and death together over the years. He loved his brother, and he knew him well. He simply could not believe that Mark would deliberately allow her to come to harm.

Or could he?

***

Alixandrea was dressed and waiting for Matthew when he arrived back at their chamber. It was warm and cozy inside, the fire blazing brightly in the hearth now that the sun had gone down. Clad in a soft white shift with a heavy and elaborate gold brocade surcoat, Alixandrea looked absolutely magnificent. The sight literally took Matthew's breath away when he walked in the door and saw her.

"My God," he breathed. "You are a glorious creature."

Standing by the cluster of fancy chairs, she grinned humbly. Mary Joan had curled her hair with a heated iron and cascades of spiral curls tumbled down her back while the front of her hair was secured off her face with a shell comb. Her face was scrubbed clean and rosy and her lips were saturated with the lip ointment she always used. She could see by the look on Matthew's face that her efforts had been worth the results.

"I hope you like it," she said. "I wanted to give a proper appearance our first night here."

"Have no doubt, lady, that you do," he moved towards her, drinking in the sight. "I will be the envy of every man in the room."

"Will you not dress?"

"I am," he held out his arms; in full armor, he looked every inch the fearsome warrior, not the elegant diner.

She frowned. "You intend to go like this?"

"Of course. How else would I go?"

She thought a moment and realized she really did not know. She had never been to a feast at the Tower and the knights she had known over the years had practically lived in their armor. It was common for them to dine in pieces of mail and protection.

"I suspect not all men will be dressed for doing battle with their beef knuckle," she said. "Or do you expect a military offensive tonight in the great hall?"

He laughed at her. "One never knows in this place. The Tower is known for its turmoil and treachery and I would rather be prepared." He took a step towards her, towering over her petite size. Taking her hands, he held them tightly in his own, bringing them to his lips for a kiss. "But for this night, I can guarantee that every eye in the hall will be trained on you. I have never seen such beauty."

She blushed delightfully. "You flatter me, my lord."

He moved down to kiss her but she turned her head and he ended up kissing her cheek instead. "I have ointment on my lips," she smacked her lips together. "Can you not see it?"

He lifted his eyebrow at her, disappointed. "I see it."

"I do not want to rub it off."

"You mean that you do not want for me to kiss you."

She smiled, putting her soft hand against his bristly cheek. "I always want for you to kiss me," she murmured. "But if you do, you shall come away with red lips. That would not do."

"I shall take my chances."

She giggled as he swooped down and kissed her deeply, tasting her sweetness with his unrelenting tongue. When he came away, it was to wipe his lips with his fingers and look at them.

"You still retain your red lips, madam, for I seem to have escaped them." As she laughed softly, he collected her wrap from the nearby chair. "If you are ready, Lady Wellesbourne, we should depart. A plethora of gluttony and extravagance awaits."

She allowed him to place her matching wrap over her shoulders and escort her from the room. The corridor outside was dim, lit only by occasional iron sconces spaced in intervals along the wall. She also noticed that there were several Wellesbourne soldiers lining the hall. As they drew near one end, John and Luke were waiting.

The youngest Wellesbournes rushed forward, pushing each other aside until Luke gave the final hard shove and managed to take his place on Alixandrea's free side. Dejected, John straightened his askew armor and his backbone and followed.

"My lady looks beautiful tonight," Luke said smoothly.

Before Alixandrea could reply, Matthew growled. "What did I tell you about flattering my wife?"

To everyone's surprise, Luke actually held his ground. "You had better become used to it, brother. Men will be salivating over her all evening."

Matthew glared at him menacingly but refrained from replying. Luke was, after all, correct. With a few Wellesbourne men-at-arms in tow, the four of them descended the steps in the Wakefield Tower and entered out into the cool evening of the courtyard.

The moon was nearly full, creating a ghostly glow across the landscape as they made their way to the White Tower. Mounting the wooden steps, they entered the second floor of the keep and into the great dining hall at the end of the short corridor.

The corridor had been relatively quiet, making the appearance into the great hall a bright and overwhelming experience. The hall was unusually hot, lit by a massive hearth that belched heat and smoke into the room. It was also littered with people, sitting at tables, clustered in groups talking, or just milling about. Servants were everywhere, carrying trays of alcohol to keep the diners happy until the king, and the food, arrived. It was, already, a hugely busy scene.

With Luke on one arm and Matthew on the other, Alixandrea walked into the room and nearly tripped on the rushes. They were in bunches around the floor. But Matthew's strong grip steadied her as he took her fully into the room, making sure to cross right through the center of the hall so that every man and woman there would see who had come. He continued to walk down the center of the room in full view, his hawk-like gaze sweeping the chamber, making note of who was in attendance and who was not. The White Lord of Wellesbourne had arrived and he would have no one mistake his presence. The major artillery in the arsenal of Richard had arrived.

To Alixandrea, it felt a little bit like a parade. She felt the gaze of everyone in the massive hall and she was torn between pride and the desire to hide. It was a fast introduction into the life of the Tower and ready or not, Matthew brought her full-force into it. All she could do was hold her head high and hold Matthew's arm tightly.

They made their sweep of the room and settled at a table near the royal dais. Matthew took her wrap and helped her to sit, carefully arranging the yards of material that comprised her surcoat. Luke was about to take a seat next to her but John, biding his time, beat him to it.

"Would you like some wine?" Matthew asked her, watching Luke rough up John's hair.

Alixandrea could see what the two younger brothers were doing out of the corner of her eye and she shook her head at the spectacle, amusing though it was. She could hear John yelp.

"I would."

He winked at her and motioned to a nearby servant, who introduced a rich red liquid into their chalices. He took his seat just as his cup was filled and he collected it, turning to his wife with a toast on his lips.

"To you," he said quietly.

She held her cup aloft also, her bronze eyes glittering. "To us."

"Even better."

They drank deeply of the heady port. All around them, the hall was bustling and Matthew sat very close to his wife, his eyes constantly on the move. Alixandrea alternately watched her husband and watched the room, finding it interesting how much his demeanor changed the moment they had entered the hall. Matthew was perpetually friendly, easy to smile, and companionable. But the moment he penetrated the room, it was as if a lever had been lifted and a curtain descended. His manner, his expression, turned hard. He changed into something dark and different. She wasn't sure if she liked it.

Gaston arrived a short time later. With him was a woman, very tall. She would have been beautiful had she not been so severe looking with her tight wimple and fussy clothes. Her features were fine and delicate, but there was little loveliness. Gaston introduced her as Lady de Russe. She coldly greeted Matthew, barely nodded to Alixandrea, and ignored Luke and John completely. From the moment she and Gaston sat at the table, they ignored each other as well.

While Gaston and Matthew settled into muted conversation, Alixandrea turned to John and Luke on her other side.

"Who are all of these people?" she asked. "Do you recognize anyone?"

John nodded. "There are many prominent people here," he pointed off to the right. "There is Lord Grey. He's from Northumbria, a kin to the Percys. He's a very powerful man. And there's Arundel off to his right."

Alixandrea's head bobbed and weaved as she attempted to get a good look at the small, fat Lord Grey and subsequently the short and red-haired Earl of Arundel. John sudden jabbed his finger in front of him, across the table.

"There's Sir John Tomalyn," he said. "He's a ferocious supporter of the crown. He spends most of his time with Robin of Riddesdale, but I do not see him yet."

Alixandrea had heard these names for most of her life. But fostering at Pickering and then sequestered at Whitewell had not given her the opportunity to experience anything other than short stories and tales of valor of these men. To her, they were faceless individuals. Now, the reality was materializing right in front of her and it was exciting.

"My lady," John's voice was suddenly low. "Don't look now, but I think we have a visitor."

She had no idea what he meant until she caught him rolling his eyes, directing her to look behind her. Slowly, she turned, wondering what on earth he could mean. She soon found herself gazing down at a skinny gray dog, sitting against the wall behind her. The moment she looked at the beast, its tail began thumping timidly against the floor. Big dog eyes glistened pitifully at her.

"God's Bones," she breathed, as if just suffering a great relief. "I thought it was something awful."

"It *is* awful. It is a dog and, as I recall, you do not like them."

She pursed her lips, passing the mutt another glance. "That may be true, but they certainly seem to like me. I could not seem to be rid of them at Wellesbourne. And now, with all of the people in the hall as targets, this dog picks me to harass."

John was grinning. "The dogs at Wellesbourne must be missing you horribly."

She simply shook her head, turned away from the dog, and reclaimed her chalice. She was about to take a sip when a voice from across the table caught her attention.

"Your garment is lovely, Lady Wellesbourne," it was a low female tone that addressed her. "Wherever did you get it?"

Alixandrea looked up into the tight face of Lady de Russe. "Thank you for your kind question, my lady," she replied steadily. "The fabric was purchased in Leeds and my maid sewed the gown."

Lady de Russe's dark eyes roved the surcoat appraisingly. There was a haughty manner about the woman. "Leeds, you say?"

"Indeed."

"I would have thought Paris."

"Nay, my lady."

With one last look, she turned her head as she spoke. "Stunning."

Alixandrea bobbed her head. "Your approval is most flattering."

That was apparently all Lady de Russe intended to discuss. She turned back to her wine, her dark eyes finding interest in everything other than the table she sat at. Alixandrea watched her profile for a moment, wondering how such a beautiful woman could be so frosty. It was clear that she had no use for anyone at the table, especially her husband, which Alixandrea found strange considering Gaston was extraordinarily attractive. She, too, turned back to her wine only to notice that the skinny gray dog was now seated at her elbow. She looked down at the beast and shook her head.

"See there," Luke suddenly hissed, leaning into John and practically shoving him over onto Alixandrea. Luke was pointing at something he very much wanted the others to see. "Dennis la Londe. Do you see him over there?"

Alixandrea had no idea who Luke was speaking of, but she obediently turned in the direction he was indicating. There were several people standing around, lords in their fine silks and a few fighting men who had not bothered to change from their armor as Matthew had done. In the midst of the group, she spied a large blond man whom she recognized.

"Which one is he?" she asked Luke.

Luke was not being very discreet as he pointed. "The big brute in armor. Blond hair. See him? He is a French mercenary with a bloodlust for English knights and a want to become powerfully rich. Rumor has it that he serves Henry Tudor directly."

Alixandrea realized they were speaking of the man that she recognized. "I know that man," she said. "His name is Phillip of Ypres. He has visited my uncle on occasion."

Luke and John looked at her as if she had lost her mind. John actually looked frightened. "Are you certain?" Luke asked.

"Of course."

"And he called himself Phillip?"

"Aye. Who is Dennis la Londe?"

Luke reached around her and tapped Matthew on the shoulder. Annoyed that his conversation with Gaston should be interrupted, Matthew gave his brothers an impatient glare.

"In a moment," he told them.

"Nay, brother, *now*," Luke said, firmly enough that Gaston's attention was upon them too. He pointed over at the group with Dennis in it. "The big knight in the middle of that group. Who is that?"

Matthew looked over, as did Gaston. When Matthew spied the object of their attention, his eyes narrowed dramatically. "You know who that is."

"I do indeed. But your wife seems to think it is someone else."

Matthew's attention riveted to her. "Do you know him?"

Alixandrea was actually intimidated by his tone. She had no idea what could possibly be wrong. "That is a knight who has visited my uncle on occasion. His name is Phillip of Ypres."

Matthew stared at her. "Are you sure?"

"Positive. I have dined with him once."

Matthew did not reply for a moment. He looked at his brothers, then finally at Gaston. "I thought you got rid of him," Matthew said to him.

Gaston's smoky eyes were steady, deadly. "I could not locate him. This is the first I have seen him."

Studying the expressions around the table, it was not difficult to discern what they were all thinking. If there had ever been any lingering doubt about Lord Ryesdale's change in loyalties, then it had just been irrevocably proven.

Dennis la Londe was Henry's loyalist to the core. Even so, Matthew could tell that Alixandrea truly had no idea about the man; she gazed up at her husband, wide-eyed, waiting. Under the table, he took her hand.

"That man," he began," is Sir Dennis la Londe. He is a mercenary knight, one of the most vicious men I have ever come across. He serves Henry Tudor, presumably because of the rewards Henry has promised him should he ever assume the throne. He is powerful, skilled, and extremely deadly."

Alixandrea looked back over at Dennis; the man was speaking seriously with a short man in ruby silks. She shrugged weakly. "If that is true, then I am at a loss for words," she said after a moment. "I truly had no idea."

"Did you have much contact with him?" Matthew asked, more gently.

She shook her head. "Nay. I have really only seen him twice and spoke to him briefly on both occasions. He seemed typical enough. He certainly never came across as a deadly mercenary."

"Because he is brilliant that way," Matthew said. "I will be honest when I say that I respect the man's abilities as a warrior and knight almost as much as I respect Gaston's. There are few peers at our level of expertise and Dennis is one of them."

Alixandrea looked away from Dennis, gazing up at her husband with an expression that caused him to feel inherent pity for her.

"I feel so foolish," she said quietly. "You have pointed out many men that are loyal to Henry Tudor whom I have seen within the walls of Whitewell. Had I only been more aware, more worldly, perhaps I would have known what my uncle was planning before I came to Wellesbourne and unknowingly attempted to bring ruin upon you. I swear, Matthew, I would have never come had I known."

He smiled at her, his blue eyes glimmering. "And I would have never had the joy of knowing you. Thank God you were not more aware."

She returned his smile, though there was little joy in it. "I am serious," she murmured, squeezing his fingers under the table. "I feel terrible about this."

He brought her hand up and kissed it, his gaze moving back to the room. "No need, love. 'Tis not your fault."

He continued to hold her hand as he resumed his conversation with Gaston. Meanwhile, King Richard made his grand entrance and worked the room as the pope would have worked an adoring congregation. Though Richard tended to be a suspicious and reclusive monarch, apparently this night he felt comfortable enough with the legions of armed men surrounding him to welcome his guests.

Both Matthew and Gaston noted that he seemed to be in a particularly good mood. They rose when the king approached the dais and went over to him as he took his seat. There was no mistaking the message that The White Lord of Wellesbourne and The Dark Knight were sending to the rest of the room; the king's greatest warriors were indeed present and they would tolerate nothing out of the ordinary this night. It was a show of force.

As the food was brought forth, it occurred to Alixandrea that Mark and Caroline where apparently not going to join them for the feast. She was lonely in that she did not have Caroline to talk to, for the only other female at the table, Lady de Russe, had left the table and disappeared into the crowd. John and Luke were playing some sort of game beside her and punching one another intermittently, and Matthew was busy with Gaston. There was no one for her to talk to.

But she did not feel too sorry for herself. As she nursed her wine, servants descended on their table and adorned it with all manner of succulent food. A roast bird was the highlight, set in the middle of the table and festooned with glorious feathers to simulate that it was still a living bird. Luke and John immediately plowed into the fowl and destroyed the careful decorations before Alixandrea could get a good look at the artwork. John plopped a leg on her trencher and thought he was doing a splendid job of playing host. She smiled her thanks and took a helping of the boiled apples.

Plate full, she looked to her husband, still on the dais talking to the king, to patiently wait for his return. After several minutes, it was clear that he was not returning any time soon so she decided to eat before her food cooled. In the gallery, a group of minstrels began to play, filling the warm, smoky hall with music. In all, it seemed to be settling down into a glorious evening. She only wished she could have enjoyed it more with Matthew.

Out of the corner of her eye, she caught sight of Mark, Caroline, and an unidentified woman entering the hall. It did not matter that they were late; she was glad to see them and waved. But Mark did not see her and she elbowed John so that the young man could catch their attention.

Finally, Mark noticed them and headed in their direction. Caroline and the mystery woman followed. The closer they came, the more Mark seemed to be intently searching for someone. He ignored the Wellesbourne table completely. That wasn't unusual in itself, but Caroline's expression seemed to be; Alixandrea noticed that the woman hadn't looked at her once. She and the unknown woman held each other by the arms, pacing after Mark. As the group neared the table, Mark located Matthew on the dais and apparently found who he was looking for. He went straight for the platform and the women followed.

Alixandrea watched curiously as Mark addressed Matthew, who turned from the king to face his brother. But what she wasn't prepared for was the expression on Matthew's face; his eyes widened, then hardened, and his entire face seemed to tense. She could not hear the words being spoken, but she could tell by his expression that he clearly was unhappy. Alixandrea put her knife down and stopped eating; she wondered what had Matthew so upset. After a few exchanges, Mark, Caroline, and the nameless woman left the hall. Matthew watched them go. Then he looked at Alixandrea.

She was gazing up at him with those great bronze eyes. Matthew suspected she had seen everything; from her expression, he could tell that she had. Struggling for composure, he went back to their table and took his seat beside her. Before she could ask questions, he picked up the wine pitcher.

"More wine, love?" he asked even as he poured into her cup.

"Where did Mark and Caroline go?" she asked the obvious. "Why did they not stay?"

Matthew set the pitcher down and reached for a side of bird. "Caroline is not feeling well."

Alixandrea did not believe him; moreover, there was something strange in his manner. Odd suspicion crept into her veins, intangible yet unmistakable. "She looked fine," she said slowly, watching his features for any reaction. "Did you have sharp words with Mark again?"

Matthew had a mouthful. "Nay."

He was being evasive and it inflamed her. He had barely spoken to her all night and now he was being ambiguous. She turned back to her plate, though she did not eat. Matthew was fully into his meal before he noticed that she was not partaking.

"What's wrong?' he asked. "Why are you not eating?"

She looked away from him. "I am not hungry."

He studied her, noting her body language, sensing she was miffed. He swallowed the food in his mouth.

"What is the matter?" he asked, more softly.

"Nothing."

The room around them was full of food, fragrance, conversation and music. But it all ceased to exist as Matthew focused on his wife's crisp manner. The mood was bad between them and he did not like it. He felt responsible somehow, uncertain. When he should not have cared, he found that he did, very much. He abruptly stood up and collected her wrap.

"If you are not hungry, then I shall escort you back to our apartment."

Furious for reasons she did not quite understand, she stood up, accepted the wrap, and allowed him to take her from the hall. Something was building in her veins and she was unsteady with it. The moment they left the White Tower and entered the cool, dark yard, Matthew spoke.

"I will say something here and now, madam," his voice was a rumble. "If this is to be a successful marriage, then there must be total truth between us. You are obviously upset over something and I would know what it is."

She came to a halt, facing him. Her lovely face was taut. "How dare you lecture me on truth. You did not tell me the truth when I asked you if you and Mark had exchanged more harsh words."

He cleared his throat. "We did not exchange harsh words. We...."

She turned on her heel and began to march away. But Matthew lashed out and grabbed her arm, snapping her back against him. He held her fast, his face looming menacingly above her own. For the first time, Alixandrea could see the deadly warrior in him. This was the man that all men feared. It was harsh and terrifying.

"You will never walk away from me in anger," he growled. "Is that clear?"

"Or what?" she asked. "Will you unleash your deadly power on me as you would an enemy?"

He stared at her, his eyes narrowing. She could see that he was genuinely baffled. "What have I done to make you so angry with me?"

It all came spilling out. "You must ask this question? You

ignore me all evening and when I ask you why Mark and Caroline do not stay, you are deliberately evasive with me. What am I to you, Matthew? Just a pretty woman on your arm, a wife in name and body only, or do you intend to make me a confidant and companion as well? Tell me now, husband, so that the next time you parade me around for show, I will know that it is only for show and not because I have your true love, respect and intimate trust. Tell me now what you truly expect of me so that I will not ask questions in the future that you have no intention of answering."

His gaze lingered on her. The grip on her arms loosened and she pulled away when she thought she could get away with it. She heard him sigh heavily.

"I expect you to be my wife."

"What does that mean?"

"Precisely that. I told you that I loved you; wasn't that enough?"

She thought she could respond with confidence and maintain her composure. But his simple words had her heart breaking and she broke into quiet tears. Matthew could not stand to see her weep and he went to her, standing so close that he could smell her.

"What have I said?" he begged softly. "What have I done now?"

She sobbed into her hand. "I do not want to be a wife in name and body only," she wept. "Forgive me, but I want to be the person closest to you in every way. I want to know your thoughts, your fears, your hopes, and your dreams. If I ask you a question, I want the respect of an honest answer without hesitation. I want to be a part of you, Matthew, as you are indelibly a part of me. I would deny you nothing. I want to be all to you as you are all to me. To tell me that you love me is not enough. It is not enough at all."

He put his arms around her, willing to take the chance that she would resist him. But she did not, collapsing against him and pressing her sweet body close. He rested his chin on the top of her head, feeling her soft and heaving flesh in his embrace.

"It is you who must forgive me," he whispered. "This is all so very new to me. I have not the experience in this territory to know enough to plot a smooth path. To tell you of my love for you was the biggest step I have ever taken, but I suppose that I do understand it is not enough. There is so much more. I would tell you my dreams and hopes and fears, but you must be patient with me. There may be times when it does not occur to me to do so out of sheer ignorance. And if I do not tell you something, perhaps it is because I am trying to spare you. You have very quickly become my all for living and I pray that you forgive my ineptness in showing it. I will endeavor to do much, much better if you will only make gracious allowances, madam. You are far wiser in these matters than I."

She looked up at him, her cheeks wet with tears. As always, Matthew knew the right thing to say. It was becoming a habit with him.

"I am not wiser," she sniffled. "Perhaps I want too much, what you cannot give."

"I will give you whatever you want, I swear it."

She smiled wanly and he wiped her cheeks with his thumbs, kissing the moisture away from her wet eyes.

"Now tell me the truth," she said quietly. "Why did Mark and Caroline leave?"

The warmth in his eyes faltered. "Because I asked them to."

"Why?"

There was no way around it. He had to tell her if there was ever any hope of having the marriage they both seemed so badly to want. "I was attempting to spare you, love."

"Spare me what?"

He swallowed hard; she saw him. "The woman with them is Lady Caroline's cousin."

It meant nothing to her. "And?"

He seemed to hesitate. "Caroline's cousin is Lady Mena."

At first, it did not register. Her gaze remained steady. Then, her eyes widened and he could see the naked struggle within her not to react. It was a difficult task. But she held herself admirably in possession of knowledge that, had the situation had been reversed, he might not have held so steady. He admired her control greatly.

"I... I did not get a good look at her," she said evenly. "Caroline never mentioned that Mena was her cousin."

"Perhaps because she did not feel it was her place. That should have come from me and it never seemed to be the right time to bring it up."

"I see," Alixandrea's jaw flexed. "Did you know she would be here tonight?"

He shook his head. "I have not seen her in almost ten years. I had no knowledge that she would be here. The last I heard, she had married and moved to Bath."

She believed him. Matthew was not the lying kind. Taking a deep breath to steady her composure, she forced a smile. "Then you should have asked them to join us. Since you thought so highly of her, I would be delighted to meet her."

He gazed down at her, a finger coming up to stroke her cheek, her chin, and finally her lips. When he was unsatisfied with his finger on her mouth, he leaned down and kissed her.

"Perhaps you shall," he murmured against her mouth, "for certainly, I would be proud to introduce you."

They embraced in the darkness, enjoying the continued discovery of one another. Alixandrea realized that their infant relationship had already suffered several issues that could have greatly upset another couple, one less durable. But they seemed to work through the matter and grow stronger with it. As long as they were willing to talk, and as long as they held each other in such regard, she was confident their progression would continue.

As they wandered back to their apartment for the night, eyes were watching them from the shadows. It was a single figure, large, that had no intention other than to observe for the moment.

La Londe would wait to make his move.

CHAPTER THIRTEEN

Alixandrea sat with her hands over her face, terrified to peer out of her splayed fingers. Alone in the lists at the tournament field about a mile to the west of the Tower of London, she was supposed to be watching Matthew practice. But she hadn't been able to summon the courage to do so. Every time he garnered a starting position along the guide of the joust rail, she would cover her eyes and lower her head.

Matthew made three passes against John without incident to either one. He was well aware of what his wife was doing. It only made him grin. After the third pass, he directed his massive charger up against the lists.

"Alix," he admonished softly. "Take your hands from your eyes, love. Look at me."

She did, blessing him with a radiant smile. He laughed at her. "What are you doing?"

She grimaced. "I am watching you practice."

"Nay, you are not."

"Trust me, I can see everything."

He just shook his head, still laughing. "I do not know how that is possible, considering every time I have seen you it has been with your hands pressed so tightly to your face that you must surely be losing circulation."

She started to laugh. "I told you that the joust frightens me."

"If this gentle game upsets you so, how are you going to react when you see me compete in the mêlée? That can be even bloodier."

"I shall watch that spectacle the same way I watch this one. Through my fingers."

His wriggled his eyebrows. "Perhaps that is because you do not understand these events," he said helpfully. "I should be happy to explain the rules of the joust so that you will not be so fearful of it."

She stood up, winding her way through the benches until she reached the edge of the platform. "Very well, husband. Explain. Though I will not guarantee it should ease my fears."

He pulled off a heavy glove and reached out, taking her hand.

"Allow me to try, at least," he said. "A match is comprised of three passes against your opponent, or glances as they are called. You may score one point for breaking a lance between the waist and neck. You may score two points for breaking your lance against the helmet or for actually knocking off a helm. Once a helm is off, your opponent cannot replace it, increasing the chances of forfeiture and, consequently, your victory. Three points are awarded for knocking your opponent off his horse. Additionally, should you unseat him you not only win the match, but his horse as well. Do you have any questions?"

She looked thoughtful. "What if you do not break a lance at all? What if you simply pass each other and no harm is done?"

"Then no one scores."

"And no one gets hurt."

His grin was back. "True enough. But where is the fun in that?"

She feigned horror, watching him laugh at her. He brought her hand up to his lips, kissing the soft flesh gently. "Go take your seat, love. Gaston should be here any moment and it has been years since we've squared off against one another."

Her horror remained, only now it was real. "You are not going to practice against him, are you? Matt, he's enormous. He'll... he'll..."

"He'll...what?" he lifted an eyebrow, urging her to finish her sentence. "He cannot unseat me. He never has."

She did not look entirely happy. He kissed her hand again, put his glove back on, and spurred his charger back to the corner where Luke and John were congregating along with a host of Wellesbourne squires. Alixandrea resumed her seat in the lists; this time, she put her pocket kerchief over her head to cover her face completely. She could hear Matthew laughing all the way across the field.

His laughter made her smile. She sat there, listening to it, gazing into the white fabric in front of her face. Suddenly there was movement on the seat next to her and she pulled off the handkerchief to find Caroline standing there. On the field, Mark entered from the gates on his red destrier and charged across the field in the direction of his brothers. She smiled up at Caroline.

"Good morn to you," she said. "I was simply taunting Matthew with my fear for his safety."

She waved the kerchief around to prove her point and Caroline smiled wanly. "I do not like tournaments, either. They are brutal things."

Alixandrea nodded, noting that Caroline looked rather pale. "I missed you last night. You left before we could speak."

Caroline's weak smile faded. She stammered. "I... that is to say, I...."

"Where is your cousin?" Alixandrea would not let the woman suffer for one moment. It was apparent that she was uncomfortable. "I was looking forward to meeting her."

Caroline's pale face washed with surprise. She fidgeted a moment before pointing weakly behind her. "I have brought her," she said, almost painfully. "She does not know anyone and I thought it would be rude to leave her alone and..."

Alixandrea stood up, catching her first real glimpse of Lady Mena standing several feet behind Caroline. It was a bit of a shock, but not too terribly. In fact, she was rather curious. Mena was indeed a pretty girl with auburn curls and green eyes. She had a delicate face that held a timid expression. Alixandrea waved the woman over.

"Come, my lady," she invited. "Sit with us. We are about to watch a horrid spectacle."

Mena seemed to relax. In fact, she smiled, a pretty gesture. Alixandrea could see why Matthew had been smitten with the woman; she was indeed an appealing little thing. And she oddly felt no jealousy at all. In fact, she was quite happy to make the woman's acquaintance.

"Thank you, Lady Wellesbourne," Mena said gratefully. "It is indeed an honor."

Alixandrea was feeling rather proud of herself for handling the situation so well. Caroline was at ease, Mena was at ease, and she was sure they would all become great friends. That is, until Mena held out her hand in the direction of the steps, motioning to someone who was apparently standing just out of her line of sight.

Suddenly, a blond-haired girl leapt onto the lists and clasped Mena's hand. The child could not have been more than eight or nine years of age and when the little girl turned to look at her, Alixandrea felt all of the blood rush out of her face. She could not breathe. For staring at her from the face of that small child were Matthew's eyes. They were absolutely unmistakable and the wave of shock that washed over her almost had her reeling.

But she fought it. She would not let the blow claim her, no matter how severe. *'Tis not possible,* she thought as she gazed at the tow-headed girl. But her logical mind told her that there could be no mistake. Alixandrea's composure slipped rapidly as the child approached. Her heart was pounding so loudly in her ears that she could hardly hear the introduction.

"My lady," Mena said. "This is my daughter, Audrey. I hope you do not mind if she joins us also. She is eager to see her first tournament."

Alixandrea felt dizzy. The child even had Matthew's mother's name. The little girl dipped into a practiced curtsy and spoke in a soft, sweet voice.

"Greetings, Lady Wellesbourne."

Head swimming, overwhelmed with what she was confronted with, Alixandrea somehow managed to respond. It was a sheer testament to her willpower.

"Welcome, Audrey. What... what pretty hair you have."

Audrey grinned brightly. It was Matthew's grin. Alixandrea nearly came apart; it took every ounce of control she possessed to maintain her poise. As Mena and Audrey sat down, she turned her attention back to the field where her husband and his brothers were congregated.

Alixandrea could see Matthew speaking with Mark; she could further see when Matthew's helmed head snapped in the direction of the lists. He drove his spurs into the side of his charger so hard that she was positive that he had gored the animal. The beast jumped violently and raced across the field, almost crashing into the lists in its haste.

Matthew threw up his visor, his blue eyes enormous pools of astonishment as his gaze moved from Alixandrea to Mena and finally to Audrey. He did not say a word; he did not have to. He just gawked. But his actions, at that moment, told Alixandrea everything she needed to know.

He hadn't known.

Shaking, unsteady, Alixandrea stood up. She did not know what else do to. "My lord, I believe you already know Lady Mena. This is her daughter, Audrey."

Matthew stared at the little girl as she stood up and gave him a smart curtsy. He still did not speak, clearly unable to. The women sat with bated breath, wondering how he was going to react to the obvious; each and every one of them, in their own way, knew the situation for what it was. But no reaction was immediately forthcoming from Matthew.

After what seemed like an eternity, he pulled off his gloves, dismounted his steed, and vaulted onto the platform. He stood before the ladies, silently towering over them. When he finally did sit down, it was directly in front of Alixandrea. He reached out and took her hand; his grip was clammy and quivering. She held his hand tightly.

It was a pivotal moment. Alixandrea could see what had happened, and all that had happened. Matthew was shaken to the core at what he was confronted with. Perhaps Lady Mena had come to tell him last night at the feast and Matthew, fearing for Alixandrea's reaction, had chased her away. He never gave her the chance. Perhaps Mark had also been trying to tell him, but he sent his brother away. Matthew said he hadn't seen her in almost ten years, so he surely could not have known about the daughter he had clearly fathered.

Alixandrea did not know all of the facts or reasons, but one thing was clear; Matthew needed her support, not her distress. She squeezed his hand tightly for strength, for comfort. He responded by squeezing so tightly that he almost broke her fingers.

"Lady Audrey has never seen a tournament before," Alixandrea said to Matthew. "Surely you are honored that she has chosen to make your match the very first."

Matthew cleared his throat; even so, his voice was hoarse when he spoke. "Of course," he said. His eyes were riveted to the child. "Is this your first time to London also, my lady?"

Audrey was, in every sense of the word, an adorable child. She smiled, displaying a shadow of her father's dimples.

"It is," she said. "Mother and I came to visit and we saw that Cousin Caroline was here also. Yesterday, we saw a circus with monkeys and dancing horses, and today I am going to see a tournament!"

Matthew looked as if he were going to cry. Alixandrea looked at him, watching his eyes grow moist at the first sound of his child's voice, and she hastened to lighten the mood for his sake. He was an emotional man as it was and she did not want him to embarrass himself.

"Surely you must come and visit us at the Tower," she said to Audrey, to Mena. "Where are you staying?"

"In town, with my husband's sister," Mena said; she, too, was having a difficult time looking at anything other than Matthew. "She lives a few miles from the Tower."

"Is your husband here?"

"He has business at the ports." Mena tore her gaze away from Matthew long enough to look at Alixandrea. "He is a merchant, my lady. Usually he comes to London on buying trips alone, but this time, we begged to come and he agreed. We saw the Wellesbourne army arrive two days ago and I sent word to the Tower to see if Caroline was in residence. Fortunately, she was. I have not seen my cousin in many years, and she has never even met Audrey."

It explained a great deal. Alixandrea felt no anger, no jealousy, only tremendous pity for her husband and the little girl he never knew. She thought that, perhaps, Matthew needed a private word with Mena. It would seem that much had happened he did not know about, and she had not told him. She was undisturbed at the thought of leaving them alone for a few moments. It was the right thing to do. Abruptly, she stood up.

"Audrey, do you like custard?" she asked.

The little girl nodded. "Aye."

Alixandrea held out a hand to her. "May I take you to the custard vendor? He is just around the corner. I saw him earlier. I have been dying for sweets all morning. Would you like to come?"

Audrey jumped up eagerly, but rightfully remembered her mother. "Mummy, may I?"

Mena was clearly unsteady, but she nodded. "Not too much, darling. It will give you a belly ache."

Alixandrea took the little girl's hand, simultaneously reaching down for Caroline. "You, too, my lady," she said crisply. "I may want more than one sweet and I will need more hands to carry them. Come along."

Caroline did not argue. She bolted up from her seat and dutifully followed Alixandrea and Audrey from the lists.

Suddenly alone, Matthew and Mean simply sat there, each one of them not daring to look at the other just yet. It was an odd and painful silence that filled the air between them until Matthew finally shattered the spell.

"My God, Mena," he breathed. "Why didn't you tell me?"

She smiled, with irony. "Tell you that I was pregnant when we parted or tell you before now that you had a daughter?"

He did look at her, then. "Both," he hissed. He reached up and unlatched his helm, pulling it off irritably and setting it at his feet. "You should have told me you carried my child. It was my right to know."

"Why?" she whispered. "You could not marry me. Your father had already betrothed you to Lady Alixandrea. What good would it have done other than to make you miserable and guilty?"

He could not disagree. "At least I could have taken care of you."

She smiled sadly, shaking her head. "I did not need to be taken care of. I needed a husband and Audrey needed a father."

"I *am* her father," Matthew blurted, then caught himself before he could say too much. He was bordering on anger and resentment. "You even named her Audrey, after my mother."

She nodded. "Lest you forget, I knew your mother, Matt, and I adored her. She is like my Audrey in every way."

Matthew did not know if he felt better or worse. He could only imagine his father's reaction if he knew, a blond girl that looked exactly like his dead wife. But the thought was too overwhelming for him at the moment and he chased it away. His mind was brittle enough.

"And your husband?" he asked. "Does he know the child is not his?"

"He knows," she said, averting her gaze. "We met after Audrey was born. I told him that my husband had died and he raised Audrey as his own. She has known no other father but him."

Mathew could see the logic in that but it still hurt. "But she is mine."

"In blood only, Matt."

He did not have a good argument to that. He knew she was right but he was struggling against it. "Is... is he good to her?"

"He could not love her more if she was his own flesh. She is very much spoiled."

Tears sprang to his eyes but he blinked them away, quickly. "She's beautiful," he said hoarsely. He looked up at her. "And she's a Wellesbourne."

Mena stood her ground. "She is a Cuthbert."

"She's my child."

"She's *my* child."

His emotions were reeling, feeding his mounting frustration. "So you would keep her from me?"

"I will not disturb the only life she has ever known," Mena said steadily. "Matt, had we not happened to contact Caroline, you still would not know about her. It was my intention that you should not because I know how you are. You are possessive. And I shall not let you take her away from me."

He softened somewhat. "I do not want to take her away from you. But I think it only right she knows who her real father is."

"Right for who? For you?' Mena shook her head. "You must think of Audrey. To tell her that right now would completely disrupt her life. Is that what you want? To upset her so?"

He just sat there, thinking on her words, not wanting to admit she may be right. He reached down and picked up his helm. "Nay," he breathed. "I would not upset her."

Mena could see how badly he was hurting. She was hurting, too, but she was also doing what she believed best for her child.

"Perhaps I will tell her someday, Matt," she said softly. "But not right now. She is too young. She would not understand."

He could feel the tears and did not try to stop them. He looked up at her, his eyes brimming. "May I at least talk to her?"

Mena reached out and touched his hand; he put his big one over hers. It was simply a comforting touch of old friends. "Of course," she said softly. "I would encourage you to. She's a wonderful child."

He wiped at the tears quickly, struggling to recover what was left of his shattered self-control. Mena, thankful he was calming, removed her hand.

"Your wife seems like a lovely lady," she said, changing the subject. "She is quite kind."

"Aye, she is," Matthew wiped at his nose and plopped his helm back on his head. "I am very fortunate to have married her."

Mena grinned. "Sorry to say, that is not what you thought ten years ago."

He looked at her, sharply, but they both knew that she was correct. He broke down in a weak smile. "Indeed. But I was wrong. More wrong than you can know. She is a magnificent woman."

"Then I wish you all of the happiness in the world," Mena said sincerely. "May you have many Audreys in the future."

"Now you sound like Aunt Livia."

"Is that old bird still alive?"

"Still."

They shared a nervous laugh just as Alixandrea, Audrey and Caroline returned. Alixandrea's concerned expression was eased when her husband called her over. She slid her hand into his outstretched one, her gaze moving anxiously between Mena and her husband.

"Is everything well?" she asked him quietly.

He nodded, standing up and kissing her hand more tenderly than she could ever remember. His blue eyes were warm and loving upon her; she could literally feel his adoration reaching out to embrace her. But before she could say any more, he looked to Audrey, now happily shoveling custard into her mouth. His gaze softened as a twinkle came to his eye.

"Young lady, if you have come to see a match, let me see if I can give you a good one," he said as he moved to the base of the platform. "I shall unseat all of my brothers just for you."

"And take their horses?" she asked, her mouth full.

He laughed. "So you know something of tournaments, do you?" he said. "Well, I shall try, but I doubt my brother Mark will go down without a fight. He will try to unseat me first."

"Send him to the ground, my lord," she instructed, extending her wooden spoon at him imperiously.

"It shall be done."

Audrey exclaimed gleefully as Matthew mounted his charger and rode off across the field. Alixandrea could not remember ever seeing him so happy about anything.

***

He thrust into her repeatedly, listening to her soft moans with every contact, every hint of friction. The firelight from the dying hearth illuminated her beautiful breasts as they quivered with every measured stroke he delivered. It became mesmerizing to watch her move, her eyes closed to the joy of his touch, experiencing the magic he seemed to cast upon her.

Matthew's hands were on her buttocks, holding her to him as he drove into her time and time again. Alixandrea's hands were on his neck, holding him fast as their bodies melded into one heart, one soul. When he finally found his release, she was able to match him. Bodies shuddered, sweat glistened, and Matthew gathered her up against him and held her close.

It was the fourth time they had made love that night. It had started just after supper and now continued well after midnight. Matthew was insatiable; she had been naked and in bed since sunset with his body over her or in her one way or another.

There was more than passion to his touch; there was wonder and excitement and an odd desperation. Though she did not mention it to him, she could feel it. Somehow, he was feeling pain and she thought she knew why. When he flipped her over onto her stomach and took her a fifth time for the night, she simply surrendered. He did not want to talk, he wanted to touch, and she would let him for as long as he needed to.

Somewhere during the night, they slept wrapped in each other's arms. Alixandrea awoke to him making love to her again, and he took her twice as the sun rose. By the time the dawn was upon them, she was exhausted but in a good way. She thought to herself that she would need to sleep all day to recover from the active night.

He never let her out of his arms, his face buried in her neck. They were swathed in linens, burrowed warm and cozy in the heavy bed. She rolled over onto her left side, gazing at his dozing face. He looked so peaceful. His blue eyes finally opened and fixed on her.

"Good morning, Lady Wellesbourne," he murmured.

"Good morning, my lord," she smiled at him. A hand came up to touch his cheek, his brow, moving across his face. "You surely must be exhausted."

He grinned, his eyes closing. "Not at all. I feel remarkable."

"You have a tournament today."

"Indeed I do. Are you planning on watching or will I have the shame of my wife in the lists with her hands over her eyes?"

She giggled. "I will watch, I promise."

He pulled her close, kissing her until he grew hard again and his passion begged for release. He took her for an eighth and final time, listening to the birds outside the window as the day began to deepen.

Alixandrea lay in bed, spent, as he rose to relieve himself in the chamber pot. There was a basin of cold water and a cake of soap on the vanity near the massive wardrobe; she studied his naked body as he made his way over to the water and proceeded to wash himself. He had magnificent form; tight buttocks, muscular legs, a slender waist and wide shoulders. Though she'd never before seen a naked man, she had very quickly learned to admire Matthew's nude form and he wasn't shy about parading around in it.

With a small bronze mirror and sharp edged razor, he shaved in the cold water, remarkably not cutting himself. He did not care if the water was warm or not and did not want the interruption of a servant bearing hot water. Properly cleaned and shaved, he faced his wife as she lay wrapped up in the linens. He smiled at her.

"Are you going to lie there all day?"

She stretched wearily. "I would if I could."

He went over to the bed and smacked her lightly on the backside. "You cannot," he said firmly. "The tourney is in two hours and I need you up and dressed."

She sat up, her glorious bronze hair mussed and her delectable white shoulders revealed. He looked at her and groaned.

"God's Bones," he muttered. "Hurry up and get dressed before I am back in that bed with you."

She grinned. "Are you saying that you have not had enough of me yet?"

"I will never have enough of you. Get up before I get you out of bed myself."

She started to crawl out of bed, the linens still wrapped around her. "It is cold and I want a bath. I promise I shall make it fast."

He found his leather breeches and pulled them on. "You'd better." He went in search of his tunic. "I have to go over to the field but I shall return in time to escort you there. Can you be ready in an hour?"

"Hour and half."

"Hour and fifteen minutes."

"Very well."

"Good girl."

He found the tunic, pulled it on, and went for his boots. He sat on the edge of the bed to pull them on and she crawled next to him, watching. When he was done, he gazed at her as if beholding something more beautiful than anything man could have ever created in his mind. He cupped her face gently, kissing her tenderly.

"I shall be back for you."

He went to the door but she stopped him before he could leave.

"Matt?"

He paused. "Aye?"

"Please be careful today. I would have you safe and whole in my arms by evening's end."

He grinned. "I shall endeavor to do my best."

"I do love you, husband."

"And I love you."

The door closed behind him. Alixandrea leapt out of bed, still wrapped in the linens, and rang for Mary Joan and Anne. Within fifteen minutes, she was in a hot tub and in danger of a vigorous scrub-down.

***

The day was brilliant for the tournament and the lists were jammed with nobility and peasants alike. Banners waved in the breeze, snapping against the clear blue sky. The southern end of the field was standing room only and it was packed with peasants that had not been able to get into the lists. All along the outskirts of the field, people milled and vendors wandered through the crowd, selling mulled wine and other food items. It was already a busy, exciting day.

Alixandrea sat in the lists off to the left of the king's box. Clad in a pale blue silk surcoat with an undertone of green, she was accompanied by Audrey, Caroline and Mena. Audrey sat between Alixandrea and her mother, chewing happily on spun sugar and pointing out all of the knights that she could see. Some were cantering in around the field to warm up the horses, but most were stationed on the north edge of the field, preparing for their match. Alixandrea had a clear view of Matthew and his brothers, gathered near the north entrance. Every so often, he would look over at her and wave. She would wave back.

There would be twelve knights competing in the first round. Since this was such a highly contested tournament, only the best of the best were competing. Champions from Arundel, Somerset, Devon, Caernarfon, Leicester and other big houses were slated against one another. Matthew rode for Thomas Beauchamp, Earl of Warwick, while de Russe rode for Richard himself. Even though Alixandrea hated tournaments, the excitement was catching. Everyone seemed so happy and thrilled. This promised to be the biggest tournament of the year and the enthusiasm in the air was palpable.

But there were more houses competing that were well known Tudor loyalists. When announcing the first rounds, Dennis la Londe was representing the Earl of Richmond, who happened to be Howard Terrington's nearest neighbor and Tudor ally. He was scheduled to ride against the Earl of Westmoreland's champion, Sir Thomas de Norville. The entire first round of matches were Tudor against Plantagenet, although Alixandrea did not know it at the time. She would only find out later how tense those first rounds were for the participants. Everyone had something to prove.

When the horns sounded and the first match commenced, it took all of Alixandrea's strength not to cover her eyes. The crowd was screaming around her, thrilled at the spectacle of competition. She could only sit there and feign interest. When the lances made contact, however, she closed her eyes so that she could not see if splinters put out an eye or severed an artery. She hoped Matthew could not see that she was breaking her promise to watch the matches, but she suspected he knew.

After the first match ended in favor of Arundel, Lady de Russe arrived in the lists with a young, dark haired lad who was introduced as Trenton de Russe. He seemed to be a very nice boy and paid particular interest to Audrey, who was a year older than he. Lady de Russe was her usual snobbish self, with barely a pleasantry before she took her seat and found interest elsewhere.

As the second match took place, Alixandrea found herself interacting with Trenton and Audrey and paying little attention to the sport. She rather liked talking to the children, and anything was better than watching men trying to gore one another.

By the third round, someone got hurt. Robert Montgomery, champion of the Earl of Somerset, took a splintered lance to the shoulder and had to be carried off the field. The fourth round was Dennis la Londe against de Norville and he hit the knight so hard on the head that his helm flew off into the crowd. Knocked unconscious, de Norville was also carried off the field. The next round was Matthew's.

He entered the north end of the field astride his big gray charger, adjusting the strap that stabilized the lance against his arm. His opponent was the Earl of Wrexham's son, Andrew St. Héver, Viscount Tenbury.

The young Viscount, quite full of himself, entered onto the field with glorious banners cascading from his charger, working the crowd into a frenzy. He believed himself quite the hero until Richard's own herald announced Matthew. Then, the crowd burst into a deafening roar, drowning out any illusions of popularity the young Viscount might have entertained.

Alixandrea smiled proudly at the reaction. People were absolutely mad for The White Lord of Wellesbourne. Luke, John and Mark were standing around Matthew's charger, helping him with the final preparations. They were not going to compete at all, instead focusing on their brother's matches. He was, after all, The White Lord, and his popularity with the masses was clearly acknowledged. They had all heard the same tales that Alixandrea had, stories where myth and truth intermingled and gave way to a god-like being. Now he was here, their hero in the flesh, and they were crazy for him.

The crowd began to grow restless, waiting for the field marshal to drop the signal flag. Alixandrea's palms began to sweat, waiting for what was surely to come. Mark seemed to be having difficulty with a strap on the charger's plate armor and she watched, the entire crowd watched, as Mark struggled with it. She thought she could stand the anticipation no more when suddenly Mark succeeded, raised his arm to the field marshal, and the man dropped the flag. In that split second, her husband spurred his charger to the joust guide and lowered his lance.

She almost forgot her promise not to cover her eyes. They were halfway to her face before she realized it and she abruptly threw them back in her lap. The horses thundered towards each other and she could hear Audrey cheering beside her.

The crowd roared, the women screamed, and somewhere in the middle of it was a huge crash and lances splintering in all directions. Alixandrea jumped at the sound of snapping wood, watching her husband reel slightly in his seat as his opponent shattered his lance against his shield. But Matthew remained mounted and the massive gray charger made a wide turn at the far end and thundered down the field in front of the frenzied fans.

He was all right. Alixandrea swallowed hard, saying a brief prayer of thanks. She smiled at him as he made a pass by the lists, knowing he was looking for her through his lowered visor. She even managed a wave. But he did not acknowledge her as he went back to his starting point where his brothers were gathered. Someone handed him a fresh lance and they started all over again.

The Viscount went down with the next pass. He went flying off of his horse to the shouts of approval from the crowd. As Matthew turned his steed around and made another run before the wildly cheering crowd, the young Viscount stood up and staggered off the field with the help of his men. Alixandrea clapped her approval long after her husband left the field. She was glad she hadn't closed her eyes or she would have missed his magnificence.

De Russe came after him and literally obliterated the Earl of Leicester's champion, John Stanhope. Though the man appeared seasoned and skilled, he was no match for The Dark Knight. One pass, one strike to the helm, and they carried Stanhope off in pieces.

The morning passed into afternoon as more matches were held. The glances themselves took little time; it was the preparation between each one that took most of the time. The field marshals had to remove and replace banners, count points, and other details. Matthew roared through his second match by unseating Artur de Soulis on the first glance. He truly was powerful, cunning, and skilled, and Alixandrea's fear of tournaments began to turn into a love for them. As long as Matthew continued to win and continued to come through unscathed, she was delighted.

But she hadn't been keeping track of those winning and those losing other than Matthew. The field marshals covered the shields of the men who were no longer competing until Matthew, Gaston, Dennis and Caernarfon's shields were the only ones left. Only then did she realize that Matthew might have to go up against Gaston, and the fear that had been forgotten now roared back with a vengeance.

"He cannot go against Gaston," she hadn't meant to say it out loud.

"Why not?" Caroline asked.

She looked startled that someone had answered her. She did

not want to appear as if she lacked faith in her husband, but she had been watching Gaston all afternoon and the man was unbeatable.

"Because... because they are friends," she tried to talk her way out of it. "They will not want to injure each other."

"Such is the love of the sport, my lady," Lady de Russe actually turned around and spoke to her. "They have competed against each other before."

"Who has won?"

"Both of them, though Gaston has the upper hand. The last time, he broke Matthew's shoulder. Matthew should be in fine form today to exact his revenge if indeed they do ride against one another."

Lady de Russe sounded completely unemotional or unconcerned about it. It only served to infuriate Alixandrea. She stood up quickly and gathered her skirts.

"Where are you going?" Caroline asked, tugging on her sleeve.

Alixandrea did not want to tell her the truth. She did not want to look like a fool, nor did she want Matthew's reputation damaged somehow by a concerned wife.

"I must find the privy," she lied. "I shall return."

They let her go and she left the lists, heading with determination for the north side of the field where her husband was. She was not exactly sure what she was going to say to him when she found him, but she would surely say something. People were crowding the area and she wove in and out of the mob, finally coming to the big gates that separated the rabble from the competitors. There were several royal guards at the gate. She announced herself and demanded entry.

They did not believe her at first. Only by sheer fortune did John happen to pass by the gates and confirmed her identity to the guards. John ran ahead to tell Matthew of her arrival, leaving Alixandrea alone to find her way through a field of tents, men and servants. She wasn't particularly concerned for her safety until she heard a heavily-accented voice behind her.

"Lady Alixandrea, what a pleasure," Dennis la Londe came

upon her, his faded blue eyes narrowed and appraising. "I have not seen you in quite some time."

She froze, gazing up into his handsome face and remembering everything she had been told about him. Looking into his sharp face, she could easily believe all of it. "Sir Phillip," she greeted. "Or should I call you Sir Dennis?"

He grinned sheepishly. "Ah, so you have discovered the difference."

"How could I not, sitting in the lists and hearing a man I knew as Sir Phillip announced as Dennis la Londe?"

He scratched his head. "In my defense, I will say that many men use assumed names. It is safer sometimes, especially in wars and politics. It means nothing, truly."

She had little patience for him. "I see," she gathered her skirts again. "If you will excuse me, I must go and find my husband."

"Wait," la Londe stopped her. "Allow me to congratulate you on your marriage to Wellesbourne. He is a fine knight."

"Aye, he is," she said crisply. "If you will excuse me, my lord."

"Since when did your manners become so rude?" he asked, following her. "Your uncle would be very displeased."

She paused again, eyeing him. "That is none of your concern. Furthermore, I am Matthew Wellesbourne's wife now and answer only to him. Good day, my lord."

She turned away from him once more only to run headlong into Matthew. She almost smashed her nose against his breastplate. He grasped her arms gently to steady her but when she looked up, his focus was purely on la Londe. It was the look of a predator sighting prey.

"Has he been harassing you, love?" Matthew asked steadily.

She shook her head, suddenly afraid. "Nay," she said. "Come along, Matt. I would speak with you."

"Your wife and I are old friends, Wellesbourne," la Londe knew very well that he was treading on thin ice. "Did she tell you that? I am a friend of her uncle's."

"She told me that she has met you," Matthew replied. "Friendship has nothing to do with it."

Dennis grinned, a malevolent gesture that sent chills of horror down Alixandrea's spine. She did not like anything about the man and tugged gently on Matthew.

"Come along, darling," she begged softly. "Let us go."

"In a moment," Matthew patted her hand. He wasn't finished with la Londe yet. "Did you have something more you wished to say to her? Or is your boldness only present when she is alone?"

Dennis seemed to enjoy the challenge to his courage. "There is much that I could say to her, with or without you at her side. In fact, she may as well become accustomed to me, for I may very well be a fixture in her future."

Matthew's gaze, his expression, remained steady. "I cannot possibly imagine what you mean," he said. "And if all you have are delusions to spout, then I have no time for you."

La Londe clucked softly. "Did you not know that her uncle had a list of husbands for her? You are at the head of the list and the current victor. But there are many others awaiting the opportunity should something happen to you." He took a step towards them and his voice sudden dipped, low and threatening. "Were you to pass on, the lady would return to her uncle as his ward, and all of the Wellesbourne property with her. Did you not know that was a part of your marriage contract? Your father does. He agreed to it because Ryesdale is such a valuable ally. He trusts him. Therefore, it would make your wife a very wealthy widow. And very valuable. Do you believe her uncle would allow her to remain unmarried?"

Matthew refused to react. He had known the terms of his marital contract; he'd been advised of the entire thing but the terms hadn't truly occurred to him until now. When the contract had been written, Ryesdale was indeed a valuable ally. But it had clearly been established recently that he was not. Matthew was greatly disturbed to know that la Londe was aware of the private details of things that did not concern him.

"Surely you have a point to all of this," he said, making a very good show of being indifferent.

Dennis shrugged lightly, crossing his arms. He was rather

surprised, and disappointed, that Wellesbourne had not reacted. "The point is that if you pass, I am next on the list. 'Twill be me with the Wellesbourne riches *and* your wife. And, I must say, you will pass her into eager arms."

Beneath her hands, Alixandrea felt Matthew tense. She was terrified that he was going to charge la Londe and there was no way she could stop him. She squeezed, tugging him away from Dennis.

"I have a great need to speak with you, husband," she pulled harder. "Please come with me. This cannot wait."

Matthew wanted nothing more than to pull Dennis apart with his bare hands. He really did. But he wasn't so blinded by hatred that he did not hear Alixandrea's soft pleas. He allowed her to remove him from the confrontation that la Londe was trying so hard to create, knowing it was for the best but wishing it wasn't.

"*Au revoir, la belle fille,*" la Londe called after her. "Until we meet again."

"Please, walk with me," Alixandrea got a good grip on her husband and they moved further and further away. "Let us walk and calm ourselves."

"I am perfectly calm," Matthew said. "But I would like to know what you are doing here."

She shifted her hands so that one was on his elbow while the other wound tightly around his gloved fingers. "I came to talk to you."

"About what?"

"About...," She slowed her pace, suddenly ashamed. It seemed so foolish now. "I... I came to tell you that you have been magnificent. I loved watching you."

"Thank you," he said. "Is that all?"

"And... and I do not want you to compete against Gaston."

"Ah," he came to a stop and looked at her. "So that's it. I knew you did not come here just to compliment me."

Her lip stuck out in a pout. "That is not true."

"Aye, it is."

She relented, falling forward against him and throwing her

arms around his waist. "Aye, it is. I am terrified for you to go against him."

He smirked, wrapping his armored arms around her as best he could without hurting her. He kissed the top of her head. "Wife," he sighed. "You worry overly. Gaston cannot harm me."

She looked up at him, his strong face against the blue sky. "Why not?"

"Because I do not compete against him next."

She looked surprised; she did not know much about matches and the thought hadn't occurred to her. She had been singularly focused on Gaston. "Then who do you go against?"

"La Londe."

Her face lost all color and her mouth flew open. "No," she rasped. "Matthew, you cannot, not after what he just said. He will try and kill you!"

He held her tightly, attempting to quiet her. "He cannot kill me." When she opened her mouth to protest, he covered it with his own. Every time she tried to speak, he would only kiss her more deeply. He soon discovered that there were tears on her cheeks and he wiped them away with a gloved hand.

"No, love, no tears," he murmured. "Everything will be fine, I promise."

Her weeping was growing worse. "Please, Matt. Please do not compete against him. I am begging you."

He smiled at her, his hands on her face, knowing how terrified she was. He could see it in her eyes.

"Do you love me?" he asked softly.

"More than my life."

"Do you trust me?"

"Without question."

"Then you must trust me now." He knew that she did not understand so he explained. "If I were to forfeit the match, la Londe would think that I was afraid of him. Is that true?"

She sniffled. "Of course not."

"So I must compete if only to prove the point that not only am I unafraid of him, I can and will dominate him and he shall never have you, or anything about you. Is that clear?"

Her tears faded and she sniffled again, nodding her head. "It is. But I am still afraid."

"I know. And so does Dennis."

"I am sorry," she swallowed what was left of her tears. "He will not see it from me in the lists, I swear it."

"Just don't cover your eyes. Or close them."

She gave him a sheepish look. "I will not."

"Good." He kissed her again and whistled to John, who ran over to them. "Johnny, take her back to the lists and stay with her. Please."

There was something in his tone. John understood; he knew that Matthew was asking him a particular favor. If something did indeed happen to him, he wanted John at her side to tend to her. John took Alixandrea by the elbow and escorted her back to the entrance to the lists. Matthew stood there and watched them until she took her seat.

"Matt," Mark was standing beside him. "You are up next. Time to get mounted."

With a lingering glance at his wife, Matthew turned back to the cluster of Wellesbourne men waiting to assist him. He did not say anything to his brother about la Londe's pledges and promises. He did not have to.

They all knew the stakes.

***

Even Gaston was watching from the north side of the tournament field as Matthew and Dennis took their places against each other. The crowd, having heard the final match ups, had swelled enormously as more people joined the spectators.

Alixandrea's eyes never left Matthew as he secured the lance and waited for the field marshal to drop the flag. Dennis seemed to be taking some time in finishing his preparations, causing a delay. But it was a calculated delay; the longer his opponent was kept waiting, the more likely he was to become nervous. Dennis was as devious as he was skilled.

The crowd was ripe with anticipation. Alixandrea had to make a conscious effort to shut out the noise around her. Even John seemed nervous, which did not help her state. Audrey was tired and had a belly ache from too many sweets, so Caroline and Mena took her from the lists. Alixandrea was glad; with all of the tension surrounding this match, she did not want the little girl to see something that might upset her.

Lady de Russe and her son were still seated in front of her, now further off to the right and next to the royal box. Mari-Elle was even talking to the king. As the unrest of the crowd grew, Alixandrea caught movement from the corner of her eye and noticed that Gaston was now standing just below the platform, almost directly in front of her. He turned to look at her and caught her attention. Then he extended a hand to her. Realizing that he wanted her to come to him, she rose from her seat and obediently went.

He did not say a word as he took her by the hand and lifted her off the platform to stand beside him. She had a closer, far better view of the field from this position. He took her hand and tucked it into the crook of his elbow, all the while remaining stoic and silent. But Alixandrea was no idiot; she realized he had done it because he was concerned. He wanted to be with her if something should happen to Matthew and the knowledge that he was apprehensive scared her to death.

"You are worried, my lord," she said to him softly.

He did not look at her. "I simply thought you might like a better view."

"I could see fine from where I was sitting."

"Would you rather go back?"

"Nay," she studied his strong profile. "I would rather stand here with you."

He did look at her, then. The smoky gray eyes were intense. "He shall be victorious, my lady."

"Then why do your eyes tell me otherwise?"

The corners of his mouth twitched and he looked back on the

field in time to see the flag drop. The knights gored their chargers and the beasts thundered towards one another, collectively thousands of pounds of flesh and bone and armor hurling through space. It was much louder where she was standing and far more frightening. Dennis broke a lance on Matthew's hip and Matthew broke a lance on Dennis' shoulder. Splinters went flying and the crowd went mad.

Matthew made his customary wide circle and made a thundering pass before the lists. Alixandrea could hear them chanting his name and it gave her courage, thousands of people giving encouragement to her husband. She started chanting his name, too. Matthew slowed his horse when he came to where she was standing with Gaston and flipped open his visor.

"What are you doing down here?" he asked.

"Gaston invited me," she said. "You were wonderful."

Matthew's gaze moved from her to Gaston and back again. He knew exactly why Gaston had hold of her; should Matthew become injured or incapacitated, Gaston wanted Lady Wellesbourne close at hand to make sure she was safe. It was a gesture only a comrade of Gaston or Matthew's magnitude would understand. It was what true friends would do for one another. Matthew nodded his thanks to Gaston, flipped down his visor, and continued back to his starting point.

The second glance was benign, though Matthew managed to get a piece of Dennis' shoulder again. It put Matthew ahead in points and the crowd could smell blood. Alixandrea was actually fairly calm by this point, watching Dennis and her husband prepare for their last glance. When the lances were finally in place, the field marshal dropped his flag again.

The horses thundered. The crowd screamed. The lances went down and aimed for the opposing bodies. But at the last second, Dennis lowered his lance into the chest of Matthew's charger and the beast impaled itself upon the wood.

The horse collapsed in a flying mass of flesh and armor, tearing into the guide and pitching Matthew off. Dennis was caught in the calamity of his own doing as the momentum carried both Matthew's charger and the guide straight into him, throwing him and his horse towards the lists in a huge cloud of dust and wood.

It had all happened in a split second. The crowd screamed in terror. Alixandrea heard herself shriek and instead of covering her eyes, she began to run. She heard Gaston calling after her, too loaded down with armor to sprint after the very fast Lady Wellesbourne. The dust still hadn't settled by the time she reached the center of the field, but her eyes nonetheless beheld the devastation.

Matthew's horse was a dead, bloody mess, twisted in the wreckage of the guide. Dennis' horse, having been struck by the violent tumbling of Matthew's steed, lay several feet away with an obviously broken leg. Dennis was half buried under his charger and already men were trying to move him out from under the horse. The guide was in ruins and she leapt over it, spying Matthew on the ground about twenty feet in front of her. Men were running at him from all directions. She raced to him as fast as her shaking legs would carry her.

"Matthew!" she cried. "*Matthew!*"

Luke and Mark were the first to reach him. They fell to their knees beside him, as did Alixandrea a split second later. Matthew was moving; that much was certain, and Mark reached down to unlatch his battered helm. It was dented and stuck, and it took both Mark and Luke to pull it free. Matthew's dazed, bloodied face greeted them.

"Matt," Mark's voice was full of concern. "Are you hurt, man? Where are you injured?"

Matthew lay there a moment, blinking unsteadily. Flat on his back, he looked upward and could see his wife's distraught face looking down at him. She was a mess and he lifted a weak hand in her direction.

"I... I do not believe I have broken anything," he rasped, trying to move all of his limbs. "Alix, do not cry. I am all right, love."

She was trying desperately not to sob. One hand went over her mouth and the other reached out to grab the gloved hand that he was extending at her. Gaston loomed over her shoulder.

"That was one of the better spills I have seen on the tournament circuit," he said it as if it were something to be impressed about. "Are you sure you are all right?"

Matthew took a deep breath and felt a stabbing pain in his torso. He grunted. "Perhaps I spoke too soon," he groaned. "Get me on my feet."

"Where do you hurt?" Gaston reached down to take one arm as Mark took the other.

"My ribs," Matthew grunted. "I may have cracked one or two."

They managed to get him into a sitting position. By this time, John had joined them and he helped to steady his brother. The crowd, seeing that The White Lord was at least sitting up, began to cheer wildly and chant his name.

Matthew sat a moment, struggling with his breathing, before allowing Gaston and Mark to pull him to his feet. Luke stood behind him, lifting him under the shoulders as the others pulled. He was extremely unsteady on his legs, but managed to walk out of the arena under his own power. There is no way in hell they were going to carry him out; the only way that would happen is if he were unconscious or dead. Moreover, he had promised Alixandrea that all would be well in the match. He did not want to have to admit he had been wrong. For her sake more than anything, he had to walk out on his own two feet.

They walked past his horse on the way out. He paused by the beast, gazing down at the mess.

"He was a good horse," he muttered. "What a damn waste."

Alixandrea was following behind, deliberately looking away when he stopped next to the destrier. She did not want to see it. Off to her right, someone took a hammer and put Dennis' horse out of its misery. The loud, sickening thud echoed off the lists. The last she saw, they were dragging out the carcass as another group of men went to work untangling the remains of Matthew's horse. It was a nauseating sight.

By the time Matthew left the field, he was feeling slightly better. His head wasn't swimming so terribly, but his ribs were killing him. Gaston had a good grip on him so that he would not fall, but Matthew assured him that he was steady enough. He was, in fact, more concerned about his wife than for himself. Once clear of the field, he stopped walking and turned to her.

She was still behind him, head down, carrying his dented helm. He reached out a hand to her.

"Come here, love," he said gently. "Walk with me."

Alixandrea went to walk beside him, furiously blinking away the tears that threatened. For as frightened as she was, she had done a good job of keeping her hysterics in check. Gaston took the helm from her and took a position behind both her and Matthew. He wanted to be close should Matthew stagger.

"I do believe that I am done for the day," Matthew said to her. "I am looking forward to a good meal and a warm bed."

"What about your ribs?" she could hardly speak. "We must find a physic."

"We will," he said. "I have had enough broken ribs to know that it is not serious. Perhaps just a crack or two."

"What about Dennis?" Luke asked no one in particular. "Did anyone see how he fared?"

Gaston cast a glance back toward the field. Dennis had long since been removed. "He was walking unassisted when I last saw him, so it could not have been too bad."

"Bastard," John snarled. "He deliberately drove his lance into Matthew's charger. Instead of going for the knight, he killed the horse. I saw everything clearly."

"And he shall be disqualified for it," Gaston said steadily; he suspected that Lady Wellesbourne did not want to hear all of this. "But for now, Matthew is in one piece and we can all be thankful."

Matthew suddenly faltered and he pitched onto his knees before anyone could grab him. Mark and Luke held him steady as Gaston began unlatching his armor.

"Help me get this off of him," he said to Alixandrea. "He cannot breathe with this heavy armor restricting him."

Alixandrea unstrapped the stays on his dented breastplate as

Gaston pulled it free. She wasn't very good with armor and Gaston and John ended up taking off most of it. She simply stayed next to her husband, holding his arm steady as if to support his weight. He smiled at her, wearily, as his brother and friend yanked off pieces of metal.

"Forgive me for giving you such an exciting end," he said. "It did not go exactly as I had planned."

She returned his smile, reaching out to stroke a rough cheek. "It does not matter. You did as I asked. You finished whole and in one piece."

He lifted an eyebrow, not saying what he was thinking; when the charger went down, he was positive that he was about to break his neck. He was, in truth, astonished that he hadn't. The last piece of armor came off and he signaled the group that he was ready to stand again.

"Someone take my wife and I back to our apartment," he said. "I have an overwhelming desire to lie down."

Luke and John went off in search of a carriage. Mark, holding on to Matthew's right arm, noticed that the field marshals were attempting to get Gaston's attention. He nudged the big knight.

"Gaston," he said. "They've cleared the field. Your bout is up."

Gaston had almost forgotten. "Will you be able to handle Matthew?"

Mark nodded. "I have for thirty-four years."

Gaston lifted a dark eyebrow. "Take him, then. And take care of the lady, too. Mind that she does not run off somewhere in the chaos."

Mark looked at him, puzzled and defensive at the same time. Gaston met his gaze steadily, silent implications in the smoky eyes. He did not even have to say Rosehill for Mark to know what he had meant. They both knew. Mark wondered if Matthew knew, also.

"You needn't worry about the lady," Mark finally said, collecting Matthew's dented helm as Luke and John brought around a flat-bed wagon they had borrowed from another competing knight. "Nothing will happen to her."

"I will take you on your word," Gaston replied, hoping that was enough. "Get Matthew settled and find a physic to tend his ribs. I will see him when I am finished destroying Caernarfon."

"What about Dennis?"

Gaston's smoky eyes took on a distant look as if he could see things the others could not. He was The Dark Knight, after all, and there were those who said he conjured. Perhaps he was conjuring now, divining the future as he would have it.

"Rest assured, his time will come when he least expects it."

Mark did not doubt Gaston for a minute. In the mêlée the next day, Dennis la Londe met with an unfortunate accident at the hands of Gaston de Russe that rendered him forever unable to father a child.

CHAPTER FOURTEEN

August 4, 1485 A.D.

London in August was filled with sticky heat, day and night. Alixandrea was not sleeping well these days, miserable with humidity she was not used to. She tossed and turned so much that she kept Matthew awake, and he was miserable enough with four cracked ribs from his bout with la Londe.

Never one to be selfish, however, he was more concerned with Alixandrea's discomfort and had taken to rubbing her back when she could not sleep in the hope that it would relax her enough to doze. The trick usually worked, but then he was left wide-awake staring at the ceiling, his mind working over the increasing movements of Henry Tudor.

He had met with the king several times a day over the past week, going over a surfeit of information that was sometimes clear, sometimes not. Even so, it all pointed to one thing; everything that Matthew had predicted seemed to be happening and the tension within Richard's ranks was mounting.

It was early in the morning on the fourth day of August. Alixandrea had been up most of the night and was now sleeping soundly in the cool early dawn. Matthew, however, was awake, his hand still on her back where he had left it after massaging her skin for what seemed like hours. She was sticky to the touch, as the humidity from the river was heavy even in the early morning and it promised to be another sultry day.

He rose slowly, partially so as not to disturb her but also because he wasn't able to move very quickly with his healing ribs. He removed his hand from her back carefully but could not resist touching her head in an affectionate gesture. She was so beautiful when she slept.

Quietly, he found his breeches and went into the sitting room, closing the bed chamber door softly behind him. Mary Joan was already stoking the fire to warm some water for her lady's morning toilette. Matthew sent the woman for fruit and cheese as he walked over to one of the massive lancet windows that faced into the courtyard of the Tower.

There was little activity outside at this time of the morning, mostly wild creatures scrounging for a meal. He gazed up at the blue sky, cloudless, thinking of his father. He'd not heard from him since they had left Rosehill and he wondered on his health. He was still standing at the window, gazing into the dawn, when someone knocked softly on the chamber door and, without prompting, entered.

Matthew turned around to see Gaston. He looked as if he hadn't slept all night and Matthew sensed immediately that something was amiss.

"What is it?" he asked.

Gaston's smoky eyes were shadowed. "Henry Tudor sailed from Harfleur two days ago," he said. "We just intercepted a message he sent to one of his supporters asking to meet him at Shrewsbury. As you predicted, he's expected to make landfall in Wales in a few days. Richard has ordered the army to Nottingham to anticipate his arrival."

"When do we leave?"

"Today. And Matt... he's riding with us."

Matthew's eyebrows lifted. "The king is going Nottingham?"

"Indeed. It seems that he has determined that he will take command of the forces to repel Henry. He even intends to go into battle with us."

Matthew looked at him a long moment before letting out an agitated hiss. "This only complicates matters, Gaston. The man is *not* a warrior."

"But he *is* the king and by rights has command of his army." The last exchange was strongly spoken between the two of them. Gaston finally shook his head. "We cannot stop him. He rides with us whether or not we like it."

So it had come. The hammer had finally sounded. Matthew wasn't surprised, but he must have looked in the direction of the bed chamber because Gaston's next words to him were swift and quiet.

"Send her back to Wellesbourne immediately," he said. "She must not stay here. 'Tis not safe. Norfolk was set upon this morning in the Deveraux Tower and barely escaped with his life. His wife was injured."

Matthew cast him a long look. "Wellesbourne is not far from Nottingham. 'Twill be in the line of fire between Richard's base and Henry's army."

"You have no choice. You cannot leave her here. Besides, Wellesbourne is well fortified and should not be of particular interest to Henry. Warwick to the north would be of more interest to him."

Matthew sighed heavily, calming now that the reality of the day's expectations were settling. Moreover, he knew that Gaston was correct, about most things. He was able to think more clearly.

"I knew this time would come," he said softly. "My wife will be on her way to Rosehill before the morning is out. I will have my father and John take her home and stay there should the castle need defending."

"Johnny will not want to go."

"I know. But he will if I ask it of him." He glanced up at his friend. "What of Mari-Elle and Trenton? Where will they go?"

"Back to France," Gaston replied, trying not to think on how long it would be before he saw his son again. "They will be safe there."

Matthew nodded in agreement. "Indeed." He paused, seemingly prepared to say something further. He faltered twice before finally bringing forth the words. "Lady Mena is in London these days."

Gaston wasn't stupid; he'd known that all along although they had never spoken of it. He knew that Matthew would talk about it when he was ready. Gaston had been around those years ago when Matthew fancied himself in love with the petite auburn-haired lady.

"I have seen her," Gaston said casually. "With a lovely blond girl child, too."

Matthew looked at him, a thousand unspoken words between them. Although Matthew did not have to verbally acknowledge what they both knew, he did so anyway. "She looks a good deal like me, doesn't she?" he said.

"A perfect image. Trenton is quite taken with her, by the way."

"Keep your son away from her," Matthew jabbed a finger at him. "I shall kill him, I swear it. And I do not care if he is only seven years old."

Gaston just laughed. Matthew did, too, breaking the tension that had been so prevalent since Gaston's arrival. It felt good to laugh, if only for a brief moment.

"I would like for you to arrange for Mena and Audrey's travel back to Bath," Matthew continued his original train of thought. "I do not want either of them in London at this time. 'Tis far safer for them at home."

"It will be my pleasure. Anything else?"

"Have you told my brothers of Richard's plans?"

"Nay. But we should, immediately."

Matthew pushed himself off the windowsill and headed for the bed chamber. "Rouse my brothers and have them meet here in fifteen minutes," he said. "For my part, I must break the news to my wife."

"That could take longer than fifteen minutes."

Matthew cocked an eyebrow at him, his hand on the door latch. "If you hear screaming, pay no attention," he deadpanned.

Gaston smirked as he quit the room. Matthew took a deep breath before opening the door. It was dark inside, the oilcloths hanging heavy over the windows. He went to the bed where Alixandrea was still sleeping soundly. He was loath to wake her but he had little choice if she was going to pack and leave the Tower by noon.

He sat down on the bed next to her and began stroking the

bronze head gently. After the third or fourth stroke, she inhaled deeply and her eyes opened. Rolling onto her back, her sleepy gaze found Matthew.

He smiled at her. "Good morn."

She smiled in return, stretching. "Good morn," she sighed. "What time is it?"

"Time for you to get up and start packing," he said. "You have a long day ahead of you."

She looked at him curiously. Matthew decided in that moment he was going to make this discussion as easy as possible; no heavy emotions, no serious going-to-battle last words. He would, of course, tell her everything he needed to say, but he would do it in a way that left her comforted rather than rattled. At least, it sounded good in theory.

"Why am I packing?" she asked. "Where am I going?"

He leaned over and kissed her. "The answer to both of those questions is Wellesbourne."

"Wellesbourne?" she sat up, eyes wide. "Why are we going back home?"

He stood up and went to the wardrobe where some of her smaller capcases were stored.

"You are going back home with my father and Caroline," he said. "As for me, it would seem that I am required to head up the welcome committee for Henry Tudor."

Her expression darkened. "What does that mean, Matt?"

He took out a capcase and set it on the floor. "It means that Richard is moving his army to Nottingham today. Henry Tudor sailed from France two days ago and is expected in Wales in a matter of days. We must be there to greet him."

Surprisingly, she did not break down. She sat there a moment, seemingly dumbfounded. Matthew continued to pull her cases out until there were none left.

"I will have the servants bring your larger cases out of storage," he said as casually as if they were packing for a holiday. "Mary Joan and Ann can start packing immediately. I must have you out of the Tower before the army moves out."

Instead of weeping, she simply seemed depressed. Rising from bed with the linen sheet still wrapped around her, she padded over to where he stood and pressed herself against him. Matthew wrapped his arms around her, holding her tight and fast. She was warm and sweet and soft, and the pangs of separation were already starting to bite at him.

Cupping her face, he kissed her hair, her forehead, her cheeks, her nose, and finally her mouth. It was a long, sweet, tender kiss that rocked him to the core. He began to wonder if he would be strong enough to see the day through. Although war was his life, as he was born and bred to it, he'd never before had to leave behind someone he deeply loved. This was an entirely new experience and not one he relished.

"Gaston and my brothers will be here shortly," he said. "I must go and meet with them, but it should not take long. I will try to stay with you as long as I can."

Though she was quite proud of herself for maintaining her composure, inside, Alixandrea was dying. But Matthew did not look as if he could take any hysterics today. He had enough on his mind without her falling apart and she resolved to stay strong, at least until she was well away from him. When he could not see her tears.

"Oh, Matthew," she breathed. "I suppose I knew this day would come, but now that it is here, I find that I am ill prepared for it."

He stroked her cheeks with his thumbs. "I am not sure if any manner of preparation is ever enough for this kind of thing."

Her hand reached up, touching his scratchy face where he had not yet shaved. "There is nothing I can say that I have not already said. I do not want you to go, but you already know that. Anything more… it will not change the way of things."

"Nay, it will not."

"I have known since the day I married you that you were meant to do this."

"Indeed."

She sighed, snuggling back into his warm embrace and savoring it. "Will you at least see me off?"

"Not only will I see you off, but I shall ride with you all the way to Wellesbourne," he replied. "John and my father shall stay with you there."

"And then what?"

"You will wait for my return."

"When will that be?"

It was an honest question. He struggled to give her an honest answer. "It could be weeks or months. I have no way of knowing."

"Will you at least send word and let me know how you are?"

"As often as I possibly can."

"I will miss you horribly."

"And I shall miss you with every breath."

They gazed at each other for a long, bittersweet moment, a million emotions filling the space between them. Just when it seemed there was nothing further to say, Alixandrea softly spoke.

"Do you remember when I asked you once what you liked to do?"

His blue eyes twinkled, remembering that magical afternoon not so long ago. "I do. Why?"

Her fingers toyed with his armor, his mail. "Perhaps when this is all over, and when peace is finally attained, we... we can go fishing."

He smiled, touched that she would remember such a thing. But he repeated the word just to make sure he heard her correctly. "Fishing?"

"Aye," she grasped for words. "But there is a reason why I wish to do this. You told me once that fishing signified peace, far removed from the horror of battle. I think... I think it is something we should do when this insanity is finished."

"To signify peace?"

"In the hope that we shall always live with it."

His smile broadened. "I would like nothing better."

"Promise?"

"Promise."

A warm understanding settled, something to look forward to, however symbolic, when this madness had passed. Matthew wanted to go out on a pleasant note, so he kissed her again and went for the chamber door.

"I shall send the maids in to you," he said as he lifted the latch. "Perhaps if you dress quickly enough, you may come out and join us for the morning meal."

She nodded, watching him close the door quietly behind him. When a stray tear trickled down her cheek, she quickly wiped it away.

She had to stay strong.

***

The room was filled with more legendary fighting men than Matthew had seen in a long time. These were not the high nobility of England, but the rank and file knights upon which this entire endeavor would depend. Each and every man had fought with Matthew and Gaston at different times, and Matthew felt humbled in their company.

Gazing around the small, stuffy chamber, he counted the likes of Richard Radcliffe, Percival Thirwall, James Harrington, Thomas Pilkington, Robert Percy and Marmaduke Constable. It was a gathering the likes of which had seldom been seen, and in the middle of it sat a small man whose very life would depend on the strength of these knights. King Richard did not take the gathering lightly. He took charge.

"We must send word to the Duke of Norfolk, the Earl of Surrey, the Earl of Northumberland, the Stanley brothers, Thomas and William, and also Richard Brackenbury. These men command massive forces and it is imperative they leave for Nottingham right away to join us."

Francis Lovell said what they were all thinking. "I worry for Thomas Stanley, Your Grace. His wife is Margaret Beaufort and it is quite possible he will desert you in your hour of need."

The king seemed unfazed. "He is loyal to me, as is his brother," he insisted. "Henry Tudor may be his stepson, but I have had his support for years. Moreover, he and Margaret have not lived together in some time. I do not believe there is any loyalty there to her or to her son."

Lovell simply lifted an eyebrow, looking over at Matthew and Gaston. They were standing near one another, one of them leaning back against the wall and the other standing with his arms crossed. It always seemed Matthew was leaning and Gaston was cross-armed, stiff-legged, like a guard dog. The young chamberlain's gaze begged for support.

"Perhaps if one of us went personally to summon him, his loyalty would stay in check, Your Grace," Gaston suggested. "He would not refuse a representative from your inner circle of knights."

"He would not refuse me as it is," Richard snapped back, angered that his knights appeared to question his judgment. Deep down, he worried over Stanley's loyalty, too, but he would not let them know that. "Send a rider to him right away. I would have him assemble and move for Nottingham within the week."

"As you say, Your Grace," Gaston replied steadily.

With a lingering glare at de Russe, purely for effect, the king turned back to the map laid out before them. Recently crafted by his royal cartographers, it was a beautiful spectacle of color and detail. He thumped his finger on the vellum.

"We already know that Henry has sent dispatches to his faithful," he said. "Had we not intercepted one, we would have never known that he left France two days ago. Now the whole of England should be on the move very shortly with Tudor and Plantagenet forces, waiting to confront each other. We must make it to Nottingham to make it a foundation from which to strike at Henry; from there, we can quickly intercept him from his base in Wales wherever he may decide to strike."

"Do we know the strength of the force that Henry brings with him from France?" Robert Percy asked the question; having just arrived from Lincolnshire, he had not been privy to much of the information already discussed over the past several days.

"Two thousand," Gaston replied. "Mostly French mercenaries."

"Plus one thousand Irish mercenaries that were holed up in

Gloucester about three weeks ago," Matthew stepped forward and traced his finger up the path of the Severn River. "We found out last week that they had moved out of the city and to the north. I originally believed that Henry was going to make Gloucester his rally point, but it would seem that I was wrong."

Gaston jabbed a finger at the map, stating the obvious. "Leicester or Nottingham."

"There is no other possibility. It would seem that Henry would position himself in the middle of England to create a noose in which to separate north from south. If he can do that, we are in serious jeopardy."

By this time, the knights had huddled around the map, watching Gaston and Matthew drag their fingers all over it. Richard slapped his hands against the table, as much to gain their attention as it was a frustrated gesture.

"He cannot do it if we are one step ahead of him," he said firmly. "No more discussion. I want your armies to be ready to leave by noon. Is that clear?"

The knights and nobles agreed in unison, watching the king flee the room with Lovell on his tail. When he was gone, it was if the fighting men could finally breathe. They looked around the room, at each other, losing themselves in one or two man conversations. Gaston turned to Matthew and Robert Percy.

"Lovell will undoubtedly send out the riders for Northumberland and the others," he said. "The rest of us should check on our men and be in the saddle by the bell of the nooning hour."

"You do not believe that one of us should ride for Stanley?" Robert Percy was the Controller of the Royal Household. He had been in Lincolnshire on a royal errand to the earl of Lincoln, the king's potential heir, and shared the concerns of the other knights even if the king did not. "I have fought with Thomas before; he tends to side with his brother, and William had a confrontation with Richard six months ago over a taxation issue that was never resolved. That in and of itself causes me great alarm."

Gaston could do nothing more than shrug. "Our king insisted that sending one of us is unnecessary to ride for Stanley. If we disobey him, there could be consequences. He is already unnerved enough and this build up against Henry is too important to involve ourselves in petty disagreements."

If Percy agreed, it was not clear. He simply shut his mouth and left in search of the weary troops he had brought with him from Lincolnshire. Gaston and Matthew watched him leave, standing silent until most of the room had cleared.

"I have thirty of my men taking Lady Mena, her husband and daughter back to Bath today," Gaston finally said, his voice low. "I was not aware that the lady's husband did not know of your former relationship with his wife."

Matthew shrugged. "It is not my business what the lady tells her husband."

"He is under the impression that Audrey's father is dead."

"Again, not my doing but the lady's."

"You could have told me," Gaston showed some irritation. "It would have saved me from a few awkward moments, as the man had no idea why my men were there to escort his family back to Bath. I finally had to tell the husband that I was an old friend of the lady's father and had promised the old man that I would look after the daughter in times of trouble. With Henry on the move, this happened to be one of them. I doubted he believed me. It was most uncomfortable."

Matthew chuckled. "I would have liked to have seen that."

"No, you would not have," Gaston replied, annoyed. "I had to lie to the man to basically save his life. He has no idea he's connected to The White Lord and, consequently, the politics of the crown. By the way, I should tell you that I intend to enter into negotiations for a marital contract between Audrey and Trenton."

"You must be mad."

"Not at all. I assume that with the massive dowry you shall provide for her, secretly of course, I can retire and live off of my son's fortune. I shall be rich off of your money."

Matthew's smile vanished and his eyebrows flew up, outraged. He was about to verbally abuse his friend when Gaston broke down in snorts and headed for the door. Matthew could see he was baiting him in vengeance for not having mentioned the nature of familial understanding of Lady's Mena's husband. Half-amused, half-disgusted, he followed him from the room.

***

Adam was healing slowly from his injuries. Unbeknownst to his sons, the broken leg had to be amputated at the knee due to a severe infection that had taken hold. When Matthew's army reached Rosehill, it was clear that Adam was in no condition to travel much less act as protector to Alixandrea. The normally robust old knight looked old, weak and fragile.

But his mind was still sharp. Matthew gave his father all of the latest intelligence on the approach of Tudor. It seemed to him that his father had aged tremendously in the short time they had been apart, falling apart before his very eyes.

Saddened at the prospect of facing a battle without his father, Matthew left Adam in the care of Livia and her servants and continued on to Wellesbourne.

The focus now shifted to John as the protector of Lady Wellesbourne, but Matthew did not broach the subject with him until the day they arrived at the castle. He supposed it would not go over well and delayed for as long as he could.

The storm began to brew four days later when Alixandrea's last case was offloaded from the wagon and taken into the keep. Alixandrea was greeted as soon as she went inside by the pack of happy dogs while John, Mark, Luke and Matthew remained in the ward, making sure the men were fed and watered before continuing the sixty mile trek to Nottingham.

As the meal at noon commenced on a surprisingly mild August day, Matthew pulled John aside. They went to the solar, finding comfort among the yellowed, pocked map and heavy furniture. But without Adam to anchor the room, it seemed strange and alien. Things were different now; they could all feel it.

"I have a most important task for you, Johnny," Matthew said as his brother sat in their father's usual chair. "As you know, father is not here to administer Wellesbourne as I had planned. I believe you understand that we must have a knowledgeable knight here to secure the castle."

John's young face was curious. "Why?"

"Because Henry Tudor is gathering to our west and the army of Richard is amassing to our east. If Wellesbourne is somehow caught in the middle, I will have need of an experience man to direct the defenses of the castle."

"We have many seasoned soldiers here."

"But we need a knight."

John's normally-placid expression stiffened; he may have been young, but he was not slow. "Surely you are not suggesting...?"

"I am not suggesting. I am asking."

John was outraged. "Then the answer is nay. I am a knight; I go where the fighting is. I will not sit here and wait for it to come to me."

It was surprising for John to become so animated, but he was growing older, and with that age he was gaining confidence. Matthew respected that he was standing up for himself, but the fact remained that Matthew was not merely his brother, he was his commander. If Matthew gave the order, John would have to comply. But Matthew was trying to give John a choice, forced though it might be.

"I appreciate your position, truly," Matthew said evenly. "But the fact remains that there are only four knights at Wellesbourne and one must remain behind for this duty; it is out of the question for me to stay. Mark is far too strong with a sword to leave behind, which leaves you and Luke. As much as I will miss either one of you, I must make the difficult choice."

John was red around the ears. "So you think me less than a knight than Luke?"

"Nay. I think you more of a knight because you think before you act. Luke is often too rash. That is why I must trust you with

Wellesbourne."

It was a compliment and, for a moment, John was flattered. But he was on to his brother's game and felt tricked.

"What you ask of me is not fair," he retorted, miffed at being manipulated. "If there is a battle, I must fight it. You have said so yourself, Matt. Do not diminish what I am."

"I am most certainly not, Johnny," Matthew said sincerely. "But I must think of what is right for Wellesbourne. If I am killed in this coming skirmish, if Mark and Luke are killed, then I must die with the comfort of knowing that the best and brightest Wellesbourne is still alive to ensure that our family survives. And that hope is you. Do you not see the logic in this?"

John began to show signs of relenting. "You have never left anyone behind before. We have all gone off to fight together. Why now?"

"Because this is perhaps the greatest conflict we've yet faced and Wellesbourne is sitting far too close to the action. Moreover, there is father and Alixandrea and Caroline to think about. Who will take care of them if the rest of us are gone?" Matthew braced his massive arms against the map table, leaning over so that he could look his brother in the eye. "Please, Johnny. This task is far more important than any combat we may face with Henry Tudor. Will you not do this for Wellesbourne? For your family?"

John squirmed like a miserable child. "Matt...."

"John, I must have your pledge. And for something else."

"God's Bones, what else could there be?"

"Alixandrea," Matthew said. "If I should fall in battle, I want your pledge that you will marry her."

John's eyes widened, all of the displeasure gone from his movements. "*Marry* her?"

Matthew nodded; it was difficult for him to think about it and even more difficult for him to spit out.

"She must stay a Wellesbourne," his voice was low. "Father had it written into the marriage contract that if something was to happen to me that she, and all of Wellesbourne, would become a ward of Howard Terrington. This cannot happen."

Obviously, John did not know any of this. He sat a moment, stunned, seeing the motivation behind Matthew's request. "Is... is that really why you are leaving me here? As a husband to her in case you should die?"

"I am leaving you here for the reasons I stated. But if something should happen to me, I would die with the comfort that my beloved wife will be well taken care of by my beloved brother."

John did not look happy in the least, but he was forced to see the reasoning his brother was presenting. He could no longer meet his gaze and looked to his lap, fidgeting with a hole in his breeches. He tore a bigger hole contemplating his brother's request, pulling at the leather until he grew frustrated and emitted a heavy sigh. Only then did he look back at his brother, who was still hovering over the map table. The mood between them was as sharp as a knife, as brittle as kindling. John felt disappointment more than anything.

"As you say, Matt," he finally said. "But if you survive this battle, do not ever expect me to stay behind again. Consider this the one and only time I shall do this, and not because you forced me to."

Matthew was more relieved than he let on. "I did not force you, Johnny. But I would be lying if I said that I did not feel a far sight better at this moment than I did when we first entered the room."

John just made a face of distaste and went back to fumbling with the hole in his clothes. "Next time, leave Luke."

"I am not sure that would be wise. Luke would take far too much pleasure in marrying my widow."

John shrugged in agreement, finished picking at his breeches, and stood up. Matthew slapped him on the back in an affectionate gesture as they left the solar.

"It is your castle now, Johnny," Matthew said. "Do what you must to make her strong."

His castle. John rather liked the sounds of that. As the youngest brother of four, there was rarely a chance for him to play lord and master. As he went outside to begin assessing the wall strength of what was now *his* castle, Matthew had eyes only for the stairwell that led to the upper floors. He knew Alixandrea was up there and it was time he bid her farewell. Time was pressing and Richard's army would be expecting him. More than his meeting with John, and more than his looming confrontation with Henry Tudor, he did not relish this moment. With a steadying breath, he mounted the stairs.

He knew where she was simply by the dogs lying in the landing outside of the room; she was in the larger chamber on the third floor that was situated directly across from Adam's smelly chamber. This had been the chamber that Adam and Audrey had occupied together long ago; now it was simply vacant and dusty.

Matthew pushed the cockeyed door open to admit his bulk, his gaze falling on Alixandrea on her knees with her face shoved into the hearth. Her hair was pulled back with a kerchief and she had a heavy apron on. Caroline and another serving woman stood slightly behind her, sweeping and cleaning up old ashes and cobwebs. Matthew stood in the doorway with his hands on his hips.

"You have been here less than two hours and already you are cleaning this place?" he shook his head. "Must I say my farewells to a dusty bunny instead of my lovely wife?"

She rocked back on her heels, grinning at him. There was a smudge of soot on her forehead, but it only made her look more charming.

"I do apologize," she said as she stood up and wiped her hands off. "But I simply could not stand the filth in here. It looks as if it has been unlived in for a hundred years."

"So you would clean up one hundred years of dirt all in a day?" he went to her, putting his arms around her. "You could have at least waited until I left."

She pointed to the cases in the corner and out in the hall. "I need to unpack and it cannot wait."

He gave her a peck on the nose. "Remove that apron and come

to the ward with me. The army will be pulling out soon and I would say my farewells."

She dutifully took off the apron and pulled the dusty kerchief from her head. Taking his arm, they were to the door when Caroline spoke.

"God speed, Matthew," she said. "I will pray for your safe return."

They paused to look at her, the thin, pale redhead. She had spent the days in London with her cousin and Audrey; Mark had kept himself occupied with others and Caroline had made sure she was far away from her husband and his indiscretions. Mark had wanted it that way. The ride back to Wellesbourne had been quiet, uneventful, and Mark had barely said two words to her. Now, she was back at Wellesbourne and her husband was going off to war with his brothers. They all knew that Mark probably would not bid her a farewell, as that was his usual habit. Therefore, Matthew left his wife to go and embrace his sister-in-law, so badly in need of human contact.

"Take care of yourself," he told her, squeezing her small body tightly. "And watch over my wife. I would leave her in your care."

Caroline was truly fond of Matthew; he had always been inordinately kind to her. "I will take excellent care of her. And, Matthew?"

"Aye?"

"Take care of Mark."

He winked at her as he let her go and went back over to Alixandrea. "I always do."

Alixandrea blew a kiss at Caroline as she and Matthew quit the chamber. The wolf pack greeted them at the landing and wagged their tails at the sight of Alixandrea, who reached down to pet the big wolfhound sniffing her skirt. Silently, Matthew, Alixandrea and the canine escort descended to the second floor. Matthew almost tripped over one of the smaller dogs when it got in his way. The second floor hall was quiet, smelling like old smoke and rushes. As the dogs milled around their feet, Matthew and Alixandrea faced one another in the dimly lit area near the entry.

Neither one of them wanted to admit how much they had been avoiding the emotions of this moment. But now, it was upon them. Alixandrea had given a good act back at The Tower when Matthew had told her of Henry Tudor's advance. She had put up the good front of a valiant wife. Now she struggled to maintain that same presence as Matthew's soft blue eyes gazed down at her.

"So," she pressed up against his body, craning her neck back to look up at his face. "Do you go straight to Nottingham from here?"

He nodded, wrapping his big arms around her. "Sixty miles. Hopefully we can make it by late tomorrow if I push the men."

"Where is Gaston?" she asked. "He did not accompany us from London."

Matthew shook his head, pulling her closer. "He has gone to rendezvous with some of our allies. I shall meet up with him at Nottingham."

Alixandrea started talking about Nottingham, the berg she passed through on her way to Wellesbourne from York, but Matthew did not hear her; his thoughts were on Gaston, having gone to meet up with the Stanley Brothers in spite of the king's admonition not to do so. Both Matthew and Gaston decided that it would be in the king's best interest for one of them to do so, and with Matthew occupied, the logical choice was Gaston.

Matthew wondered what sorts of opposition or indecisiveness The Dark Knight had run up against. With Thomas Stanley married to Henry Tudor's mother and William Stanley in a financial dispute with Richard, Matthew had serious doubts about their loyalty.

"Matthew?" Alixandrea's voice suddenly pierced his thoughts. "Did you hear me?"

Snapped from his train of thought, he smiled sheepishly. "I am sorry, love," he bent down to kiss her. "My thoughts are elsewhere. What did you say?"

"Nothing of importance," she sighed, closing her eyes at the feel of his lips against her flesh. She suddenly threw her arms around his neck. "Oh, Matt, I shall miss you so."

"And I, you," he pulled his face from the crook of her neck, looking at her. "I am leaving John here with you. He shall be in charge while I am away."

She shook her head. "I am sure he would much rather go with you."

"Protecting you is more important."

She stared at him, sensing a multitude of thoughts he seemed unable to say. His mind was already engaging Henry even if his body was here, with her. She put her hands on his cheeks.

"Will you be honest with me?"

"I always am."

"How bad will this be?"

He kissed her palm. "I do not know. But with the size of force that Henry is bringing, it promises to be a big fight."

She stroked his cheeks with her thumbs, running her fingers along his smooth lips and memorizing every curve of his face. She was suddenly aware of the lump in her throat and she battled furiously against it.

"Do not forget your promise to send me word whenever you can," she reminded him softly. "I will be here, watching the horizon every day for your return."

He stroked her face, her hair, feeling pangs that he had never before known. She could see it in his eyes.

"I will be fine," she assured him, grasping at the last threads of courage before they left her completely. "Caroline and John and I will get along quite well. Do not worry over anything."

"I do not worry over anything here at Wellesbourne," his voice was oddly hoarse. When he looked at her, Alixandrea swore she saw tears glistening in the blue depths. "But we must have a serious discussion."

"About what?"

"I must say this so that we are clear on things," he was trying to be firm with her without sounding grave. "If something should happen to me, you will...."

She suddenly threw her hands over her ears and pulled away

from him. "Nay," she cried softly. "Do not say such things. I cannot hear it from your lips. Only by God's grace do I stand here with even an ounce of courage at your departure. If you say things like that, I will surely crumble."

He grasped her, more firmly so that she could not get away. His muscular arms went around her, holding her still and tight. Alixandrea clung to him.

"You must hear me, Alix," he murmured. "If I fall in battle and I have not told you all that I must, I fear for your life and safety more than you can know. Please hear me out."

She only nodded, but it was enough. He continued. "If I should not return, John has instructions to marry you immediately. This will keep you at Wellesbourne and ensure that your uncle does not gain control of you or my inheritance. It also ensures that you will be well treated and well cared for the rest of your life. John will make a fine husband. Those are my wishes, love, and I would ask that you abide by them."

It was too much. Her resolve to remain courageous unraveled completely and she was a soft, warm, sobbing mess against him. Matthew rocked her gently, his face in the top of her head. He sighed heavily, wishing with all of his heart that he did not have to leave her. But time was short, and he had to say everything that was on his mind whether or not she wanted to hear it.

"I love you, Alixandrea Terrington St. Ave Wellesbourne," he murmured, feeling his eyes sting with tears. "The man that existed before the day you walked into that tavern was dark, humorless and dull. You are the spark that gave him a meaningful existence and for that, he shall be eternally grateful. To have known a scant month with you has made his entire life worth living."

His sweet words only made her weep harder. He put his hands on her face, lifting her tear-stained cheeks to his lips. He kissed her softly, gently, across the nose, forehead, cheeks, chin, and each eye. Her salty tears were delicious upon his lips.

"Alix," he murmured. "Open your eyes and look at me, love."

She obeyed, the great bronze eyes slowly opening. He wanted

one last, strong, enduring look into her soul to sustain him.

"If I have any control over my own fate and any leverage with God, I swear to you that I will return," he whispered. "But if it is decided that my time has come, know that I wait for you to join me on the other side. Look for me when you enter the great golden gates of Heaven, for surely, I will be standing there."

Her weeping had faded, the pull of emotion now too strong for tears. She stared at him a long moment before speaking. "That gives me more comfort than perhaps anything you have said."

"Good. I meant that it should."

There was nothing left to say. Their final embrace was too strong, too powerful, too full of unspoken words. When Matthew finally let her go and moved to quit the keep, she ran after him and they embraced once more, heated kisses and murmurs of love between them. He forced himself to let her go and descended the steps into the ward below.

Alixandrea stood in the doorway, watching him mingle with Mark and Luke, eventually barking orders as the entire bailey began to move with fighting men preparing for battle. It brought her tremendous comfort to watch him in action, confident with his skills as a warrior and knowing that he would indeed do everything possible to return home to her whole.

She stood there as the army formed ranks and began to move out. Matthew occasionally turned and waved to her. Alixandrea had no idea how long she had been standing there before she realized someone was beside her.

John stood next to her, his blue eyes fixed on the departing troops. She put her hand in the crook of his elbow.

"I am glad you are staying here with me, John," she said, meaning to be of comfort. "Perhaps we can even begin rehabilitating your mother's garden while we wait for them to return."

But he did not find much consolation in the statement. "Perhaps," his gaze lingered on Matthew, just leaving the gate with the massive army behind him. "Did my brother tell you what he has asked of me?"

"He did."

"If it comes to that, I just want you to know that I am sorry," he said to be of comfort.

Alixandrea did not find any consolation whatsoever in his statement. When her husband disappeared through the gates, somewhere inside of her, it was as if a candle blew out. She felt dark, lonely, and anxious.

There was nothing left to do now but wait.

CHAPTER FIFTEEN

August 21, 1485 A.D.

Nottingham Castle was a massive place, more of a fortified city than a castle proper. It was normally full of people going about their daily business, but with the assembled armies of King Richard, the entire castle and surrounding berg was jammed with bodies. Norfolk and Surrey had joined the king's forces, as well as a host of other lesser knights and houses. It was quite a conglomeration of forces and at council, most of the ranking nobles demanded to be heard. This could make the meetings long and loud.

Matthew had spent most of his time with the king during this time and one thing was becoming increasingly apparent; Richard did indeed plan to take command of his army and ride to battle with them. Matthew had no idea how this would complicate things or shift the focus of the battle and he fervently wished that Gaston would soon join them, as much for his counsel as for his sheer presence. But The Dark Knight was still noticeably absent, much to the displeasure of the king. Matthew had sent several riders to find him bearing messages and as yet, none had returned. He could only assume they had found Gaston and that the man was on his way.

They had received word the previous day that Henry Tudor's enormous army was moving to Atherstone, having crossed the Welsh Marches without resistance. This had Richard's entire army on the move to Leicester to intercept him. War was imminent and Matthew had been in battle mode since leaving Wellesbourne ten days earlier. He ate little, slept even less, and focused only on the coming conflict. He could smell it in the air, especially on the evening of August twenty-first.

It was warm and sultry, but more than that, it was tense with battle preparation. Richard's entire force of around five thousand men was camped on Ambion Hill, south of Leicester and directly in the path of Henry Tudor. When dawn broke on the morning of August twenty-second, the battle had finally come.

The morning at Bosworth Field was clear but for some lingering fog created by the heavy evening moisture. The White Lord took his troops with Norfolk to create the front lines. Matthew set up three rows of archers just ahead of the cavalry, nearly one thousand strong. It would have been far better for him had Gaston been here with his contingent of Welsh archers, but he could not wish for what was not available. Norfolk had mostly cavalry and infantry, lingering just behind Matthew's troops. In the distance, they could see an army approaching, standards flying high.

"Do you see who it is?" he asked Mark, astride his fat red charger.

Mark's visor was lowered. "Nay," he turned to Luke. "Can you see the colors?"

Luke squinted in the early morning sun. "It looks like green and white pennants."

Matthew heard him. "Oxford," he hissed. "He is leading the charge. Archers ready!"

His voice boomed across the field. The soldiers with the red pennants that, once waved, would set off a deadly volley of arrows, stood at the ready. As Luke charged off to supervise the archers, Mark remained at Matthew's side, studying the incoming tide of men.

"Any further orders before I assume my position?" he asked.

Matthew shook his head. "When the foot combat begins, return to my side. We must stay united if we are to survive."

Mark nodded, but still he lingered. Matthew was focused on the approaching Oxford pennants when Mark spoke quietly.

"This is more than likely not the appropriate time, Matt, but I feel I must speak."

Matthew glanced over at him. "What of?"

Mark cleared his throat, his gaze suddenly uncertain. "Your wife," it was difficult for him to bring forth the words. "I... I have not been very kind to her. I have said terrible things. I want you to know, before this battle begins and our lives may be cut short, that I am sorry. I am sorry for the cruelty I have thought of her."

He had his brother's full attention now. "It is unnecessary to apologize," Matthew said, watching emotion flicker across Mark's face. "I know you, brother. I know that you did not mean what you said."

Mark lifted a dark eyebrow. "That is where you are wrong. I meant everything I said, at least at the time." He was uncomfortable with his confession and slammed his visor down. "I was jealous, I suppose. Jealous she had you, jealous you married a woman that you could love. But that is all over now. I just wanted you to know that should anything happen, you do not have to worry over your wife. I shall take care of her if it comes to that."

Matthew's gaze was intense. "Why?"

"Why what?"

"Why the change of heart?"

Mark would not look at him; he was focused on the approaching army.

"You have always been an excellent warrior, Matt," the helmed head turned in his direction. "But she has made you an excellent man. I have seen changes in you but do not ask me to describe them, for I cannot. But know that I have seen you change for the better. You are blessed, and as my brother, I am pleased. God knows you deserve some happiness in this world. I am glad that you have found it."

Matthew could only smile. "Your wife adores you, too, Mark. Perhaps you should give yourself the chance for happiness such as I have found."

"Perhaps."

Matthew held out a gloved hand. Mark caught it and they held each other tightly, drawing strength from their brotherly bond. But the moment was cut short as they realized the archers were still waiting for the signal to let fly. Matthew was preparing to bellow the order when a messenger suddenly approached him from the rear. He recognized the man as having been sent for Gaston several days prior. Matthew passed his command over to Mark and went immediately to the messenger.

"Where's de Russe?" Matthew asked before the man could speak.

"He is to the north with the Stanley armies, my lord," the man was clearly exhausted. "They are lingering just out of battle range."

Matthew's eyebrows drew together. "What is he doing there? The battle is beginning."

"He says to tell you that he must speak with you, my lord," the man replied. "I am to take you to him."

Frustrated, Matthew was forced to leave his post. Mounting his newly purchased Belgian charger, he tore off after the already-mounted messenger.

Gaston was more than a mile to the north, on a ridge overlooking the distant field of battle. He was there with the Stanley brothers and their army of over five thousand men. It was nearly as big as the contingent on the field in the distance. Matthew found Gaston dismounted, helmless, standing next to his charger and quite calmly watching the far-away battle commence. The thunder of cavalry and the shouts of men could already be heard.

Matthew's charger kicked up clods of wet earth as it came to a rough halt. He dismounted heavily, his armor banging against itself as he walked straight for Gaston. It was a purposeful and perplexed march. The Dark Knight turned to him as he approached.

"Matt," he greeted.

Matthew flipped open his visor, his blue eyes full of bewilderment. "What goes on here? What are you doing?"

Gaston was quite composed. "I am waiting for you."

"So here I am. Why have you not joined Richard's forces? The battle has begun."

Gaston glanced back to the skirmish in the distance. "I can see that," he said. "Oxford is leading the charge. Who is heading the front line of the opposition?"

Matthew did not quite catch the meaning of "opposition". "Norfolk and myself. You should be there also."

"And so I am not," Gaston turned back to Matthew, an odd gleam to his eye. "Matthew, we have serious matters to discuss."

"Now?" Matthew took another step, ending up very close to him. "I do not understand. What we have been anticipating for years is in front of our face. Why are you lingering here on the outskirts?"

"Because my fealty is no longer with Richard."

It took Matthew several long, painful moments to process what his friend had said. Then, he could only manage one word. "What?"

Gaston remained collected, almost casual. He turned away from Matthew and began to pace, his massive boots leaving the wet grass smashed.

"Precisely that," he replied. "My loyalty has turned. When Thomas and William Stanley move to support Tudor's lines, I shall go with them."

Matthew had no idea how to react. He shook his head as if he had not heard correctly. "If this is a joke, it is a very bad one. You must get mounted immediately and come with me."

"Matt," Gaston said his name as a hiss, as if to get his attention. "It is not a joke. And I have very valid reasons for this. I would hope, as my friend, that you would hear them."

Matthew just stared at him. "If this is not a joke, then I cannot believe my ears. This is insane."

"Will you hear me?"

"Hear what?" Matthew threw out his arms beseechingly. "What is to hear? That you have betrayed your king on the cusp of battle?" When Gaston averted his gaze, looking at the ground like a stung child, Matthew could feel all of the blood rushing to his head. *This cannot be,* he thought. "What, in God's name, could you possibly tell me?"

Gaston cocked his head, a sidelong glance to Matthew. "I do not have to review my record for service to Richard," he said quietly. "It is impeccable. I was there at the death of King Edward, the father. I was there when the young princes were murdered. It was I, in fact, who carried the Duke of Gloucester's body to his final resting place, murmuring prayers in the boy's ear that he would forgive his uncle and forgive me. Do you not recall that?"

Gaston's manner had gone from calm to passionate in a matter of seconds. Though they had never discussed the incident of the young princes, Edward and Richard, Matthew knew how Gaston had felt about it. It had been the ultimate act of loyalty to Richard and Matthew knew that Gaston had always hated the king for it. Murdering the father for his throne was one thing. Murdering helpless boys was quite another.

"I recall," Matthew responded steadily.

"You were not there."

"I was at Wellesbourne at the time, else I would have been just as guilty as you."

Gaston nodded his head as if convinced. "With all of Richard's petty squabbles and paranoid commands, I was there to carry them out. Never did I question, never did I refuse. I convinced myself that I was serving the last of the Plantagenet line, just as you were. We were both convinced that we were preserving a royal legacy. But I have recently been the recipient of a raw and devastating revelation, something so catastrophic that it would cause me to question my entire existence." He moved closer to Matthew now, his dark face intense. "The murder of a king could not convince me. The murder of the sons could not convince me. But something else has."

"What could that possibly be?"

Gaston met his gaze a moment longer before looking away. He turned back in the direction of the battle, now gaining in intensity. "Do you recollect that I mentioned my wife keeping a lover in London?"

Matthew's mind was brittle; he had not the patience or energy to follow opposing trains of thought. "What does that have to do with anything?"

"Do you recall?"

"I do."

Gaston turned to him, then, his face a mask of barely contained emotion. "It was Richard."

Matthew did not react at first. Then, his eyebrows lifted as if to stretch out his entire face. "The king?"

"Aye," Gaston said softly. "And do you know what our king said to me when I confronted him?"

Matthew could only shake his head and Gaston continued. "He told me that it was none of my concern. He further told me that if I should choose to protest the affair, he could not guarantee the safety of my son and would see to it that The White Lord took care of the boy. You see, he is convinced that your loyalty to him supersedes our friendship and the bounds of common decency. He is convinced that you would harm my son to punish me if he gave the order. To spare you that horrible choice, I have ended my fealty to Richard, sent my wife and son to my holdings in France, and sworn my oath to Henry Tudor."

Matthew's mouth was a tight line of astonishment and outrage. He had known Gaston for twenty years; the man had never lied to him, not once. Word from Gaston was as good as word from God. He must have stopped breathing because when he finally drew in a breath, it was loud and ragged. His chest hurt.

"I have never heard anything more contemptible in my life," he breathed. "Are you sure, Gaston? There could be no mistake?"

"None."

"So when you went to find the Stanley brothers to make sure their loyalty to Richard remained true, in reality, you were going to join them and Henry Tudor."

"Correct."

"Why did you not tell me this before now?"

Gaston shrugged. "I am not sure," he said. "Pride, perhaps. Confusion, I do not know. Perhaps I was afraid that you would not believe me."

"When have I ever doubted you?" Matthew fired back softly.

"No matter what you say or what you have done, you have not ended our friendship. It is still there, stronger than ever. And no matter if the king ordered me to harm Trenton, I would not do it."

"Even at the expense of your fealty to Richard?"

"Even so. I would go to the executioner before I harmed your son."

Gaston knew that. He nodded his head, weakly, struggling against the fatigue and despair that threatened. "Even if you would not, others would."

"I would kill them all."

Gaston reached out, slapping a massive hand on Matthew's shoulder. "I know, my friend," he assured him quietly. "But what of your family, your wife and father and brothers? Do you have any idea how this would affect them?"

"They would understand. And we would adjust."

"Then I tell you now," Gaston looked pointedly at him, "that the man we have sworn to serve is not worthy of your loyalty."

"And Tudor is?"

"The lesser of the evils."

A gleam came to Matthew's eye. "Did you summon me to convince me to switch my allegiance?"

"Nay. I summoned you to tell you of mine."

"And how did you expect that I would react?"

Gaston lifted his big shoulders. "I do not know. Kill me, perhaps."

Matthew hissed in disgust. "I would sooner throw myself on my own sword," he said. But his blue eyes were fixed on Gaston, almost painfully. "What I cannot seem to understand is why you did not tell me any of this sooner. I always thought you and I were closer than brothers, no secrets between us. I guess I was wrong."

Gaston had been experiencing guilt over that same thought. But it was more than that. "Perhaps my deepest shame was something to be kept to myself. It was not meant as a betrayal to our friendship."

Matthew was hurt, bewildered and grieved all at the same

time. He would have never expected this from someone he had known most of his life, someone who thought exactly as he did. Or so he believed.

"Surely Tudor must know the reasons for your new loyalty," he said.

Gaston braced his legs slightly apart and crossed his massive arms, his traditional and favorite stance. "Not strangely, when I found the Stanley brothers, they had an offer for me straight from Henry's mouth. It gave me the opportunity to use it as an excuse for my change in fealty."

"What is the offer?"

"Yorkshire should Tudor emerge the victor. And there is an offer for you, too."

Matthew was torn, not wanting to hear it, wanting to hear it. "What is that?"

"Herefordshire and the Southern Marches."

Matthew inhaled a long, deep breath. It was an endeavor to steady himself but it wasn't working. Gazing into the smoky eyes of his closest friend, his mind was sorting through many a thought; Alixandrea, Wellesbourne, Richard, the future, and Henry Tudor. He found himself asking a question that would have only come from his heart and not his head.

"What is your opinion on the outcome of this battle?"

Gaston glanced to the north, where a black line of soldiers await in the distance. "Henry's forces outnumber Richard's. He has the strength of Northumberland."

Matthew blanched. "Northumberland is riding to meet Richard."

"No, he is not."

"And you knew this?"

"Only a few days ago, from Thomas Stanley. Northumberland sides with Tudor now."

That betrayal alone cost Richard over a thousand supporting troops. Matthew could see what was happening. They were all turning, for various reasons or perhaps none at all. Richard's support was crumbling. He sighed deeply.

"I am sure Northumberland has his reasons," he said. "As do you. I do not dispute them. But I have no such reasons. My oath is my bond and once given, cannot be retracted. I must do as I pledged. I must protect the king."

Gaston had known what his answer would be the moment he saw him approach from Richard's lines. Matthew Wellesbourne was a man of his word. It was a bitterly sad moment, friend with friend, not warrior against warrior.

"Is there nothing I can say that would convince you to join me?"

"Would that I could, my friend. Yet honor holds me bound."

"But you are outnumbered, Matt," Gaston sounded very much as if he were pleading. "This cannot go well in Richard's favor. I do not want to see your end."

"Nor do I," Matthew said. "But I must do as I must."

A heavy silence fell as both men pondered their immediate future. "I would ask you a question, then."

"Ask."

"If Richard had set sights on your wife, what would you have done?"

Matthew snorted. "You are far better in control of yourself than I would have been. I would have killed him."

Gaston took a step closer to him and lowered his voice.

"Then know that he did set his sights on her when you first brought her to The Tower those weeks ago," he rumbled. "He had been watching the gates from his chamber as he so often does and saw her when she disembarked her carriage. Twice he sent me to retrieve her while you were occupied in war council. When I refused, he sought out Mari-Elle instead. You must understand that Richard's lust for Alixandrea precipitated this chain of events. He bedded my wife to punish me for refusing to bring him yours. Though you are a man of honor, Matt, you are bound to a man that has none. He would have taken your wife and threatened you when you resisted, as he did me. Now, are you still as loyal to our king as you were only a moment ago?"

Matthew was embroiled in perhaps the greatest internal

struggle he had ever known. Never did he doubt Gaston's word. Now it was a matter of pride for him, too. But it was more than that. Alixandrea had been at stake and Gaston had done something completely unselfish to protect her, which had worked horribly against him.

Gaston had sacrificed himself to save Matthew's life and happiness. Perhaps there were times when true friendship and the safety of one's family meant more than the breaking of a bond. Perhaps it was Matthew's turn to sacrifice something for Gaston, perhaps for all of the wrong reasons, but reasons nonetheless. *I must do as I must....*

"My wife means more to me than anything in this world," Matthew said, his voice choked with emotion. "If what you say is true, and I have no reason to doubt that it is, then in spite of my loyalty to Richard, he has none to me. This I cannot abide."

Gaston almost collapsed in relief. He closed his eyes, lowering his head in a small prayer of thanks.

"Then you shall join us?" he asked softly.

Matthew sucked in a long breath. "This is not about Herefordshire and the Southern Marches. This is not about believing in Henry over Richard. This is not even about England. This is about you, a man who would destroy his life and reputation to save mine. This is all about my wife and the lengths I will go to for her protection. What I do, Gaston, I do for you, and no one else. You have saved her, in more ways than one. Let me repay the debt."

"What will you tell your brothers?"

"The truth. And that they shall gain holdings in Herefordshire and the Southern Marches when this is over."

It was done. Without another word, Matthew re-latched his helm, mounted his charger, and rode off towards the battle in the distant field. The sun was rising steadily now, casting pale golden light on the green fields. Gaston watched Matthew for a moment before motioning to one of his men, hovering a good distance away. Patrick's familiar shape came riding upon him.

"Did he understand?"

"He did."

"Did he accept?"

"He did. Spread the word; as soon as we see Henry's standard approach, we move."

Patrick was gone. Gaston lingered a moment longer on the turn of events before mounting his charger and following.

It would prove to be the longest, bloodiest day of his life.

CHAPTER SIXTEEN

Early September

The bushes were trying to come back. Little buds had begun to form and Alixandrea inspected them yet again before she watered that particular hedgerow. The entire length of shrubs that Audrey had planted against the western wall of the garden were showing signs of life after the weeding and pruning and cutting that she, Caroline and John had done. Finally, the garden was emerging from its dormant stage with water and attention. Every day, Alixandrea could see a marked improvement.

This day was no different from any of the others, except perhaps it was a little cooler. The seasons were beginning to change and she hoped to keep the garden flourishing through the colder months to come. Caroline joined her shortly, dressed in her heavy linen garments and having come to do battle with the prickly garden. She saw Alixandrea stooped over a bush, pouring a bucket of water onto the roots.

"Alix," she came over to her, her manner wrought with exasperation. "You should not be carrying that heavy bucket. Let me have it."

Alixandrea shook her head even as Caroline wrestled her for the pail. "Caroline, I am fine, truly," she let Caroline win the tussle. "I am perfectly capable of watering the garden."

Caroline frowned. "You should be resting."

"I feel fine."

"But you must take care of that baby."

Alixandrea grinned. She had done an awful lot of grinning lately, most noticeably, since the day she realized that she was pregnant. That had been almost three weeks ago. No menses, tender breasts, a strong aversion to meat and a strange firmness of her lower belly told Alixandrea all she needed to know. Caroline, much more knowledgeable about such things, confirmed it. From that point on, there had been much joy within the walls of Wellesbourne at a time when there was little to be joyful about.

"Go tend the camellias," Caroline instructed her. "That bush near the gate needs some pruning."

Since Caroline had taken Matthew's words literally and was seeing to nearly every aspect of Alixandrea's life, she simply shrugged and went over to the camellia bush that was beginning to sprout deep green leaves. Sitting on the padded leather cushion that John had fashioned for her, she was in the process of trimming a dead branch when John entered the small garden. Head down, she could still see his feet.

"Ah, Johnny," she said. "Just in time. Could you perhaps have the stable boys provide more horse droppings today? Just look what it has done for these camellia bushes. The flowers are thriving."

John did not reply immediately. Alixandrea lifted her head and turned around. "John?"

He just stood there, looking at her. It was an odd stance. For some reason, it unsettled her. Unsettlement turned very quickly into fear.

"John, what is the matter? Why do you look so?"

John sighed heavily and took another few steps into the enclosure. By now, he had both ladies' undivided attention.

"We... we just received a missive," he said.

Alixandrea leapt to her feet and rushed towards him. "What did Matthew say?"

"It was not from Matthew."

In her state, emotions were more prevalent than normal. Tears sprang to Alixandrea's eyes.

"John, for the love of God, tell me what has happened," she was trying not to weep. Caroline grabbed hold of her and they huddled together in fear. "Who sent the missive and what did it say?"

There was a carved wooden bench against the wall, put there by Adam for his wife those many years ago. John directed the ladies to sit. When they did, he knelt before them, taking Alixandrea's hands tightly.

"Alix," he said softly, firmly. "I need your calm attention, not your hysterics. Please do this. It is important."

She nodded, though she was struggling. "Please tell me."

John passed a glance at Caroline before continuing. "The missive was written by Viscount Lovell. Henry met Richard south of Leicester almost three weeks ago in a massive battle."

"What happened?"

John did not know where to begin. He was still reeling from the news, making it difficult to relay. "Richard was defeated," he said, hardly believing it as he said it. "We have a new king."

"What about Matthew?" Alixandrea practically shouted. "Where is he?"

John patted her hands to calm her. "As near as Lovell can tell, he survived the battle."

"What do you mean as near as he can tell?"

John sighed heavily again, grasping for words. "He saw him towards the end of the battle and he was still alive, as was Mark. But Luke...," John abruptly faltered, wiping at the tears that suddenly sprang to his eyes. "Luke fell towards the beginning of the battle. Struck down by archers."

Caroline sucked in a sharp breath and closed her eyes. Alixandrea, strangely, seemed to calm though there were tears on her face.

"Luke," she murmured. "God be with him. What more did Lovell say?"

John struggled to compose himself. "He said that Matthew and Gaston sided with the Stanley brothers and came charging in when Henry took the field. They fought for Tudor, Alix. The Wellesbournes fought against Richard."

Alixandrea's eyes widened to the point where they threatened to pop from her skull. "That is not possible."

"Lovell would not lie."

"But... why? I do not understand any of this."

John let go of her hands and stood up, agitation in his manner. "Oh, Alix, it was a mess. I do not know why my brothers changed their fealty on the day of battle, but the fact remains that they did so. Together with Gaston and the Stanleys, they turned the tide in Henry's favor. Richard fell and Thomas Stanley took the crown off the dead king and crowned Henry right there on the field."

"But Matthew is alive," Alixandrea said as if she had not heard anything else. "We are sure that he survived?"

John snapped at her. "Is that all you are concerned with? Do you not understand that we now have a new king?"

She met his fury. "Of course that is all I am concerned with. I care not who rules this country so long as my husband is still alive and we are allowed to raise our family in peace. To the Devil with this battle for the throne. I would be lying if I said I wasn't glad it was over."

John was clearly upset. He was reeling over the death of Luke and the change in loyalties.

"Matthew must have made the decision to support Henry," his tone was almost accusing. "He always makes the decisions; the rest of us merely following, trusting that the great White Lord of Wellesbourne knows what is best. Well, I do not know if I would have changed so easily. I do not know if I would have followed Matthew."

"Do you not trust your brother?"

"I trust him, but I have my own mind as well," John was twitching with anger, bewilderment. "Matthew must have promised Mark and Luke something great if they would change their loyalties."

"Are you saying that he bribed them?"

"What else could he have done? Or... or perhaps he was bribed himself by Henry. Perhaps The White Lord was bought."

Alixandrea struck him across the face, a sharp slap that echoed off of the garden walls. It was a brutal, sudden action and completely unexpected.

"You will never again express such doubts of my husband's

honor," she hissed. "If he did in fact change loyalties, then he must have had a very good reason. You will not doubt him."

John glared at her, but in the same breath, he knew she was correct. If Matthew sided with Henry, it must have been a sound and wise decision as he saw it. John adored Matthew; upon reflection, he knew there could be no other possibility.

"I must send word to my father," he turned away from Alixandrea, evidently not wanting to discuss it further. "He does not know what has happened."

Alixandrea grasped his arm before he could get away. "Did Lovell say where my husband is?"

"He did not. He only said he saw him towards the end. He did not say that he saw him leave the battlefield alive."

John's words struck her just as her small hand had struck his cheek. He had only said that because he was disturbed, too, about Luke, the conflict, about everything. All Alixandrea seemed concerned with was Matthew and not the overall implications of the battle. But as soon as he said it, he was sorry.

"I am sure he is well," he said quietly. "Matthew is stronger than you know."

Her face was pale, her lovely features twisted in thought and dread. "When did you say this battle took place?"

"Around the twenty-second of August."

"Then if that is true, Matthew has had almost three weeks to come home. Leicester is less than fifty miles away. It would not take him three weeks to travel fifty miles." Her features suddenly tightened with fear. "John, where is he? If he survived, *where is he?*"

She was starting to become hysterical again. John grasped her hands tightly. "I do not know, Alix. Perhaps he has gone to London with the new king."

"You must go and find him," she insisted. "You must find him and you must also bring Luke home to be buried next to his mother. Johnny, you must."

John's mind was muddled. He needed to get away from the weeping women and think clearly. But as he tried to pull away again, Caroline came at him.

"And if Mark is also alive, why has he not come home?" she asked. "You must find out where they are, John. You could be the only Wellesbourne left."

The only Wellesbourne left. Alixandrea could not hear anymore. She turned away from them both and went back to her camellia bush. Picking up her pruning knife, she resumed her steady cutting. The battle was over and Matthew was not home. If he was alive, surely he would have sent word. But word had only come from Lovell. The more she cut at the bush, the more brittle her mind became.

***

It was sundown and Alixandrea was still in the garden, still tending the shrubs. She had not come inside all day. When Caroline had tried to force her, she had actually shoved the woman away. Nothing anyone could do or say could convince her to leave the garden and come inside.

The old garden of Audrey Wellesbourne had become a sanctuary, a therapeutic environment in which to exercise her demons. Right now, that demon was Matthew's whereabouts. She could focus on nothing else. She had very nearly convinced herself that he had died on the field at Bosworth and now lay buried in a common grave with his brother. Thinking of her strong, wise, sweet husband in a pauper's grave nearly destroyed her. He did not belong there. If John could not find him, she would not rest until she did.

As the sun set, she began working the ground with her hands. A servant had brought more horse manure and she used her fingers to work it into the soil that surrounded some dormant bulbs. It was smelly, dirty work, but she did not care. She dug until her fingers bled and still, she dug. At some point, the tears came. She wept deeply as she continued to till the soil, her tears mingling with Wellesbourne earth. This was the place that had bred her husband. It was odd that she felt close to him here, her hands in the dirt of the fortress that he loved.

To her right against the garden wall sat the grave of Audrey Wellesbourne. Though the woman should have rightfully been buried in the chapel, Adam had chosen to bury her in the garden she had loved so well. Tears blurring her vision, Alixandrea looked over to the grave with the carved stone marker. If she could not find Matthew's body, it was the closest thing she would ever have to his grave, the woman who had given birth to him. On her hands and knees she crawled to the plot and lay atop it.

The sun went down as she lay against the cold earth and cried. She did not care that Caroline was standing near the garden gate, weeping softly at the sight. She'd come to bring Alixandrea some warm broth but stopped when she saw what had happened. She did not know what to do, or how she could give the woman comfort in a time like this. Alixandrea was distraught and surely no one could bring her comfort but the appearance of Matthew himself.

Somewhere in the dark, a sentry shouted from the wall. Caroline heard the commotion but was too consumed with Alixandrea's grief to care. The gates rolled open on their great chains and the activity of the soldiers picked up somewhat. Because Caroline was tucked back behind the keep and away from the gates, she had no idea that the Wellesbourne army was finally returning. It was the moment they had all waited for with great anticipation and, sadly, no one was aware of it. Caroline had no idea her husband had come home until she saw him some time later, standing at the gate that led into the kitchen yards.

Mark looked worn and beaten, but he was alive. Caroline caught sight of him, thought she was seeing a ghost, and dropped the broth in her hand. Mark smiled weakly and walked to his wife, standing before her and gazing into her eyes for a long moment. Caroline stared back at him, words stuck in her throat. She wanted to throw her arms around him but dare not do so. He was not the embracing type.

"Welcome home, husband," she said. "I am pleased to see that you are well."

Mark's response was to lean over and kiss her on the cheek. Shocked, Caroline put her hand to her cheek where he had kissed her. Mark chuckled softly, wearily. "It is good to see you, also."

Dazed, Caroline struggled to retain her senses. "Did... did you just arrive? I am sorry that I did not greet...."

He shook his head to quiet her. "I am glad to find you here."

Caroline suddenly remembered her sister-in-law, curled up on the ground. Her heart leapt. "Is Matthew with you?"

"No," Mark said shortly. "And I caught Johnny just down the road. He has returned with me."

"But he has gone to find Matthew and Luke."

"No need. I know where they both are. I have brought Luke home with me for burial."

"Thank God. And Matthew?"

Mark avoided answering her. "Where is Alixandrea?"

Caroline could only point to the garden. Mark's eyes gradually adjusted to the darkness and he could see a figure lying on the ground amongst the carefully clipped bushes. Puzzled, and deeply concerned, he went to her.

"My lady," he knelt beside her. "What is the matter? Are you ill?"

Alixandrea had not heard him enter. Shocked by his sudden appearance, she sat up, her hands instinctively grabbing at him as if to convince herself that he was not a ghost.

"Mark," she gasped. "You are alive."

He nodded. "Indeed," he replied, noting even in the darkness that she had a wild look about her. "What are you doing on the ground? You should be inside where it is safe and warm."

He was trying to pick her up but it was like trying to hold on to sand; she kept slipping through his fingers.

"Where is Matthew?" she begged.

Mark stopped trying to stand her on her feet; he looked at her, wondering if she was strong enough to understand what he had to say. He'd ridden a very long way to tell her personally. He drew a deep breath, ignoring the cold night around them, praying she would comprehend his words and the seriousness of them.

"My lady, I must tell you something and I pray that you will listen and take heed," he said. "For whatever I have thought of you in the past, for whatever I may have said in jealousy and anger, I would ask for your forgiveness now."

She looked at him, not genuinely comprehending what he was saying. "What have you done?"

"It does not matter now. All that matters is that I was wrong. About everything. And I am very thankful that my brother has married you."

"Mark, where is he?"

Mark took another deep breath. "In London."

Her entire face went alight. "He is alive?"

"Indeed."

"Then why did he not send word to me?" she suddenly cried. "He promised that he would."

She wasn't particularly hysterical, merely distraught. Mark looked her in the eye. "I need for you to be strong, my lady. What I am about to tell you will require strength of will and character. I do not doubt that you have either of these. Can you do this?"

Something told her that an ominous bit of news was coming. It was more in his manner than in his words. She nodded, slowly. "I can. What has happened to my husband that he would not send me word?"

Mark's jaw flexed; she could see it, even in the darkness. "Lovell told you what happened at the battle, did he not?"

"How do you know about Lovell's missive?"

"Johnny told me."

"Lovell said that the Wellesbournes fought for Henry."

"And he was correct," Mark said. "The reasons for our shift in fealty do not matter. Suffice it to say that it was a matter of honor more than you can comprehend, and we all agreed. But to Matthew, it was far more. He fought like I have never seen him fight, my lady. It was as if Gabriel himself had come out of Heaven to vanquish Richard. Matthew was magnificent. You would have been proud."

She could see Matthew's performance through Mark's eyes. A

weak smile lit her face. "I *am* proud," she whispered. "Now you will tell me what has happened to him."

She knows. Mark gazed back at her, wondering how he was going to tell her what he must. He felt so guilty for every hideous thought he'd ever had of her. The day she ran off from Rosehill, he should have gone after her. He could only thank God that Gaston had found her, righting his sin.

"One moment, he was fighting as if possessed," Mark said, his voice quieting. "He dropped several powerful knights with hardly an effort. I know this because he was near me and we were watching out for one another as we normally do. And then... then de Russe's charger went down and de Russe with it. Gaston was trapped beneath the wounded charger and vulnerable. Matthew saw the threat before I did."

Her heart was thumping in her ears. "What threat?"

"La Londe heading for Gaston."

Alixandrea's eyes widened. "La Londe was at Bosworth?"

Mark nodded with bitter irony. "He was indeed. He was fighting for Henry amongst Richmond's troops. But when Gaston fell, la Londe went after him. You are aware that there has been bad blood between them ever since Gaston emasculated him in the mêlée at Richard's tournament. We could see him moving towards Gaston, but I could not get to him in time. But Matthew could; he was closer. Gaston was trying to get to his sword, hearing our shouts that la Londe was upon him. I swear to you, my lady, it happened in the blink of an eye. Before la Londe's sword came down, Matthew threw his arm out to prevent la Londe's strike from cutting off Gaston's head. That gift of time gave Gaston a chance to reclaim his sword. Yet the damage had already been done. La Londe cut off Matt's left hand before Gaston could raise his sword and cut off Dennis' head."

The story abruptly ended there. Alixandrea gazed at Mark, digesting his words, coming to realize that somewhere in the middle of it, Matthew had lost a hand. For some reason, it did not have nearly the impact that it should have, that it clearly had on Mark. Her gaze grew steady.

"Is that why he did not send word to me?" she asked. "Because he lost his hand?"

Mark nodded. "He wanted to, every minute of every day. He was just unsure how to tell you. Then he decided that he must tell you in person, but the new king has kept him busy in London and he's not had the opportunity to leave. So he sent me to tell you that he is alive and more deeply in love with you than he has ever been. And he said to tell you that he is sorry."

"Sorry for what?"

Mark shrugged. "On that, he was not clear. For perhaps not sending word sooner or for perhaps losing his hand; I do not know. But one thing is certain; Gaston would not be alive had Matthew not sacrificed his hand. It was the most selfless act of loyalty I have ever seen."

A warm, fluid feeling swept her. It made her weak. "As I would expect nothing less from The White Lord," she murmured. "Mark, is he somehow afraid that I will love him less without his hand?"

"He is diminished."

"Nay, he is not. Matthew Wellesbourne is greater than he ever was."

"Then he will need you to convince him of that. He did not want me to tell you about his hand; he will be arriving soon and would tell you himself. He merely wanted me to tell you that he was alive and well, but I knew when I arrived that I could not keep such news from you. Perhaps this way, it will be less of a shock."

Alixandrea felt such relief, such comfort, that she very nearly collapsed. "Then if my husband will be home soon, I must make sure that Wellesbourne Castle is ready to receive The White Lord."

Mark could only nod his concurrence. Alixandrea sat for a moment, pondering all of the news this day had brought her. It occurred to her that it was cold and dark in Audrey's little garden. She rose with heavy assistance from Mark. She was having difficulty standing, difficulty digesting the events of the day. But one thing was certain; Matthew was alive and he was coming home. If nothing else in her life had ever given her even a moment's sweet joy, this one thought did.

Mark held on to her arm to steady her as they walked from the garden. When they reached the gate, he even held out a hand for Caroline. The petite red head took his arm, affectionately, as if the two of them had been doing it all of their lives. He leaned over and kissed her once again, so very glad to see her. The events of the last few weeks had made him re-think everything in life. He knew he had been wrong.

Mark had finally come home.

CHAPTER SEVENTEEN

The dawn was shades of pink and blue, splashing hues across the night sky as the sun threatened to rise. It was a peaceful morning.

Alixandrea was sleeping soundly until a massive body suddenly climbed into bed next to her. Huge arms pulled her close and there was hot breath in her ear. Startled from a deep sleep, her momentary shock was replaced by elation.

She could smell her husband's distinctive musk, warm and masculine and comforting, before she ever saw his face. She could only pray it was not a dream for she would surely die to awaken from this bliss and find it unreal.

Rolling onto her back, she was confronted by a very familiar, very weary face. Matthew Wellesbourne smiled warmly at her, his blue eyes glimmering with unshed tears of joy. Alixandrea's first reaction was to throw her arms around his neck and squeeze him like a vise.

"Matthew," she gasped.

He laughed softly, his face buried in her neck. "Good morn to you, love. Did you sleep well?"

Half-asleep and emotionally brittle, she burst into tears. "Matthew, I do not care what has happened," she wept. "I love you more than anything in the world. You are my husband and I would be lost without you. Whatever you are, whatever you may be, I will never leave you."

It all came out as a rambling mess. He pulled back, gazing down at her with a serious expression. "That was quite a speech. Is there anything else?"

She wept in response and he smiled gently, kissing her cheeks, her nose, her wet eyes. He could not seem to stop kissing her.

"No more tears, sweet girl. I am home to stay, I promise." He gathered her up tightly against him, relishing his first feel of her in ages. It was sweeter than he had remembered. "I am so sorry, Alix. So sorry you had to go through all of this turmoil. But I am back now and all shall be well again, I swear it."

She touched his face, feeling the stubble. It was the most wonderful feeling in the world. "I love you, Matt," she sobbed softly. "I am so glad... so glad...."

She could not finish. He cradled her against his powerful body, holding her with two good arms and one good hand. He could feel her arms moving over him as if inspecting him to see if he was indeed sound and whole. The sobs were like music to his ears. Then, one hand began to move down his left arm. He knew what she was seeking and lifted his arm to show her before she could find it.

His left arm was stumped at the wrist. A soft linen sock fit over the top of it, like a glove, extending up to his mid-arm. It simply covered the nub. Her sobs lessened as she inspected it, carefully and silently.

Matthew closed his eyes as she did so; it was a strong moment, and a defining one. He had been dreading it for weeks but now he thought himself an idiot. Alixandrea responded exactly as he had expected her to; not with revulsion, but with interest and tenderness. He did not say a word as she ran her hand over the cleaved edge of his wrist, becoming acquainted with it. Then she kissed it.

"I would see your flesh," she sniffed as she went to remove the glove.

He shook his head. "Not now," he murmured as he pulled his arm away. "It has not healed completely and knowing your weak stomach when it comes to wounds, I would rather you wait."

She grinned, knowing he was more than likely correct. He knew her well. But it did not stop her curiosity. "Did you... did you find your hand?"

"Aye." He held up his right hand and she could see the silver wedding band flashing on the third finger. "Gaston retrieved it for me. I would not leave the field until he found it."

"Your hand?"

"My ring."

The man had just lost a hand in a horrendous battle and all he was worried about was retrieving his wedding ring. It was the only thing he carried on his person that his wife had given to him and Alixandrea was touched beyond words by his respect for that little silver band.

"I would have bought you another," she said softly.

"It would not have been the same."

She gazed up at him, her eyes wet. The frenzy of their reunion began to settle as she reached up to touch his face once again. She could not stop touching him, as if repeatedly convincing herself that he was real.

"You do not seem surprised that I already knew about your hand," she murmured.

He lifted an eyebrow. "I did not doubt that Mark would tell you no matter how much I told him not to. The man cannot keep a secret to save his life." The hand that was on her arm moved to her belly. "Speaking of secrets, how are you feeling?"

Her mouth flew open. "He told you!"

"I told you that he could not keep a secret." His eyes twinkled as his hand drifted over the gently rounded mound. "He blurted it out the moment I entered the gates. I ran all the way from the ward just to see you."

She smiled, seeing the obvious joy in his expression. "Then you are pleased."

He leaned down, kissing her so sweetly that the tears returned. She put her hands on his face, sobbing softly, relishing the feel of his lips over her cheeks.

"I have not the words to describe the joy in my heart or my love for you," he murmured. "I am humbled, Lady Wellesbourne. Truly, deeply humbled. And Aunt Livia will be pleased."

She laughed, a joyous sound in the midst of her tears. Her arms were wrapped around him as if to never let him go and she squeezed tight. They lay there for a small eternity, his lips against hers, his hand moving up her belly, reacquainting himself with her delicious body. It had been far too long. But more than her touch or the physicality of their relationship, he had missed her wit and charm and companionship. There was so much he wanted to tell her.

"Much has happened since we saw each other last, husband," she said as if she could read his mind. "There is much to say."

"Indeed." He shifted so that they lay side by side on the pillow, their faces an inch apart. His blue eyes were soft on her. "Much that you may already know, I was told."

"Did Mark tell you about Lovell's missive?"

"He did. But I had already heard about it through my sources in London."

Her bronze eyes grew intense. "Why did you not send word yourself? You promised that you would. Why did I have to hear these things from Lovell?"

He sighed, touching her cheek. "Because I was incapacitated with this wound after the battle. I lay unconscious from blood loss for several days. Mark did not tell you that detail, did he?"

She looked horrified. "He did not. Oh, Matthew, I...."

He put his fingers on her lips to quiet her. "It is of little matter. But it took nearly two weeks for me to feel well enough to move about."

"You still could have sent word."

He was remorseful. "You are correct. I could have. And I would beg your forgiveness for not contacting you as soon as I was able. Believe me, many a time I had a scribe begin a missive, every day in fact, but I was unsure what to say or how to tell you what had happened. I wanted to tell you personally, but I was not well enough to travel. I just did not feel as if I could tell you all that I needed to in a missive. I had to tell you face to face."

"But you sent Mark."

"Just as I was preparing to return home, the king summoned me. I knew that I could not delay any longer and sent Mark ahead to tell you that I was alive and would soon return."

Her gaze was steady, without the earlier tears. "Then what Lovell told us is true."

"It is."

"But why, Matt? The White Lord of Wellesbourne is sworn to Richard and the bitter enemy of Henry Tudor. Why did you turn?"

He could not explain to her all of the reasons. It was too complicated, too twisted, and perhaps too frightening for someone like her who was unused to the dealings of politics. She would never know that it was Richard's lust for her that set off the chain of events that would eventually claim his throne and his life. He had to tell her in terms she would understand, and in a way that would bring her comfort.

"You said once that you did not care who sat upon the throne so long as you and I could live in peace," he said quietly. "Perhaps I saw that chance with Henry more than Richard. Perhaps I finally realized that my family was more important than my fealty to a king."

"But Gaston turned, too."

"He realized the same thing."

She pondered that for a moment. "Do you believe that the wars are over for now?" she asked softly. "Do you really believe we will have the opportunity to live in peace?"

"I risked my life and reputation just for that very hope," he said. "Nothing is more important than you and our child, Alix. I would kill a million men and betray a thousand kings just to provide my family with a safe world. Do not doubt that for one moment."

"I do not," she said, believing him without question. Snuggling closer, she allowed herself to feel the thrill of realizing that he was indeed home to stay. "What of Gaston? Where is he?"

"Henry has sent him to York, to a castle called Mount Holyoak. He has control of Yorkshire for now."

"Will we see him again?"

"Of course. De Russe and I are irrevocably connected, as he is now to you, too."

"What do you mean?"

He could not tell her what he really meant. "Suffice it to say that you did the improbable," he touched her cheek. "You made a friend of the man."

It was a pleasing thought and she was very glad, although she did not know what she'd truly done to deserve such an honor. She was silent a moment, contemplating the new future before them.

"What will happen now?" she asked softly.

His embrace tightened and he inhaled deeply of her faded violet scent. He had missed it painfully. "Now, we await the birth of my son in the spring."

She smiled. "There must be more than that."

"Of course there is," he thought a moment on something other than the immediate future. There was so much more ahead of them, things he found himself looking forward to. "With Henry the Seventh upon the throne, I will send Johnny to Rosehill to bring father home. I will also send Mark to Kington Castle on the Welsh Marches to assume the position of garrison commander."

"Garrison commander?" she repeated with surprise. "He is leaving Wellesbourne?"

"Aye," Matthew replied. "As the Earl of Hereford, I have appointed my brother the garrison commander of my holdings. Three of them, in fact, all active border castles. Mark will have his hands full but I have confidence that he can control the Welsh."

Her eyes opened wide. "Earl of Hereford?"

His eyes twinkled. "Did I forget to mention that? Henry rewarded me for my exemplary service at Bosworth. A mighty legacy to pass along to our son, don't you think?"

Alixandrea was overwhelmed. Her husband was home, a new earl no less, a baby was on the way, and Matthew seemed confident that peace would hold. The War of the Roses would soon become a thing of the past and a new era of harmony glimmered on the horizon. It was almost too good to believe.

On that day those months ago when she had entered the *Head O'Bucket* in Newbold and saw a mountain of a man brooding in the corner, she could have never imagined her life to turn out as it had. It seemed like a dream. The White Lord and Lady of Wellesbourne had passed into a new age and she was ready, more than willing, to face it so long as Matthew was by her side.

Her touch spoke of untold emotion and tenderness as she gently kissed her husband's lips. Gazing into his blue eyes, she knew that she would never be able to fully express what was in her heart. With all they had lived and died for, all she cared about was that the man was safe.

"I think our son will have a remarkable legacy," she kissed him again, more firmly this time. "And I think he has a remarkable father."

Matthew could feel her warmth burning deep inside of him. She was delicious and he tasted deeply of her. "Not nearly as remarkable as his mother."

"Matt?"

He did not want to talk; he only wanted to taste her. "Aye?"

"There is something I would like to do."

He thought they were of the same mindset. "I am about to do it."

When his palm closed over her breast, she put her hand over it, stopping him. Her eyes glittered. "Not that."

He looked surprised. "Not that?"

"Nay."

"Then what?"

A wonderful smile spread across her lips. "You promised."

Her grin was catching. He smiled at her but did not know what she meant. "What did I promise?"

"Is this really the end of Richard's wars?"

"It is."

"Then there is something we must do for our children to signify that we have truly achieved peace."

The following May and after two days of labor, Lysabel-Audrey Wellesbourne was born healthy and fat. Her father had been so relieved after the long and difficult birth that he had wept uncontrollably for an hour when it was over. Lysabel was followed in close succession by siblings Rosamund, James, Thomas, Emeline, Daniel and William.

All of the Wellesbourne offspring learned to fish before they could walk.

ABOUT THE AUTHOR

Kathryn Le Veque has always been a writer. From her first "book" at the age of 13, Kathryn has been writing prolifically. A strong interest in History and adventure has added to her stories, most of which take place in the Plantagenet period of England. She also writes contemporary romance and adventure, as evidenced in the Kathlyn Trent/Marcus Burton Archaeology Adventure/Romance Series.

The White Lord of Wellesbourne was originally called *The Four Horsemen*, but it became apparent very early on that the focus and strength of the novel was Matthew, The White Lord. He is, to this day, the author's favorite hero, and with little wonder. Alixandrea is a very lucky woman.

Visit Kathryn's website at www.kathrynleveque.com for more novels and ordering information. Kathryn currently has 48 novels published on Amazon and Barnes and Noble.

Bonus Chapters of the exciting Medieval Romance **TO THE LADY BORN** to follow.

1388 A.D. - The Lady Amalie de Vere is the sister to the Robert De Vere, Duke of Ireland, Earl of Oxford, and personal confident and lover to Richard II. When trouble arises between the king and Henry of Bolingbroke, the Duke of Ireland flees for his life, leaving his sister behind and at the mercy of his enemies. Bolingbroke confiscates Hedingham Castle, the duke's seat, and Lady Amalie along with it.

Enter Sir Weston de Royans. A powerful, pious knight from a good Yorkshire family, his first introduction to Lady Amalie is a shocking one. But he eventually comes to know a beautiful, intelligent and humorous young woman who is in great torment and harbors a terrible secret. However, Weston harbors secrets of his own, deep family secrets that he has tried to run from for all of these years.

As Weston and Amalie fall deeply in love, the two of them must reconcile themselves to these secrets and find understanding and forgiveness. For four years, they live happily and peacefully. Then, the situation changes and Weston's demons resurface again when his grandfather dies and Weston inherits a baronetcy. Weston and Amalie find a new life with Weston's new title that leads them into danger, vengeance, murder, and a brutal showdown on the tournament fields of Yorkshire where Weston risks his life seeking justice for his beloved Amalie

Amazon Reviews:

5 Star review:

"... this story covers some very controversial and emotional issues. The Lady Amalie has been abandoned by her brother. She is in the hands of a brutal enemy. One of the household manages to hide her and send for help. By the time Weston comes to take over the control of the garrison Amalie is suicidal. Weston has a very difficult job trying to save her from herself. The way women were treated in those days (and for hundreds of years) was awful. This story shows us love can bloom in the most difficult of times and change people almost beyond recognition. A beautiful love story with some vicious battles." – Petula Winmill

Another 5 Star review:

"...I love a good medieval romance and Le Veque does them best. I couldn't put the book down, I laughed and cried. I rarely do that. 5 star read for sure." – Rachel

CHAPTER ONE

Hedingham Castle
January, Year of Our Lord 1388

He was coming.

She knew he was approaching and she knew why. Dear God, she knew and there was nothing she could do to stop him.

He'd been watching her for weeks with a lascivious look to his eye and at sup tonight, he couldn't take his eyes from her. His gaze had made her skin crawl, the dirty fingers of his mind reaching out to touch her. After the meal, he had ordered her to her room under guard and there was no way she could escape. He had her trapped. Heart pounding, tears threatening, it was a struggle not to panic. She knew he was coming for her.

God help me, she thought.

The halls of Hedingham Castle were sturdy and big, the corridors thick and smoky with the haze of greasy torches. The keep of the mighty de Vere family reflected the power of the family and the prominence. But tonight, it reflected the instability of the de Vere future. Troops from Bolingbroke filled the halls and grounds since the Robert de Vere's flight to Ireland and to safety to avoid the barons closing in on him. But he left behind his sister, vulnerable to the enemy troops that now manned the battlements. Her punishment was now approaching.

The walls were so thick that she couldn't hear the voices of the guards in the hall. She couldn't hear when he approached, the garrison commander, her jailor, a man as vile as Lucifer and twice as ugly. As she sat huddled on a chair near the fire, fear eating holes in her, she was only aware that the man was upon her when the door rattled and jerked open. Old iron hardware squeaked as the garrison commander slithered into the room.

His brown eyes fixed on her and she met his gaze as bravely as she could. Her green eyes watched him, heart pounding in her ears, as he gave her a lewd grin and quietly closed the door. When he threw the bolt, she knew she was in trouble. Her palms began to sweat and it was a struggle not to scream. But she held her ground, courageously and foolishly, as he approached her. She could tell by the look in his eye that her life, as she had once known it, was over.

He was drunk. She could smell it on his breath from where she sat. When he ordered her to stand and remove her clothing, she refused. Unable to abide disobedience, the garrison commander grabbed her slender wrist and fractured the bones as he yanked her up from the chair and tossed her onto the bed. She tried to scramble off, to run, but she was a small woman against a large man and he didn't care how much he hurt her in the process. He grabbed an ankle and struck her on the side of the head to still her.

As he tore her undergarments to shreds and threw his big, smelly body on top of her, Amalie Leighton Rossington de Vere screamed at the top of her lungs, fighting with every ounce of strength she had to resist. But the garrison commander was too strong and too big; he quickly overwhelmed and trapped her, wedging himself between her supple legs and ramming himself into her virginal body. He grunted with pleasure as she screamed in pain.

The agony went on long into the night. When he wasn't raping her, he was beating her. By the time morning arrived, the garrison commander had raped his captive four times and beat her so badly that her right eye was swollen shut. When dawn arrived, he calmly replaced his clothing and left her chamber as if nothing was amiss. But clearly, a good deal was amiss. In his wake, he left blood and weeping.

A sympathetic guard, a very young man with sisters of his own, made sure the lady was tended and put to bed. When the garrison commander began to speak loudly of his conquest at the nooning meal, the sympathetic guard was sickened in to action. Before the day was out, he sent a message to their liege, Henry of

Bolingbroke.

Until a reply was received, he took the lady and hid her deep in the tunnels of Hedingham so the garrison commander could not abuse her again. The garrison commander roared and threatened, but no one would tell him where the lady was, mostly because no one knew but the young guard. He kept his mouth shut, praying for a swift reply from Bolingbroke.

Within a few weeks, his prayers were answered; the garrison commander was immediately recalled and another man assigned. All men knew and cheered the new commander, a knight of immense power and reputation, who was both feared and respected. Sir Weston de Royans was a man of supreme talent and strength, newly returned from the siege of Vilnius, a military action supported by Henry of Bolingbroke. Weston had led Henry's armies in their attempts to defend the Duchy of Vilnius, but the battle was still ongoing. It had been for years.

Now, Weston was coming to assume command of mighty Hedingham Castle, stronghold of the Earls of Oxford and the Duke of Ireland. It was no small assignment during this dark and volatile time.

But de Royans wasn't due to assume his position for more than a month, so the sympathetic guard spent the next forty-four days guarding the Lady Amalie against those who would resume where the banished garrison commander left off. Such were the orders of Bolingbroke, and the lady was allowed to heal from her ordeal physically. Mentally, it was another issue altogether.

For the occupants of the castle, including the Lady Amalie, the tides were about to turn with the appearance of Sir Weston de Royans.

CHAPTER TWO

He wasn't simply big; he was a colossal man among men, a Samson among average warriors, and was treated with all due respect. With his cropped blond hair, dark blue eyes and granite-square jaw, Weston de Royans was truly a sight to behold in a land of dark and colorless peasants. He was handsome, powerful, and intelligent, a devastating combination for the feminine palate.

It wasn't so much his size and physical strength that garnered respect from even the mightiest of men; it was also the way he handled himself, his well-spoken and calm manner, his wisdom when all else was chaos. He could pull a man's head off with his bare hands or gut with one stroke of his serrated-edged broadsword most impressively.

Quite simply, Weston was a man of brains as well as brawn. Henry of Bolingbroke had learned to depend heavily on him and had sent him to Hedingham Castle with the caveat that he could, and would be recalled at any time. But until such time, Weston was needed at the volatile de Vere castle.

It was a cloudy day, threatening snow, as Weston and his column approached the massive de Vere bastion. The destriers were fatigued from a long day's ride across muddy and sometimes rainy roads and the knights astride them were only marginally less fatigued. At the head of the group, Weston's dark blue eyes beheld Hedingham for the first time and his dark brows, arched like raven's wings, lifted.

"So this is Hedingham?" It was a rhetorical question. "I had heard it was a massive structure but surely that description did not do it justice."

His voice was deep, rippling up from his toes and vibrating through the massive muscles. Riding slightly behind him, a big knight with shoulder-length red hair replied.

"My uncle served the Earl of Oxford years ago," he said. "He said that Hedingham has great caverns beneath it."

"I have heard tale that it can hold out indefinitely during a siege." Still another knight, riding behind Weston, spoke up. He was muscular and bald. "I heard a story once that when King John laid siege to this place, they held out for months, eventually throwing fresh fish at John's army to prove that they were not starving."

Weston wriggled his eyebrows. "I would believe that."

The knight with the red hair spurred his charger up beside him. "What is the first order of business, my lord?"

Weston glanced at his second; Sir Heath de Lara came from an old and distinguished family. He was young and capable, trying to make a name for himself in troubled times.

"Gather the troops in the bailey," he said. "I will address them immediately and then we will observe Mass. Then find whoever had been in charge for the past month and I would meet with him privately."

"Sorrell was in charge," Heath replied. "I heard that he killed a de Vere relative and that was why Henry recalled him."

Weston cocked an eyebrow. "Sorrell has the self-control of a rabid dog," he muttered. "He should have never been left in charge of something this important."

"He has good family ties."

"His mother was a Bigod. A good family does not make the man."

Heath fell silent, glancing back to the big, bald knight behind him; the two exchanged glances, wondering what mess they were going to find in Sorrell's wake.

The man had always had a destructive and immoral reputation. Heath, and his counterpart, Sir John Sheffield, had as much tolerance for unscrupulous knights as their liege did. If de Royans had instilled one thing in them, it was the value of virtue in a world where not much of that seemed to exist. Chaste women and honest men were very important to de Royans because that was the code he lived by. Anything else was a lower life form and unworthy of his respect.

The one hundred man army passed through the small village that surrounded the castle. The road was muddy and uneven, and peasants scampered to get out of the way of the incoming army.

Being January, it was colder than usual and as the column passed through the town, snow flurries began to fall. They clung to Weston's blond eyelashes as he led his column through the muddy, dirty town and to the powerful castle on the north end of town. He could see Hedingham's mighty keep rising four stories to the sky, a truly enormous structure made from pale stone.

Crossing the great iron and wood bridge that hovered above a ditch surrounding the castle, they were admitted through the gates and into the outer bailey beyond. The ground was frozen and the snow flurries were building up on the roofs of the outbuildings. The stables and all other structures other than the keep were in the outer bailey, while the keep sat perched atop a giant motte surrounded by its own walls.

Weston took the army to the stables, dismounted, and sent his men about their duties. Eight days traveling in inclement weather had the men anxious to settle down and find some warmth. Weston paused for a moment as he gathered his bags from his charger, gazing up at the keep that was truly an impressive Norman structure.

Off to his left he could see a small lake surrounded by bushes and trees, suspecting that the pond was the fresh fish supply that John had been speaking of. As men and horses disbanded around him, he brushed the snow off his raised visor and began to walk.

He would eventually make his way in to the keep but at the moment, he wanted to see the size and details of his garrison. His analytical mind absorbed the size of the lower bailey, the capacity of the stables, and the outbuildings that housed the smithy and the tanner.

Weston digested the size of the keep, the slope of the motte and the strength of the walls. Nothing escaped his detailed examination as he made his way along the eastern edge of the outer bailey. To the right was the small lake and he headed in that direction to take a look.

The snow was beginning to fall harder now, sticking to the ground in a white dusting. Weston's massive boots made equally massive footprints as he moved through the brush that bordered the lake, gazing out over the half-frozen pond. He actually found it very peaceful and lush, this little lake, and he liked it a great deal. With the gray skies above and the white-dusted foliage, it was surreal and calm. He could imagine it in the summertime when the grass was green and the bugs danced along the surface. He wondered if he'd have the opportunity to see it.

Wiping the snow off his enormous shoulders, he was in the process of turning for the keep when something caught his attention. He could see a woman several yards away, dressed in a dark and heavy cloak that covered part of her face.

The woman was partially hidden by the snowy brush but he could see that she was of petite stature. She apparently didn't notice him because she didn't look up or give him any indication that she was aware of his presence. She was staring at the lake. Not interested beyond a cursory glance, he was turning to resume his path to the keep when the woman suddenly tossed off the woolen cloak.

Weston came to a halt as his gaze beheld the lady; the cloak had concealed a woman of unearthly beauty, with long, silken blond hair to her buttocks and a body of full breasts and slender torso beneath a simple linen surcoat. Once the woman's cloak came off, it was apparent that she was poorly dressed for the elements. Weston could see the outline of her torso and buttocks through the thin fabric, luscious features that caused him to move in for a closer look. .

He moved to within several feet of her, stealthily, his dark blue gaze fixated on her. As delicious as her body was, it was her facial features that had his interest; he could see a pert little nose and rosebud lips set within a porcelain-like face. Even at this distance he could see that she was an exquisite creature. As he paused amongst the trees and watched, captivated, the woman looked up to the sky, her eyes blinking rapidly as snow crystals fell against them. She seemed to look at the sky for quite some time, perhaps praying; he could not be sure. All he knew was that he had never seen such a beautiful woman.

He didn't even stop to think why she pulled off her cloak in this frigid weather. He was so focused on her lovely face that he was caught off guard when she plunged into the pond.

CHAPTER THREE

Startled, Weston burst through the brush as the woman's blond head went under the water. His first instinct was to go in after her but he knew, with his armor, he would sink straight to the bottom and drown.

He began shouting for his men as he yanked off his helm and tossed it to the ground, followed by his tunic. Pieces of plate armor began flying off and he broke several fastens in his attempt to quickly remove it. By the time he reached his hauberk, Heath was by his side and Weston bellowed at the man to pull on his mail. Heath, confused and concerned, did as he was told as Weston bent over by the waist and extended his arms. Heath pulled the mail coat off smoothly, leaving Weston clad in his heavy tunics, hose and boots.

Weston was still overdressed but couldn't waste more time removing the rest of his clothing. Time was passing and the lady's life was draining away the longer he delayed. As Heath watched in shock, Weston dove into the half-frozen pond and disappeared beneath the surface. John joined Heath at the water's edge, along with several men at arms, and they watched with apprehension as the ripples in the pond stilled and the surface began to smooth over. There was no sign of Weston and John turned to Heath, his round face full of horror.

"What happened?" he demanded. "Where is he?"

Heath, his brown eyes full of concern, pointed to the water. "Under there."

"Why?"

Heath shook his head. "I do not know," he pulled off his helmet when, seconds later, Weston had not reappeared. "He must need help."

Heath began to rip his tunic and plate armor off, falling over when he lost his balance in the process. John, unwilling to wait to disrobe, was already walking into the pond. He had no idea what had happened to Weston other than he was underwater and he was terrified that Weston was drowning. Before he could get too far, Heath grabbed him and yanked him back onto the snowy shore.

"No," he roared. "You fat ox, you'll sink to the bottom with all of that steel on your body. Think, you idiot!"

Anger added to the mix as John shoved at Heath, sending the man toppling over into the frigid water. Just as Heath righted himself and balled a fist to shove into John's face, Weston abruptly broke the surface of the water. But he wasn't alone.

"Take her!" he bellowed.

He was lifting a woman up in his enormous arms, keeping her head out of the water. Heath thrust himself forward, grabbing the lady from his liege as Weston struggled to move; his limbs were nearly frozen and he was having great difficulty moving his arms and legs. Heath, mired down in mud that had his boots wedged in, handed the lady off to John who managed to climb out of the lake with the limp lady in his arms.

"Blankets!" Weston roared as Heath reached out to help him. "Get blankets and wrap her up before she freezes to death."

The men at arms went on the run as John grabbed the nearest dry piece of clothing he could find, Weston's tunic, and struggled to wrap the lady up in it. His hands were freezing, too. Meanwhile, Heath pulled his half-frozen liege out of the pond.

Steam rose into the air from Weston's enormous body as he gave off heat against the frigid air temperature. He stumbled out of the pond and over to John, who had managed to wrap the woman up tightly in the heavy woolen tunic bearing the blue and yellow colors of Bolingbroke. A couple of the men at arms suddenly burst through the snowy bramble; one had a giant horse blanket and the other one had a woolen tarp. Weston grabbed the horse blanket.

"Pick her up," he commanded John.

The knight obeyed, collecting the woman into his arms as Weston took the dusty horse blanket and wrapped the lady up in it. Nearly frozen himself, he didn't react when Heath tossed the woolen tarp over his shoulders; he was more concerned about the lady. Her face was gray, eyes closed, and he cocked an ear over her mouth to see if she was even breathing. After several long seconds, he could feel faint breath, hot and sweet, against his ear.

Exhausted, freezing, he began to stumble towards the keep with the lady in his arms.

"Go to the keep and tell them to fill a tub with warm water," he commanded his men, his blue lips quivering against the cold. "Find out if they know who she is."

Heath bolted towards the keep while John stayed with Weston, carrying the precious cargo towards the towering keep of Hedingham. They made quite a procession marching through the increasing snow, struggling up the slippery path up the motte before finally mounting the snowy, slippery wooden staircase that led to the second floor level. It was the entry level and a blast of stale, heated air hit Weston in the face the moment he entered the door.

A cavernous hall opened up before him, two stories tall. Great Norman arches lined the hall as they supported a minstrel gallery on the second floor above. Weston charged into the room as servants began to rush towards him, and somewhere in the middle of it, Heath was shouting orders to the servants who were overwhelmed with what was happening. Two older women, both in tight wimples that nearly strangled them, pushed forward in the midst of the chaos.

"Lady Amalie!" one woman cried, reaching out to touch the pale, gray face. Feeling that it was like ice, she drew her hand back in shock. "She is dead!"

Weston pushed through them even though he had no idea where he was going. "She is not dead," he snapped. "I ordered a hot tub. Where is it?"

The other servant woman began pointing toward the alcove that housed the narrow spiral stairs. "This way, m'lord," she was practically jumping up and down as she attempted to lead the way. "Bring her this way."

Weston charged after the woman with Heath, John and two men at arms following him. The group entered the small, dark alcove and he followed the serving woman up the slippery, narrow steps, trying not to smack the unconscious lady's head on the wall in the process. With his bulk, stairs such as this were difficult enough without the added awkwardness of carrying a limp body.

It wasn't an easy trip. The third floor contained the minstrel gallery so they were forced to take the treacherous stairs to the fourth floor of the keep. They spilled out into a small corridor that had two doors; one immediately to the left and one further down the hall. The flighty servant indicated the far door and Weston proceeded in.

The room was spacious and warm, with a roaring fire in the hearth and furs on the bed and cold wood floor. It was a room that suggested the wealth of the de Veres, something not lost on Weston. He paused in the middle of the room as several servants finished hurriedly finished filling a big copper tub near the hearth.

It was only partially filled with steaming water but Weston didn't want to wait. He lay the lady down on the big, fur-covered bed and began unwinding her from the horse blanket and tunic.

"Who is this?" he demanded from the serving women assisting him.

The younger of the pair, a woman with crinkled skin and missing teeth, spoke as she unwound the horse blanket from the lady's feet.

"The Lady Amalie de Vere," she told him. "She is the earl's sister."

Weston pulled the horse blanked free and tossed it back to one of his men at arms. His gaze moved to the unconscious woman's features, puzzlement registering on his face. She was absolutely exquisite, even gray and wet. Her face was sweet, with a gently pouting mouth and long-lashed eyes that were closed and still. As he continued to gaze at her, he felt something stir within his heart that he couldn't begin to describe - there was interest there, delight, and utter fascination. But there was also great confusion.

Not wanting to make a fool out of himself by staring at the woman, he pulled off the tunic with the help of the two women.

"She is nearly frozen," he said as he lifted her off the bed and turned for the heated tub. "She must be warmed immediately."

He laid her in the tub as servants continued to pour hot water into the mix. Weston was freezing, too, but at the moment he was more concerned with the lady. His knightly sense of chivalry was more important than his health at the moment but one of the two female servants, the plump one, brushed against him and noticed.

"M'lord," she had a hand on his muscular forearm. "You are nearly frozen yourself."

She began to shout commands to the men who were bringing buckets of water into the room, demanding warmed wine and blankets. Weston tried to wave her off but as he opened his mouth to do so, the lady in the water came alive.

Great gasps came forth and her eyes flew open. She began thrashing violently, as if trying to swim or save her life as the last thing she remembered, the icy grip of the lake, closed in around her. A hand flew up and caught Weston in the mouth, driving his teeth into his lip and bringing blood. Weston put his enormous hands on Amalie's shoulders and tried to steady her.

"You are safe, my lady," he said steadily, trying to break through her haze of fear. "You need not fear; you are safe."

Amalie gradually became lucid, realizing she was in her chamber with a few familiar faces. The haze was clearing yet her panic was not eased; there was so much fear and distress in her heart that nothing could soothe her. Adding to the fear was the square-jawed, enormous man hovering over her that she did not recognize. She began to fight viciously.

"Nay!" she cried, struggling to climb out of the tub. "Leave me alone!"

Weston had her in an iron grip. "Be at ease, lady," he assured calmly. "No one will hurt you. You are safe."

Her panic was expelling itself in harsh little pants; it was as if she did not understand his words. Weston caught Heath's wide-eyed expression over the top of the lady's head and he jerked his head in the direction of the door, silently ordering the man to vacate. Heath took the hint and ushered the men at arms out as he went. The younger of the serving women slammed the door behind the unfamiliar knights, racing back to her position next to the tub as Amalie struggled to climb out.

"Ammy," she put her rough hands on Amalie's face, forcing her to look at her. "Look at me, lamb; you are safe, I promise you. This knight... he brought you here. He rescued you."

Amalie's green eyes were wide on the serving woman but at least she was calming. Weston was relieved. But his relief was short-lived as the woman suddenly began to weep.

"Nay," she breathed, her lovely face crumpling. "Nay... I ...I...."

She dissolved into distraught tears. By this time, she had stopped struggling and Weston removed his big hands from her shoulders when he was sure she wasn't going to bolt from the tub. He stood unsteadily, shaking because he was still soaking wet and nearly frozen, but his gaze never left Amalie and he had no idea why. As the plump servant tried in vain to comfort the lady, the other serving women went to Weston and gently grabbed a cold elbow.

"Come and stand by the fire, m'lord," she encouraged. "You are nearly frozen. Come and be warmed."

He did as he was told but his eyes remained on the woman in the hot tub, weeping as if her heart was broken. His confusion grew.

"Who is she?"

The servant was trying to wring the water out of his sleeve. "The Lady Amalie de Vere," she said, realizing she wasn't doing any good with his wet clothing. "She is the earl's sister."

Weston regarded the lady a moment; he still wasn't sure what he was feeling at the moment because the lady was so overwhelmingly beautiful that he couldn't seem to feel anything other than complete fascination. The serving woman jolted him from his thoughts.

"May I take your wet clothing, m'lord?" she asked. "You must change into something dry before you catch your death of chill."

Weston was still gazing at the weeping lady as he pulled off his wet tunic with the automatic response of a child responding to his mother's command. He handed the woman the heavily padded tunic, exposing his magnificent torso to the weak light of the room. He was brilliantly muscular with a thick neck and shoulders, enormously big arms and chest. His waist was narrow, disappearing beneath his leather breeches.

But the old serving woman didn't notice; she was more concerned with drying out the sopping tunic. There was a soft knock at the door and one of the male servants appeared with two cups of steaming wine in hand. The old serving woman took it from him and closed the door once more. She handed one of the cups to Weston, which he accepted gratefully.

"What is your name?" he asked the woman.

"Esma, m'lord," the women replied, then indicated her counterpart still kneeling by the tub comforting the sobbing lady. "My sister, Neilie."

Weston sipped the hot wine, still staring at the lady in the tub. "Why would Lady Amalie throw herself into the lake?"

Esma's wrinkled eyes widened with shock. "She... she threw herself into the lake?"

Weston nodded. "I watched her," he said frankly. "She removed her cloak and jumped in. Naturally, I went after her. I could not stand by and watch her drown."

Esma's astonished gaze moved to the lady in the tub. "'Tis not true," she gasped. "You must be mistaken, m'lord."

"I am never mistaken."

The servant didn't argue with him; his statement left no room for doubt. More troubling than that, she believed him. She blinked rapidly as if blinking back tears.

"God help her," she whispered. "My poor little lamb."

Weston looked at the woman; she seemed more saddened than shocked, as if not particularly surprised. She didn't give him much of an argument on what he had suggested regarding the lady's behavior. His analytical mind began to kick in.

"What do you know about this?" he asked her.

She looked at him, shocked. "I... I would know nothing, m'lord."

He didn't believe her for a minute; now she had his full attention. "My name is Sir Weston de Royans," he told her. "I am the new commander of Hedingham. In order for me to command effectively, I must know the truth of what has gone on before my arrival. Do you understand so far?"

Esma looked terrified. "Aye, m'lord."

"How long have you served de Vere?"

"Since before the lady was born, m'lord."

"How old is she?"

"Nineteen years, m'lord."

"Then you know everything that goes on at this place."

She nodded timidly, as if he was trying to trick her with his statement. "My sister and I assist the lady in her chatelaine duties."

"Then you will tell me why she threw herself into that lake."

Esma was torn; she eyed the now-sniffling lady in the tub, watching as her sister forced Amalie to sip at the warmed wine. She didn't want to divulge too much to this knight she did not know, but on the other hand, perhaps in doing so he would understand the fragility of Lady Amalie and treat her accordingly. The man had saved Amalie from a watery grave; perhaps that meant he was better than the last man that had held his position. Esma could only pray.

She moved closer to Weston, wringing her hands nervously. When she spoke, her tone was so soft he could barely hear her.

"I can only tell you what I know, m'lord," she whispered. "The last of Bolingbroke's commanders was a brutal man with no great love for the de Vere's. He was personally offended by the earl's flight to Ireland to escape Bolingbroke's wrath and took his frustrations out on Lady Amalie."

Weston was studying the woman intently, seeing the pain ripple across her face as she spoke.

"What did he do?" he asked.

That brought tears to the old woman's eyes and she began wiping at her nose, dragging mucus across her cheek.

"He... he beat her severely one night," she whispered. "He broke her wrist and nearly killed her. After that, one of his men hid Amalie so the commander could not hurt her again. He also sent word to Bolingbroke of the man's actions. Until the commander was recalled by Bolingbroke, we spent weeks hiding Lady Amalie in caverns, holes and tunnels so the commander could not find her. She was living like an animal for weeks."

Weston's gaze moved to the beautiful creature in the tub, now calmly sipping her warmed wine. His gaze moved over her delicate features, the silken blond hair; knowing his predecessor as he did, he could only imagine what the man did to her. As he thought on that, disgust and fury such as he had never known began to surge through his big body.

With the heat of the fire upon him, he actually began to sweat from both the physical heat and the emotion he was feeling. The actions of unchivalrous knights always set his blood to boiling, fiends who hid behind their vows to mask vile actions. Men like that gave decent knights a bad name.

"That still does not explain why she threw herself into the lake," he said quietly. "My predecessor has been gone for weeks. Surely she feels safe now."

Esma looked at Weston with some surprise, wiping at her nose.

"Why should she?" she snapped softly, realizing too late who she was speaking to and demurring accordingly. "When we received word that Bolingbroke was sending a new commander to oversee Hedingham, you can imagine her fear. Perhaps... perhaps she is afraid you will do to her what the other one did."

It made perfect sense. He began to suspect why she had submerged herself in the lake and began to feel a good deal of sorrow as well as some revulsion. He downed the rest of his wine in one swallow and thrust the cup back at Esma.

"Go," he commanded softly. "Take your sister and go."

Startled, Esma began to feel the same desperation she had felt

351

when the previous commander had made the same request of her once. That was the worst day of her life. She was starting to think she had been too bold in speaking the truth to him; she did not know the man or anything about him. Perhaps she had offended him.

"Please, m'lord," she began to beg, tears in her eyes. "She cannot... you cannot... please do not hurt her. She cannot..."

Weston waved her off. "I will not harm her in any way," he was moving towards the tub. "You and your sister will go."

Esma was weeping softly as she scooted to the tub and pulled her sister to her feet. The old serving women clutched at each other, whispering between themselves as Esma pulled her sister to the door. It was apparent that the older woman did not want to leave but Esma forced her through the door. When the women vacated and Weston shut the door behind them, he returned his attention to the tub near the hearth.

His dark blue gaze fell on the back of a blond head, now drying in the heat of the room. Amalie hadn't moved a muscle; she sat in the big copper tub, still dressed in her thin linen surcoat, staring at the surface of the water.

Weston made his way to her, hesitantly, wondering what he was going to say. He was coming to realize that everything they had suspected about Sorrell was the truth and this woman was at the heart of it. Sorrell hadn't killed the de Vere relative as rumored but, as Weston gazed at the face of the pale woman, he'd probably come close. Before he could speak, her soft voice filled the air.

"Did you fish me out of the pond?" she asked.

He was struck by the tone of her voice - smooth, silky and honey-like. In spite of the serious circumstances, he found it exceedingly delightful.

"Aye," he said quietly. "My name is Weston de Royans. I am the new garrison commander for Hedingham."

Amalie continued to stare at the surface of the tub, her green eyes, usually so beautiful and full of life, now dull with sorrow.

"You should not have done that," she murmured. "I will only

do it again."

Weston's brow furrowed and he crouched beside the tub; he could only see her delicate profile as she stared at the water. She wouldn't look at him and he could feel her shrinking from his gaze. Not that he blamed her given her past experience with Bolingbroke men.

"Why?" he finally asked, baffled.

She lifted her face to look at him and Weston felt the physical impact as their eyes met. It was as if her great green eyes swallowed him up, holding him in a trance that he was unable to free himself from. All he could do was stare at her.

"Because I must," she said simply.

He was even more baffled, trying to figure out why she was so determined to harm herself. He should have, at the very least, been disgusted with her weakness. Given what Esma told him, however, and what he knew of Sorrell, he couldn't bring himself to lose respect for the woman. In fact, he felt strongly compelled to ease her mind.

"My lady," he said in his rich, deep voice. "I understand that you have not been treated kindly since your brother fled to Ireland and I will say now that it is a cowardly man who would leave his sister to the clemency of the enemy, but you must understand that I will not behave as my predecessor did. I have no intention of laying a hand on you. Under my command, you will be treated with respect. This I swear."

Amalie stared at him, emotions undulating behind the veil of the green eyes. It was almost as if she could not understand what he was telling her. But the glassy expression began to fade, the one so dull with sorrow, and he could see her lovely features twist with emotion. The great green eyes filled with tears again, spattering like raindrops against her porcelain cheeks.

"Please," she sobbed softly. "Please take your sword... please... will you not do me this one small mercy and end my torment?"

He stared at her, horrified by the suggestion. "I will not," he replied, standing to his considerably height. "Why would you ask such a thing?"

Her weeping grew stronger and she suddenly stood from the warm tub, water sloshing out onto the floor. Stumbling from the tub, she ended up on her knees at Weston's feet. She grabbed his leg, her forehead against his knee.

"Please," she begged him, weeping. "You are a knight. You are sworn to obedience. You must do as I ask."

He looked down upon her blond head, appalled and distressed by the request.

"I will not help you kill yourself," he reached down and grasped her arms. "Get up, now. You are simply overwrought. You need to rest."

He easily lifted her to her feet; she was weak, sobbing and wet, so for lack of a better action, he pulled her over to the fire to warm her up and dry her out. But she struggled against him, slugging at his hands, trying to push him away. Afraid she might try to throw herself in the fire, he tried to stay between her and the open flame.

When her behavior should have disgusted him, all he could feel was great concern. Whatever Sorrell did had seriously damaged the woman and his animosity towards the man increased.

As Amalie struggled and he continued to keep himself between her and the fire, he'd finally had enough. He couldn't stand here and scuffle with her all night. In a bold move, he put his enormous hands on both cheeks and forced her to look at him.

"My lady," Weston's tone was sincere, firm. "I understand you are afraid and I understand that in times past, you were treated with great disregard. But you must understand that this is no longer the case. I am here now and things will be different. You must not despair."

Amalie found herself gazing into a powerfully handsome face and eyes that were hard yet kind. It was an odd combination, one that, for a moment, stilled her raging despondency. Her tears inexplicably began to fade as their gazes locked. For the first time, they were able to get their first real look at each other without all of the snow, terror and chaos.

"Disregard?" she repeated, suddenly sounding very lucid. "Disregard would have been preferable. He used his fists on me as one would on an enemy. He cracked bones in my wrist. He hit me so hard in the face that my eye swelled shut. He did... unspeakable things. Is this what you call disregard, Sir Weston? For, quite clearly, it was more than that."

It was the first coherent statement he'd heard from her, one that had his disgust surging and his heart strangely twisting. She was well spoken and seemingly intelligent.

Weston had been a fully sworn knight at twenty years old and had seen many things in the thirteen years since. But what he was feeling as he gazed into the pale, beautiful face was something beyond compassion. He wasn't sure what it was yet but he knew it was different. Something in that pathetic little face moved him.

"Then I apologize for my misstatement," he said in a low voice. "Now that you have explained things, I do not consider what happened to you mere disregard. But I assure you that it will never happen again."

She held his gaze a moment longer before pulling away, firmly; he had no choice but to drop his hands from her face as she moved towards the fire again.

He bolted forward when she held her hands out against the flames to warm them, afraid she was going to try to jump into it. He still didn't trust her. Amalie saw the swift movement from the corner of her eye and it startled her. When she looked at him, he had his big arm between her torso and the fireplace. When their gazes met, he lifted a dark blond brow.

"Burning is a horrible death, my lady," he told her. "It is not swift or merciful. I would not recommend it."

She just looked at him, holding his gaze a moment, before looking away. "Then what would you recommend from a professional standpoint, of course?"

He couldn't tell if there was humor in that statement but one might have interpreted it that way. There was a funny little lilt to her tone. But he would not be lulled into a false sense of security with her manner, no matter how calm she seemed to be at the moment.

"I would not recommend anything for your purposes," he said. "The church frowns upon the taking of one's life no matter what the circumstances."

"What does the church know of my pain?"

"God knows of it; what God knows, the church knows. You must have faith."

As upset as she was, the knight's manner and words were making some impact. In spite of everything, he was settling her and she had no idea why; perhaps it was the fact that he had saved her from drowning herself. Or maybe it was because she saw something in his eyes that insured honesty. Whatever it was, she could feel herself calming. But it did not erase her sense of hopelessness at her situation.

"Have faith in what?" she asked, her voice soft and hoarse. "I am a prisoner in my own home. When you leave, who is to stay that the next commander will not resume where the other one left off? You cannot insure my safety for always."

He eyed her, the gentle slope of her torso as it descended into rounded buttocks, now outlined with the damp and clinging material. He'd never seen finer.

"I can swear to you, on my oath as a knight, that you will be safe from harm as long as I have breath in my body," he told her flatly. "No female under my protection will ever be mistreated, I swear it."

She turned to look at him; now that she was regaining her senses, she had an opportunity to take a good look at him. It hadn't occurred to her until this moment that he was without clothing from the waist up. He was a tall man but it wasn't his height that was impressive; it was his sheer bulk. He had an enormous neck and shoulders, and his arms were the biggest she had ever seen. His chest was muscular and beautiful, his waist trim. But the sight made her heart race and she wasn't sure why; all she knew was that it made her uncomfortable.

"You will understand if I am dubious of your declaration," she said, moving away from him. "The last knight I came into contact with displayed less than chivalrous behavior."

He watched her move away, shivering even in the radiant heat of the blaze. He wasn't offended by her statement because he understood her point of view.

"Perhaps time will prove my trust, my lady," he said. "But until that time, I would ask one thing."

She glanced at him, now at a safe distance from his delicious naked torso. "What would that be?"

"That you not make any more attempts to, shall we say, swim in a frozen pond."

She averted her gaze, looking back to the dancing flames. She seemed to get that glassy look again.

"My apologies to have troubled you," she said quietly.

He couldn't help but notice she hadn't given him a direct answer.

"You did not trouble me," he said. "But I have enough on my mind with a new command without the additional worry of the Lady of the Keep condemning herself to a watery grave."

She didn't say anything. He took a step toward her to make sure she heard him. "Lady Amalie?"

She looked up from the fire to notice he was much closer. Instinctively, she flinched and moved away from him. Her hands went up as if to protect herself.

"I will do my best not to cause you additional worry," she assured him quickly.

He could see the panic in her face and he stopped his advance.

"I have faith in the word of a lady," he replied, eyeing her a moment and realizing that she was still quite damp. He indicated her dress. "I will send your serving women in to help you change from those wet garments."

Amalie nodded briefly, watching him with her great green eyes as he collected his wet tunic from the stand near the hearth and proceeded to the door. Weston's eyes lingered on her a moment before quitting the room silently. Even after he was

357

gone, she simply stood there, depression swamping her and her sense of desolation returning full-force. Whatever the knight said, she was sure he was lying. They all lied. They were all animals.

Amalie went to her dresser where, inside a lovely bejeweled chest, lay a delicate dirk that her mother had given her long ago. She collected the weapon, fingering it, feeling the sharp edge and wondering what it was going to feel like when it cut into her chest.

In her opinion, she had no choice. Better to take her life and end her torment than to bring a bastard into the world. That was one little element she had left out of her conversation with de Royans; she couldn't take the shame, more dishonor to be heaped upon the House of de Vere. That was something that men like Weston de Royans could never understand.

When Esma and Neilie came to the chamber several minutes later with food and more wine, Amalie was gone.

$$\wp$$

Read the rest of **TO THE LADY BORN** in Kindle format or in paperback at Amazon.com or Barnes and Noble.